The Best American Mystery Stories 2008

GUEST EDITORS OF
THE BEST AMERICAN MYSTERY STORIES

1997 ROBERT B. PARKER

1998 SUE GRAFTON

1999 ED MCBAIN

2000 DONALD E. WESTLAKE

2001 LAWRENCE BLOCK

2002 JAMES ELLROY

2003 MICHAEL CONNELLY

2004 NELSON DEMILLE

2005 JOYCE CAROL OATES

2006 SCOTT TUROW

2007 CARL HIAASEN

2008 GEORGE PELECANOS

The Best American Mystery Stories™ 2008

Edited and with an Introduction
by **George Pelecanos**

Otto Penzler, *Series Editor*

HOUGHTON MIFFLIN COMPANY
BOSTON • NEW YORK 2008

www.houghtonmifflinbooks.com

ISSN 1094-8384
ISBN 9780618812660
ISBN 9780618812677 (pbk.)

Printed in the United States of America

VB 10 9 8 7 6 5 4 3 2 1

These stories are works of fiction. Names, characters, places, and incidents are products of the authors' imagination or are used fictitiously. Any resemblance to actual events, locales, or persons, living or dead, is entirely coincidental.

"Mist" is reprinted with the permission of Simon & Schuster Adult Publishing Group from *Jesus out to Sea: Stories by James Lee Burke.* Copyright © 2007 by James Lee Burke. Originally appeared in the *Southern Review.*

Michael Connelly, "Mulholland Dive," from *L.A. Noir,* Akashic Books, 2007. Copyright © 2007 by Michael Connelly. Reprinted by permission of Philip G. Spitzer Literary Agency, Inc.

Robert Ferrigno, "The Hour When the Ship Comes In," from *L.A. Noir,* Akashic Books, 2007. Copyright © 2007 by Robert Ferrigno. Reprinted by permission of the author.

Chuck Hogan, "One Good One," from *Ellery Queen's Mystery Magazine,* March/April 2007. Copyright © 2007 by Chuck Hogan. Reprinted by permission of Multimedia Threat, Inc.

Rupert Holmes, "The Monks of the Abbey Victoria," from *Dead Man's Hand,* edited by Otto Penzler, 2007, Harcourt. Copyright © 2007 by Rupert Holmes. Reprinted by permission of Rupert Holmes.

Holly Goddard Jones, "Proof of God," from *Epoch,* Vol. 56, no. 1, 2007. Copyright © 2007 by Holly Goddard Jones. Reprinted by permission of the author.

Peter LaSalle, "Tunis and Time," from *Antioch Review,* Winter 2007. Copyright © 2008 by Peter LaSalle. Reprinted by permission of Peter LaSalle.

Contents

Foreword

GOING BACK TO THE nineteenth century, Houghton Mifflin has been an independent publishing house primarily interested in high-quality literature. It started to publish *The Best American Short Stories* as an annual volume in 1915 and inaugurated *The Best American Mystery Stories* in 1997. By the standards of the present day, it is regarded as a medium-size house. Last year, its parent company acquired the parent company of Harcourt, another old and distinguished publishing firm, and the two imprints have been combined. Even together, they are still dwarfed by giants such as Random House, Viking, Hachette, and Simon & Schuster. This appears to be just fine with them and should be cause for silent celebration by all readers who care about good books.

Neither of these elegant publishers was noted for its ten-million-dollar advances to popular writers, or for its overhyped million-dollar advertising and promotion campaigns for the latest fad-diet book. They have placed their share of books on national and regional bestseller lists the old-fashioned way, by publishing outstanding works and giving them realistic and appropriate support. They have remained independent and successful by following this course, and there is cause for hope and even exaltation that this merger will strengthen both firms.

This, the twelfth edition of *The Best American Mystery Stories,* is the first to be published since the merger, and so far, so good. Two publishing houses with a sense of history, notable for their integrity, are savvy enough to turn profits (the indispensable element in any business that is necessary to keep the doors open) on a regular basis. No editor or executive has knocked on the door to offer "suggestions" about changes, no memos have appeared in the mailbox with advice on how to improve the "product" (a repugnant word I have never heard from anyone at Houghton Mifflin regarding this series, or at Harcourt, where I have a crime fiction imprint). So, barring a sudden change of philosophy or priorities, I expect we'll keep on tooling along for a while, trying hard to bring the most outstanding mystery stories of the year to readers for the foreseeable future.

And a good thing, too, as there were more submissions and discovered stories than in any year to date. More stories in electronic magazines, more editors of literary journals submitting greater numbers of stories, more short story collections and anthologies filled with mystery tales, all combined to produce a bumper crop of outstanding fiction from which to make the ever more difficult decision about what can be contained in these pages.

As frequent readers of this series are aware, each annual volume would, I am convinced, require three years to compile were it not for the uncanny ability of my colleague, Michele Slung, to read, absorb, evaluate thousands of pages in what appears to be a nanosecond. After culling the nonmysteries, as well as those crime stories perpetrated by writers who may want to consider careers in carpentry or knitting instead of wasting valuable trees for their efforts, I read stacks of them, finally settling on the fifty best — or, at least, my fifty favorites — which are then passed on to the guest editor, who happily this year is the supremely talented George Pelecanos.

The author of more than a dozen mystery novels, including the Edgar Allan Poe Award nominee *Drama City,* Pelecanos has written and produced numerous episodes of the HBO series *The Wire,* for which he won an Edgar and was nominated for an Emmy. The generosity of this distinguished author, giving up countless hours to read the finalists and select the top twenty stories, cannot be overstated, and the same debt of gratitude is owed to the previous guest editors: Robert B. Parker (1997), Sue Grafton (1998), Evan Hunter/Ed McBain (1999), Donald E. Westlake (2000), Lawrence Block (2001), James Ellroy (2002), Michael Connelly (2003), Nelson DeMille (2004), Joyce Carol Oates (2005), Scott Turow (2006), and Carl Hiaasen (2007).

The search has already begun for suitable stories for next year's edition. To qualify, a story must be — duh — a mystery, by which I mean any work of fiction in which a crime, or the threat of a crime, is integral to the theme or plot. It must be written by an American or Canadian and have had its first publication in the calendar year of 2008 in an American or Canadian publication. If you are the author of such a work, or its editor, or any interested party (your credentials will not be reviewed), please feel free to submit it. Every word of *Ellery Queen's Mystery Magazine* and *Alfred Hitchcock's Mystery Magazine* is read, and it is unlikely that we will miss a story published in an anthology entirely devoted to mystery stories, so there is no need to call these to our attention. If the story was first published online, only hard copies will be read; these must include the name of the e-zine, the date on which it was published, and contact information. No unpublished stories are eligible, for what should be obvious reasons. Submitted material will not be returned. If you do not trust the U.S. Postal Service to deliver the book, magazine, or tear sheets, please enclose a self-addressed post card to receive confirmation.

The earlier submissions are received, the less hurriedly will they be read. If your story is one of fifty or sixty or more delivered during Christmas week, it may not receive quite the same respectful reading as those submitted in less crowded months. Because of the unforgiving deadlines necessarily imposed on a work of this nature, the absolute deadline for receiving material is December 31. This is not an arrogant or whimsical date, but is essential in order for production schedules to be met. If it arrives on January 2, it will not be read. Sorry.

Submissions should be sent to Otto Penzler, The Mysterious Bookshop, 58 Warren Street, New York, NY 10007.

O. P.

Introduction

Recently I was asked by Otto Penzler, the series editor of this collection, to come up to Manhattan and do a reading at his store, The Mysterious Bookshop, in Tribeca. The event was to promote a huge volume of classic pulp stories that Otto had edited, Black Mask–era work from the likes of Dashiell Hammett, Cornell Woolrich, James M. Cain, Erle Stanley Gardner, Horace McCoy, and many others. Initially I was looking to read something obscure and promote an underappreciated writer, but in the end I went with a selection from Raymond Chandler's "Red Wind," perhaps his most beloved short story. To read Chandler to an audience in New York was a once-in-a-lifetime opportunity for me, and I took it.

Here's the famous first paragraph of "Red Wind":

> *There was a desert wind blowing that night. It was one of those hot dry Santa Anas that come down through the mountain passes and curl your hair and make your nerves jump and your skin itch. On nights like that every booze party ends in a fight. Meek little wives feel the edge of the carving knife and study their husbands' necks. Anything can happen. You can even get a full glass of beer at a cocktail lounge.*

Beautiful, right?

After the reading, I spoke with many of the people who had come to the event. One of them opined that "Red Wind" might have been the best thing Chandler had ever written, as the short fiction form had forced him to focus and had prevented him from meandering and losing his grip on plot, one of the few negatives critics have cited when commenting on his novels. "Red Wind" *is* a remarkable short story, though at fifty-seven pages (my Ballantine paperback edition from 1977) it stretches the definition of "short." I don't know that it can be called Chandler's best (for me, it's *The Long Goodbye,* hands down), but then "best" is subjective, up to and including the contents of the book you are holding in your hands.

Now would be an appropriate time to explain how the stories in this volume came to be chosen. The mechanics went like this: Otto Penzler and his esteemed associate combed through hundreds of crime/mystery stories published during the year and came up with fifty candidates deemed to be of the highest quality. The fifty were sent to me in a cardboard box, and I read them. From the fifty, I chose twenty stories. Biographies were not supplied. I am friendly with a couple of the writers, and know the names of several others, but I was not acquainted whatsoever with the majority of the authors whom I chose. Don't know their race, ethnicity, political persuasion, or shoe size, and in some cases could not determine their gender. I chose the stories that I enjoyed reading the most and that I hoped you would enjoy, too.

Having said that, I was asked to be the editor, and took the invitation seriously, so naturally the stories I selected are representative of the type of prose I generally read. What you will be reading here has a degree of realism to it. I liked the characters and recognized something in them that rang true. The writing, I promise you, is good, thoughtful writing.

Which brings me to my next point. There is another book out there, from the same publisher as this one, called *The Best American Short Stories.* I would contend that several stories in this collection *are* among the best American short stories of the year. So why two books? The short answer is marketing. There are folks who fancy themselves too erudite to try a volume of mystery stories. They believe that one is mere entertainment, and the other is good for you. It's my opinion that any kind of reading is good for you but, rather than reopen the literary-versus-genre can of worms, I will again defer to Raymond Chandler, from a section of his landmark essay "The Simple Art of Murder":

> *As for "literature of expression" and "literature of escape" — this is critic's jargon, a use of abstract words as if they had absolute meanings. Everything written with vitality expresses that vitality: there are no dull subjects, only dull minds. All men who read escape from something else into what lies behind the printed page; the quality of the dream may be argued, but its release has become a functional necessity. All men must escape at times from the deadly rhythms of their private*

> *thoughts. It is part of the process of life among thinking beings. It is one of the things that distinguish them from the three-toed sloth; he apparently — one can never be quite sure — is perfectly content hanging upside down on a branch, not even reading Walter Lippmann. I hold no particular brief for the detective story as the ideal escape. I merely say that all reading for pleasure is escape, whether it be Greek, mathematics, astronomy, Benedetto Croce, or the Diary of the Forgotten Man. To say otherwise is to be an intellectual snob, and a juvenile at the art of living.*

Damn, he's good.

I've leaned pretty hard on Raymond Chandler for this introduction, and there's a reason for that. Chandler, and the teacher who turned me on to his books, pretty much changed the course of my life.

I was a senior at the University of Maryland when I took a college course called Hardboiled Detective Fiction (ENGL 379X), an elective that I used to fill out my schedule, an easy three credits on the home stretch to graduation. I recall the syllabus course description as "read and discuss paperback novels," which sounded like something I could do, despite the fact that I was not even a casual reader of novels at the time.

The teacher was a bearded, bearish fellow named Charles C. Mish, an accomplished, intelligent man who did not look down his nose at the subject matter but rather sought to give us an appreciation of what he considered to be an important, uniquely American art. Twice a week he paced the aisles of our classroom, paperback rolled in his meaty fist, converting us with his enthusiasm and energy. I learned later that he was in Dutch with his academic colleagues for treating crime fiction with the same reverence as one would the classics. It made me like him even more.

The books we read that semester included Hammett's *Red Harvest*; Mickey Spillane's *I, The Jury*; John D. MacDonald's *The Deep Blue Good-by* (the first Travis McGee); and Ross Macdonald's *The Blue Hammer* (late Lew Archer). Though it is a spy novel, John le Carré's *Call for the Dead* was in there, too, probably because Mish simply liked it. And in the mix was Chandler's *The Lady in the Lake.*

I was struck at once, as if socked in the jaw, with Chandler's descriptive powers, and that he could say so much about the human condition by setting his story in a world mostly shunned by "serious" novelists (I had not yet read Steinbeck, Edward Anderson,

Upton Sinclair, A. I. Bezzerides, John Fante, or any of the other social realists I would begin to devour in the coming years). Mostly I was impressed with the clarity of his prose, obviously written to be read and understood by folks who did not know the secret handshake. It was populist literature, and I wanted to be a part of it.

From the early pages of *The Lady in the Lake*, here is the introduction to the dominant female character in the book:

> *At a flat desk in line with the doors was a tall, lean, dark-haired lovely whose name, according to the titled embossed plaque on her desk, was Miss Adrienne Fromsette. She wore a steel gray business suit and under the jacket a dark blue shirt and a man's tie of lighter shade. The edges of the folded handkerchief in the breast pocket looked sharp enough to slice bread. She wore a linked bracelet and no other jewelry. Her dark hair was parted and fell in loose but not unstudied waves. She had a smooth ivory skin and rather severe eyebrows and large dark eyes that looked as if they might warm up at the right time and in the right place.*

Those eyebrows and the "not unstudied" wave of her hair are deft shorthand for the true nature of Miss Fromsette's character. She, and the brutal cop, Lieutenant Degarmo, are two of Chandler's greatest creations. The novel ends, hauntingly, in the following manner:

> *A hundred feet down in the canyon a small coupe was smashed against the side of a huge granite boulder. It was almost upside down, leaning a little. There were three men down there. They had moved the car enough to lift something out. Something that had been a man.*

That clinical, unromantic view of death and a distrust of authority figures and politicians, hallmarks of the genre, fit the worldview of a certain segment of my generation, who had rejected the hippie-gone-yuppie lifestyle that emerged as the decade turned and the Reagan years began. The time was ripe for many of us to connect or reconnect with crime lit. Writers like Elmore Leonard, James Crumley, Newton Thornburg, and Kem Nunn were turning crime fiction on its head, implicitly telling young hopefuls with ambition that the game didn't have to be played the same way anymore. Several students in my class had come to the hard-boiled canon through an interest in punk and new wave music. Pre-punk rockers like Warren Zevon had been writing songs influenced by California crime fiction since the early seventies. Reggae and ska bands had hooked into James Bond and spaghetti Westerns, and guitar-is-back bands like the Dream Syndicate and artists like Stan Ridgway were crafting sonic, short-story valentines to Ross Macdonald and Jim Thompson. What the punk ethic meant to me and the prospect of my work was that I didn't need the pedigree of an advanced writing program degree to, at the very least, try to contribute something worthwhile to the genre. If an untrained musician could pick up a guitar and make righteous noise, I could attempt to do the same thing with a pen and notebook. The fact that I knew nothing about the craft or the business side of publishing actually went in my favor. If I hadn't been so naive, I might not have given it a try.

I know I'm not alone. If you throw a rock in a room full of modern crime novelists, it will probably hit someone who got ignitioned after reading his or her first Chandler. Or Hammett, Macdonald, Patricia Highsmith, Robert Parker, Lawrence Block, Leonard, Crumley . . . take your pick. And don't forget the teachers. I bet there is one good teacher in most of our backgrounds who at one point gave us words of encouragement.

Still, there is no obvious direct line from the grandfathers and fathers of crime fiction to the stories in this collection. I certainly don't think you will detect anyone here trying to be Chandleresque. Neither are any of the contributors writing in a faux hardboiled style. Though there are twists and surprises to be discovered, none of these stories are puzzles, locked-room mysteries, or private detective tales. I did not deliberately exclude the traditional. I simply chose these authors because of their original, unique voices. But make no mistake, we are all standing on the shoulders of the writers who came before us and left their indelible mark on literature through craftsmanship, care, and the desire to leave something of worth behind.

I hope you enjoy these wonderful stories.

George Pelecanos

The Best American Mystery Stories 2008

JAMES LEE BURKE

Mist

FROM *The Southern Review*

LISA GUILLORY'S DREAMS ARE INDISTINCT and do not contain the images normally associated with nightmares. Nor do dawn and the early morning mist in the trees come to her in either the form of release or expectation. Instead, her dreams seem to be without sharp edges, like the dull pain of an impacted tooth that takes up nightly residence in her sleep and denies her rest but does not terrify or cause her to wake with night sweats, as is the case with many people at the meetings she has started attending.

The meetings are held in a wood frame Pentecostal church that is set back in a sugarcane field lined with long rows of cane stubble the farmers burn off at night. In the morning, as she drives to the meeting from the shotgun cabin in what is called the Loreauville "quarters," where she now lives, the two-lane is thick with smoke from the stubble fires and the fog rolling off Bayou Teche. She can smell the ash and the burned soil and the heavy, fecund odor of the bayou inside the fog, but it is the fog itself that bothers her, not the odor, because in truth she does not want to leave it and the comfort it seems to provide her.

She pulls to the shoulder of the road and lights a cigarette, inhaling it deeply into her lungs, as though a cigarette can keep at bay the desires — no, the cravings, that build inside her throughout the day, until she imagines that a loop of piano wire has been fitted around her head and is being twisted into her scalp.

Lisa's sponsor is Tookie Goula. She is waiting for Lisa like a gargoyle by the entrance to the clapboard church. Tookie takes one look at Lisa's face and tells her she has to come clean in front of the group, that the time of silent participation has passed, that she has a serious illness and she has to get rid of shame and guilt and admit she is setting herself up for a relapse.

Lisa feigns indifference and boredom. She has heard it all before. "Talking at the meeting gonna get that knocking sound out of my head?"

"What's the knocking sound mean, Lisa?"

"It means he was rocking around inside the coffin when they carried him to the graveyard. I heard it. Like rocks rolling 'round inside a barrel."

Tookie is a thick-bodied Cajun woman with jailhouse tats and a stare like a slap. She is not only inured to financial hardship and worthless men, but she did a stint as a prostitute in a chain of truck stops across the upper South. She wears no makeup, bites her nails when she is angry, and doesn't hide the fact she probably likes women more than men. She is chewing on a nail now, her eyes hot as BBs. "Quit lying," she says.

Lisa can feel the heat bloom in her chest. Lisa tries to slip into the role of victim. "Why you want to hurt me like that?"

"'Cause you ain't honest. 'Cause you ain't gonna get well till you stop jerking yourself around," Tookie replies.

"The Army didn't want me to see what he looked like. All of him wasn't in the coffin. Maybe it wasn't even him," Lisa says.

"You like making yourself suffer?"

Lisa thinks she is going to break down. She wants to break her fists on Tookie's face.

"You're setting yourself up to use, girl," Tookie says. "You're gonna see Herman Stanga. I know your t'oughts before you have them."

"Least I ain't got to wear tattoos to hide the needle scars on my arms," Lisa says. "Least I don't wake up in the morning wondering what gender I am."

During the meeting Tookie keeps raising her dark eyes to Lisa's, biting on her nails, rubbing the powerful muscles in her forearms, breathing with a sound like sand sliding down a drainpipe. Lisa can't take it anymore. "My husband got killed nort' of Baghdad. I know I'm suppose to work on acceptance, but it's hard," she blurts out, without introducing herself by name or identifying herself as an alcoholic or an addict. "I got twenty-seven days now. But I start t'inking of Gerald and how he died and what he must have looked like before they shipped him home, and I start having real bad t'oughts. 'Bout scoring a li'l bit of rock, maybe, not much, just a taste. Like maybe I can still handle it. I'm saying these t'ings 'cause my sponsor says I got to get honest."

She believed her statement about her loss would suck the air out of the room and fill her listeners with shock and sympathy and in the ensuing silence make Tookie regret her callousness. But the local National Guard unit lost five members in Iraq in one day alone, and no one has a patent now on stories of wounded and maimed and dead GIs from south Louisiana. In fact, if anything, Lisa's admission seems either to antagonize or bore those who are not staring out the window, trapped inside their own desperation and ennui. She realizes that in her self-absorption she has interrupted a woman who has recently been gang-raped in a crack house. Her cheeks burn with embarrassment.

"I'm sorry," she says. "My name is Lisa. I'm an alcoholic and a drug addict."

"Keep coming back, Lisa. Those first ninety days are a rough gig. Sometimes you got to fake it till you make it," the chair of the meeting, a white man, says. Then he calls on someone else as though flipping a page in a book.

Fake it till you make it? Fake what? Being sick all the time?

After the meeting she heads straight for her car, looking neither to the right nor to the left, but Tookie inserts herself like an attack dog in her path. "What was that pity-pot stuff about?"

"I made a fool of myself. You ain't got to tell me," Lisa replies.

Tookie's eyes try to peel the skin off Lisa's face. "There's something you ain't owned up to," she says.

"My husband got blown apart. What else I got to tell you?"

"That was eight months ago. What you hiding, you? What happened in New Orleans?"

The sunshine is cold and hard on the cane fields, the stubble still smoking, the fog billowing in white clouds off Bayou Teche. Lisa wants to walk inside the great pillows of white fog and stay there forever.

"I'm okay, Tookie. I ain't gonna use. I promise," she says.

"You know how you can tell when drunks and junkies are lying? Their lips are moving. Come to my house. I'll fix breakfast."

"I'm late for my appointment at the employment office."

Tookie steps closer to her, her face suddenly feminine, tender, almost vulnerable. Her fingers rest on Lisa's forearm, her thumb caressing Lisa's skin for just a moment. "Herman will try to get you in the sack. But getting in your pants ain't what it's about. He wants you on the pipe and working his corner. I been there, Lisa. Herman Stanga is the devil."

Tookie forms a circle with her index finger and thumb around Lisa's wrist and squeezes, her mouth parting with her own undisguised need.

Herman Stanga is full of rebop and snap-crackle-and-pop and knows how to put some boom-boom in your bam-bam, baby. Or at least that is his self-generated mystique as he cruises from place to place in New Iberia's old red-light district, a leather bag hanging from a strap on his shoulder, a pixie expression on his lean face, his mustache like a pair of tiny blackbird's wings against his gold skin.

His girls are called "rock queens," although a lot of them have shifted gears and are doing crystal now because it burns off their fat and keeps them competitive on the street corner where they hook. Herman prefers them white because there are black dudes who will always pay top dollar for white bread, no matter what kind of package it comes in. But, as he is fond of saying, he is "an Affirmative Action employer. Ain't nothing wrong with giving a country girl a crack at a downtown man."

Lisa did not lie to Tookie about her appointment at the state employment office. The problem was the three hundred people ahead of her when she arrived and the piano wire that someone is now tightening around her head with a wood peg. She lasts forty-five minutes in the waiting room, vomits in the bathroom, then drives down Railroad Avenue to the first liquor store she can find. The short-dog she buys may smell like a mixture of hair tonic and kerosene, but it goes down with a rush that is one notch south of the orgasmic moment she experienced when she first shot up with brown skag.

She finishes the bottle under the shade of a spreading oak by a small grocery store. Gangbangers with black kerchiefs tied down on their heads are taking turns at a weight set under the tree, curling the bar into their bare chests, their steroid-swollen muscles almost popping out of their skin. Lisa screws the cap on the empty bottle and stares vacantly into space, then takes her time getting out of the car and dropping the bottle in a trash barrel. She has no reason to remain under a lichen-encrusted tree, in New Iberia's old brothel district, on a morning she should seek work, on a morning that somehow seems like a crossroads that has been set in her path. But the sun-spangled shade under the tree is a pleasant place to be, with her car door open to the wind, on a day that is both warm and cool at the same time, while the boys clank iron and leaves drift down on her windshield like gold coins.

She shuts her eyes and breathes the heavy odor of the fortified wine in and out of her lungs, and for just a moment, as though she is outside of her body, she sees Gerald kiss her cheek and place the flat of his hand on her belly.

Without invitation, a grinning man wearing a striped brown suit and an oxblood Stetson opens the passenger door and slides in beside her. He has two sweating cans of Budweiser balanced in his left palm and a fat package of warm boudin in the other. "Hey, darling, want to join me in a li'l snack?" he asks, already spreading the butcher paper open on the seat, filling the car with the delicious smell of ground sausage and spice and onions.

"I ain't here to score, Herman," she replies.

"I respect folks' choices. When they get clean, I say more power to them. But that don't mean I ain't their friend no more."

He peels the tab on one of the beer cans and lets the foam rise through the hole and well over the top and slide down the back of his hand. "Here you go, baby. Sip this while I cut you some boudin chunks. You found a job yet? All them evacuees is kind of messing up the labor market, ain't they?"

She is an evacuee, flooded out of the Lower Ninth Ward in Orleans Parish by Hurricane Katrina, shuttled from the Superdome to a shelter in New Iberia's City Park. In fact, she'd still be there or in a FEMA trailer camp if her aunt hadn't given her the use of the shotgun cabin in the Loreauville quarters. But Herman already knows that. Herman knows how to flatter, to imply his listener is different, special, not part of a categorical group whose presence is starting to be resented and feared.

"That Budweiser is good and cold, ain't it?" he says. "Lookie here, drive me to my crib and let me make some calls. Can you do receptionist work, answer the phone, maybe seat people in a restaurant, stuff like that?"

"Sure, Herman."

"Then let's motivate on out of here, baby," he says, lifting his chin, indicating she should start the engine and drive the two of them to his Victorian home on Bayou Teche.

Herman acquired the house from a black physician who, for unknown reasons, signed over the deed and left town. No one ever knew where the physician or his family went, nor were they ever heard from again. The wood columns are eaten by termites, the ventilated green shutters askew on their hinges, the second-story rain gutters bleeding rust down the walls. The oak and pecan trees are so thick that sunlight never enters the house and no grass grows in the yard.

But Herman is not concerned with historical preservation. The swimming pool in his backyard is a glittering blue teardrop, coated with steam, where his girls float on inflated latex cushions, where bougainvillea drips as brightly as drops of blood on his latticework, where potted lime and Hong Kong orchid trees bloom year round and assure his guests the season is eternal.

"Sit here and relax, while I call in a couple of favors from some business associates," he says out on the terrace. "Have some of them veined shrimps. Ignore the ladies in the pool. They nice, but they ain't in your league, know what I mean? Hey, if I get you on in a hostess position, it's probably gonna be twelve or t'irteen dollars an hour. You all right wit' that?"

Lisa sits in the coolness of the sunshine and tries to concentrate on what she is doing. It's only noon and she has gone from the comfort of the fog at sunrise into the meeting at the church, then to the employment office and the liquor store and the shady oak tree where boys clanked iron and admired one another's bodies as though anatomical perfection were a stay against mortality. Now she is at the home of Herman Stanga, watching women she doesn't know swim in a sky-blue pool, while Herman paces back and forth behind the French doors, talking on the phone, undressing down to a thong, kicking his trousers in a rattle of change across the room.

The bayou is chocolate brown, the sun a wobbling balloon of yellow flame trapped under its surface. The bayou conjures up images and memories she does not want to revisit. In her mind she sees people wading in chest-deep water, the surface iridescent with a chemical sheen, fecal clouds rising from the bottom, a stench crawling into her nostrils that makes her gag. Then the knocking sound starts in her head, and she has to press both fists against her temples to make it stop.

Why has she come to Herman's house? Does she really believe he wants to help her? What would Tookie say if she knew?

"I'm telling you, this is a nice lady, man," she hears Herman saying. "No, she ain't on welfare. No, she ain't got no personal problems or bad habits. What she *got* is my recommendation. Don't give me your trash, Rodney. I'm sending her over. You treat her right, nigger."

Herman clicks off the phone and slips on a blue robe that hangs on his lithe frame like ice water. He motions Lisa inside and tells her to sit on a stool at a counter that separates the living room from the kitchen. "My cousin Rodney own a couple of clubs in Lafayette and cater parties and banquets for rich people out at the Oil Center. All you got to do is supervise the buffet table and the punch bowl and make sure everybody getting the drinks they need. They want somebody know how to deal with the public. I told Rodney that's you, baby."

He's talking too fast for her. Her ears are popping and she thinks she hears voices yelling and the downdraft of helicopter blades. She realizes Herman is staring at her, his face disjointed. "You gonna get crazy on me?" he says.

"The Coast Guard helicopter took me off the roof. The blades was so loud nobody could hear. I was shouting and nobody could hear."

"Shouting what?" Herman asks. "What you talking about?"

"The Coast Guard man grabbed me around the chest and pulled me up on a cable. I couldn't t'ink. I could see trash and bodies in the water all the way to where the levee was broke. I cain't get that noise out of my head."

"What noise?"

"The knocking."

Herman brushes at a nostril with one knuckle and huffs air out his nose, his eyes flat, as though he's studying thoughts of a kind no one would ever guess at. He begins to massage the tendons in her shoulders. "You're tight as iron, Lisa. That ain't good for you. Come upstairs."

"No."

For just an instant, in the time it takes to blink, she sees the light in his eyes harden. Then he bites his lip softly and smiles to himself.

"I respect you, darling. Wouldn't have our relationship no other way."

Now he's the pixie again, his tiny mustache flexing with his grin. He places a mirror on the corner, backside flat, and begins chopping up lines on it with a razor blade, shaping and sculpting each white row like an artwork. "I still got the best product in town. I don't force it on nobody. They hurting, need some medicine, I hep them out. But I ain't the captain of nobody else's soul."

"I don't want any, Herman," she says, the words catching like a wet bubble in her throat.

"If you can get by on a short-dog and a beer now and then, I say 'rock on, girl.' I say you a superwoman."

He removes a one-hundred-dollar bill from the pocket of his robe, rolls it into a crisp tube, and snorts a line up each nostril, the soles of his slippers slapping on the floor. He grabs his thonged phallus inside his open robe and pulls on it. "Tell me them coca leaves wasn't picked by Indian goddesses."

"I got to go, Herman," she says, because she is absolutely sure the knocking sound that has haunted her sleep and that sometimes comes aborning even in the midst of a conversation is about to begin again.

At the front door he presses the hundred-dollar bill into her palm and closes her fingers on it. "Get you some new threads. You fine-looking, Miss Lisa. Got the kind of class make a man's eye wander."

He lifts her hand, the one that holds the hundred-dollar bill, and kisses it. The cocaine residue on the paper seems to burn like a tiny ball of heat clenched inside her palm.

The party she helps cater that night is held in a refurbished icehouse across the street from a Jewish cemetery shrouded by live oaks. It's raining outside, but the moon is full and visible through the clouds, and the shell parking lot is chained with rain puddles. A tin roof covers the old loading dock where years ago blocks of ice rushed down a chute into a wood box and once there were chopped into small pieces with ice picks by sweating black men. The roar of the rain on the tin roof is almost deafening, and Lisa has a hard time concentrating on her work. She has another problem, too.

Rodney, the caterer, can't keep his hands off her. When he tells her how to arrange and freshen the salad bar, he keeps his palm in the middle of her back. When he walks her the length of the serving table, he drapes an arm over her shoulder. When she separates from him, he lets his fingers trail off her rump.

"Herman tol' me you growed up here'bouts," he says, slipping his grasp around her triceps.

"My husband's daddy worked at this icehouse. He chopped up ice out there on the dock, in that wood box there," she replies.

He nods idly, as though processing her statement. "Your husband got killed in Iraq?"

She starts to answer, then realizes he isn't listening, that he's watching another worker pour a stainless steel tray of okra gumbo into a warmer. His gaze breaks and his eyes come back on her. "Go ahead," he says.

"Go ahead what?"

"Say what you was saying."

"Can I get paid after work tonight? I got to hep my auntie wit' her mortgage."

"Don't see nothing wrong wit' that," he says.

He squeezes by her on his way to the kitchen, the thick outline of his phallus sliding across her rump.

The party becomes more raucous, grows in intensity, the males-only crowd emboldened by their numbers and insularity. Four bare-breasted women in spangled G-strings and spiked heels are dancing on a stage, fishnet patterns of light and shadow shifting across their skin. Outside, the rain continues to fall and Lisa can see the black-green wetness of the oak trees surrounding the Jewish cemetery, the canopy swishing against the sky, and she wonders if it is true that the unbaptized are locked out of heaven.

Why is she thinking such strange thoughts? She tries to think about her life in New Orleans before the hurricane, before Gerald's reserve unit was called up, before his Humvee was blown into scrap metal.

She had waited tables in a restaurant in Jackson Square, right across from Café Du Monde. There were jugglers and street musicians and unicyclists in the Square, and crepe myrtle and banana trees grew along the piked fence where the sidewalk artists set up their easels. It was cool and breezy under the colonnades, and the courtyards and narrow passageways smelled of damp stone and spearmint and roses that bloomed in December. She liked to watch the people emerging from Mass at St. Louis Cathedral on Saturday evening, and she liked bringing them the steaming trays of boiled crawfish, corn on the cob, and artichokes that were the restaurant's specialty. In fact, she loved New Orleans and she loved Gerald and she loved their one-story, tin-roofed home in the Lower Ninth Ward.

But these thoughts cause her scalp to constrict, and she thinks she hears hail bouncing off the loading dock outside.

"You got seizures or something?" Rodney asks.

"What?"

"You just dropped the ladle in the gumbo," he says.

She stares stupidly at the serving spoon sinking in the caldron of okra and shrimp.

"Take a break," Rodney says.

She tries to argue, then relents and waits in a small office by the kitchen while Rodney gets another girl to fill in for her. He closes the door behind him and studies Lisa with a worried expression, then sits in a chair across from her and lights a joint. He takes a hit, holding it deep in his lungs, offering it to her while he lets out his breath in increments. Her hand seems to reach out as though it has a will of its own. She bends over and touches the joint to her lips and feels the wetness of his saliva mix with her own. She can hear the cigarette paper superheat and crinkle as she draws in on the smoke.

"I got to pay you off, baby."

"'Cause I dropped the ladle?"

"'Cause you was talking to yourself at the buffet table. 'Cause you in your own spaceship."

Someone outside twists the door handle and flings the door back on its hinges. Tookie Goula steps inside, the strap of her handbag wrapped around her wrist, her arms pumped. "You put that joint in your mout' again, I'm gonna break your arm, me. Then I'm gonna stuff this pimp here in a toilet bowl," she says.

Moments later, in Lisa's parked automobile, Tookie stares at Lisa with such intensity Lisa thinks she is about to hit her.

"Next time I'll let you drown," Tookie says.

Lisa looks at the Jewish cemetery and the oak trees thrashing against the sky and the rain puddles in the parking lot. The puddles are bladed with moonlight, and she thinks of Communion wafers inside a pewter chalice, but she doesn't know why.

"What do you know about drowning, Tookie?"

Tookie seems to reflect upon Lisa's question, as though she too is bothered by the presumption and harshness in her own rhetoric. But the charitable impulse passes. "Get your head out of your ass. You want to fire me as your sponsor, do it now."

Lisa still has the hundred-dollar bill Herman Stanga gave her, plus the money she was paid by his cousin Rodney. She can score some rock or crystal or brown skag in North Lafayette and stay high or go on an alcoholic bender for at least two days. All she has to do is thank Tookie for her help and drive away.

"Where you think limbo is at?" she says.

"What?"

"The place people go when they ain't baptized. Like all them Jews in that cemetery."

Tookie stares wanly at the parking lot, her face marked with a sad knowledge about the nature of loss and human inadequacy that she will probably never admit, even to herself.

The next morning Lisa stands at the speaker's podium at the A.A. meeting in the Pentecostal church, her eyes fixed on the back wall, and owns up to drinking, using, and jerking her sponsor around. She says she intends to work the steps and to live by the principles of the program. Both the brevity of her statement and the sincerity in her voice surprise her. She receives a twenty-four-hour sobriety chip, then watches it passed around the room so each person at the meeting can hold it in his palm and say a silent prayer over it. She lowers her head to hide the wetness in her eyes.

"Eat breakfast wit' me. Up at the café," Tookie says.

"I'd like that," Lisa says.

"You gonna make it, you."

Lisa believes her. All the way to 3:00 P.M., when Herman Stanga pulls up to her shotgun house in the Loreauville quarters and kills his engine by her gallery. His car hood ticks like a broken watch.

"You ain't gonna unlatch the screen for me?" he says.

"I ain't got no reason to talk wit' you, Herman."

"Got me all wrong, baby. I done a li'l research on your financial situation. You should have gotten at least a hundred t'ousand dollars when your husband was killed. The gov'ment ain't paid you yet?"

She swallows and the tin rooftops and the narrow houses that are shaped like boxcars and the trees along the bayou go in and out of focus and shimmer in the winter sunlight.

"Gerald's divorce hadn't come t'rou yet," she says.

"What you mean?"

"His mama and his first wife was the beneficiaries on the policy. He didn't change the policy," she says, her eyes shifting off of Herman's, as though she were both confessing a sin and betraying Gerald.

Herman feeds a stick of gum into his mouth, smacks it in his jaw, and raises his eyebrows, as though trying to suppress his incredulity. "Tell me if I got this right. He's putting the blocks to you, but he goes off to Iraq and fixes it so you ain't gonna have no insurance money? That's the guy you moping 'round about?"

He begins to chew his gum more rapidly and doesn't wait for her to reply. "So what we gonna do about the eight-t'ousand-dollar tab you got? Also, what we gonna do about the twenty-t'ree-hundred dollars you took out of Rodney's cashbox last night?"

"Cashbox?"

His head bounces up and down like it's connected to a rubber band. "Yeah, the cashbox, the one that was in the desk in the office where Rodney said to sit your neurotic ass down and wait for him. You t'ink you can rip off a man like Rodney and just do your nutcase routine and walk away?"

"I didn't steal no money. I don't owe you no eight t'ousand dollars, either."

"'Cause you was so stoned out you got no memory of it." Then he begins to mimic her. "'Tie me off, Herman. Give me just one balloon, Herman. I'll do anyt'ing, Herman. I'll be good to you, Herman. I'll pay you tomorrow, Herman.'"

How does he speak with such authority and confidence? Did she actually say those things? Is that who she really is?

"I ain't stole no money out of no office."

"Tell that to the sheriff when Rodney files charges. Open this goddamn door, bitch. You fixin' to go on the installment plan."

She attacks his face with her nails, and he hits her with his fist harder than she ever believed a human being could be hit.

During the next six weeks Lisa comes to believe the person she thought was Lisa perhaps never existed. The new Lisa also learns that hell is a place without geographical boundaries, that it can travel with an individual wherever she goes. She wakes to its presence at sunrise, aching and dehydrated, the sky like the watery, cherry-stained dregs in the bottom of a Collins glass. Whether picking up a brick of Afghan skunk in a Lafayette bus locker for Herman or tying off with one of his whores, sometimes using the same needle, Lisa moves from day into night without taking notice of clocks or calendars or the macabre transformation in the face that looks back at her from the mirror.

She attends meetings sometimes but either nods out or lies about the last time she drank or used. If pressed for the truth about where she has been or what she has done, she cannot objectively answer. Dreams and hallucinations and moments of heart-pounding clarity somehow meld together and become indistinguishable from one another. The irony is, the knocking sound has finally stopped.

Sometimes Tookie Goula cooks for her, holds her hands, puts her in the shower when she is too sick to care for herself. Tookie has started to smoke again and some days looks haggard and hung over. At twilight on a spring evening they are in Lisa's bedroom, and the live oaks along the bayou are dark green and pulsing with birds against a lavender sky. Lisa has not used or gotten drunk in the last twenty-four hours. But she thinks she smells alcohol on Tookie's breath.

"It's codeine. For my cough," Tookie says.

"It's a drug just the same," Lisa says. "You go back on the spike, you gonna die, Tookie."

Tookie lies down next to Lisa, then turns on her side and places one arm across Lisa's chest. Lisa doesn't resist but neither does she respond.

"You want to move in wit' me?" Tookie asks. "I'll hep you get away from Herman. Maybe we'll go to Houston or up nort' somewhere, maybe open a café."

But Lisa is not listening. She rubs the balls of her fingers along one of the tattoos on Tookie's forearm.

"A mosquito bit me," Tookie says.

"No, you're back on the spike."

She kisses Tookie on the mouth and presses Tookie's head against her breast, something she has never done before. "You break my heart."

"You're wrong. I ain't used in t'ree years, me."

"Stop lying, stop lying, stop lying," Lisa says, holding Tookie tightly against her breast, as though her arms can squeeze the sickness out of both their bodies.

It begins to rain and Lisa can smell fish spawning in the bayou and the odor of gas and wet leaves on the wind. She hears the blades of a helicopter thropping across the sky and sees lightning flicker on the tin roofs of her neighbors' homes. As she closes her eyes, she feels herself drifting upward from her bed, through the ceiling, into the coolness and freedom of the evening. The clouds form a huge dome above her, like that of a cathedral, and she can see the vastness of creation: the rain-drenched land, a distant storm that looks like spun glass, a sea gone wine-dark with the setting of the sun.

Gerald loved me. We was gonna be married by a priest soon as his divorce come through, she says to Tookie.

I know that, Tookie says.

Down there, that's where it happened.

What happened?

My sister was trying to hand up my li'l boy t'rou the hole in the roof, and they fell back in the water. I could hear them knocking in there, but I couldn't get them out. My baby never got baptized.

These t'ings ain't your fault, Lisa. Ain't nobody's fault. That's what makes it hard. You ain't learned that, you?

Directly below, Lisa can see the submerged outline of the house where she and her family used to live. The sun is low on the western horizon now, dead-looking, like a piece of tin that gives no warmth. Beneath the water's surface Lisa can see tiny lights that remind her of broken Communion wafers inside a pewter chalice or perhaps the souls of infants who have found one another and have been cupped and given safe harbor by an enormous hand. For reasons she cannot explain, that image and Tookie's presence bring her a moment of solace she had not anticipated.

MICHAEL CONNELLY

Mulholland Dive

FROM *Los Angeles Noir*

BURNING FLARES AND FLASHING RED and blue lights ripped the night apart. Clewiston counted four black-and-whites pulled halfway off the roadway and as close to the upper embankment as was possible. In front of them was a fire truck and in front of that was a forensics van. There was a P-one standing in the middle of Mulholland Drive ready to hold up traffic or wave it into the one lane that they had open. With a fatality involved, they should have closed down both lanes of the road, but that would have meant closing Mulholland from Laurel Canyon on one side all the way to Coldwater Canyon on the other. That was too long a stretch. There would be consequences for that. The huge inconvenience of it would have brought complaints from the rich hillside homeowners trying to get home after another night of the good life. And nobody stuck on midnight shift wanted more complaints to deal with.

Clewiston had worked Mulholland fatals several times. He was the expert. He was the one they called in from home. He knew that whether the identity of the victim in this case demanded it or not, he'd have gotten the call. It was Mulholland, and the Mulholland calls all went to him.

But this one was special anyway. The victim was a name and the case was going five-by-five. That meant everything about it had to be squared away and done right. He had been thoroughly briefed over the phone by the watch commander about that.

He pulled in behind the last patrol car, put his flashers on, and got out of his unmarked car. On the way back to the trunk, he grabbed his badge from beneath his shirt and hung it out front. He was in civvies, having been called in from off-duty, and it was prudent to make sure he announced he was a detective.

He used his key to open the trunk and began to gather the equipment he would need. The P-one left his post in the road and walked over.

"Where's the sergeant?" Clewiston asked.

"Up there. I think they're about to pull the car up. That's a hundred thousand dollars he went over the side with. Who are you?"

"Detective Clewiston. The reconstructionist. Sergeant Fairbanks is expecting me."

"Go on down and you'll find him by the — Whoa, what is that?"

Clewiston saw him looking at the face peering up from the trunk. The crash test dummy was partially hidden by all the equipment cluttering the trunk, but the face was clear and staring blankly up at them. His legs had been detached and were resting beneath the torso. It was the only way to fit the whole thing in the trunk.

"We call him Arty," Clewiston said. "He was made by a company called Accident Reconstruction Technologies."

"Looks sort of real at first," the patrol officer said. "Why's he in fatigues?"

Clewiston had to think about that to remember.

"Last time I used Arty, it was a crosswalk hit-and-run case. The vic was a Marine up from El Toro. He was in his fatigues and there was a question about whether the hitter saw him." Clewiston slung the strap of his laptop bag over his shoulder. "He did. Thanks to Arty we made a case."

He took his clipboard out of the trunk and then a digital camera, his trusty measuring wheel, and an eight-battery Maglite. He closed the trunk and made sure it was locked.

"I'm going to head down and get this over with," he said. "I got called in from home."

"Yeah, I guess the faster you're done, the faster I can get back out on the road myself. Pretty boring just standing here."

"I know what you mean."

Clewiston headed down the westbound lane, which had been closed to traffic. There was a mist clinging in the dark to the tall brush that crowded the sides of the street. But he could still see the lights and glow of the city down to the south. The accident had occurred in one of the few spots along Mulholland where there were no homes. He knew that on the south side of the road the embankment dropped down to a public dog park. On the north side was Fryman Canyon and the embankment rose up to a point where one of the city's communication stations was located. There was a tower up there on the point that helped bounce communication signals over the mountains that cut the city in half.

Mulholland was literally the backbone of Los Angeles. It rode like a snake along the crest of the Santa Monica Mountains from one end of the city to the other. Clewiston knew of places where you could stand on the white stripe and look north across the vast San Fernando Valley and then turn around and look south and see across the west side and as far as the Pacific and Catalina Island. It all depended on whether the smog was cooperating or not. And if you knew the right spots to stop and look.

Mulholland had that top-of-the-world feel to it. It could make you feel like the prince of a city where the laws of nature and physics didn't apply. The foot came down heavy on the accelerator. That was the contradiction. Mulholland was built for speed but it couldn't handle it. Speed was a killer.

As he came around the bend, Clewiston saw another fire truck and a tow truck from the Van Nuys police garage. The tow truck was positioned sideways across the road. Its cable was down the embankment and stretched taut as it pulled the car up. For the moment, Mulholland was completely closed. Clewiston could hear the tow motor straining and the cracking and scraping as the unseen car was being pulled up through the brush. The tow truck shuddered as it labored.

Clewiston saw the man with sergeant's stripes on his uniform and moved next to him as he watched.

"Is he still in it?" he asked Fairbanks.

"No, he was transported to St. Joe's. But he was DOA. You're Clewiston, right? The reconstructionist."

"Yes."

"We've got to handle this thing right. Once the ID gets out, we'll have the media all over this."

"The captain told me."

"Yeah, well, I'm telling you too. In this department, the captains don't get blamed when things go sideways and off the road. It's always the sergeants and it ain't going to be me this time."

"I get it."

"You have any idea what this guy was worth? We're talking tens of millions, and on top of that he's supposedly in the middle of a divorce. So we go five by five by five on this thing. *Comprende,* reconstructionist?"

"It's Clewiston and I said I get it."

"Good. This is what we've got. Single-car fatality. No witnesses. It appears the victim was heading eastbound when his vehicle, a two-month-old Porsche Carrera, came around that last curve there and for whatever reason didn't straighten out. We've got treads on the road you can take a look at. Anyway, he went straight off the side and then down, baby. Major head and torso injuries. Chest crushed. He pretty much drowned in his own blood before the FD could get down to him. They stretchered him out with a chopper and transported him anyway. Guess they didn't want any blow-back either."

"They take blood at St. Joe's?"

Fairbanks, about forty and a lifer on patrol, nodded. "I am told it was clean."

There was a pause in the conversation at that point, suggesting that Clewiston could take whatever he wanted from the blood test. He could believe what Fairbanks was telling him or he could believe that the celebrity fix was already in.

The moonlight reflected off the dented silver skin of the Porsche as it was pulled up over the edge like a giant beautiful fish hauled into a boat. Clewiston walked over and Fairbanks followed. The first thing Clewiston saw was that it was a Carrera 4S. "Hmmmm," he mumbled.

"What?" Fairbanks said.

"It's one of the Porsches with four-wheel drive. Built for these sort of curves. Built for control."

"Well, not built good enough, obviously."

Clewiston put his equipment down on the hood of one of the patrol cars and took his Maglite over to the Porsche. He swept the beam over the front of the high-performance sports car. The car was heavily damaged in the crash and the front had taken the brunt of it. The molded body was badly distorted by repeated impacts as it had sledded down the steep embankment. He moved in close and squatted by the front cowling and the shattered passenger-side headlight assembly.

He could feel Fairbanks behind him, watching over his shoulder as he worked.

"If there were no witnesses, how did anybody know he'd gone over the side?" Clewiston asked.

"Somebody down below," Fairbanks answered. "There are houses down there. Lucky this guy didn't end up in somebody's living room. I've seen that before."

So had Clewiston. He stood up and walked to the edge and looked down. His light cut into the darkness of the brush. He saw the exposed pulp of the acacia trees and other foliage the car had torn through.

He returned to the car. The driver's door was sprung and Clewiston could see the pry marks left by the jaws used to extricate the driver. He pulled it open and leaned in with his light. There was a lot of blood on the wheel, dashboard, and center console. The driver's seat was wet with blood and urine.

The key was still in the ignition and turned to the on position. The dashboard lights were still on as well. Clewiston leaned further in and checked the mileage. The car had only 1,142 miles on the odometer.

Satisfied with his initial survey of the wreck, he went back to his equipment. He put the clipboard under his arm and picked up the measuring wheel. Fairbanks came over once again. "Anything?" he asked.

"Not yet, sergeant. I'm just starting."

He started sweeping the light over the roadway. He picked up the skid marks and used the wheel to measure the distance of each one. There were four distinct marks, left as all four tires of the Porsche tried unsuccessfully to grip the asphalt. When he worked his way back to the starting point, he found scuff marks in a classic slalom pattern. They had been left on the asphalt when the car had turned sharply one way and then the other before going into the braking skid.

He wrote the measurements down on the clipboard. He then pointed the light into the brush on either side of the roadway where the scuff marks began. He knew the event had begun here and he was looking for indications of cause.

He noticed a small opening in the brush, a narrow pathway that continued on the other side of the road. It was a crossing. He stepped over and put the beam down on the brush and soil. After a few moments, he moved across the street and studied the path on the other side.

Satisfied with his site survey, he went back to the patrol car and opened his laptop. While it was booting up, Fairbanks came over once again.

"So, how'z it look?"

"I have to run the numbers."

"Those skids look pretty long to me. The guy must've been flying."

"You'd be surprised. Other things factor in. Brake efficiency, surface, and surface conditions — you see the mist moving in right now? Was it like this two hours ago when the guy went over the side?"

"Been like this since I got here. But the fire guys were here first. I'll get one up here."

Clewiston nodded. Fairbanks pulled his rover and told someone to send the first responders up to the crash site. He then looked back at Clewiston.

"On the way."

"Thanks. Does anybody know what this guy was doing up here?"

"Driving home, we assume. His house was in Coldwater and he was going home."

"From where?"

"That we don't know."

"Anybody make notification yet?"

"Not yet. We figure next of kin is the wife he's divorcing. But we're not sure where to find her. I sent a car to his house but there's no answer. We've got somebody at Parker Center trying to run her down — probably through her lawyer. There's also grown children from his first marriage. They're working on that too."

Two firefighters walked up and introduced themselves as Robards and Lopez. Clewiston questioned them on the weather and road conditions at the time they responded to the accident call. Both firefighters described the mist as heavy at the time. They were sure about this because the mist had hindered their ability to find the place where the vehicle had crashed through the brush and down the embankment.

"If we hadn't seen the skid marks, we would have driven right by," Lopez said.

Clewiston thanked them and turned back to his computer. He

had everything he needed now. He opened the Accident Reconstruction Technologies program and went directly to the speed and distance calculator. He referred to his clipboard for the numbers he would need. He felt Fairbanks come up next to him.

"Computer, huh? That gives you all the answers?"

"Some of them."

"Whatever happened to experience and trusting hunches and gut instincts?"

It wasn't a question that was waiting for an answer. Clewiston added the lengths of the four skid marks he had measured and then divided by four, coming up with an average length of sixty-four feet. He entered the number into the calculator template.

"You said the vehicle is only two months old?" he asked Fairbanks.

"According to the registration. It's a lease he picked up in January. I guess he filed for divorce and went out and got the sports car to help him get back in the game."

Clewiston ignored the comment and typed *1.0* into a box marked *B.E.* on the template.

"What's that?" Fairbanks asked.

"Braking efficiency. One-oh is the highest efficiency. Things could change if somebody wants to take the brakes off the car and test them. But for now I am going with high efficiency because the vehicle is new and there's only twelve hundred miles on it."

"Sounds right to me."

Lastly, Clewiston typed *9.0* into the box marked *C.F.* This was the subjective part. He explained what he was doing to Fairbanks before the sergeant had to ask.

"This is coefficient of friction," he said. "It basically means surface conditions. Mulholland Drive is asphalt base, which is generally a high coefficient. And this stretch here was repaved about nine months ago — again, that leads to a high coefficient. But I'm knocking it down a point because of the moisture. That mist comes in and puts down a layer of moisture that mixes with the road oil and makes the asphalt slippery. The oil is heavier in new asphalt."

"I get it."

"Good. It's called trusting your gut instinct, sergeant."

Fairbanks nodded. He had been properly rebuked.

Clewiston clicked the enter button and the calculator came up with a projected speed based on the relationship between skid length, brake efficiency, and the surface conditions. It said the Porsche had been traveling at 41.569 miles per hour when it went into the skid.

"You're kidding me," Fairbanks said while looking at the screen. "The guy was barely speeding. How can that be?"

"Follow me, sergeant," Clewiston said.

Clewiston left the computer and the rest of his equipment, except for the flashlight. He led Fairbanks back to the point in the road where he had found the slalom scuffs and the originating point of the skid marks.

"Okay," he said. "The event started here. We have a single-car accident. No alcohol known to be involved. No real speed involved. A car built for this sort of road is involved. What went wrong?"

"Exactly."

Clewiston put the light down on the scuff marks.

"Okay, you've got alternating scuff marks here before he goes into the skid."

"Okay."

"You have the tire cords indicating he jerked the wheel right initially and then jerked it left trying to straighten it out. We call it a SAM — a slalom avoidance maneuver."

"A SAM. Okay."

"He turned to avoid an impact of some kind, then overcorrected. He then panicked and did what most people do. He hit the brakes."

"Got it."

"The wheels locked up and he went into a skid. There was nothing he could do at that point. He had no control because the instinct is to press harder on the brakes, to push that pedal through the floor."

"And the brakes were what were taking away control."

"Exactly. He went over the side. The question is why. Why did he jerk the wheel in the first place? What preceded the event?"

"Another car?"

Clewiston nodded. "Could be. But no one stopped. No one called it in."

"Maybe . . ." Fairbanks spread his hands. He was drawing a blank.

"Take a look here," Clewiston said.

He walked Fairbanks over to the side of the road. He put the light on the pathway into the brush, drawing the sergeant's eyes back across Mulholland to the pathway on the opposite side. Fairbanks looked at him and then back at the path.

"What are you thinking?" Fairbanks asked.

"This is a coyote path," Clewiston said. "They come up through Fryman Canyon and cross Mulholland here. It takes them to the dog park. They probably wait in heavy brush for the dogs that stray out of the park."

"So your thinking is that our guy came around the curve and there was a coyote crossing the road."

Clewiston nodded. "That's what I'm thinking. He jerks the wheel to avoid the animal, then overcompensates, loses control. You have a slalom followed by a braking skid. He goes over the side."

"An accident, plain and simple." Fairbanks shook his head disappointedly. "Why couldn't it have been a DUI, something clear-cut like that?" he asked. "Nobody's going to believe us on this one."

"That's not our problem. All the facts point to it being a driving mishap. An accident."

Fairbanks looked at the skid marks and nodded. "Then that's it, I guess."

"You'll get a second opinion from the insurance company anyway," Clewiston said. "They'll probably pull the brakes off the car and test them. An accident means double indemnity. But if they can shift the calculations and prove he was speeding or being reckless, it softens the impact. The payout becomes negotiable. But my guess is they'll see it the same way we do."

"I'll make sure forensics photographs everything. We'll document everything six ways from Sunday and the insurance people can take their best shot. When will I get a report from you?"

"I'll go down to Valley Traffic right now and write something up."

"Good. Get it to me. What else?"

Clewiston looked around to see if he was forgetting anything. He shook his head. "That's it. I need to take a few more measurements and some photos, then I'll head down to write it up. Then I'll get out of your way."

Clewiston left him and headed back up the road to get his camera. He had a small smile on his face that nobody noticed.

Clewiston headed west on Mulholland from the crash site. He planned to take Coldwater Canyon down into the Valley and over to the Traffic Division office. He waited until the flashing blue and red lights were small in his rearview mirror before flipping open his phone. He hoped he could get a signal on the cheap throwaway. Mulholland Drive wasn't always cooperative with cellular service.

He had a signal. He pulled to the side while he attached the digital recorder, then turned it on and made the call. She answered after one ring, as he was pulling back onto the road and up to speed.

"Where are you?" he asked.

"The apartment."

"They're looking for you. You're sure his attorney knows where you are?"

"He knows. Why? What's going on?"

"They want to tell you he's dead."

He heard her voice catch. He took the phone away from his ear so he could hold the wheel with two hands on one of the deep curves. He then brought it back.

"You there?" he asked.

"Yes, I'm here. I just can't believe it, that's all. I'm speechless. I didn't think it would really happen."

You may be speechless, but you're talking, Clewiston thought. *Keep it up.*

"You wanted it to happen, so it happened," he said. "I told you I would take care of it."

"What happened?"

"He went off the road on Mulholland. It's an accident and you're a rich lady now."

She said nothing.

"What else do you want to know?" he asked.

"I'm not sure. Maybe I shouldn't know anything. It will be better when they come here."

"You're an actress. You can handle it."

"Okay."

He waited for her to say more, glancing down at the recorder on the center console to see the red light still glowing. He was good.

"Was he in pain?" she asked.

"Hard to say. He was probably dead when they pried him out. From what I hear, it will be a closed casket. Why do you care?"

"I guess I don't. It's just sort of surreal that this is happening. Sometimes I wish you never came to me with the whole idea."

"You rather go back to being trailer park trash while he lives up on the hill?"

"No, it wouldn't be like that. My attorney says the prenup has holes in it."

Clewiston shook his head. Second-guessers. They hire his services and then can't live with the consequences.

"What's done is done," he said. "This will be the last time we talk. When you get the chance, throw the phone you're talking on away like I told you."

"There won't be any records?"

"It's a throwaway. Like all the drug dealers use. Open it up, smash the chip, and throw it all away the next time you go to McDonald's."

"I don't go to McDonald's."

"Then throw it away at the Ivy. I don't give a shit. Just not at your house. Let things run their course. Soon you'll have all his money. And you double dip on the insurance because of the accident. You can thank me for that."

He was coming up to the hairpin turn that offered the best view of the Valley.

"How do we know that they think it was an accident?"

"Because I made them think that. I told you, I have Mulholland wired. That's what you paid for. Nobody is going to second-guess a goddamn thing. His insurance company will come in and sniff around, but they won't be able to change things. Just sit tight and stay cool. Say nothing. Offer nothing. Just like I told you."

The lights of the Valley spread out in front of him before the turn. He saw a car pulled over at the unofficial overlook. On any other night he'd stop and roust them — probably teenagers getting it on in the back seat. But not tonight. He had to get down to the traffic office and write up his report.

"This is the last time we talk," he said to her.

He looked down at the recorder. He knew it would be the last time they talked — until he needed more money from her.

"How did you get him to go off the road?" she asked.

He smiled. They always ask that. "My friend Arty did it."

"You brought a third party into this. Don't you see that — "

"Relax. Arty doesn't talk."

He started into the turn. He realized the phone had gone dead.

"Hello?" he said. "Hello?"

He looked at the screen. No signal. These cheap throwaways were about as reliable as the weather.

He felt his tires catch the edge of the roadway and looked up in time to pull the car back onto the road. As he came out of the turn, he checked the phone's screen one more time for the signal. He needed to call her back, let her know how it was going to be.

There was still no signal.

"Goddamn it!"

He slapped the phone closed on his thigh, then peered back at the road and froze as his eyes caught and held on two glowing eyes in the headlights. In a moment he broke free and jerked the wheel right to avoid the coyote. He corrected, but the wheels caught on the deep edge of the asphalt. He jerked harder and the front wheel broke free and back up on the road. But the back wheel slipped out and the car went into a slide.

Clewiston had an almost clinical knowledge of what was happening. It was as if he was watching one of the accident re-creations he had prepared a hundred times for court hearings and prosecutions.

The car went into a sideways slide toward the precipice. He knew he would hit the wooden fence — chosen by the city for aesthetic reasons over function and safety — and that he would crash through. He knew at that moment that he was probably a dead man.

The car turned 180 degrees before blowing backward through the safety fence. It then went airborne and arced down, trunk first. Clewiston gripped the steering wheel as if it was still the instrument of his control and destiny. But he knew there was nothing that could help him now. There was no control.

Looking through the windshield, he saw the beams of his headlights pointing into the night sky. Out loud, he said, "I'm dead."

The car plunged through a stand of trees, branches shearing off with a noise as loud as firecrackers. Clewiston closed his eyes for the final impact. There was a sharp roaring sound and a jarring crash. The airbag exploded from the steering wheel and snapped his neck back against his seat.

Clewiston opened his eyes and felt liquid surrounding him and rising up his chest. He thought he had momentarily blacked out or was hallucinating. But then the water reached his neck and it was cold and real. He could see only darkness. He was in black water and it was filling the car.

He reached down to the door and pulled on a handle but he couldn't get the door to open. He guessed the power locks had shorted out. He tried to bring his legs up so he could kick out one of the shattered windows but his seat belt held him in place. The water was up to his chin now and rising. He quickly unsnapped his belt and tried to move again but realized it hadn't been the impediment. His legs — both of them — were somehow pinned beneath the steering column, which had dropped down during the impact. He tried to raise it but couldn't get it to move an inch. He tried to squeeze out from beneath the weight but he was thoroughly pinned.

The water was over his mouth now. By leaning his head back and raising his chin up, he gained an inch, but that was rapidly erased by the rising tide. In less than thirty seconds the water was over him and he was holding his last breath.

He thought about the coyote that had sent him over the side. It didn't seem possible that what had happened had happened. A reverse cascade of bubbles leaked from his mouth and traveled upward as he cursed.

Suddenly everything was illuminated. A bright light glowed in front of him. He leaned forward and looked out through the windshield. He saw a robed figure above the light, arms at his side.

Clewiston knew that it was over. His lungs burned for release. It was his time. He let out all of his breath and took the water in. He journeyed toward the light.

James Crossley finished tying his robe and looked down into his backyard pool. It was as if the car had literally dropped from the heavens. The brick wall surrounding the pool was undisturbed. The car had to have come in over it and then landed perfectly in the middle of the pool. About a third of the water had slopped over the side with the impact. But the car was fully submerged except for the edge of the trunk lid, which had come open during the landing. Floating on the surface was a lifelike mannequin dressed in old jeans and a green military jacket. The scene was bizarre.

Crossley looked up toward the crestline to where he knew

Mulholland Drive edged the hillside. He wondered if someone had pushed the car off the road, if this was some sort of prank.

He then looked back down into the pool. The surface was calming and he could see the car more clearly in the beam of the pool's light. And it was then that he thought he saw someone sitting unmoving behind the steering wheel.

Crossley ripped his robe off and dove naked into the pool.

ROBERT FERRIGNO

The Hour When the Ship Comes In

FROM *Los Angeles Noir*

ONE GOOD DEED . . . One good deed is all it takes to get a man killed. One good deed, one step in front of the other. Yancy staggered down Pomona toward the beach, straightened his shoulders, and kept walking. Not far. Pomona ran parallel to Alamitos Bay, close enough to smell the waffle cones at the ice cream parlor on Second Street . . . and the strawberries. He had stopped for a Jamba Juice before they hit the house on Pomona. Mason had complained, eager to get started, but Yancy insisted. A large Strawberry-Kiwi Zinger with protein powder and spirulina. No idea what that shit did, but why take a chance. Full of antioxidants and nutrients specially formulated to increase longevity . . . LIVE FOREVER, the sign said. Yancy laughed, and pain shuddered through him.

Beautiful day in Belmont Shore. The yuppie jewel of Long Beach. Late afternoon, the hard chargers on the freeway now, heading home from the job. They spent so much for the Belmont Shore address that they were hardly ever there. Working late. Cardio classes at the gym. Cursing their way through traffic, radiators boiling over. Spinning the wheel, faster and faster, hamsters in Porsches. Beep-beep.

Three young mothers wheeled their babies down the street. On their way back from the bay. Towels wrapped around their waists, breasts cupped high and tight in their bright bikini tops. Coconut oil glistening. Talk, talk, talk, while their babies lolled in the shade of the strollers, hands next to their sleepy pink faces. Husbands on the way home. Mexican maid cooking dinner. Just enough time for a yoga class.

One of the wives looked at Yancy, saw him watching. She smiled, and Yancy smiled back. He stepped onto the grass, let them pass. Half tempted to bow. Some sweeping flourish. Probably fall on his face. He watched them glide down the sidewalk. The one who had smiled stared at something on the sidewalk. Blood. She looked back at him, hurrying now, and Yancy hurried too. Get to the beach. He wanted to walk on the sand. Listen to the waves. He wanted to walk down the beach until he got to the *Queen Mary.*

Here he was, born and raised in Long Beach and Yancy had never set foot on the *Queen Mary.* Fucker had been docked in Long Beach Harbor for thirty years, but he had always dismissed the idea of visiting. Tourist trap. Floating mall. Overpriced and snooty to boot. Assholes dressed as commodores selling post cards and saltwater taffy. So here he was now . . . at the end of it all, determined to make it aboard. Maybe the guy from the fish-and-chips stand would pipe him aboard. The *Spruce Goose* had been parked right next door when Yancy was a kid. Parked in a huge dome. Awesome fucking airplane. Bigger than the biggest jumbo jet and made out of wood. Yancy used to imagine the *Spruce Goose* busting out of its dome some Halloween night, jumping the *Queen Mary,* the two of them going at it like Godzilla and Mothra. The *Spruce Goose* was long gone. Moved to Oregon or Kansas or some state far away, after flopping with the tourists here. Not enough shit to buy. Just a giant airplane that some guy actually built and flew once, skimming across the waves in Long Beach Harbor. One time, a hearty fuck-you, and then he landed and never flew it again. Yancy had gone to see it three or four times, brought his younger brother James, the two of them standing there for hours just looking at it.

Sirens in the distance as Yancy crossed onto the beach, sand crunching underfoot. Police or ambulance. Headed to the house on Pomona probably. What a mess. He had asked Mason if he was sure about the address. Asked him twice. Mason was sure. Mason was always sure. New guy, PJ, was jumpy. Mason's nephew. Bony kid who talked too much, like he was afraid if he stopped jabbering they would see the fear in his eyes. As if Yancy could miss it.

The beach almost empty this time of day. Just a few windsurfers making the best of it and families of Mexicans from inland who didn't like mixing with the Anglos sunbathing on the bay. The offshore oil rigs pumped quietly a few thousand yards off the coast, the rigs planted on fake islands painted in pastels of green and pink and blue. They looked like cheap condos out there. Yancy walked along the bike path that wound through the beach, a twisting path to the *Queen Mary*. Couldn't be too far. Couple of miles maybe. He could do that. Good to have goals, that's what that English teacher told him one time. What was his name? Yancy shook his head. Mr. Something . . .

The house on Pomona . . . supposed to be the usual crash and bash. Knock on the door, then bust it open with the swing-arm and rush inside. Mason had bought the swing-arm from some junkie who boosted it out of the back of a SWAT van. Twenty-five-pound steel battering ram. Your tax dollars at work, that's what Mason used to say before he broke down a door. It had only been funny the first time he said it, but that never stopped him. The three of them had clustered around the front door on Pomona, PJ hyperventilating, Yancy trying to calm him down, and Mason rearing back with the swing-arm — here we go, men, your tax dollars at work.

Must have been thirty or forty pigeons on the bike path ahead, pecking away at bread crumbs that some asshole had left. So much for survival of the fittest. Yancy walked right through them, the birds squawking as they gave way, then closing in behind him to return to the bread. Yancy kept moving. Making pretty good progress. The *Queen Mary* visible in the distance, just beyond the pier. His feet hurt. The concrete too hard. Better to feel the sand. Better to be barefoot.

A wino rummaged through a trash can nearby, pulling out half-eaten burgers and loose french fries. Yancy held on to the trash can while he took off his boots. Eight-hundred-dollar Tony Lama lizardskin. Custom-made for Yancy's flat feet. The boots worth every penny. He handed them to the wino.

"I don't shine no shoes," said the wino, a french fry dangling from his mouth. "I got my pride."

"They're for you. Keep them."

The wino didn't react at first, then warily took the boots. He grinned, started to put them on. Stopped. Shook one of them. It made a sound. He turned the boot upside down and blood splashed onto the sand. The wino jumped back, stared at Yancy, backing off now.

Yancy peeled off his socks. One white. One red. Tossed them into the trash can and walked toward the water. The sand warm between his toes. Unsteady now. The sight of blood. It never bothered him . . . unless it was his own.

The house on Pomona was supposed to be fat with coke and cash, but Yancy knew as soon as they got inside that it was a mistake. Three guys sitting on the couch drinking cans of Diet Pepsi and watching tennis on TV. Never met a dope dealer that didn't crave sugar . . . and *tennis?* Give me a fucking break.

Where is it, motherfucker? PJ had shouted, waving his gun. Turn it *over,* motherfucker, or I'll blow your fucking brains out!

Which was *way* too Tarantino, even if it was the right house. Yancy had gone over everything with the kid beforehand. Gone over it ten or twenty times. *Yancy* did the talking. We bust down the door, flash the fake badges, and always speak in a soft, polite manner. Violence, then calm. Violence to get their attention, calm so they did what you wanted them to. After they gave up the dope and money, *then* it was back to the violence. A fast finish and out the door. Last thing Yancy wanted was some doper with a grudge looking for him. Unacceptable. No witnesses was the order of business, except when you broke into the wrong house. Times like today, when it happened, and it *did* happen, you just apologized, put away the badges, said *send a bill to the city,* and hauled ass. No muss, no fuss, no bother. Not today though.

Yancy lurched across the sand, the beach dotted with clumps of brown oil from the offshore rigs. He splashed into the ocean, walked in until it reached mid-calf, then headed north, paralleling the shore, straight for the *Queen Mary.* Cool water, real tingly, a nice little wake-up. He bent down to roll his pants up, lost his footing, and flopped down. Sat there soaking his ass in the ocean. Yancy saw a family of Mexicans eating dinner on a blanket, radio blasting, *niños* playing in the sand. *Mamacita* pointed at Yancy — look at that silly *gringo*! — laughing, and Yancy waved back. He stood up, put his hands on his knees until his head cleared. Walked on. Soldiered on down the beach. A small plane cruised overhead, trailing a *SECOND ST. SPORTS BAR $2 TEQUILA SHOTS* banner. Yancy kept his eyes on the big boat. Man needed a focus. Something to aim for. *Queen Mary* was the biggest thing in the area.

Getting hard to breathe. Little gurgly sounds every time he took a breath. Tempted to take off his bulletproof vest, but no telling what that would do. The cinched vest probably the only thing holding him together. Shallow breaths helped. First time in his life he had ever been winded. Yancy lettered in football, baseball, and track in high school. Couple of his records still unbroken at Long Beach Poly. Go Rabbits! Yancy laughed and it hurt worse than ever. He got a scholarship to Cal State, Long Beach, but only lasted a semester. Long enough for Mason to call him *college boy.* Like Yancy was supposed to be ashamed for not moving his lips when he read a newspaper.

Splash splash splash in the shallows. He left a light chum of blood trail in the water. A geezer in plaid Bermuda shorts approached, a sunburned beachcomber working his way along the tideline with a metal detector, moving it back and forth, back and forth. Yancy's uncle did the same thing every weekend after the crowds were gone. All along the beach, head down, earphones cupped in place, oblivious to everything but the *beep-beep* that signaled the mother lode. Or a buried beer can. Uncle Dave . . . the treasure hunter. Man had gone to every one of Yancy's football games, cheered himself hoarse, then told him afterward every mistake he made, every dropped pass, every poorly chosen cutback.

"Any luck?" called Yancy.

The beachcomber lifted one earphone.

"Any luck?" repeated Yancy.

The beachcomber glared at him. Shook his head. Moved on.

Right, pops. Keep your secret stash. Guy probably found a class ring with a glass stone a month ago and now claimed the beach. His old lady was probably glad to get him out of the house, packing him tuna-fish sandwiches with the crusts cut off. A seagull screamed at Yancy, swooping low. Could be worse. He could be drawing buzzards.

More sirens now. Meat wagons on the way.

Yancy had waved his badge at the yokels watching the tennis match, started to apologize for ruining their front door when PJ barreled over to the couch, started pistol-whipping the biggest one. Yokel went down like a bag of shit.

Yancy had looked over at Mason, like, You brought this asshole to the party, you vouched for him, now jerk his leash. Mason just rolled his eyes.

Maybe if the yokels had taken the beating, things might still have worked out okay, but this buff dude with a Rolex, probably the guy who owned the home, this buff dude grabbed PJ, and just like that, PJ capped him. Just jammed the gun in his face and *pow pow pow.* Guy's head made like a melon. Nothing for Yancy to do at that point except let nature take its course. PJ had his rage on full throttle. No way you could get in the way of that. The other guy on the couch had his hands up, like, Don't shoot, man, I surrender. PJ shot him in the eye. Tapped a couple into the pistol-whipped guy on the floor. You would have thought it was Fourth of July, what with the sound and PJ grinning, bouncing around, stepping on teeth, face sprayed with blood. Yancy turned away, watched the tennis player on TV holding up a gold trophy, his clothes so white . . . Yancy turned at the sound of a toilet flushing. A girl came out of the bathroom.

Yancy stayed in the water as two young men in black suits approached. Bible patrol. They hit the beaches every day, trolling for converts. Or maybe it was easy duty to score points with God. The Bible boys stayed on dry land, stepping back every time the waves rolled in. Doing the hokey-pokey. Ugly-ass shoes on the boys. Big black shoes with thick crepe soles. Jesus could walk on water, but they didn't want to put it to the test.

"Could we talk to you for a minute, sir?" asked the one with the dusting of pimples across his cheeks.

"I'm in kind of a hurry."

"Always time to hear the good news," said the other one. The one with the frayed collar and the thin lips. "We just need a few moments. Could change your life."

"My life's already changed."

"Are you all right, sir?" said the one with the pimples.

Yancy walked on. The one with the pimples kept pace for a few steps, then gave up. Other fish in the sea. Yancy was a lost cause. He believed in God . . . *his* God, not theirs. That was the problem. No way God forgave everything you did. What kind of a chump would that make God? You do all kinds of evil shit your whole life, then at the last minute you say you're sorry and the pearly gates swing wide? No way. Heaven would be filled with con men and hustlers if that were the case. No, God was a referee. He kept score, that's it. At the end of the day, you were either in positive or negative territory. God didn't hear sorry. He didn't hear boo-hoo. He just added things up. You had to respect that motherfucker.

He was tired. Now I lay me down to sleep . . . the prayer his mother taught them, him and James . . . Now I lay me down to sleep, I pray the Lord my soul to keep. God bless Mama and James and Yancy. Good luck with that last one. Better to trust putting one foot in front of the other.

Would be nice to call James. He was probably still at work. Welder at the port. Sucking in lead fumes for eighteen dollars an hour and benefits. Rented apartment and a car with rust on the door panels and maybe a movie once a month. Amazing the things that made people happy. Wife and a little girl, Cleo. Another one on the way. Kathy sexy and skinny when he married her, now her hips were spreading like a jumbo jet. Yeah, amazing the things that made people happy. Yancy had gone over there for Christmas, bought too many toys for Cleo. Too many expensive toys. James and Cleo exchanging looks. Yancy making excuses why he had to leave early.

Limping now, he walked under the pier. Concrete piling crusted with barnacles. Cigarette butts floating on the water. Voices from the pier echoed around him. Vietnamese fishermen trying for dinner, casting their lines with easy flicks of their wrists. Skaters and skateboarders rolling. Music, music, music . . . Keep walking. The *Queen Mary* closer now, the railings edged with silver. Three smokestacks stark against the sunset.

Everything would be different if the girl hadn't walked out of the bathroom back at the house on Pomona. She hummed as she closed the door behind her, clutching a baby. Must have been changing it when the killing went down. It . . . he, she, whatever. Yancy didn't know from babies. What he knew was taking down dopers and getting away clean.

Yancy tried to make her disappear, make her go back into the bathroom, pretend she hadn't seen anything. Mason knew better. He had his faults, but he knew what he had to do.

The girl stood there, mouth moving like a fish, no sound coming out. Eyes shifting from the bodies on the floor to Mason. She half-turned her body as Mason raised his pistol. Half-turned her body, as though that would protect the baby.

Maybe that's why Yancy had done what he did. Stupid thing. No explaining it really. Just as Mason tightened on the trigger, Yancy shot him in the head. He shot PJ too, but not before PJ shot him four times. Kid was quick, you had to give him that. Three of PJ's rounds hit Yancy in the vest, but the impact of the rounds twisted him, and the fourth bullet slipped under his arm, bounced around inside him, tumbling like a load of laundry in a dryer. Good thing PJ liked a 9mm Glock. All the young guys did. That's what they saw in the movies. Yancy preferred a .45. He felt the comforting heft of the .45 in his jacket with every step. Mean gun, no grace to it, but one shot in a vital area and you were dead. Case closed. 9mm had no stopping power. Man could walk forever with a 9mm slug in him. Yancy was proof of that.

The girl was unhurt. Hysterical, of course. She found her voice after he killed Mason and PJ, the girl screaming so loud he could hardly wait to leave.

Funny . . . he had made such rapid progress toward the *Queen Mary* at the beginning, but now he seemed to be moving slower and slower. He walked along the edge of the water, where the sand was hard-packed. He kept walking but didn't seem to be getting any closer. It was like . . . he was being allowed to approach his goal, get it in sight, but there were limitations. Like the *Queen Mary* was off limits. Going to be dark soon. At this rate . . . he was never going to get there.

He just wished he could figure out why he did what he had done at the house on Pomona. Killing Mason . . . how could he explain that? Mason was making the right move. The girl had seen them. Could ID them. Rules were rules. Mason followed the rules . . . it was Yancy who had broken them. PJ was a hothead and Yancy knew he wouldn't work with the kid again, but Mason and he had partnered for three years. Mason had thrown him a party when Yancy killed his twelfth man. His first dozen. Mason made a big deal about it, rented a suite at the Four Seasons and hired a couple of hookers for each of them. Top-quality ladies too. Mason talked too much and stank up the car with fish tacos and jalapeño burritos, but Mason was dependable. Yancy was the one who'd had a change of heart, and that bothered him. It was like his whole life up until now was *wrong* somehow.

The girl didn't remind him of anybody. She wasn't particularly pretty or gentle or sad or any of that other crap that always made the movie bad guy spare her life. And that bit about her trying to protect the baby . . . he didn't even *like* babies, and besides, that was just a reaction on her part. No courage or nobility to it. She probably didn't even know what she was doing. Yancy coughed, spit blood into the water. He was too tired to convince himself, but what he had done in that split second at the house gnawed at him. Throwing away his life, that's what he had done. Nothing wrong with his life . . . nothing . . . and yet he had tossed it aside with the squeeze of a trigger. Blowing away Mason and PJ . . . Now what was he supposed to do? Ask James to get him a job at the port?

Yancy stumbled up onto the dunes. Soft sand with not a speck of oil on it. Sand like sugar, heaps of it . . . and he had a perfect view of the big boat. He sat down. Just a little break. A little rest before starting back up again. He lay back on that pure white sand. Stretched out his arms, scooped them back and forth. Made sand angels. He and James used to do that when they were kids. Spreading their arms wide, the two of them making flapping sounds. Wings big enough to carry them to heaven. Now, though, his sand angel was sloppy and uneven . . . broken somehow. Yancy lay still, arms poked out at a crooked angle. Just a little rest, that's all he needed. He watched the *Queen Mary* floating there in the blazing sunset. Every seam and rivet in sharp focus. Ship of gold. Close enough to touch.

CHUCK HOGAN

One Good One

FROM *Ellery Queen's Mystery Magazine*

MILKY GOT HOME ABOUT NINE THAT NIGHT, sweating and shivering like he had the flu. Which he did. He had the street flu; he was in a bad way. He opened the door to the house on O Street *(Best thing about living on O Street? You only have to walk a block to P.)*, trudged up the stairs to the third-floor apartment, and watched his shaky hand try to fit the key inside the lock.

Ma was at the table. In her housecoat. Her close-set eyes were red-rimmed from crying, and Milky knew instantly.

"Why, Eddie?" she said. Grief tuned her voice up a notch. "Why?"

Edward Francis Milk felt his gut drop, like a sack of garbage hitting the floor.

He said, "What, Ma?"

"You *know*." Her hands, worn like old dish towels, gripped her crossed arms tightly in hopeless self-consolation. "I know it when I see it."

"Ma."

"Eddie, you promised me. You always promised. My little boy . . ."

The guilt. Milky was thirty-one years old, still living with his mother. Then the anger. *Milky was thirty-one years old, still living with his mother.* "What were you doing in my room, Ma?"

"You been away two days. No phone call, no nothing. I'm scared, I'm all alone. What'm I supposed to do? Sit here and wait?"

"Not go through my *things*."

"I was going to call the police. Report you missing. You should thank the man above I didn't."

"I was . . . I was working."

"You used to want to be a cop." She wept for him now. "You'd put on Dad's shirt and hat and pretend you was him . . ."

This memory had lost all traction with him, the number of times she retold it. "Ma."

"Jimmy's passing *killed* him. Not the grief of it. The *shame.* Having it in our house? In *his* house? He told me, your father did, he said, 'Eddie ever does it, Eddie ever follow in Jimmy's footsteps, out of my house he goes. Put him right the hell out.' You know I got to honor that, Eddie." She looked at Eddie's father's picture, framed and standing on top of the stove. Him in his transit-cop uniform. A smaller photo of Jimmy laughing on the front steps was next to it. "This is still his house."

"Ma."

"Now I got to put you out." She pushed herself up from the chair, and in her housecoat nearly flew to the sink. She clung to it as though hands from the floor had her by the ankles, pulling her down. "My baby boy. I should of dragged you to church with me. Should of *dragged* you. You're leaving me all alone in the world!"

"Ma." He just couldn't do this now. "Ma, sit down."

"Where you been all this time, Eddie? Where?"

"*Working,* Ma." He hit his chest where the letters *MBTA,* for Massachusetts Bay Transportation Authority, were stitched over the pocket. Milky had been fired five months before, but still left the house most mornings dressed for work. For her sake.

"Two days straight, and no call?"

"Work is work, Ma."

"How could you bring this evil down upon me? You're all I got, Eddie! Daddy's in heaven and Jimmy's in the ground and you . . . you . . ."

She felt her way back into the chair, a handkerchief clutched in her hand over her heart. She looked gray. She wasn't breathing right.

"Ma. Ma, listen to me. Where is it? Tell me what you did."

"How you could bring it in this house after your only brother . . ."

"Ma, where'd you put it?"

"I didn't touch it!" Her arm fell dead on the table. "I don't touch that stuff. *I* know better."

"Ma." Milky grabbed a seat, pulled it near. Her voice was like raccoon claws scraping at the insides of his eyes. He ran his hand through his hair and it came back wet with scalp sweat. He wasn't moving out. He wasn't going nowhere except down the hallway to his room to cook a foil and do up. "Listen to me, Ma."

"Both my boys, these drugs . . ."

"Ma, *shut up!*"

He wasn't yelling at her. He was yelling at himself.

"Look," he said. "This is something I'm not supposed to tell. Not to anyone. Not even my own mother. No one, you understand?"

He got right up again and paced in the kitchen. His angst was real. This was a leap off a cliff. A Hail Mary pass. The kind of lie that had no end, but he knew he had to follow through anyway, and hope for some miracle. He was too dopesick to argue with her. He was sweating like an egg left out on the counter.

"Ma, it's this way, okay? I'm a cop. Not really a cop — not a full cop. Not yet. But I'm on that track. I'm working for them now, you see? Under cover. And this — this breaks every rule in the book, me telling you here. If only you hadn't gone into my room . . ."

He spun around, gripped a handful of his own hair. He wished he could rip it out. Focus the pain on his flesh, instead of underneath where it wriggled through him like bloodsucking worms.

"But Eddie, how could —"

"I worked it out with them. They know Dad, of course — they remember him, they all still talk about him. And they approached me about maybe doing this . . . and I tell them, I says, 'I got some priors, some trouble in my youth, maybe a little even beyond juvie.' And they says, 'That little stuff we can work out. If you can show and demonstrate who you are now. Make up for those mistakes, balance the books. If so, then clean slate.'"

She said, "They talked about Dad?"

"I told them up-front, I says, 'I don't want to coast. Don't bring me in on the old man's reputation alone.' Because who could live up to that anyway? But they says, 'Milky' — or, actually, it's 'Eddie' they call me. 'Eddie, you got to be your own man. We know that. There's room for you with us if you work hard now. But it's dangerous, this thing. This is lion training without no whip. You'll be in that ring all alone.'"

He could see emotion tugging at her face. Like waves washing seaweed forward and backward. She wanted to believe him. To commit to this. To crash onto the sandy beach of good news.

He felt the crinkle of the Summons to Appear still in his back pocket, from just having been cut loose of the Suffolk County Jail. "Here," he said, taking out the pink form, folding it so that she could see only the official seal and the lettering above his typed name. "See that? City of Boston, right there. Boston Police Department." He put it away again before she could reach for it. "I'm breaking rules left and right here, Ma. I'm jeopardizing my place with them as it is, just telling you this. Risking everything. So you gotta trust me now. Please. And for chrissakes, stay outta my stuff from here on in."

"Eddie . . . I just don't know. I remember Jimmy, all his lies."

"That's just it, Ma. It's because of Jimmy that I went to them. That's what this thing is. Bringing those others to justice."

"Who?"

"I can't say. I can't tell you nothing more, Ma, we won't discuss these things. In fact, we should never talk about any of this again. Ever. Let it be an understanding."

"The department, Eddie? For real?"

"I'm trying not to count my chickens too hard. Things haven't panned out for me before. But they been good to me so far, and I'm trying to be good to them. Only now I got the added stress of worrying about you knowing."

"No, Eddie."

"This is a long-term project I'm on, understand. Nothing's going to break overnight. They tell me these things take months, maybe years. But I'll do what they say, however long it takes. This is my shot here, and I know it."

These last words he felt in his chest. Felt them like they were the truth.

Ma was sitting back now, breathing easier. The strange look in her unfocused eyes, faraway yet so close: It was pride. It was love.

"Come here," she said.

He did. He went and leaned down, and she placed her warm and trembling palms on his clammy cheeks. Her pale lips quivered as she stared at him, drinking him in like medicine. This clinch was as close as they ever got. The Milk family version of a hug and a kiss.

"My boy," she said.

Milky hated himself then, and loved himself at the same time. A terrible sort of dreadful euphoria, as though he had shot his own mother up with smack. Tied her off and injected her himself and watched her eyes go liquid, and let her thank him for it, for delivering her from suffering. Delivering her from pain. Turned out both of them had needed to get high.

"You're not going to tell no one," he said.

"No, no."

"Not until I let you know the time is right."

"Then I shout it from the back porch. I dance up Broadway in heeled shoes."

He had her soaring. Pipe dreams worked for everybody. He stood straight again, his mother sitting back.

"I thought I'd lost you, Eddie. Thought my best boy was gone from me forever."

Milky squeezed her hand and stole a glance down the narrow hallway toward his room, needing to do up so badly right now.

The walk was an informal thing that, over time, had become consecrated. All the old war widows (staying married in Southie, that was a war) met at the rink down on the Point and walked Day Boulevard to Castle Island, around and around the old fort there at the edge of the harbor. Two shifts, a late-morning walk and a late-afternoon walk. A gang of gray ladies in white Reeboks and duck-brimmed visors, walking laps around the belly-ringed teenagers promenading their baby buggies.

That morning, there were only two of them. There was Rita and, wasn't it just her luck, Patty Milk. Patty had stopped walking for a long time after her youngest boy Jimmy died up on their roof. Now she tagged along every once in a while, rarely with anything to say. Always a step or two behind the pack, just walking and looking out to sea.

The story was that Patty's father had nodded off drunk one afternoon at Cushing Beach. Somebody else found Patty, who was only two or three at the time, face-down and floating in the surf. They pulled her out and got her to Mass. General, but she was never right after that. Growing up, she had that look, the chubby face, eyes a little off-kilter, her mouth, thin-lipped and cornered down. The father insisted she was fine and was content to let the neighborhood raise her. No special schools. After puberty, she developed an infatuation with men of the cloth. Stalked them over at St.

Brigid's like a girl after a boy band. Many nights, the cops had to come pick her up for tapping on the rectory windows. It was scandalous. She should have been sent away.

Over time, her obsession switched to cops. The uniforms, Rita figured. And Jimmy Milk, he took what was offered him. For that, he was made to marry her, a shotgun wedding with the neighborhood and not the father holding the gun. But Jimmy Milk never regretted it. She waited on that man hand and foot, worshiped him as if he walked on water and cured the sick. Her boys, too, Eddie and Jimmy Jr. Three men spoiled by a damaged woman, raised in a rent-controlled O Street walkup on the salary of a transit cop too timid to grift.

Patty would often ask Rita about Rita's son Billy. Going on about how proud she must be, her eldest son a builder, living up in Swampscott. And Rita always told her, not rubbing it in but trying to give the poor woman some hope: *All you need is one good one.*

"Ain't that the truth," answered Patty this day.

That was strange. Patty had a little extra spring in her step, Rita noticed. She wasn't trailing behind like the runt of the litter. And didn't Rita hear that Eddie Milk lost his T job some months back?

"You have news?" said Rita, these being the most words the two women had exchanged in the last five years.

Patty gazed out at the sea, the gulls coasting with their dirty wings spread wide in the salt air, and Rita realized that Patty Milk was positively bursting.

Derrick sliced up the whiskey bread his mother had baked. Irish soda bread with raisins soaked overnight in Hennessy's. When the mood struck, she would bake up a few loaves for neighbors and friends, whoever was on her good list that month, and always one to take by Marian Manor, where she worked. The bread was soft enough and safe enough for the elderly patients to gum, and the raisins put them right to sleep.

Derrick paused a moment, realizing that the knife in his hand, the one with the splintered handle, was the same knife he had used to slice up Sulky Nealon. But that was a month or so ago, and besides, the blade had been washed and dried.

His mother baked bread today because Billy was home. Derrick's brother, the golden boy who married a fat girl from the North Shore and moved out of Southie. Today he had returned for a rare Sunday dinner.

"Slice that thicker, Derr," said Rita, Derrick's mother. And for some reason, he did. He had a lot of patience today. Because there was something good on his horizon. Something big.

"You get down to the Island today, Ma?" he asked from the kitchen.

"I got my walk in, yeah," she said, from the parlor. To Kelly, Billy's pregnant wife, seated next to her on the divan all polite and shit, she said, "Good for my lungs."

"Still rollin' with the gray ladies?" said Billy, an inch taller in new, heeled shoes.

"I'm to be the fifth grandma in the bunch," said Ma. "Today out there, it was just two of us. Me and Patty Milk."

"Milky's ma, huh?" said Billy, some of that North Shore condescension crawling into his voice. "Good old Milky. What's that mope up to these days?"

"That's the thing," said Ma. "Derrick, you hear anything about Eddie joining the force?"

Derrick almost laughed out loud. "Eddie what?"

She went on, to Billy, "I was telling Patty about you putting up the new development in Wilmington. She said her Eddie had some good news coming. That he was working for the police on something, a special project. I figured MBTA, but she seemed to say no. Derr, didn't you tell me he got clipped from the T?"

Derrick had stopped slicing. He was staring down at the sliced bread, the whiskey-soaked raisins swollen, yellowed. He set the knife down on the carving board.

Derrick stood with Milky outside Hub Video. Milky was scratching lottery tickets with his thumbnail and dropping the losers to the sidewalk, one after another.

"Still playing, huh?" said Derrick.

"You kidding me?"

"I quit that." Derrick shoved his hands deep into his pockets. "I'm quitting a lotta things. Thinking about it."

"Yeah? What's up?"

"Don't know exactly. Change in the air around here, I guess."

Milky dropped his last scratch ticket. He looked concerned. "Well, maybe that's a good thing."

"I think it is. Like, you getting pinched again a couple of days ago. Not good. How'd that thing go?"

"The usual. Except they forgot about me in there and I was in longer than I should've. I pay this fine, I avoid the thirty days. Which I have to do. My ma."

"Yeah," said Derrick.

"I was going to see, maybe, if you could front me some. Against this thing at the end of the month."

Derrick said, "You want some up-front?"

"Fine's twelve-fifty."

Derrick's eyebrows climbed. "That's steep."

"I need the dough to stay out here. Think you can do?"

Derrick put one sneaker tread flat against the brick wall behind him and crossed his freckled arms. "Pushy. This ain't like you, Milky."

"I'm walking a tightrope here, you know?"

"How's your ma doing, anyways?"

"Her? She's good. She's all right. She's got her TV. Her chair."

"Been walking with mine out on the Island."

"Yeah? I didn't know that. Good. Keep her from turning to stone."

Derrick watched Milky step foot to foot on the sidewalk in the cooling night air. Milky was straight now, but the dancing-in-place told Derrick he didn't intend to be for much longer.

"So, can you front me? Or any chance of moving this thing up?"

Derrick said, "Now you want me to move it up."

"If I go away for thirty, how can I help you with this thing?"

Derrick looked out at Broadway, the parked cars lining both sides of the broad avenue. A white van turned past them onto Emerson, and Derrick stared it down. Then he figured that wasn't very smart. He had to play this cool.

"I'm pushing that thing back," he said. "Maybe indefinitely, I don't know. I'm starting to think there's a better way out here, you know? Things are changing. Don't look it, but they are."

"A better way?" said Milky.

"Twelve-fifty, huh?"

"In five days' time."

Derrick nodded. "But your ma there, she's good?"

"She's good, Derr, yeah. She's good."

"Good," said Derrick. "That's good."

Yarrow stopped with the darts pulled out of the board. He turned. "What?" he said.

Derrick said, "I'm telling you."

"This is based on what?"

"And I been going dizzy here trying to think back, all the things I told him. Trying to think, has he ever been inside this house without me around? You know — listening devices and such."

Yarrow returned to him from the wall, Derrick pulling another Killian's Red from the old Coleman cooler. Yarrow toed the chalk line on the basement floor and readied a dart. "You're getting paranoid."

"Think back on him. Think hard."

Yarrow threw a nineteen. "You been smoking too much."

"It explains things. Little things going wrong recently. Something's in the air, a buzz. He's all into me for this coming-up thing."

"What does he know?"

"He knows. Not every particular. I don't spread much around, that's not my style. But he gets it. He come to you for money?"

"He did, yeah."

"See? Wanted an advance against the take. First of all, I ain't loaning money to nobody. I ever float a loan you know of?"

"Negative."

"Ain't gonna happen. So why's he so pushy all of a sudden? Asking to move up the timetable? Getting into us for cash? That's us showing intent."

"He said it was Get Outta Jail money."

"Maybe it's not money he needs to get out." Derrick's finger went back and forth between them. "Maybe it's us."

Yarrow scowled. "I think he's probably fine."

"'Probably fine.' You're not careful."

"How am I not careful?"

"You're too trusting."

"Who do I trust?"

"Too many."

"'Too many.' Who do you trust?"

"I don't trust nobody. Except who I trust."

"You trust me?"

"I don't trust Milky."

"You never liked that kid."

"I liked his brother. Liked his brother a lot. His brother was the shit. Wish he had been *my* brother. You didn't know Jimmy."

"Not well."

"Before you came back to town. The shit, he was. Until Oxy turned his head into a friggin' butterfly cage. Never saw anyone in such a hurry to die."

Yarrow launched his last two darts in quick succession, having lost his taste for the game. Fourteen and a triple-ring eight. "Milky, though. What's he gonna do? He dimes us, how's he gonna show his face around town again?"

"Witness relocation or some such. They're forcing him into it, don't you see? They pushed a deal across the table, and he took it because he's a weak sister. Because he's strung out like Silly Putty, and because of his ma. That's why they picked him up on the possession charge. The fix was in on this from the start."

"What fix?"

"Don't you see? Busting him, breaking him down, using him to get to you and me."

"Who told you this?"

"About him? I know."

"Who told you exactly? I think I need to know."

"This came from very close, and it was pure happenstance how I got it. I was lucky. I still got a guardian angel left somewhere."

Yarrow collected the darts. "She's your last one, that's for sure."

Derrick swigged his Killian's and said, "I want to go over there right now and beat the shit out of him. Beat the *truth.*"

"That would not be wise."

"This throws everything into question. How can we make a move, period? If everything we say . . ." He waited for Yarrow to return, then lowered his voice. "If everything we say and do is being taken down. The friggin' Invisible Man could be in this room with us."

"Then we said too much already. We got to know for sure. So how do we do that? Search him for a wire?"

"Forget that. They sew those things into the clothes now, they're so small. Nothing would be taped to his chest. They hide that shit anywhere."

"Even if you freeze him out, then what? He already knows what he knows. If you seriously have a question, you need to keep him close."

"Friggin' right. Like *The Godfather.*"

"The thing is what, eleven days off? That's some time."

"Don't upset the cart. That's what you're saying."

"Eyes on the prize, baby."

"All right." Derrick took the darts from Yarrow, readied one. "But if Milky turns out dirty, I swear to God, I'm gonna smoke him."

It would have been cooler if he'd thrown a bull's-eye then, instead of a lousy six.

Pendleton and Kyter stopped by O Street before lunch, double-parking outside. Two winding flights up the narrow staircase, Mrs. Milk answered the door holding her housecoat robe together with one wrinkled hand.

Pendleton badged her. "We need to see Eddie."

Mrs. Milk smiled at the sight of them, shuffling backward to welcome them inside. "I don't know where he is right now. Out working hard, I'm sure. You can leave a message for him with me. He'll want to get right in touch with you as soon as he can."

Pendleton smelled buttermilk, looking up and down the narrow hall. "Sure he will."

Mrs. Milk's eager smile was not the welcome they got from most mothers whose grown sons were in trouble with the police. "Can I get you two something to drink?"

Kyter said, "I don't think so, Mrs. Milk."

"Eddie is working very hard," she said, stepping closer, speaking confidentially. "He wants to do well. To prove to you that he can."

"Prove he can what?" said Pendleton, hiking up his pants. "Stay out of jail?"

"See," she said, ignoring the comment, "I know he wasn't supposed to tell me, but . . ."

They waited. "Tell you what, Mrs. Milk?"

"Well, that he's working for you."

Kyter looked at Pendleton. "Working for us?"

"Working *with* you. But please, don't fault him. You know a mother has ways of finding things out. His secret's safe with me." She looked at a framed photograph hanging on the wall, a man with two young boys fishing off a pier. "He's going to look so handsome in uniform."

The detectives looked at each other.

"Okay, Mrs. Milk," said Kyter. "Tell Eddie we came by. Tell him to do himself a favor and get in touch."

"He will." She touched the glass front of the frame as she spoke. "He has a lot to live up to now."

The detectives were pissed off going downstairs, as though they had been the ones lied to.

"That little shit," said Pendleton, out at their car. "That weasel."

Kyter said, "I'm sick of this shit. Sick of getting the thumb from him. We come by here like a taxi service?"

"He's working for us, huh? Working *with* us?"

"Imagine that day."

Pendleton looked at him over the roof of the car. "I think now it's time we teached him a lesson."

The traffic stop went down in Andrew Square. They brought a marked cruiser with them, full rack lights, big show. Everybody out, hands on the roof.

Pendleton patted down Derrick Shanahan. "You don't got any warrants there, Shanahan, do you?"

Kyter took Chippie Yarrow, kicking out one leg and bouncing him against the once-white Mazda. "How 'bout you, Yarrow? Any outstandings?"

Derrick said, "What is this?"

"Inspection sticker," said Pendleton, tapping the corner of the windshield of the beat-up Mazda. "Twenty-nine bucks would have done it. Gotta keep up."

Kyter said, "Downtown we'll tell you all about how it works."

Eddie Milk stood with his hands on the car roof, very quiet, very nervous.

"You," said Pendleton. "Milky."

Milky said nothing, eyes staying down.

Pendleton said, "Go ahead, take off. Get outta here."

Milky blinked like there had been a mistake, relief coming into his eyes. Amazed at his good fortune, he started away before they could change their minds, glancing back over his shoulder as he walked fast into the crowd.

Derrick stared at the roof of the Mazda as if he was trying to remove the paint finish using only the heat from his eyes.

Yarrow looked at the detective facing him as handcuffs clasped around his wrists.

Yarrow went alone to Milky's place. He wanted to get to him before Derrick did.

Milky's mother answered the door, said she didn't know where he was.

"Look, Mrs. Milk. Did two plainclothes detectives come by here a couple of days ago?"

She clammed up then. She looked worried.

Yarrow said, "How long has Milky been gone?"

Kyter was standing at his desk, waiting for Pendleton when he came in. "He called, all pissy."

Pendleton spilled down his mobile and his keys. "I expected that."

"Says he's gonna call us on it. Gonna write it up."

"Bullshit. So we got a little creative. Who knew?"

"He wants a favor. Demands it."

"What the hell now?"

"Not for him. For the mother, he says."

"For her?" said Pendleton. "What's that get us?"

"Gets us nothing. But he's holding our feet to the flames here."

"To do what?"

"Just show up. Make an appearance."

"Walk in there?"

"Make like it's out of respect. The woman's all alone now. Widow, one son OD'ed. He says she needs something good to cling to."

"What are we now, Santa Claus?"

"It's a gesture. For my own conscience, too."

"Christ."

"Don't hard-ass me. You know we dicked this up. We wanted to put Eddie Milk in his place. Put him on the outs with his little crew there. Well, it big-time backfired. If this is how we pay, if this is the sum total? Then we get off cheap."

Pendleton said, "He was a weasel. Who got thrown under an Amtrak."

"Fine," said Kyter. "Put on your tie."

In the back room of O'Connor's, the black-awninged funeral home on Broadway, men sat on padded folding chairs sipping whiskey and paying their respects. In the main parlor, Mrs. Milk sat in a brocaded chair wearing a black crepe dress and white Reeboks. The closed casket was peacocked with a ragged assortment of flowers, the largest wearing a white sash reading SON.

The conductor had seen an obstruction on the tracks. He hit the brakes and the body was dragged two hundred feet, sparks igniting its clothes. Between those burns and the wheel cuts, the coroner was at a loss. Milky's death was ruled a suicide, like his father.

Pendleton and Kyter walked in close to eight. They stood in the receiving line, staring down a couple of punks waiting their turn. Mrs. Milk recognized the two detectives and rose to her feet. They took her aside and spoke with her quietly. Kyter even held her hand.

In the back room, Derrick grabbed Yarrow's jacket lapel. "You see that shit? Right there."

Yarrow watched Kyter patting Mrs. Milk's shoulder as she convulsed into a black hankie.

Derrick said, "I knew I was right to top him."

Yarrow froze, the Dixie cup of whiskey in his hand. "What'd you say?"

Derrick stared hard. He wore a grin on his face like a look of sick determination, his breath smelling flammable. "End of the month is officially back on."

Later, after the mourners had thinned out, Yarrow went up to the bier, kneeling before the walnut veneer of the no-frills casket. Mrs. Milk sat alone in her chair, humming a church hymn to soothe herself. She had her hero now, a martyr to look down over her from the wall in that third-floor walkup on O Street. She would be consoled. Those two bumblers had done something right for a change.

I knew I was right to top him.

Admission of murder. It didn't matter now whether or not the end-of-the-month deal went down.

Yarrow made like he was crossing himself, feeling the sweat-dampened front pleat of his shirt, the thin wire that was sewn in there. Under his breath he muttered something — a prayer for Milky, and for all the wayward sons of the town — that only the passive electronic ear could hear. "Never lie to your mother." Then he stood, touched his fingertips to the coffin's cool finish, and walked away.

RUPERT HOLMES

The Monks of the Abbey Victoria

FROM *Dead Man's Hand*

HEADS HAD BEEN KNOWN TO ROLL in the RCA Building like cabbages in a coleslaw factory. The maroon hallway carpet on the twenty-first floor often doubled as conveyor belt to the waiting express elevator, which was always eager to facilitate an executive's plummet back down to the street. I'd hardly been at the network a month when I found my own fair-haired cranium poised fetchingly on the chopping block. But at least I didn't lack for company.

"This memo in my hand."

Ken Compton, Vice-President of Programming but second to no network chieftain in his wrath, flourished the document for the four of us to see. The four of us were attorney Shepard Spitz of Practices and Standards, Matty Dancer from Variety and Specials, Harv Braverman in Public Relations, and myself, Dale Winslow, from the catchall hopper dubbed "Broadcasting." As department heads, we formed the quartet that reported directly to Compton, with News, Sports, and Original Programming having their own hierarchy within both the network and the building. I'd been brought on board to achieve the goal of broadcasting in compatible color from sign-on right up through "Sermonette." Even the National Anthem and the test pattern were going to be in color.

"This memo in my hand," Compton reiterated. "It's worth more to our enemy up the block than the sum total of your lifetime incomes, including retirement benefits. That's without even factoring in the possibility that one of you won't be working here tomorrow."

We sat across his desk, four boarding-school students caught smoking behind the sports-equipment shed.

"Let me tell you how ultra hush-hush this memo was." He leaned forward as if betraying troop locations in Korea. "I typed it myself."

There could be no clearer proof of how seriously Ken Compton feared intranetwork espionage than that he would endure the humiliation of sitting at his secretary's desk to hunt and peck on her electric typewriter. He'd had this fixation since Ted Thissel, my immediate predecessor, had been suspected of selling the previous season's fall schedule to CBS, forcing Compton to relocate some audience favorites to unfamiliar time slots, a last-minute move which many thought had cost us dearly in the ratings.

"Do you know where I found this memo?" he asked. "Let me tell you where I found this memo. Propped behind a bottle of Vitalis above the sink in the executive washroom. If I hadn't been the next one in there, this document could have been filched by the cleaning lady and sold to those vipers at CBS."

The image of our Mrs. Dawkins sitting patiently in William Paley's outer office, bucket and mop at her side, was the only thing amusing about the moment.

"Spitz, I gave it to you first. Who had it last?"

I knew the answer to this question and sorely wished I didn't. The memo — which listed by title the films we'd acquired from Paramount that we planned to run as specials against our rivals' strongest shows — had been addressed to the four of us only, and Compton had intentionally made no carbons or photostats. We were each to read the memo, check off our own name, and hand it to one of the others. The last to read it was to return it personally to Compton.

Harv Braverman's name was the only one that hadn't been checked when I'd given the memo to him, but now it was as ticked off as Compton was with us. I looked at Harv, who was peering about the office as if the identity of this incredibly careless executive was an enthralling enigma to him. I turned back to discover the others staring at me. After all, I was the new fellow on the block, a refugee from Ogilvy and Mather. The others were lifetime NBC men. Their blood ran peacock blue.

Spitz said, correctly, that there was no way for him to know. Matty Dancer said he couldn't remember, as did the blameworthy Braverman, who then turned my way with raised eyebrows.

I could have tried to exonerate myself but, being ridiculously new at the network, I thought it politic not to state my case at Braverman's expense. I hadn't even been assigned a secretary yet, and my office still contained the embarrassing scent of fresh paint.

"I have to be honest," I said, which I thought was as good a way as any to begin a lie. "I've been dispatching so many memos since coming aboard that I can't recall where I was in this particular sequence of events. If it's any help, I'm strictly a Brylcreem guy."

Our uniform dim-wittedness left Compton with nothing to tango or tangle with. "Honor among thieves. Fine. Then I'll deal with you like I'm Ali Baba. Here's our fall schedule."

He tossed it onto his desk blotter. We hadn't expected to see it for at least two more weeks. Reflexively, Dancer reached for it, and Compton slapped at his hand. You heard me. He slapped at his hand.

Compton transferred the memo to a lower drawer and locked it with a little key. "So here's how it works. If you want to consult the schedule, you come in this room, you ask me for the specific information you want, I will look it up and tell you. Until then, no one sees it, holds it, or gets a copy of it. Not my secretary, and not you four."

I got the feeling we were being listed in order of trust.

"Mighty white of you, Winslow," Braverman mumbled in the hall as he tucked neat pinches of cherry blend tobacco into his briar pipe. The stem made little clacking noises as it rolled against his side teeth. "Not everyone in your position would have kept mum. As new man here, suspicion was likely to fall on you first."

I said something about the time I'd sent a line drive through Mr. Overmeyer's window and been finked on by Ricky Yatto, when it would have cost him nothing to cover for me.

Braverman offered in stumbling fashion, "This Saturday. A little shindig me and the missus throw each year. Cocktails, canapés, more cocktails, sit-down barbecue. Been meaning to invite you. You're married, I've heard?"

"Fourteen years, three months, two weeks," I joked, a stock line that I updated every now and then.

It evoked an understanding laugh from Braverman. "Ever get time off for good behavior?"

"Not a chance." I smiled.

"Donna at Reception will be sad to hear that," he said.

This statement instantly made Braverman one of the most interesting people I'd ever met. "What do you mean?" I asked, trying to sound casual about Donna at Reception, who bore a passing resemblance to starlet Joi Lansing in every department. This bears repeating. *Every* department.

"Didn't you know?" he asked. "She's been waving semaphore signals at you since you started here."

I smiled. "She'll lose her enthusiasm when she finds out I'm married."

Braverman lowered his voice. "I already broke the news to her, buddy boy, and her reaction was 'What else is new?'"

I couldn't help looking down the hallway, where Donna at Reception was stationed behind a low-cut reception desk. She smiled my way, then arched her back and stretched her arms above her head. I expected the Sweater Police on the scene any moment to charge her with assaulting an angora.

"I just invited her to my party," Braverman added. "You know what she said?"

"What?"

"She said she'd come stag and asked if you'd be there, too."

"Joanie," I said to my wife as she changed for the party early that Saturday evening, "if you're really feeling under the weather, I'll understand if you want to stay home."

She was wearing a navy blue strapless cocktail dress and applying roll-on deodorant that I hoped would not glisten so much by the time we got to the party. "I didn't say I was feeling under the weather," she corrected. "I said I was exhausted from shopping. It's Saturday night. I wouldn't think of you going without me."

Braverman was a hi-fi buff and had built himself a great rig. He was putting it through its paces with one of those stereo demonstration disks, *Provocative Percussion* or *Persistent Percussion* or something. Braverman centered me and kept pointing from the right to the left as bongos or claves would ping-pong to either speaker, while an accordion throbbed "Misirlou" straight down the middle.

He and his wife, Linda, were serving gimlets, with the color and taste of a Charms lime lollipop but one hell of a kick. Braverman revealed himself to be some kind of barbecue nut, complete with one of those aprons that proclaimed "I'm the chef!" With his straight briar pipe clenched between his teeth, the only thing he said to anyone for an hour was "Too rare for you?"

Donna from Reception was wearing a tight canary yellow dress that had undoubtedly brought a pleased smile to her lips when she first saw it in the changing-room mirror at Saks. Every time I looked her way, she was already looking at me. She made impatient little arcs with her eyes, urging me to step out onto Harv's patio to chat with her, for pity's sake, but Joanie intercepted one of Donna's glances and instantly asked to be introduced to my closest associates at NBC. I was sure she didn't consider Donna to be one of my closest associates, nor did I want her to.

Harv, Shepard Spitz, and Matty Dancer couldn't have been more gracious to my wife, clearly going out of their way to make her feel accepted within the NBC community. Her merest quip regaled them, and she flushed with pleasure at their attention and approval.

While Braverman was otherwise doubled up with laughter at what I thought was a fairly commonplace observation on Joanie's part, he managed to catch my eye and redirect my attention to the sight of Donna leaving the party. She had apparently phoned for Rye Taxi to take her back to Manhattan. As she left, she gave me the most eloquent shrug, causing her cleavage to speak volumes.

Round about ten thirty, Harv signaled to me from the doorway of his den. It was a room I would have treasured, centered around my idea of rustic: a wide stack of hickory logs ablaze in a natural stone fireplace with an Emmy on the mantel above it.

Braverman smoothly locked the door from the inside. Turning, I discovered that Dancer and Spitz were already seated, holding big-fisted Scotches on the rocks. There was the stilled air of ceremony in the room.

"We've been impressed with you, Dale, virtually since the moment you started," said Dancer.

"And we've agreed to extend you an offer." Spitz used his best attorney voice. "Braverman has nominated you into the Order of the Monks of the Abbey Victoria."

Dancer chimed in, "We think it's a whale of an idea, and we've made it unanimous."

"I have no idea what to say," I said appropriately, since I had no idea what they were talking about. I thought it wise to add, "I'm very honored, of course."

Harv Braverman smiled and began to fill his pipe. "You of course have never heard of our Order, and we like it that way. Membership is offered only to those who have displayed discretion and proven themselves trustworthy. One unexpected demise and another member's retirement had brought our membership down to four. Then Thissel got the boot, and we three were all that was left. Until you showed us this week that you have what it takes."

Dancer handed me a Scotch identical to his own. "Look, we'll explain it all to you at the initiation ceremony. Can you get free and clear of your wife this coming Monday night?"

They saw the hesitation on my face.

"Tell her we've asked you to join our weekly poker game," Spitz advised. "You won't be lying."

"American men still possess certain inalienable rights, even as we depart the Fabulous Fifties," asserted Dancer. "Our wives have their mah-jongg nights, bridge clubs, and canasta. In return, an unwritten law has been left on the books that married men like ourselves are allowed to play poker one night a week, excluding Friday through Sunday."

Dancer advised, "You might let her know the stakes are penny ante. Nickel a chip."

"Joanie, the guys want me to get together with them for their weekly poker night," I said as I hung my suit on the overnight valet in our bedroom.

To my surprise, Joanie wasn't taken aback. "Oh, yes. Linda Spitz was telling me about it. Molly Dancer, too." She was in the bathroom, shedding her strapless cocktail dress in an efficient manner, clearly transmitting that tonight was not the night. "It's on Mondays?"

"I'm lousy at poker," I said.

"They might be insulted if you turn them down," Joanie cautioned. "I know you don't like playing office politics, Dale, but it's NBC, after all."

The Abbey Victoria was that dowdy one-star Michelin hotel you'd find in Chartres or Rouen, where you were expected to leave your passport with the front desk and the restaurant would close by nine. Except that somehow this prim, bourgeois hotel had drifted off to sea and foundered upon the corner of Fifty-first and Seventh in midtown Manhattan. You'd hardly notice it alongside the gleaming Americana (which to me had always looked like the UN with a coat of whitewash). The Shabby Abbey, as some called it, was crammed full of chambers with little twin beds that had been purchased in a time when everyone was shorter and two businessmen found nothing odd about sharing a room to halve their expenses.

A number of the Abbey's bedrooms had adjoining parlors so that they could be rented as suites. But if the Abbey wasn't full (and these days it never was), you could book the drawing room alone. Apparently, parlor room 622, situated between bedrooms 620 and 624, was regularly reserved on Monday nights by the Order of the Monks of the Abbey Victoria.

The door swung open and Dancer greeted me. He'd changed since work into a blue turtleneck and tan chinos. He looked at his watch.

"Seven-oh-six," he noted. Dancer had never struck me as the punctilious type, but my time of arrival seemed to please him. "You're the first — other than me, of course."

A table from room service had been wheeled into 622, its two hinged leaves locked in the up position. A green felt cloth served as cover to the now-circular table. Presumably, ours was not the first poker game ever to have been played at the Abbey. Alongside a few red-backed Bicycle decks, still sealed, were colored plastic chips neatly nested in a circular caddy, the kind you'd see in a Sears Roebuck catalog.

"What beer do you like?" Dancer indicated a pewter bucket filled with crushed ice and a modest supply of bottled beer. Pilsner glasses were inverted alongside the bucket. He inventoried the supply. "We have Piels, Schlitz, Knickerbocker, and Miller."

I wasn't much for beer, but when in Rome. "Miller," I opted.

"The Champagne of Bottled Beers," he affirmed. So far the conversation was scintillating. There was a knock at the door and he again looked at his watch. "Seven-ten, and my money says that will be Shep."

If there was anyone who did not resemble a "Shep," it was the fellow in the doorway, attorney Shepard Spitz, still in his three-piece suit. He entered, giving no indication he might remove his jacket or loosen his tie.

"I want you to know I turned down ringside seats at the Garden to do *this,*" he complained without preamble. "Where's Harv?"

"I'm here," said Braverman, entering right behind him. "Don't make it sound like such a chore, Shepard. This is a big night for Dale. For all of us."

Spitz sat himself at the circular table. "Sorry, Winslow. Welcome to the fold."

"And fold-wise" — Braverman used his best ad-agency parlance — "let's hope you have the decency to fold once or twice when there's a big pot, right? Who's dealing?"

"Host is always dealer," said Dancer, sliding into a vacant chair. "You know that full well, Harv, and I note that whenever you've been host, you win more hands. Just a comment." He broke the seal of the blue tax stamp on a Bicycle deck. "The game is straight poker, brethren. No improvements, wrinkles, exceptions, or exclusions, and nothing is wild. I will now accept a five-dollar offertory from all members of the congregation in return for chips."

We each tossed a bill his way. As he slid our chips toward us, he cautioned, "For the benefit of Brother Dale, let me remind you that the Monks of the Abbey Victoria observe a vow of silence about current work and current events, including sports, motion pictures, TV shows, and hit records. Our purpose is to shrug away the world that is too much with us, to speak only of our experiences in the past and the lessons we may have learned from these experiences. Ante up, fellow Monks."

It seemed an odd set of restrictions on conversation. And considering that the purported reason for our get-together was to have a pleasant time, the evening passed fitfully, as if we were all fulfilling some sort of obligation. Surely life was too short to spend every Monday night this way.

"Don't you think you've had enough?" asked Spitz as I tried to improve my spirits by reaching for a second beer.

I looked at him in bewilderment. "I've only had the one."

Spitz nodded at the others' glasses, from which only a few token sips had been taken. "Best to keep your wits about you. Poker requires a clear head, especially when the stakes are high."

I took a glance at the current pot, which totaled about eighty cents and was unlikely to achieve a dollar, but the others nodded silent assent. I forsook the beer.

"Hey, did you see the outfit Donna was wearing today?" ventured Harv.

"Not permitted," Dancer said quietly. He seemed to take his role as chairman seriously.

"Sorry," Harv muttered. "Can I talk about her in general?"

Dancer raised the pot another nickel as he pondered the question. "For the moment, I'll allow some general discussion," he ruled.

"Sometimes I could swear she's not wearing a bra."

"Of course she wears a bra," said Spitz. "Call."

"But today, when she was leaning over, in that peasant blouse —"

"Not permitted," Dancer said. "Specific to time. Let's move off this general topic, anyway. It's fraught with difficulty. Anyone hungry?"

I hadn't had dinner and said as much. The others agreed that food was in order. I walked to the phone. "I assume room service is still open? It's not even ten."

Dancer shook his head. "We don't like the room service here, except for beer and peanuts. Food's lousy. And the kitchen's had citations from the Department of Health. Who wants Chinese?"

There was some grousing about which Chinese restaurant in the immediate neighborhood was best. Harv was big on Bill Hong's, whereas Spitz said he'd been going to the New Bamboo Palace, a place I didn't know myself, since the night of his high school prom in Amityville. Matty Dancer insisted Ho-Ho was the finest and Canton Village the cheapest, at least in midtown. I suggested the one I considered classiest: China Song at 54th and Broadway.

The discussion stopped dead. "We can't go to China Song, Dale," Braverman said quietly. "That's CBS territory. It's wedged in between Studio 50 and Studio 52. They've got paintings of Garry Moore and Durward Kirby hanging over the bar, for chrissakes. If Ken Compton sees any of us at China Song, he'll think we've gone over to the other side. We *can't* go to China Song, Dale. Even for takeout."

Apparently, the Abbey Victoria had a policy against food deliveries from the outside, but they allowed guests to bring food in. So Spitz took down our order and volunteered to pick it up for us at the New Bamboo Palace. Braverman said he'd accompany him, which left Dancer and me alone.

It was strange to find myself sitting late at night in a frilly little hotel room with Matty Dancer, a man I barely knew. "It's nice to have you for company, Dale," he commented and started to tidy up, cleaning out the four little blue glass Abbey Victoria ashtrays that rested by our packs of cigarettes and Braverman's pipe. "We alternate as hosts each week, but it seems as if every time it's my turn, the others go out for food, leaving me to mind the roost. Of course, I'm the neat one."

I nodded slowly, hoping this was as far as Dancer was going to bare his breast to me. He was married, of course, and his wife, Molly, was lovely. Still, it's a funny world.

"How long have you been married, Dale?" he asked, and I gave him the same stock answer I'd given Braverman, adding a few days to the total. He nodded solemnly. "These Monday nights are very important to *my* marriage, I have to tell you. They provide me with a much-needed . . . interruption. The same way our viewers sometimes look forward to a commercial, so they can get some ice cream from the freezer, or see if the kids have turned out their lights, or take a leak. Even Shakespeare had intermissions, for God's sake. So should marriage. Any good, healthy, sound marriage. You know?"

The phone rang, a long "hotel ring" via the switchboard, and he picked it up. "Yeah. Okay, I'll ask him." He turned to me. "It's Harv, he's calling from the New Bamboo Palace. He can't remember if you wanted almond gai ding or moo goo gai pan."

I had opted for the former and said so.

In theory, I agreed with the case Dancer was making for a once-weekly break from connubial "togetherness," as was the newly coined term for marital constancy. But if the offered respite was four sullen men playing dreary nickel-and-dime poker and taking little sips on ever-flattening beer while eating one from Column A, I did not see this as the ideal alternative.

Spitz and Braverman returned with two brown-paper bags. We made no shared feast, but ate our individual orders, each from his own white cardboard box, maintaining the relative silence of those who find the food more interesting than the conversation.

Blessedly, midnight arrived at last. Harv commuted from Rye by car and both Spitz and Dancer lived in Manhattan, but I relied on the New York Central to get me home. So I had no problem rising to my feet and saying, "Well, guys, it's been a great night, but I have to catch the twelve thirty-five to Pelham."

"Sit down, Dale," Spitz said gravely. "You've not been installed or initiated."

I could feel the temperature in the room drop by a good ten degrees.

Spitz looked at the others. "Are we ready?"

Dancer and Braverman nodded assent and turned their chairs to face me. Spitz, who had courtroom experience, opened: "Dale. Tell us what we did tonight."

I looked around the room. "Uh . . . we played poker."

Spitz shook his head slowly. "No, Dale, don't disappoint me. I want you to give us a detailed account of what we did tonight. For example, what time did you get here?"

I remembered Dancer's greeting when I'd first walked in. Perhaps he'd been so specific about my arrival time for the very purpose of this oral exam. "Seven-oh-six."

"Who came next?"

"You. Followed by Harv."

"What brand of beer did each of us drink?"

I pride myself on having above-average recall and rarely came up empty-handed during the interrogation. I accurately synopsized the run at the table, with Dancer playing aggressively and (I said in all candor) foolishly. Spitz had been conservative, folding his hand often; thus, when he did stay in, we assumed he had the goods. This ultimately cost him, as we didn't allow big pots to build when he stood by his cards. I'd played inconsistently, pushing a few weak hands further than I should have and not riding a trio of sixes as far as I might. The most impressive winning hand had been Braverman's. He had broken up a pair of eights in successful search of an inside straight and had gone on to be the big winner for the night, apologizing after each victory. He would be departing nearly ten dollars richer than he'd started.

As for conversation, I had little problem reconstructing the general thrust of our discourse. Past histories had come into play, Spitz recounting his years as a civil-defense attorney, Braverman the winning of the Colgate Toothpaste account by some fairly devious means, Dancer his prior career as a producer of off-Broadway revues. We'd recalled college days. Braverman was Princeton orange and black, Spitz had been Fordham Law, Dancer boasted of being kicked out of several Ivy League schools, and I tried to make the most of my class standing when I graduated from Michigan State.

As I recapped the convoluted path of our unmemorable exchanges in such detail that it alarmed me (surely there was something more noteworthy to occupy the vacancy between my ears), I noticed knowing glances cast among my associates. I wrapped up with "Harv, you accompanied Shepard to his favorite, the New Bamboo Palace, at something like nine forty-five —"

"Forty-two, but who's counting?" said Braverman.

Increasingly peeved, I rattled off, "You brought back egg rolls for three, shrimp toast for Harv, who also ordered sweet and sour pork, Matty had lung har gai pan, Shepard had steak kew, and I had the almond gai ding. Matty and Harv had pork fried rice, I had white, Shepard didn't eat his, now may I *please* ask what this inquisition is in aid of?"

Dancer stood and ceremoniously raised his pilsner. "Gentlemen, I believe we have ourselves a brother. Welcome, Frère Dale."

"Frère Dale," echoed Braverman and Spitz.

Dancer clapped an arm around my shoulders. "I suppose we must have you pretty confused. Sorry about that. We'll be delighted to enlighten, but first we need your word as a fellow Monk of the Abbey Victoria not to disclose on pain of death what we are about to tell you. Not to NBC, to your neighbors . . . not even to your wife."

"I know how to keep a secret," I said.

"You showed us that the other day," acknowledged Braverman.

Dancer nodded. "So we've had ourselves a pleasant evening" — he looked at the others and grimaced — "all right, let's say we've had ourselves a harmless evening, consisting of poker, beer, Chinese food, and some of the most tedious conversation any of us have ever endured, most of which you've just now recounted in impressive detail. A typical weekly edition of our informal men's club. And now, Brother Dale, I am pleased to inform you it is very likely we will never assemble like this again."

Spitz added, "Until such time as necessity dictates. Hopefully, not for months to come."

"Amen, Brother," murmured Braverman.

I looked at their serene expressions. "I don't understand —"

"We won't reconvene until we have a need to," Dancer explained. "You see, Dale, the reason we got together tonight was so that all of us, including you, could identically describe exactly what transpired this evening, with — what's the word, Spitz?"

"Verisimilitude."

"For what purpose?" I asked.

"Freedom," said Dancer. "We're all of us married, tethered, seven days a week every week of the year. However, as members of the Order of the Monks of the Abbey Victoria, we get one gorgeous night each week to do whatever we wish."

Spitz elaborated. "Meaning, Winslow, that we are the poker club that does *not* play poker. Or even convene. We go our own way, free from wives, neighbors, and each other, to pursue whatever secret pursuits spring to mind."

"Not to say," rushed in Harv, "that we do something *bad* on that one day a week."

"Perish the thought," said Dancer. "It might be that Spitz here feels like hanging around the Shandon Star all night to watch the Dodgers. On that same evening, maybe I opt to see a Mamie Van Doren feature at the Trans-Lux that my wife doesn't approve of, ogling the screen in pleasant solitude."

Braverman lit his pipe. "It's the adult version of playing hooky, Dale. Every Monday night from here on in, we all do whatever we like without having to account to anyone, even if it's as harmless a distraction as going back to the old neighborhood to have a chocolate malt while reading a comic book. Simple, innocent pleasures."

There was a significant pause. Then Braverman added, "Or you can do something bad."

"Very bad," Dancer instantly affirmed with a wicked grin. "Very bad indeed." I had the impression he had specific images in his mind, and I was glad I couldn't see them for myself.

"What does 'bad' really mean, after all?" Spitz waxed philosophically. "A life without experience is a life hardly lived." Then he glared at the room. "But what we do on our Mondays is nobody's business. Correct, gentlemen? Even amongst ourselves."

"Even amongst ourselves," Dancer repeated, clearly for my benefit. "As far as any of us are concerned, we are all here every Monday, playing poker. If anyone significant in our lives happens to ask us how the evening went, we will merely try to do as admirable a job as Brother Dale just did in recounting whatever details — very *real* details, to be sure — are needed. Thus, should our wives or others compare our stories, they will jibe harmoniously."

I tried to understand what they were telling me. "So we're supplying each other with an" — I couldn't think of another word — "alibi?"

Spitz fidgeted. "The term *alibi* would imply that one or more of us might need one, because we had done something illegal. Think, rather, of the Monks of the Abbey Victoria as a cover story, and that we spend our Mondays . . . under cover."

"So how does it work?" I asked, already wondering how I might occupy myself next Monday evening.

Spitz said, "We don't meet here again until we have to. The innocuous events of this evening will serve as what transpires here every Monday until one of us is obliged to recount the details to another person, in which case we will reluctantly reconvene to create a different real evening to describe."

Dancer was moving the used glassware to the ice-bucket tray. "Each week, one of us mans this outpost. Today was my turn, next week is" — he mentally went through the alphabet — "is Shepard, then you, Winslow, then Harv, and then it's back to me."

"And what do I do when it's my turn?"

"The same thing we all do," Matty Dancer said. "You check in for the four of us, order up some beer and a card table, and sit here alone for the rest of the night. You watch TV or read a book, but you must stay here. Mid-evening, the three remaining members phone in, just like Shepard did from the Chinese restaurant, to make sure the coast is clear. If one of our wives has called the hotel, either because of an emergency, an errand, or simply to check up on us, that week's sentry will tell them their spouse is out getting food for the others. When that husband checks in at mid-evening, the sentry advises him to call his wife as soon as possible. We all check in a second time at midnight, just in case."

Harv chimed in, "If anyone presses us about what we did, what we discussed, how the poker game went, we just describe the last time we were together. That's why we never discuss current events, TV, movies, things that might date our evening. Under ideal circumstances, we may not have to meet more than once or twice a year."

"That's fine with me," Spitz murmured.

"If you like, I'll help you on your first shift as sentry," Dancer offered as he and I left Room 622 and walked to the elevators. Braverman and Spitz had already left, staggering our departures to draw less attention to ourselves.

"But won't that mean you'll lose out on one of your Mondays?" I asked.

He looked almost embarrassed. "Oh, I'm afraid I don't have any really exciting prospects at the present. Not like some of us." He pushed the elevator button. "Our receptionist Donna, for example. She likes you, damn your eyes."

"You work too hard, Mr. Winslow," Donna said that Friday. She'd volunteered to bring me a cup of coffee before she left for the night, and I'd had no problem accepting her gracious offer.

"Call me Dale, please," I requested. "After all, I call you Donna."

"But you don't," she said.

"Don't what?" I asked.

"Call me." She set the cup on my desk, accidentally brushing the right side of my body. "My number's in the book, you know."

"And what would we talk about?" Oh, I was enjoying this.

"About where you might want to take me for dinner after we go to the planetarium."

"You're interested in astronomy?" I asked.

"I'm interested in dark places. On a first date, the planetarium is as far as I go."

I was certain if I asked how far she went on a third date, I'd get yet another answer I'd never forget, but my conscience nagged at me almost as much as Joanie does when I'm not helping her around the house. I indicated my wedding ring, which suddenly weighed a ton.

"I'm married," I heard myself say.

Someone knocked at my office door and opened it without waiting for my response. I would have bitten his head off if he hadn't chosen to be Ken Compton.

"Winslow, am I hallucinating, or is there simply no ethical behavior on this avenue anymore? You will not believe who was just coming on to me, and I mean coming on strong."

Reflexively I looked at Donna, but Compton answered his own question. "Those little worms at CBS. Paley's man Denham. Inquiring if I wouldn't be happier with *them,* maybe I could do a little better for myself *there.* Insult to my intelligence and ego. It's the damn schedule they want, that's all. They know we've got them beat this season. If you get any calls from anyone at CBS, I want you to put them directly through to me. That's official, got it?"

A second later, Donna and I were alone again. "Where were we?" she asked.

Compton's exit seemed to trigger her need to fidget with the buttons on her blouse, and I was fighting a similar urge. "I'm afraid I was reminding you I'm married," I reprised.

"I know," she said. "So many people in this country are. It must be the reason for the skyrocketing divorce rate."

Give me credit. At least I was no longer a foolhardy kid who couldn't foresee an absolute disaster in the making. At least I now had enough willpower to resist temptation, no matter how appealingly it was offered.

"You doing anything Monday night?" I asked.

Joanie shouted to me through the bathroom door, "How much longer are you going to be using the shower? My makeup's in there."

"Help yourself!" I called out cheerfully, being in a better mood than I am most Monday mornings.

As she entered, she turned her head away so as not to see me through the translucent shower curtain. It wasn't as if I were deformed or something, I was just naked.

"Where's my makeup mirror?" she asked.

"Sorry, I was using it," I apologized. "I was shaving in the shower. I read somewhere you get a much smoother shave that way." I turned off the water, wrapped a towel around my waist, handed the magnifying mirror to her, and reached for the bottle of Aqua Velva I'd bought on Sunday, ladling its contents onto my face.

"Take it easy with that stuff," she said. "It's expensive."

"Sorry yet again. I'll try to defray the expense by winning a few big hands tonight."

"It might be more diplomatic to come home on the losing side," she counseled. "These fellows can help you at NBC. There's no need to make them look bad."

I slapped my cheeks hard as the alcohol pleasurably burned my face. "Okay, honey. I'll try not to get too lucky."

The planetarium had a bank of pay phones by the corridor that led into the Museum of Natural History. The last Star Show had ended, as had (for the moment) whatever groping and nuzzling I'd been having with Donna, judging by the fact that she was now fixing her makeup. I used this hopefully momentary lull to place my check-in call to the hotel, asking the Abbey's operator for Room 622.

"Hello?" Shepard sounded bored and a little dozy.

"It's Brother Dale," I informed him. "Anything I need to know?"

"Nope. No one's called except Dancer and Braverman to ask the same question. But make sure you check in again before you head home. The first time you don't call here will almost certainly be the one time your wife does."

I thanked him for minding the fort, and he assured me I'd be returning the favor next Monday. I kind of hoped he'd ask how my night had been going, so that I could boast a bit about my partial conquest, but he honored the tenets of the Brotherhood and made no personal inquiries.

Donna was checking her makeup in the reflection of a glass case containing a portion of a meteorite that had landed in a Kentucky farmyard in 1928.

"I'm ready for dinner," she said. "Necking makes me hungry. Do you have somewhere nice in mind?"

I suggested we not go where either of us might be recognized by someone from work.

"I appreciate your concern for my professional reputation," she nodded, her tongue planted as firmly in her own cheek now as it had been in mine just a few minutes earlier.

"Do you know anyone from Queens?" I asked as we stepped outside.

She shrugged that well-researched shrug of hers. "I've never met anyone who went to Queens who ever came back."

"Good. I took the liberty —"

"You sure did," she said, not altogether disapprovingly.

"— of reserving us a table at a romantic spot with candlelight dining. We'll just ask them not to light the candles." I waved for a cab, simultaneously using my arm to hide my face from passersby in the strong light of the streetlamps.

"Hello, angel," I greeted Donna at her reception desk the next morning. "Did you have pleasant dreams?"

I was a half hour late, having missed my regular train from Pelham. I'd stayed in bed later than usual, debating if I'd been brilliant or an imbecile not to press my luck with Donna after supper. On consideration, I felt I'd done the wise thing. She'd seemed pleasantly surprised that I hadn't tried to translate our racy dinner conversation into action at her apartment in lower Manhattan. But Donna was someone to be nurtured, brought along slowly. At least until next Monday. (I was already hoping I could convince the supportively disposed Braverman to trade turns with me, so I'd not lose precious momentum with her.)

"I thought about you all the way in to work," I now told her smoothly. She gave me an icy look that was not sugar-frosted and, keeping her voice low, spoke as if her words tasted of Acromycin. "I made myself a big mistake last night, *Mister* Winslow, and thank God it only went as far as it did. NBC would can me and your wife would brain you if either party found out about our date. So let's not ever talk about it again. In fact, let's not ever talk, 'kay?"

I was horrified, I mean *horrified*. That she despised me was all over her face, and I'm sure her face and the word *despised* were rarely to be found in the same sentence. I frantically searched all memories of the previous night for what I might have said or done to turn her around so completely. As I unmanfully pleaded for an explanation, I saw Matty Dancer approaching and instantly silenced myself.

Dancer offered a far warmer greeting than had Donna, with whom I'd been necking under the projected heavens less than a dozen hours earlier. He set a manila envelope on the reception desk and asked her to see it was correctly messengered to its intended recipient. Then, under the guise of jovial chitchat, he said to me, "Hey, Ken Compton wanted to have a brief word with you, Brother Dale." He lowered his voice and added, "He's already spoken with the Other Fellows You Were With Last Night, if you catch my drift."

"Bit of a personal question, Dale," Compton began in an embarrassed manner. He rose from his desk and flopped onto the leather couch directly behind me. I swiveled my visitor's chair to face him across his Danish modern coffee table, as he began, "Forgive me, but do you mind if I ask where you were last night?"

I had no idea what this was about, but felt relieved I had a big, fat, juicy answer to offer.

"Well, I guess there's no shame involved in admitting that Dancer, Spitz, Braverman, and I were playing poker. Over at the Abbey Victoria. We have a little poker night in Room 622 each Monday. I think I arrived a few minutes after seven and left a bit after midnight. Give me a moment and I can probably be more precise."

Compton waved away my offered alibi. "No, I just wanted to hear it from you. I've already spoken to your friends this morning, and they told me about your little poker club." He leaned forward. "So will you tell me? Who's the best player among you? My money's on Spitz."

I smiled. "Well, he's very conservative, and that ultimately works against him. It was Braverman who cleaned up last night, if you can call ten dollars cleaning up."

He nodded. "Exactly as I expected. But honestly, I don't know how you guys put up with room service at the Abbey. I've heard their restaurant tends toward Italian by way of the Borgias."

I explained to him how we have to bring food in. "Last night Spitz and Braverman fetched us some chow from the New Bamboo Palace. My almond gai ding was quite good."

"Ah, the old New Bamboo Palace." Compton laughed as much as I'd ever heard him laugh. Come to think of it, I'd never heard him laugh. "I remember that place. Used to love the pu-pu platter there."

Although we were clearly alone in his office, he looked around as if to ensure our privacy. "Dale, may I tell you why I ask about your poker party? Last night someone broke into my office. Pried open the drawer where I was keeping the fall schedule. Took it. Stole it. Stole a schedule that CBS would pay somebody a fortune for. Like stealing jewelry. And there were only four people, other than myself, who knew that the schedule already existed and where it was kept."

"When did this happen?" I asked.

"The night watchman discovered the forced lock on my door when he was making his eleven P.M. rounds. I keep telling RCA they have to make people sign in and sign out around here. Anyone could have taken an elevator to a couple of floors above us, waited somewhere along the fire stairs until later in the evening, then grabbed the schedule from my office, walked down to a lower floor, and taken another elevator from there to the lobby. After that, they could walk out of here free as a bird. Or if they felt like celebrating, head back up to the Rainbow Room and dance the night away."

I agreed that the scenario was plausible. "But there must be some other explanation. Because the four people who knew where you kept the schedule were otherwise occupied last night, until after the break-in."

"Well, I know that, for gosh sake. You were all having Chinese food from the New Bamboo Palace at the Abbey Victoria." He flashed me a mirthless grin that showed me more of his teeth than I'd ever wanted to see. "It's just a damn shame they closed the New Bamboo Palace three years ago."

As my brain tried to reason how Spitz and Braverman had brought back food from a restaurant that was no longer in business, Compton discarded his genial manner and taught me how frightened one man can be of another.

"Now let me ask you, sonny: Why would you make up a pack of lies unless you had something to hide? I've already asked each of your three associates where they were last night. Their stories were impressively consistent. It seems Spitz bet like a wild man and won over a hundred dollars. They ordered in a pizza with anchovies, since the Abbey Victoria graciously allows deliveries. They arrived at six P.M. and played until two A.M. They talked about their upcoming projects at the network, compared notes on current movies, discussed rumors about Wilt Chamberlain leaving the Globetrotters to sign with the Warriors, and indulged in some fairly graphic speculation regarding the mores of a girl in the secretarial pool named Rita Truscott. Each man's story was completely consistent with the others. Whereas you, Winslow, are totally at odds with all of them. So the question is, why would you so ignorantly and desperately lie to me if there weren't something you need to hide?"

A window alongside the door to the office looked out upon the hallway. Over Compton's shoulder, I could see Donna standing at the water cooler, having herself a quick laugh with Spitz and Braverman, while Spitz was having himself a quick feel of Donna's derrière. It was a silent movie, and I was not a member of the cast. Donna was opening the manila envelope that Dancer had left with her, and withdrawing what looked to me like currency. She wore an expression of pleasure, likely the first genuine one I'd ever seen on her face, including last night at the planetarium.

I understood now. There had never been a Monks of the Abbey Victoria. Not until I came on the scene. The one meeting I'd attended of "the Order" had been the only meeting ever convened. My fellow Brothers must surely have struck a deal with someone at CBS. Perhaps they'd made a similar deal the year before, one for which my predecessor, Ted Thissel, had taken the fall.

Whatever cash from CBS they were splitting, I was certain a modest percentage of their take could be found in the envelope now in Donna's hands.

I knew. But I couldn't speak, couldn't offer my real alibi, tell anyone with whom I'd been the night before, because Donna would simply deny it. Besides, any such claim on my part would give my wife, Joanie, abundant grounds for divorce. I was caught in a fool's mate, where my king could only toggle between two squares, either of which placed me lethally in check.

"All right, maybe I got some of my facts wrong," I rasped from my suddenly dry mouth. I was about to be given the red-carpet treatment, my head bouncing down the hall, bound for the express elevator that eagerly awaited my plunge to the street. "But Compton, how would I know about the poker club, and the name we gave it, even the room number, if I hadn't been there?"

He frowned. "Your associates independently explained that, sympathetic to your being the new man here, they offered you the fellowship of their club, which you attended for the first time last week. They were stunned and insulted that, after reaching out to you in a brotherly way, you were so rude as to simply not show up last night."

I had no idea how I'd explain to Joanie that I wouldn't be working at NBC. What reason could I give her for my dismissal? How might I earn a living after this? I looked back at Compton as if I were staring into the very sun that was setting on me.

He wasn't quite done. "A very foolish bluff to try to put over, Winslow. Frankly, your friends are lucky to be rid of you." He stood without offering his hand. "You must play one lousy game of poker."

HOLLY GODDARD JONES

Proof of God

FROM *Epoch*

WHEN SIMON TURNED SIXTEEN, his father gave him his old car: a red '88 Corvette, just four years off the showroom floor. Corvettes, his father insisted, were the only American vehicle worth a goddamn anymore — and made in Bowling Green, Kentucky, at that. Good for the local economy. Also, as a businessman and a local leader — *pillar,* he'd say sometimes, if he were shitfaced — looking like a success was important. "I'm a walking advertisement," he'd tell Simon's mother, who'd pretend she hadn't heard the same bellowed proclamations two dozen times already. "Folks see me living high and know I must sell the good stuff."

Good stuff it wasn't. Jefferson Wells owned a small chain of furniture stores with locations in Kentucky and several surrounding states, and what he dealt in could only be called furniture by the most generous and perhaps naive of observers: chipboard entertainment centers with plastic veneers meant to mimic the look of wood grain; kitchen chairs with metal legs that would start to bow upon too many sittings. The name of the chain — Wells Brothers Furniture Company — was also crap. Simon's father didn't have a brother. He thought the name sounded old-fashioned, though — established — and so he put it on all of his stores in heavy Old West lettering. He told Simon that he might change the name to Wells and Son if Simon minded his p's and q's and got through a business degree at Western, and back then Simon had considered that more of a threat than an offer. He wanted to help the old man sell junk like he wanted a hole in the head.

A few weeks after Simon's sixteenth birthday, some guys from his high school trashed the Corvette. He'd been driving it to school every day, feeling good: folks at Bowling Green High School paid attention when he walked down the hall now; heads turned. One day, a couple of seniors, football players, asked him if he wanted to go down the road to G. D. Ritzy's with them after final bell, and Simon agreed, too dazed to do much more than nod and croak out a "yes." *This is how things change for a person,* he'd thought, walking out BGHS's big double doors with two of the most popular guys at school on either side of him, like bodyguards. He wished his father could see him. They rode in the Corvette with the windows down and the radio blaring Aerosmith; he wouldn't remember the song later, not for sure, but it was one of the ones with Alicia Silverstone in the video, who was, Kevin Britt proclaimed in the car that day, "hotter than sin."

They ate burgers and string fries, drank giant chocolate milk shakes in a dining room decorated with photos of fifties and sixties rock stars. Simon paid. The two older boys talked about Friday's game and about Sheila Foster's enormous tits. "Just wanna get my face between them," Ray Hunter said, putting his hands out in front of him in a honking motion, shaking his face vigorously side to side, so that his considerable jowls trembled. They all laughed. When the food was eaten, Simon dropped Kevin and Ray off back at the high school, next to Kevin's Pontiac Grand Am — a real clunker — and they raised hands to one another, made promises to do Ritzy's again next week. Simon's heart didn't slow down until he pulled off Scottsville Road and down his family's long, paved drive. He'd never been good at making friends. Being with those boys had been a joy and a torture all at once.

The next morning, his father woke him at 6:00 A.M. by flipping on the light switch. "Get up," he said, and Simon did. He knew not to make his father say something twice.

He found him outside. The sun was just an ember several hills over, and fog clung to the cow pasture like sweat. His car was where he parked it, but it looked like a murder victim, destroyed and decomposing. Unrecognizable.

"Explain this," his father said.

Simon took a few steps forward, then circled the car. None of the glass was broken, or even the headlights, but there were deep gashes in the paint on the doors, the hood, and the trunk. He'd discover later that the culprits had also pulled the old sugar-in-the-gas-tank trick, but what hurt the most — what embarrassed him to the point of nausea — was the graffiti slashed across the hood and trailing down both sides of the car: FAG, over and over again, like a curse. On the trunk door, just for variety: RICH FAG. He returned to his father's side.

"Who did this?" his father said.

Simon shook his head.

His father slapped him, a hard blow that almost knocked him off balance. "Jesus Christ," he said. "If this doesn't beat all. Can't you have anything nice?"

"It's not my fault," Simon said.

His father rubbed his lips and stared at the graffiti — that one word over and over, in purple paint, in white: BGHS school colors. He closed his eyes.

"They're just jealous, is all," Simon told his father. He looked at that word, the big one on the hood: FAG. The letters were sturdy and authoritative. "They don't like seeing somebody have something they can't."

That seemed to relax his father a little, as Simon had hoped it would. "Well, that goes along with the territory, I guess," he said. "Goddamn shame, though. I ain't growing a fucking money tree back there." He thumbed toward their property, fifty acres of farmland and woods with a small stream coursing through its center.

"No, sir," Simon said.

"You may have to hitch a ride with your mother again for a while."

Simon looked at the ground, rubbing his sore cheek. "Okay."

They went back inside, where Simon's mother was just putting breakfast on the table: bacon and fried eggs, home fries, sliced cantaloupe and tomato sprinkled in salt. Jefferson Wells liked to eat a roadhouse breakfast every day of the week, called cereal "bird food," and suffered the occasional pain in his left arm that terrified Simon but also delighted him a little. They ate and didn't speak, and Simon's mother chattered cheerily between them, a monologue that required neither response nor acknowledgment. Nobody ever listened to her. When the meal was done, she cleared the dishes and started loading the dishwasher, humming to herself. Later in his life, when she was the only person he could count on to love him — when he realized that she was probably the only person who had ever loved him, period — he'd try to remember details about her, fond memories, things they could share and laugh about. There were devastatingly few. But he'd think about how she liked to sing as she cleaned or cooked, and he understood that she must have had some personality outside the bland housekeeper role she occupied as his father's wife, because her repertoire was diverse and ever changing, old-fashioned, current: the Rolling Stones and R.E.M., Frank Sinatra, Johnny Cash. She'd loved Simon and Garfunkel, and Simon was a grown man with too many bad choices behind him, like train cars, before he realized that he was almost certainly Paul Simon's namesake — a fact his mother never confirmed and his father would have been furious to discover. One afternoon, when he was still a little kid too young to start school, she'd sung the "Bookends Theme" over and over as she hemmed pants, her voice plain, pleasant: a mother's voice.

On this morning, though, she merely hummed, an empty, cheerful tune meant to soothe his father and reassure them all. Simon felt his father staring at him.

"You aren't —" He paused, mashing a fried egg with his fork, the loose yolk running into his pile of home fries, neon and viscous. "You didn't —" He cleared his throat. "— do anything to encourage this, did you?"

Simon knew to shake his head right away. But he thought about it. He was old enough to know *what* fag meant, just like the boys who'd vandalized the car knew. He wasn't sure that he understood what *being* a fag meant, though — if it should be clear to him as hunger, if it meant that he had to feel only some things and never others — because all of that was mixed up and confused, what could excite or arouse him. None of it made sense.

What made the least sense to him was how yesterday had provoked this. He'd only taken those boys to the place they'd wanted to go, bought them some food, eaten with them, laughed with them. He hadn't touched them or said anything risky. He'd hardly spoken at all. That they were able to pin him with this word, to see something in him that he hadn't gotten sorted out for himself yet, that he hadn't even known he was transmitting — well, it was humiliating. But it also made him afraid. He felt like a wounded animal in a house with a predator.

"Okay, then," his father said, face wary. "See that you don't."

*

Simon met Marty in one of his classes at WKU: his second go at College Algebra, actually. He wasn't bad at math — wasn't bad at anything he applied himself to — but college had been good to him, and as long as his father was willing to pay for it, he was willing to take the scenic route to a degree. At twenty-three, then, he was still eighteen credits short of graduating, and he'd be lucky to finish school with a 2.5 GPA. Like it mattered. His father would give him some token position with the stores whenever he finished, and Simon thought that they were both eager to postpone that day as long as possible.

Life, for the first time he could remember, was fine. He had a small apartment off College Drive, a generous food allowance, a nice car — a black Corvette, his high school graduation gift. Not a hand-me-down this time, either. He took twelve hours every semester, the full-time minimum, and always mixed in with his general ed classes something easy and interesting, like Intro to Drawing or Intro to Philosophy. The philosophy class was his favorite, the only class he scored an A in. He'd loved learning about Descartes, with his wild ideas about the world outside yourself, how everything you believe is real could just be the work of some evil genius or puppetmaster. He'd liked Descartes' proof of God, too, though Simon himself had an idea that God was a fairy tale, that dead was dead. God must exist, this Descartes guy thought, because imperfect beings are incapable of imagining perfection. Bullshit, really. But Simon thought about his father sometimes — about how it felt to try to be the son his father wanted him to be, and how that effort made him love and hate all the more fiercely — and couldn't help but wonder.

Marty was a freshman. He was a cool guy — good-looking in an accidental, unawares sort of way, easygoing, witty — the kind of person who wouldn't have had anything to do with Simon a few years before but now gave him some respect because he was old enough to buy the beer and flush enough to pay for it more times than not. Gullible enough, too, Simon realized. But who gave a fuck? The money was his dad's, the good times just as good. And despite all of that, he felt a real connection to Marty, felt that what they had was legitimate. A friendship. He knew that Marty's mother was Mexican and barely spoke a lick of English, that Marty had been teased by other kids when he was little, called a spic and a wetback. "Words their daddies taught them," Marty had said, and

Simon commiserated, though his own father's arsenal of derogatory terms and ethnic slurs was just short of breathtaking.

They started hanging out nights and on weekends. Marty had a dorm room in Pierce-Ford free on minority scholarship, but he'd crash at Simon's place most nights after hours of drinking, or pot if they could arrange it; Marty always had those connections. They stayed up till dawn two or three nights a week, sipped beers — Natural Lights when they felt cheap and sloppy, Anchor Steam, Marty's favorite, when they had a bottle of whiskey on hand. They'd try to remember the saying about mixing the two — "Liquor before beer, nothing to fear; beer before liquor, you've never been sicker" — but got the order screwed up half the time and usually ended up doing beer and shots all at once and getting sick anyway. They'd drink and play music; or drink and sit on the front porch of Simon's building, watching the traffic; or drink and walk down to Mickey O'Shea's on Cherry Street, where you could often catch a decent band for cheap on Fridays. Sometimes they'd get in the kitchen together and chef up a ridiculous meal that somehow tasted all right anyway, like the time when all they had was saltines and banana peppers and spicy mustard. They could be together and just *be*, that was the thing. No fake conversation, no showing off or showing up. Simon had never been good with other people, so for something like this to come along — well, it felt fated. Felt like a gift, a reward for suffering so much misery and bullshit in high school.

One morning, on a Thursday — late though, nearly lunchtime — Simon woke to the smell of cooking meat, the sizzling sounds of breakfast. He'd missed his morning class, Business Ethics, five times now, and he'd be lucky if the prof didn't fail him. Marty was in the kitchen, standing over the stove. He was holding a big chunk of beef with a fork, and he laid it down carefully in the skillet, making the oil pop.

"What's cooking?" Simon said.

"Supper." Marty let the meat sit for just a few seconds, then he rotated it.

"Early for supper." Simon watched the meat cook, his stomach clenching around the alcohol he'd put away last night before crashing: six beers and the four shots of Jose Cuervo he downed for Marty's benefit. He hated tequila.

"We aren't eating it now, dumbass." Marty pulled the meat out of the skillet and set it on a pile of paper towels beside the sink. "I'm doing a roast. It won't be ready until four or five."

Simon went to the fridge and pulled out one of Marty's bottled waters. He sipped, goosebumps making a trail between his shoulder blades. *You know you're hung over,* he thought, *when even water tastes like poison.* "Maybe I'll have an appetite by then."

"Oh, you'll eat it," Marty said. "This is my mother's roast." He pulled ingredients out of a grocery bag on the counter: several spice containers and a package of bouillon cubes, red-skinned potatoes, a bag of baby carrots, one large white onion, and a bottle of red wine. "You've got nothing in this kitchen, man. I even had to buy a corkscrew." He pulled that out of the bag, too, and waved it at Simon: a cheap one, the kind that looked like a pocketknife.

"I'm not much of a wine drinker," Simon said.

"Thought you rich folks drank this shit every night."

"Dad's more of a beer man," Simon told him.

"Well, you're classy now," Marty said.

Marty started rinsing the potatoes, peeling the onion. Simon had a crock pot, though he'd never once used it — his mother had bought it for him, along with a dozen other household items that had always been in his childhood home but seemed ridiculous in his apartment: a silverware tray; the fuzzy toilet seat cover and matching floor mat; coasters, designed to protect furniture much nicer than the crap sold by Jefferson Wells; a "While You Were Out" phone tablet. Marty piled ingredients into the crock pot, topping the mess off with half of the bottle of wine. "This is good stuff," he said, taking a sip from the bottle. "Thought I'd splurge." He offered the wine to Simon, who waved it off.

"Suit yourself," Marty said. He turned the crock pot's dial over to medium and set the lid on the top. "You're gonna love me in about four or five hours, friend."

Simon looked down at his water bottle. Shocked by that word, *love,* rising so suddenly and casually between them, he admitted the inevitable to himself: he already did.

The rest of the afternoon, they sat in the living room watching a movie on A&E, *Superman,* the smell of roast filling the apartment: rich, earthy. *Love,* Simon kept thinking, panicked, daring himself with the word the way he'd once climbed trees or taken spills on his skateboard. He knew that love came in all kinds of forms and degrees, even though he'd never been on the receiving end of much of it. His father loved him, he knew, in his way: a selfish sort of love, and limited — a love that asked for more than it could return. And his mother loved him, but she was a weak, ineffectual woman, and so her love, too, was weak and ineffectual.

He thought back to that day — almost seven years ago, now — when those football players had vandalized his car, branded it: fag. When you were alone — a loner — you could put a memory like that and all of the insecurities that went along with it somewhere safe, deep within yourself; and you could build walls around it; and you could pretend it didn't exist, at least most of the time. Other people complicated that. Marty made it impossible. Simon didn't know what he was — what loving Marty might make him — but he sat on the couch with him all afternoon, their arms just a foot or so away from touching, and his heart stuttered in his chest, and his face and neck burned. In the movie, Superman was flying around the earth in reverse, fast laps meant to make time spin back so that he could save Lois Lane. "Hey, there's a party tonight," Marty said. "At the Sig Ep house. Keg passes are five bucks. You interested?"

"You know I'm not into that shit."

Marty sighed and shook his head, and Simon sensed his frustration — a frustration that Marty had managed to keep in check most of the three months they'd been hanging out but still let surface on occasion. "Let me tell you something, man. Something nobody else is gonna care enough to say to you. This ain't a fucking life, what you're doing. This is pathetic."

"You're here, too," Simon said. He wondered, not for the first time, why.

"That's the problem." Marty turned the TV off, shifting on the couch so that he was facing Simon. "It's easy to sit around and drink, and I've been letting you drag me down with you. But that's done. Let's go, all right? What do you say? Besides, motherfucker, I'm making you dinner."

"All right," Simon said. He looked at Marty's profile — the dark eyes and hair, skin the color of pie crust, the too-big, crooked nose. And he understood two things: that he wouldn't be able to go on much longer being with Marty this way, pretending brotherhood when he wanted something more; that Marty almost surely, certainly, didn't feel the same way in return.

*

Simon paid the keg fee for them both at the door. He would have done it anyway — that was how he and Marty usually worked — but he felt especially obligated since Marty had made dinner and bought all of the ingredients, including the fourteen-dollar bottle of wine. And Marty hadn't exaggerated: the roast was incredible. They'd both eaten long and well, until Simon's stomach went from hung-over-sick to food-sick. He would associate that feeling — fullness bordering on illness — with Marty long after. But at the party, as they started to wander around the Sig Ep house, he only thought of his father, who complained about indigestion a couple of evenings a week. *Best thing a man can do,* he'd tell Simon, mouth smiling but not his eyes, *is pour a beer on top of it.*

Simon decided to do just that. He took a plastic cup from the guy manning the door — a pathetic thing, really, not much bigger than a Dixie cup — and got into the keg line, which was at least fifteen deep.

Marty handed him his cup. "Fill me up, would you, buddy? I'm going to go mingle a little."

Simon wasn't surprised. He nodded.

"Don't run off." Marty smiled — all those white, straight teeth, with one crooked eye tooth to make him approachable — and raised a finger. "This is the night everything changes for you, friend."

Simon laughed and turned toward the keg. The line was moving. "Get out of here."

He hated parties. Hated the music — the mix of hip-hop and Nashville country whose only shared characteristic, far as Simon could tell, was their God-awfulness. Hated the look of a fraternity house — how a once-decent building could be transformed into a stinking hole that somehow still attracted the good-looking girls. Green, threadbare carpet, stained here and there with beer or urine or puke that had only been soaked up, not properly cleaned. Pictures of the fraternity members, framed by year, matted loosely and hanging askew over a fireplace. Maybe he hated the girls the most — not all girls, he didn't hate women — just the ones who showed up to places like this one with their fake tans and oily mascara, their bellybutton piercings and side fat. The girls who got in free, cut to the front of the keg line without hearing boo from anyone, then complained all night about the taste of beer the whole time they were getting drunk off of it. Those girls.

So he noticed the girl in line ahead of him, the one with the brownish-blond hair — dishwater blond, his mother would've called her — who waited her turn instead of cutting ahead, which she easily could have done. She didn't look any different than the rest of them; she had streaky highlights and heavy eyeliner, wore a bright yellow T-shirt that hit her mid-stomach and blue jeans cut low enough that you could see the sharp angles of her hipbones jutting out over the waistband. But she *seemed* different. Quieter, not so desperate to be on exhibit. Across the room, two drunk girls — they barely looked old enough for college — were touching each other's faces and giggling, while a handful of frat boys tried to goad them into kissing.

"These keg parties suck," Simon said, waving his little cup. He felt mortified as soon as the words came out of his mouth — what the hell possessed him to talk to this girl? — but she laughed, kindly, and shook her head up and down with enough exaggeration that Simon could tell she had been drinking.

"You got that right," she said. Her voice had the pronounced lilt of a local, oddly comforting. The line moved again, and she took a step forward, but awkwardly, with her body half-turned toward him. He could sense her uncertainty, so similar to his own, and he could tell that she wanted to keep talking — was relieved to hear a friendly voice — but was unsure about his intentions, whether he'd meant to engage her or just tossed out a random observation for anyone within earshot. It touched him.

"Simon," he said, nesting Marty's cup in his own so that he could offer his hand. He was intoxicated by his own confidence.

"Fish," she said, shaking it, and she blushed right away. "Well, Felicia's really my name. But my nickname is Fish."

"Who calls you that?" Simon said. He regretted it immediately, because the question came out disbelieving instead of charming, like he suspected she'd given herself the name. And the look on her face — the cute blush turning to scarlet, the line appearing suddenly and decisively between her eyebrows — told him that she had done exactly that. Reinvented herself.

"My friends," she said. "My friends here call me that."

"I like it," Simon told her.

"Sure," she said — sarcastically, Simon thought. She looked ready to turn around — they were almost to the keg now — when Marty returned, sipping from a bottle of Corona.

"Where did you get that?" Simon said.

Marty took another swig, a lime wedge sliding up the neck and down again. "Some guys," he said, shrugging. He noticed Fish. "Who is this?" he said, looking at her and not Simon.

"Felicia," she told him. Her cheeks were pink again, the smile back on her face. And Simon felt the shift in their attentions away from him, toward each other — monumental, it felt, disastrous, like the landscape around him was changing, the ground under his feet disappearing, sliding out beneath him.

She stepped out of line, and the keg was in front of him. He stared at the spout.

"Move it," someone yelled from behind.

"Whoa," the guy manning the keg said, putting his hand out like a goddamned police officer. "What's this two-cup shit?"

"I paid for two glasses," Simon said.

"All right," the guy said, so self-important that Simon wanted to punch him. "This time, okay. Next time, maybe not."

He put his cup under the spout, flipped the nozzle, and watched the beer trickle out, slowly filling his tiny glass. He filled Marty's, too, and when he stood, the inevitable: Marty and Felicia were gone. He got out of the line and found an empty corner to stand in.

"Two-fistin' it," a guy said, stumbling past him. He gave Simon a shaky thumbs-up. "Right on."

Simon looked down: his glass, Marty's glass. He sipped from one, then the other. In no time, the beer was gone. The young girls were kissing now as a group of boys cheered them on. Their movements were exaggerated, grotesque — heads swaying back and forth more than seemed necessary or even sexy, tongues flicking out at one another between kisses. He held the empty plastic cups in his hands and looked at the keg line, which was deeper than ever. Fucking ridiculous. And Marty, nowhere to be seen. He tossed the cups behind a recliner and left.

He stopped by Greenwood Liquors on his way back to the apartment, bought a bottle of Bushmills, and woke up to Marty's voice: "Hot, man."

Simon was sweating. He thrashed under the covers, feeling close to suffocating. His alarm blinked a single-number time, five or six A.M., he couldn't make it out, and he saw the empty Bushmills bottle on his nightstand.

"What?" he rasped.

"She was fucking hot," Marty said. "Goddamn."

I'm going to die, Simon thought. He needed to vomit, but he wouldn't — couldn't. He was going to drown in his own chest, with the taste of old whiskey and red meat in his throat. He was going to die.

At some point — then or later, he didn't know — he was rolled over, so that his chin hung over the edge of the bed.

Daylight. He blinked, eyes gummy and itchy. When the world came back into focus, he saw red: a pasta pot on the floor, last night's dinner a churned mess inside of it. He closed his eyes, sure that he was going to puke again.

The only person who'd ever know the facts of what happened three nights later in Felicia's dorm room — the facts, though not actually the truths behind them — was Simon's father. Simon had known that his father would have the power and smarts to help him, but he'd also sensed, on a level he didn't even care to acknowledge, that his father would understand. Would forgive him and maybe even support him, in a way he couldn't have done had Simon confessed to something else. Telling him the sequence of events ended up being the easy part; Simon could think of it all like some story he was making up, or the plot of a movie, and just cling to the chronology when no other connections sufficed: *We were bored, had nothing better going on. Marty told me that she was easy, that he could get me laid. We'd talked about maybe driving out on Windsor Road, where they're clearing land to build that new subdivision, and do a campfire or something. Marty put his sleeping bag in the trunk of my car, and I threw in a couple of blankets, and we just went.*

The truths, though — those he kept to himself. He couldn't explain to his father what it felt like to wake up Friday afternoon, after the party, and listen to Marty tease him about getting drunk and sick and how Simon was lucky that Marty was home in time to roll his dumb, plastered ass over. What it felt like to listen as Marty gave him every sick fucking detail about his night with Felicia: "We went to her room, and Jesus, dude, I didn't even have to play nice. She didn't put on CDs or burn incense or any of that dumb shit girls do when they're trying to talk themselves into it. She was out of her shirt before the door closed all the way."

And he could never, never tell his father the next part of the conversation — how his face must've given some of what he was feeling away, because Marty looked at him strangely, and Simon was sure that Marty had finally figured out how he felt about him, that there was a side to their friendship he'd been ignorant about all this time. So when Marty spoke — when he asked Simon, "Have you ever been laid, man?" — Simon was so shocked that he shook his head *no,* which was the truth. He hadn't.

"Jesus," Marty had said. "Goddamn, I'm sorry. I've been a jerk."

"It's no big deal." He turned on the TV, but Marty shut it off again.

"No, it is a big deal." He put a hand on Simon's knee. "We're gonna fix you up, though. You don't worry about it."

Simon felt like crying: his head howled, his stomach was rotten, and he just plain *hurt,* inside-out. He'd been lulled by the contentment of the last few months — tricked into thinking that his life could be different and better — and now he was in hell. "Please, just leave it alone."

Marty got quiet then, but Simon knew that the conversation wasn't over. So he felt no surprise when Marty approached him Monday afternoon, looking like he'd thought hard and reached a difficult decision. "Felicia," he said. "Felicia'll do it."

"Do what?" Of course he knew.

"She'll fuck you."

Simon tried to laugh. "What the hell? Did you ask her?"

Marty shook his head. "No, but if we go over there, she'll do it. We just gotta get her a little drunk first, but she won't need much convincing."

"You're crazy," Simon said.

"No, I owe you," Marty told him. "You've been good to me. Let me do this for you, okay? It ain't that big a deal. That's the first thing you need to realize. You've got this shit built up so big in your head that you're paralyzed."

"It's not really like that," Simon said.

Marty picked up his cell phone. "Trust me." He flipped the receiver open, scrolled through his number list, and looked at Simon, lifting his eyebrows. Not getting laid — that was one thing: Marty could understand that, could even commiserate. But not *wanting* to: that was something else. He nodded to Marty.

"This time tomorrow," Marty said, smiling, "you'll be a stud."

*

Marty tried calling her about four, but her roommate told him she was out running or something, he'd tell his father early the next morning, weeping, on the edge of hysterics. This was later, after, and the streetlights to his father's house had all been on their yellow caution sequence, as if none of the regular rules applied at such an ungodly hour. *Then she had to meet some guys about a group project, wouldn't be back till late. Marty said that we should just hang out a while, surprise her later on. So we went down to the corner store and got some beers, then hung out at the house for a while.*

They bought tequila, too, and a bottle of peppermint schnapps that was on the bargain rack, plus some of those prepackaged watermelon-flavored shots that cost one dollar apiece and came packaged like test tubes. They drank. Simon didn't want to. Since Friday morning he'd been in horrible shape — throwing up every couple of hours, feeling a kind of trembling ache that reminded him of the flu but was hideously worse, like comparing a gunshot to a bee sting. Friday night he was just about convinced that he needed to be in the hospital — he almost certainly had alcohol poisoning — but he couldn't bring himself to do it, knowing that his father would find out and push him with a million different questions and scoldings. So he'd lain in bed and suffered, and by Saturday night he was able to choke down a bowl of Campbell's Chicken and Stars without getting sick. By Sunday, he felt dizzy and weak, but close to normal, otherwise. Except for the depression. He'd been sad in his life lots of times, but this was different. This was nothingness: a total vacuum of hope. He'd awakened in the middle of the night, at one point — Friday or Saturday, they blended together — and thought about killing himself. The idea was a relief but little more, and if he could have reached out and pressed a button and had it done, he would have. He didn't have the motivation for anything else.

He drank Monday night because he felt weighed down by inevitability, and he didn't know another way to disconnect from what was about to happen. He wasn't going to be able to have sex with that girl, he was sure — not with Marty watching or hanging out in the hallway outside her room, maybe not at all. Even if he could, though, what would doing it accomplish? Marty wanted this for him — had gone out of his way to arrange it — and that hurt more than an outright rejection would have.

"What are you thinking right now?" Marty asked. Night had fallen, and they sat on the porch of Simon's apartment house, passing the bottle of schnapps back and forth. The blankets and sleeping bag were in the trunk. A Durex Ultra-thin condom, one of Marty's, was in his pocket.

"I don't know," Simon said.

"That's okay." Marty rocked his lawn chair back, tipped back the bottle at the same time. "I was a mess my first time. I was fourteen, and she was sixteen, lived one street over in my neighborhood. She was my sister's friend."

Despite himself, Simon felt a cold excitement. He sat very still, the blood pulsing in his temples and his groin, making his body — still feverish from his illness — thrum like a giant, beating heart.

"We'd been building up to it, you know. Second-base shit, but I didn't know what the hell I was doing, of course. I was just grabbing her tits and trying to kiss her and grope her like they do in the movies." He laughed, and a car passed by on the street ahead of them. "So when we finally got around to fucking, she pretty much took over. It was wild. And I wanted her all the time after that. It was like the first time you — I don't know — eat a steak or smoke pot. It's so good you don't know why you waited so long to try it."

"You didn't wait that long," Simon said.

"Nah." Simon could hear the pride in that one syllable. "I've never been too patient." Marty flipped his phone open and looked at the time. "It's eleven, friend. She should be home by now. You ready to cruise?"

"As I'll ever be," Simon said, his skin burning.

Marty's fingers grazed his arm in the dark. "Just chill out, okay? You're gonna love this. She's a real hellcat."

Simon closed his eyes and focused on the sensation of Marty's fingers. "Okay," he whispered. This would be over in a few hours, no matter what happened. He clung to that.

Felicia's room was on the seventh floor. Keough Hall was female-only, and male guests weren't allowed up after eleven on weeknights, but Felicia had shown Marty that there was a back way you could access through the common laundry room. Simon was out of breath after two flights — the alcohol had hit him harder than usual, and he was lightheaded — but they couldn't have used the elevator without getting spotted by the Rent-a-cop at the front desk. "Almost there," Marty kept saying. He was small and fit — he'd walked on to the soccer team in August, then dropped out a month later — and he laughed the whole way up, never once needing to rest. "Save some energy, big guy."

By the seventh floor, Simon realized that his left ear was ringing. He took a deep breath.

"No more stairs," Marty said. "She's just down the hall."

"Give me a minute," Simon told him.

Marty waited, and when Simon was feeling better — he must have looked a little better, too — Marty handed him the tequila bottle. "One to grow on," he said. "And go wash your face."

Simon took a long, shuddering drink, swallowing past the oily taste he hated. He handed the bottle back to Marty and went to the restroom, hoping he wouldn't run into anyone. The bathroom was empty. He bent over the nearest sink and splashed water on his face, ran it through his short hair, took slow drinks of it by sticking his mouth right into the flow. He didn't look in the mirror. He had his father's face — the heavy eyebrows and full lower lip, the broad nose that made him — them — look slow and mean. He didn't need to see that face right now.

In the hallway, Marty was holding the tequila bottle, now empty. "No worries," Marty said, voice thick, like his tongue was too big for his mouth. "She'll have something."

She'll just say no, Simon thought. His relief was instantaneous. Why had he assumed she wouldn't? No booze, no chance.

"Ready, man?" Marty said.

Her door was heavy oak — decorated, like the other doors on this floor, with construction-paper clowns with googly eyes, two of them: STEPH in block letters on the left, FISH on the right. They'd forgotten about the roommate, he realized; there was no way this could go down the way Marty had envisioned it. Too many unconsidered factors. He knocked on Felicia's door himself, three hard raps. He smiled at Marty. And after a pause — a bar of light appearing on the floor in front of them — the door opened. Felicia stood there, the room behind her empty. Simon could see that she had been sleeping.

"Marty?" She smiled in a confused way, looking from Marty to Simon and back again, loose ponytail swinging. She had on a tank top — no bra — and light cotton pajama pants with a drawstring waist. The pant legs were long, and Simon could see her finely shaped toes sticking out from beneath the material, nails a glossy bright blue. "What are you guys doing here?"

"Can we come inside?" Marty said.

She hesitated. Only for a second, but her eyes met Simon's, and though she never stopped smiling — a confident, breezy, college girl's smirk, the one she even knew to call upon in her half wakefulness — he sensed her unease, and shared it.

"Okay," she said, and Simon also saw what Marty was too drunk to notice: the pretty blush on her cheeks, the naked hope. Whatever she'd told Marty about their night together — whatever she'd even told herself — she'd slept with him because she liked him and wanted him to like her back. She would do whatever Marty asked of her.

Marty gave her a quick kiss on the cheek and crossed the room in two good strides, plopping down on what had to be Felicia's bed. The space was small, with identical desks and metal wall lamps, cheap chests of drawers — they could have come from the Wells Brothers showroom — and closets with no doors. Felicia's bulletin board was covered, every inch, in photographs of bright, tanned girl faces, a collage interspersed here and there with cutouts of fish — some real photographs, from magazines, some cartoons. There was a stuffed fish on her bed, too: fluffy and colorful, with a zippered pocket. Simon took a seat at the roommate's desk.

"So what are you guys doing?" she asked again.

Marty shrugged. He got up from the bed and started wandering around the dorm room, checking the fridge, pulling up the corner of the roommate's mattress. Then he grinned, grabbed the stuffed fish from the bed, and unzipped the front pocket, jamming his hand inside. He pulled out a baggie of weed and a package of rolling papers.

"Bingo," he said.

Felicia grabbed at the bag, and Marty yanked it out of her reach. "Come on, give it back," she said. "That's got to last me until I get home again, and I don't usually do it here, anyhow. The smoke detectors are really sensitive."

"Let's take off, then," Marty said. "We thought about camping out over on Windsor, close to where that drive-in movie used to be."

"I don't know," Felicia said, plopping down on the bed and pulling her legs up under her, Indian-style. "I have class at nine."

Simon noticed Marty looking at him. "We'd have you back in plenty of time," he said.

She laughed. "Are you crazy? It's already midnight."

Marty sat down beside her and leaned close, pushing her hair over so that he could kiss her neck. Simon's chest tightened, his breath cut short and painful — but there was an impatience in this pain, too, a kind of reluctant desire that was more potent for being wrong, so clearly counter to everything Simon thought he'd discovered about himself. He watched, and Marty brushed his lips lightly against her skin, raised his chin, murmured something into the cup of her ear; Simon couldn't make out what. Marty moved his hand to her stomach, working his thumb under the fabric of her tank top; from across the small room, Simon could see her chest expand with a quick breath, stomach withdrawing from Marty's touch. She looked from Marty to Simon, eyebrows knitting together.

"Skip," Marty said, loud enough this time that Simon could hear.

She sighed in an exaggerated way, leaning away from him, back against her cinderblock wall. "I can't camp, guys. If I miss my Psych class again my grade's going to drop by a letter."

Simon felt his chest loosen, his forehead cool. His relief was so powerful that it flooded him like adrenaline, and maybe that's what it was: a high, the high of realizing he had a way out. He stood. "Let's go, Marty. She's right. It's late." He added: "We could camp for real this weekend. Maybe drive out to Dale Hollow or something."

"I'd be up for that," Felicia said.

"Goddamn." Marty waved his arms in an exasperated way. "Seems like the harder I try to have a good time, the harder people make it. You two belong with each other." He rose and started for the door, a show that Simon knew to take for what it was: just bravado. Marty was always making grand exits, grand pronouncements. Especially when he was drunk. Last month, when they were drinking at Mickey O'Shea's and listening to the Friday band — Hard Knox, they were called, a name that Marty had declared was "straight-up retarded" — he'd waited for a pause between songs, a lull after the clapping, to yell in the bar-quiet, "Christ, you suck!" Most guys doing that would have gotten their asses beat. Marty got some cheers, a high-five, and a halfhearted retort from the lead singer: "Not cool, man. Grow up."

It was conviction, Simon decided. Even the conviction to be a drunk asshole got you further than none at all.

"Wait," Felicia said now, rising before Marty could swing open her door. She picked up the baggie, dangled it between her thumb and forefinger. "Don't run off. I can't camp, okay? But you guys can hang out here for a little while."

Marty motioned to the ceiling. "What about the smoke detector?"

She waved him back into the room, to her bed. He relented, smiling, and once he was seated, Felicia began a series of operations that had the air of ritual, oft-repeated and perfected: she went to the windows and turned the handles, pushing them out and open; then she unplugged a box fan that was propped up on her roommate's dresser and moved it to the windowsill, replugging it and cranking it on its highest setting, air blowing outside. She grabbed an aerosol can of air freshener, sprayed a little near her door, and sat it on the floor by her bed where she could grab it in a hurry.

"That's worked in the past," she said finally. "I usually do this at my friend's apartment or at the park, but we should be okay here."

"You sure?" Simon said. That beautiful feeling of relief from before had dissipated. The air freshener, some generic floral scent, sat heavy in the air and metallic on his tongue: mockingly cheerful, nauseating.

Felicia nodded, already smoothing a rolling paper out on some kind of monster textbook, shaking out a neat mound of bud, working the joint between her fingers and thumb and sealing the edge with her saliva. She twisted the ends expertly, a useless sort of grace that Simon couldn't help but admire. His father looked this way when he was operating the standard shift on a car, his mother when she was peeling potatoes or taste-testing a pot of her vegetable soup. And Simon himself could handle a batting cage like a major leaguer, his swings as fast and uniform as crochet stitches.

Felicia leaned close to the fan, lighting the joint. She puffed it twice, the way rich men tasted cigars in the movies, and exhaled into the blades — her hum made staccato, the funny robot-sound Simon remembered from his childhood.

"Don't hog," Marty said, taking the joint and Felicia's spot near the fan. Then Simon had his turn, and he got a bit of pleasure from the intimacy of sharing this with Marty, their lips on the same soft twist of paper, the same smoke in their chests. He finally exhaled, lightheaded. This seemed like a potent enough batch, which didn't surprise him: rich girls always got their hands on the good stuff, paying too much for it and not even knowing the difference. They were scoring from friends of their parents, not rednecks and black kids. No visits to bum-fucked Egypt to buy from a pregnant teenager, no drives down to the housing projects, where you were more likely to get approached about a rock than a dime-bag. And Felicia had money, he could tell. It wasn't a matter of how he'd seen her dressed, either — the labels and nonsense, the dainty diamond earrings — and it wasn't her room, which was no more impressive on Felicia's side than on her roommate's. The same Target bedclothes, rumpled and overdue for a wash. Similar posters and makeup cases, shower caddies and rubber flip-flops. Similar Nike tennis shoes lining the closet floors: an old pair with some wear still in them, a newer pair for going to class. *I've measured my life in tennis shoes,* Simon thought then, remembering some poem he'd read in lit class.

No, it was something else. She had the manner of a girl who'd been denied nothing, whose rebellions were safe because they were sanctioned and contained and easily remedied, even if the worst happened. Her parents would have been the type to say, "If you drink too much, give us a call. You won't get in trouble. If you're going to have sex, let us take you to the doctor. You won't get in trouble."

Three hits, a fourth, a fifth. He was feeling it. "Really, though, this stuff is fascinating," Felicia was saying, hand on the giant textbook. "I'm thinking of changing majors."

"Fascinating," Marty echoed.

It went on like this for a while, and then there was a second joint, and Simon was feeling tired, blurry. He faded out for a moment, and when he found his focus again, Felicia was on the bed with Marty on top of her, pajamas down around her knees, Marty between her hips. Music was playing lowly, some female-wailing stuff that Simon didn't recognize or much care for, and Marty's quick breaths were easily audible above the brash acoustic guitar chords. His head bobbed above her. Her fingers curled loosely in his dark hair. As Simon watched, Marty leaned down and lifted her tank top over her head, and she curled her shoulders up to make it easier for him, breasts so small that they barely stirred with the motion.

Marty finished, lifted his head, and saw Simon watching them. Simon's terror was instant but dulled — out-of-body. He felt himself slowly turning to the window, focusing on it. He had been looking that way all along. He'd been sleeping.

"Hey," Marty said. "Your turn."

This was the part he'd try to explain to his father — how nobody ever just lost everything, or crashed, or went screaming over an edge. No, you nickeled-and-dimed your way there, you took a step and felt the ground solid beneath you and then thought another was safe enough, or maybe somebody was pushing you the whole way, little pushes, the kind that felt more like reassurances than actual pressure.

He managed to get the rubber on, and Marty was pulling him over before Felicia fully registered the change, before she had a chance to replace her clothes or otherwise react. She grabbed at her sheet, not saying no, just making a low moaning sound that could have been fear but seemed less potent somehow: *unnnnnh.* Her breath quickened, yet still she didn't say anything. Simon waited for her to stop him, to ask what the hell was going on, but her eyes flitted from his to Marty's and back again, frightened but resigned, as if she knew that all of this had been decided beforehand and her vote was futile against the majority's.

He was inside her when she started to cry.

"No," she managed now. "Off. Get him off me, Marty, please, get him off me."

Simon felt Marty's hand on his lower back, intimate as a kiss would have been. "She's just wigging," he said. "Hurry up."

Simon did, no longer stimulated but sick to his stomach and moving against her, rubber tugging uncomfortably, dangling, but neither Felicia nor Marty seemed to know the difference. She was moaning again, a chilling sound, and Simon had decided that he just needed to stop, collapse on top of her — like Marty had done, with the final thrust, the hard exhalation — but out of nowhere her moans turned to shrieks, screams, and he and Marty were both trying to cover her mouth before they all got caught. He felt something pushed into his hand, the stuffed fish with the zippered pocket, and he held it to Felicia's mouth, Marty's hands pressed on top of his own, like men making a pact. "Felicia, come on, shut the fuck up," Marty was saying when Simon pulled back, tugging his jeans over his hips and zipping his fly closed. He yanked off the rubber and stuffed it into his pocket before Marty could see that he'd wasted it, still thinking that way despite his panic, because all of this seemed disconnected from the kinds of anguish he was used to feeling. They'd figure this situation out — calm Felicia down, talk her out of reporting them to the R.A. or the god-forbid campus police — but then he'd have the rest of his life to contend with, the awkwardness with Marty, and maybe Marty wouldn't want another thing to do with him. Felicia was thrashing, sheets working themselves into ropes beneath her, and her leg pistoned out, catching Simon square in the kneecap, pain quick and bright as a lightning flash.

Marty pulled back, removing the pillow, and she screamed. "Goddamn it," he said, covering her mouth again, but she was bucking now, panicked, and Simon could see that Marty was going to lose hold of her. So he leaned down, holding his weight over her legs and midriff, heart rebounding in his chest like a boxer's speed bag. "Jesus," Marty grunted, trying to keep her head still under his hands. "Fish, get it together. I thought you were into it, you stupid —" She jerked, and he pushed the stuffed fish against her face. "Fuck." He looked at Simon, his own face pale, the flesh under his eyes, always dusky, now heavy as graphite. "She's having a fucking conniption," he said breathlessly. "Fuck, fuck, I don't know what to do, man."

The rest happened very quickly. Simon would have trouble making sense of it later, because he'd remember Marty saying, "Shhh, honey," and "Please, kid, we're just gonna leave," and "Calm down, calm down," but she must have already been still by that time, and how long? He didn't know. At some point he realized that there wasn't any more tension in her legs, no resistance against him, and he said to Marty, "Hey, is she okay?" and Marty didn't answer him. And Simon knew.

"Oh my God," Simon said. He was sitting on the end of the cheap twin bed, and he thought her leg was maybe still under his hip, but he was so numb all over that he couldn't be sure. It struck him that he should try slapping her cheeks or checking for a pulse — or CPR, maybe that was what they needed to do — and there was 911, too, and that was probably the smartest idea. Get an ambulance here. Put the whole thing into more capable hands. But that was all balanced by fear — for her safety, sure, but mostly for himself — an emotion so pure it was primal.

"Marty," Simon found himself saying, voice cracking. "Marty, what if she's dead?"

Marty threw the pillow on the bed and wiped his hand on his jeans. He stared at Felicia and then the door, holding a finger to his lips. Neither moved for a moment, waiting, the only sounds their hard breathing and the fast hum of the box fan.

"We've got to do something," Simon said finally. "Right? Right?"

"Yeah," Marty muttered. He was crying, visibly desperate, and Simon ached because there wasn't an acceptable way for him to give comfort right now, or to take it. He ached, too, because this was Marty's fault, all Marty's fault, and it wasn't fucking right for him to worry right now, for him to feel anything for a man whose concern for Simon only extended as far as Simon's ability and willingness to keep him drunk. It wasn't right. But Simon couldn't change it.

"What do we do?" he asked Marty.

Marty started searching the room like he had hours before — pulling out drawers, checking the closet shelf — and Simon stood and backed toward the door, not sure what to ask, what to think. All at once Marty stopped, bent down, and grabbed the aerosol can of air freshener that Felicia had left on the floor. Before Simon could object, he stalked over to Felicia's bed and sprayed her down with it, dousing her face and her crotch most heavily and using his free hand to wipe sweat off his forehead. The air was thick with the floral scent from before, pink-smelling and nauseating, and Simon wasn't surprised when Marty turned and retched into a wastebasket.

"Oh God, what the hell," Simon said, but he guessed he understood.

Marty came to him and shoved the can into his hand, and Simon looked at it stupidly. English Rose Garden, it said. There was a picture.

"Now you," Marty told him, hand still on Simon's.

He did it, he guessed, as much for himself as for Marty. He knew this was true when the time came to make it final, and he didn't trust Marty not to bungle it. One of them would have to go get the car, which was parked a half mile up the way on University Drive, and pull it around for the other; that was the only way they stood a fighting chance of clearing the campus before the fire alarm engaged. The other had to stay here and make sure the fire caught, that the sprinklers couldn't soak it too quickly, and Simon was already seeing how that could maybe be done. But they had to get on it.

He pressed the keys to his Corvette into Marty's hand. "Get the car," he said. "You remember where it is?"

Marty nodded, visibly relieved. "Yeah," he said. "Sure."

"Wait for me at the corner, okay? I'll be there as soon as I can." It occurred to him that Marty could take his keys and drive off, leaving Simon stranded, but he decided that he'd have to risk it.

"I'll be there," Marty said, and Simon hated the sudden bloom of hope on his face. Worse than that, he hated the tone of that *I'll be there,* as if this were a favor and not simply his part. The whole time they'd known each other, Marty had managed to live off of Simon's good graces and make it seem that Simon was the one owing. He was dismayed by his own stupidity.

But Marty chose then to grab Simon, to hug him, and Simon felt the press of Marty's wet cheek against his neck. Simon hadn't hugged a man before — couldn't remember the last time he'd touched his own father, and only then for a hard handshake, or to have his back pummeled when a piece of food went down his windpipe — but he knew that this contact went on longer than it should have. Marty whispered *thank you,* still holding him, and Simon squeezed back fiercely, not wanting to let go but afraid not to be the first to pull back. So he did.

"I'll be there," Marty repeated, and in a second he was gone.

Simon pulled Felicia's desk chair into the middle of the room, grabbed the roommate's comforter, and worked as quickly as he could, bunching the material tight around the two sprinklers. He knotted loose spots with rolled-up towels, and the mass looked bloated and misshapen when he was finished, like a toadstool growing out of the ceiling, or a malignant mole. His shoulders ached when he jumped down, and he thought, absurdly, of Michelangelo.

He emptied the can of air freshener, spraying the textbook that Felicia had used for rolling joints — already that seemed like weeks ago — and placing it on the bed next to her feet. He tossed the empty can up there too, figuring it would explode when things got hot enough, help finish the job. He stayed as far from the body as he could, and only years later could he acknowledge that this wasn't just nausea or guilt, an irrational fear of the dead — it was the fear that she *wasn't* dead, that he'd get near enough to see her chest rise, and then what would he do? Could he stop what had been put into motion? Did he want to?

He started the fire with Felicia's lighter, the one she'd passed around with the joint. And when the first blue-white flame burst forth, he ran, the flames fast and hot behind him, the fire more successful, more quick, than he realized it could be. He exited the room as quietly as he could, pulling the door tight with the faintest *snick*, and then he dashed across the hallway and toward the stairwell, praying that he could get there without a door opening, without crossing the path of some girl on her late-night bathroom break. Then he was in the stairwell and circling down, no longer trying to soften his footfalls but taking the steps two and three at a time, almost falling, regaining balance, picking up speed again. In a minute or two he reached ground level, sprinting down the hallway and back through the laundry room's back entrance, into the night. He ran so hard that his thoughts stayed behind, for a little while, and he was filled with a beautiful energy and exhilaration — like he could lap the earth in reverse, spin time back, change everything.

Marty was waiting when he reached the corner, the Corvette's engine humming smoothly in the stillness. The car was in motion before Simon could slam his door closed.

Two hours later, he waited for his father's judgment.

"This Marty kid," he said. "Will he keep his mouth shut?"

"I don't know," Simon said. He'd dropped Marty off in front of Pierce-Ford barely an hour ago. They'd passed fire trucks on the way, and Marty looked shocked when he saw them, as if he hadn't really believed that Simon would finish what he'd started. As if the flashing lights and sirens were more proof than he could stomach.

"Well, it doesn't matter," his father told him. "May be better if he squeals. If you keep your mouth shut and don't give anything away. You say nobody saw you? Tell the truth, now."

"Nobody," Simon said.

"That's good." His father rose, started to pace their living room. "That's good," he repeated, rubbing his face.

"I used a condom," Simon said.

"What did you do with it?"

"Put it in my pocket."

His father stopped. "Still there?"

Simon nodded.

"We'll burn it," his father said. "And your clothes, too, while we're at it." Simon stripped down to his boxers and waited while his father went to the kitchen for a garbage bag. His father returned and held the bag open wide. "Anything else?"

"The lighter's in my pocket with the rubber," Simon said. He tossed the bundle in all at once.

His father looked in the bag. "Christ, kid. What a fucking mess."

"I'm sorry, Dad." And he was, though this sorry was much bigger than his father, or himself. A sorry he couldn't really contemplate just yet, tired as he was, numb as he felt. But he'd feel it later, Simon was sure. For the rest of his life, he'd feel it.

"Well," his father said. "A little late for sorries." But he crossed the living room and kissed Simon's forehead, holding Simon's face roughly with his big hands, then rested his chin on Simon's crown. "Your mother loves you," he said.

Simon knew what his father meant. "I know."

"Go to bed, son. I'll take care of it."

Simon did. He went upstairs to his childhood room — the one his mother kept dusted, just in case he decided to come home for a night or weekend. He climbed into his bed, and the sheets were fresh, because his mother changed them once a week whether the bed had been slept in or not. His body ached — from tonight or from the culmination of the last several nights he wasn't sure, but the soft mattress was a blessing, as were the familiar shadows of his childhood room and the familiar beam of moonlight hitting the end of his bed. He felt safe here, which was ironic, because he'd *never* felt safe in this house, or loved.

In a few moments, as he was starting to doze, the light in the room changed, started to shift and rollick. Simon sat up and looked out the window: his father was back behind the house, building up a small fire. Flames were already glowing in the center of a neat teepee of wood, and when the last chunks were arranged to his father's satisfaction, he stood, backed away a few feet, and shot a stream of lighter fluid over to the pile. It erupted, beautiful and startling, and Simon's father began to empty the bag, giving each item time to char before adding the next one: the jeans first, then the boxers and shirt. He wadded the bag into a ball and threw that on last.

His father stood back to watch. The flames climbed higher, black smoke roiling at their apex, and as a breeze picked up outside, bits of ash drifted off on a current, down toward the cow pasture, where the new day's fog was already starting to collect. The fire was a neat solution, and Simon knew that his father loved a neat solution. He'd known he could depend on that. He watched as his father crossed his arms, surveying his work and his property — the acreage, the far-off stream — like a king who had seen battle, fared well, and returned home to enjoy his spoils.

His car was vandalized a second time five years later.

He'd been at Mickey O'Shea's all evening, alone. The trial was long enough ago — coming up on three years — that most people didn't recognize him. Most people — even the angry ones who'd protested the day he was acquitted, marching with signs outside the courtroom, a hundred different photos of Felicia plastered everywhere, inescapable — wanted to move on at some point, to forget that bad things happened. Simon wanted to forget. But he came to this bar anyway, a few times a month, and thought about Marty, who'd called the police three days after Felicia's death and confessed to everything.

For the good it did.

Simon left Mickey's at one A.M. and started down Cherry Street to the gravel lot where he always parked the Corvette, remembering all of the times he'd cut this same path with Marty, both of them shitfaced but not bellowing idiots, usually just deep into some conversation about a movie or their folks or whether or not God was real. Marty believed in God. "Got to," he'd told Simon one night. "What else is there?" And Simon, knowing he'd bothered Marty by suggesting that there wasn't anything else, there was nothing, was happy that he could tell him about Descartes.

"Proof of God," Marty had said. "I like it."

"So do I," Simon had told him.

He was glad he'd given Marty that — a gift, he thought now, something to carry him through difficult times. Marty had made a deal in the year after Felicia's death, pleading guilty to rape and conspiracy to rape, plus manslaughter — a twenty to life sentence — in exchange for testifying against Simon in the big trial. Simon had done what his father had told him to do: *Stick to the alibi and don't waver, no matter what the police tell you, no matter what evidence they produce.* As it turned out, despite some bluffs during the interrogation, they had nothing: no witnesses, no DNA, only Marty's testimony, ever changing. In the end, Marty managed only to implicate himself.

Simon approached his car in the dark.

He felt the crunch of broken glass beneath his hiking boots and knew what had happened before he saw it: every window of the Corvette smashed, the headlights and taillights busted, cracks pounded into the black fiberglass with what could only have been a baseball bat, or perhaps even a mallet of some kind. No graffiti this time, but the message was just as plain as that long-ago FAG had been, just as accurate. He realized that whoever had done this could still be lurking somewhere nearby, holding the weapon, and he stood as still as possible, listening.

Nothing. There was nothing.

He pulled his cell phone out of his pocket and opened it, the small screen glowing like a distress signal in the middle of so much darkness. He dialed his father's number and waited, thinking, as he always did when despair wanted to settle on him, of Marty's touch that night: the heat in his wet cheek, the only proof Simon had ever needed, the only higher power.

PETER LASALLE

Tunis and Time

FROM *The Antioch Review*

I.

LAYTON FOUND HIMSELF WORKING a second week in the city. Everything was supposed to be routine in Tunis, just asking a few set questions of an informant named Khaled Khemir. Layton was set up comfortably enough in a white wedding-cake rise of an old hotel on Avenue de Paris, the Majestic.

It was a rundown place but with at least airs of former opulence. The cavernous lobby, all red and white marble, had a sweeping staircase and ornate chandeliers; a splattering of old clock faces on the wall behind the desk gave the hour in various major cities around the world (he kept noticing those clocks, and how it seemed that the one for New York had been replaced recently with a newer one for Karachi, perhaps understandable in an Arab World country at the moment). The manager was a handsome guy in his late thirties, muscular and mustached, his hair in a styled shag. Always wearing a tailored French suit, he had once actually played for the revered Espérance Sportif soccer club there in Tunis, his celebrity status landing him this easy job now.

Layton liked talking soccer with him, and the manager seemed to have no problem with Layton being an American.

Layton probably didn't need any formal cover in Tunis. Nevertheless, his informal one, in case anybody got nosy, was a line about being an academic researching an article on Flaubert and his time out at the ruins of nearby Carthage, which had resulted in the historical novel *Salammbô.* It wasn't the first occasion that Layton had resorted to the fact he had been a French literature major in what felt like some other lifetime indeed back at Harvard. To be frank, not much of the literature stuck with Layton, and often alone in a hotel room somewhere, a ceiling fan chugging, he seemed to recall nothing much from any of those novels very clearly, or anything, let's say, beyond the stuff that people who hadn't even read the books probably had heard of: the famous black hearse-like carriage rocking away with Madame Bovary and her young law clerk lover coupling as it rambled around the cobbled streets of Rouen, or even the famous centipede crawling up the famous bare white wall in the modern plantation house, seemingly the main action in Robbe-Grillet's static slim volume. True, little of that came back to him, yet what did often unexpectedly and repeatedly return was a memory of construction of the odd covers themselves of the Livre de Poche editions. He remembered 1966 or 1967 and leaving his rooms in Winthrop House on the river, to head over to the Square and the Coop Textbooks on a side street. And what he also definitely remembered was how those imported paperbacks for his French lit courses were coated in clear plastic, which somehow wasn't made for the New England climate, the coating soon yellowing, cracking, and peeling free completely before long. That always represented some essential flaw to Layton, and in that lavender rain and heading back to redbrick Winthrop House on the grassy banks of that Charles — yes, rain back then *could* be beautifully lavender in Cambridge, a guy like Layton *could* once be young and hopeful that he would be lucky in life, everything would turn out okay and good things were ahead of him — Layton almost asked himself before he cracked the spine of another new Livre de Poche, "How long before this one falls apart?"

Layton knew, though, he had to be careful of thinking of things like that, especially careful of thinking too much when by yourself in a hotel room in a very hot country, a place like Tunis, let's say.

As for the two blond girls from Montpellier, nearly a matching set and half Layton's age or less, Layton had noticed them around the downtown even before he got mixed up with them. Actually, how couldn't you notice them? Any tourists that there were in Tunisia seemed to stay at the resort towns beyond the city and out on the coast, a sleek bus occasionally herding a pack of them in for a morning shopping trip to buy the overpriced souvenir junk (cheaply plated hookahs, tiny stuffed camels, etc.) in the Medina, but not much more seen of their presence than that. And the usual tourists certainly weren't two svelte five-foot-nine girls wearing platform heels, designer jeans, and halter tops, tanned and made up like dolls there under an umbrella at one of the big cafés along the Avenue Borguiba, runway model material — though Layton would eventually learn that they were more than broke, that they had jumped a hotel bill up in ritzy Sidi Bou Said, that they had left France without as much as bothering to book a return ticket back to Montpellier simply because they were sure some playboy in a white yacht (okay, maybe two playboys, in their own nutty daydreaming) would eventually ferry them home, in *real* style.

The girls at an outdoor café — one of them in oversize sunglasses pushing her long fingers in a raking shove through the spill of blond hair, then the other in oversize sunglasses taking that almost as a cue, as if to say in her whispery French, near baby talk, "Wow, it's been a while since I pushed my hand through my beautifully lustrous spill of long blond hair that dusts my fine bare and tanned shoulders," and doing the same.

They were like that, Véronique and Jeanne-Isabelle.

II.

"You shouldn't have come anywhere near the embassy," Cunningham from CIA said.

"It was at night, my first one here," Layton said, "or the evening, anyway. I like to get a feel for a place, if you know what I mean. See where everything is. I just strolled up from the hotel. I could have been anybody strolling into that posh neighborhood there."

"Nobody saw you?"

Layton and Cunningham were having a late lunch in a modest enough place on Rue du Caire, good couscous. Layton knew that CIA saw FBI as yokels. And this Cunningham with his front of a job in the embassy's consular section was no different; he surely didn't like the idea that Layton was supposedly needed at the moment, and surely for Cunningham — lanky, bespectacled, and self-satisfied at forty or so — an FBI yokel could only mess things up.

Layton continued with the couscous, and he had to hand it to Cunningham concerning the meal: at a few dinars, the heap of the tomatoed stuff with squash and peppers and carrots and potatoes, the tender central chunk of lamb topping the semolina, was maybe proving to be exactly what Cunningham had promised, "Just try it and you tell me, if it isn't the best fucking couscous of your life." But cuisine wasn't the issue at hand there in the cubbyhole, where at the few tables the other men eating sat facing the window and the afternoon glare outside, schoolroom style. Cunningham asked Layton again:

"Nobody saw you?"

"Relax, will you. I walked. I passed that big, sort of art-deco old synagogue on Avenue de la Liberté that looks like a fortress, all the cops and armored Land Cruisers or whatever around it. Then I got into your embassy neighborhood, upscale and tasteful, where I must say I was surprised to see so little security, except for the concrete barriers in front. The whole operation was closed down for the day. What did I see? I saw the locked glass door to the consular section and a lit waiting room, empty. I saw a sign saying that visiting the consular section was a no-charge deal, and if anybody tried to charge anybody else waiting in line for preferred service or anything else, that it should be reported. A sign like that's a new one on me, and that's exactly what I saw, all I saw. And I doubt anybody saw me."

"Don't worry about the security. It's totally unseen."

"What's the deal on the synagogue?"

"There's still a Jewish community here, a small token one that's getting smaller. The police presence outside is just a token, too, trying to put on a good face to show outsiders that Tunisia isn't to be lumped with the rest of the Arab World."

"Which, of course, it is."

"Of course."

Cunningham appeared to be softening, appeared to appreciate how it was obvious that Layton was enjoying the couscous.

"Good, isn't it?" Cunningham said.

"Best fucking couscous of my life," Layton told him.

That a supposedly retired agent from the Bureau like Layton was in a place like Tunisia was an anomaly, to put it mildly. That Layton had even signed up with the FBI after law school was probably more of an anomaly, bordering on freak occurrence, to put it frankly.

Layton went to law school, UVA, after Harvard. He studied law maybe only because he felt that he owed the uncle who had raised him for all the man's kindness over the years — the bachelor uncle, a judge, so much wanted to see Layton a lawyer. Layton hated the drudgery of tort and contract courses. And to make matters worse, it was the 1960s, that time of evening news clips constantly showing more frightened American kids in camouflage uniforms being spilled out of teetering helicopters and onto the yellow rice paddies in Vietnam; Layton knew he would get heat from his local draft board in Rhode Island once his law school deferment expired. Layton decided to beat the government at its own game, and he joined the FBI to dodge the draft, if that made any sense. Assigned to D.C., he married a girl who was a secretary for a congressman, they had a son, but the marriage didn't work out. In truth, nothing was working out for Layton for a while; the snub-nosed girl with red hair who was so pretty and was so much fun as they relaxed on weekends with other couples at barbecues and suburban cocktail parties out in leafy Fairfax, his young wife, well, somehow her prettily snub-nosed, red-headed innate cheeriness wasn't a good mix with the darkness of Layton soon questioning most everything — the meaningless job, the dead-end of claustrophobic family life. After a complicated divorce, Layton didn't buck the transfer from Washington to Detroit; he needed a change.

Layton was one of the first agents assigned to the Arab community there, and seeing that the bulk of the community was essentially Christian then — Lebanese, Syrian — his fluent French was his credential, a language they sometimes shared. His work wasn't so much a matter of any terrorism, but just dealing with normal crime (often rings for the pilfering from warehouse loading docks of expensive color TVs or a few crates of Cutty Sark, what qualified as a federal offense because it involved interstate trucking). When monitoring of foreign students became a priority during the 1980s and more agents were transferred to those squads, Layton welcomed the reassignment to Boston, a better city than Detroit and one he knew well. After all, New England was home for him, granting it was very different now — his elderly uncle had died, even Layton's second-rate prep school on the North Shore was long gone, the staid fieldstone buildings and emerald playing fields close to the sea converted into, wouldn't you know it, condos. Layton lived in a small Beacon Hill apartment with a lot of windows, which didn't make it seem so small. He dated an attractive gray-eyed stewardess for the old TWA for a long while, then a divorced art gallery owner for a longer while. Admittedly, Layton didn't relish putting in time with her at another opening amid the usual empty small talk and usual cheap white wine and canapés lifted off a silver tray. He also didn't like to hear the woman, Marion, wheeling and dealing in canvases on the phone, because, as Layton soon learned, the peddling of art wasn't all that different from the peddling of storm windows, or even life insurance to the over-fifties crew. However, he did savor how she had a gift for spotting work by younger artists who might be the real thing, and merely to hear her say something in her raspy, authentically Vassar voice, like, "Does anybody know how successful nineteenth-century American painters were at getting at the very *essence* of black, Heade especially, does anybody have *any* idea?" — something like that was enough to convince Layton that she was rare, different from the attractive TWA stewardess or the several younger, so-called professionals he met in the Newbury Street dating bars, the quintessentially empty chatter of that scene. But he didn't marry Marion, and they went their separate ways.

There were a couple of somewhat major cases for Layton. One had been in his very first year of service in Washington when he got assigned to a Weatherman bombing squad. The other came through his contacts in Boston; Layton managed to gather solid information after Arab terrorists blew a Pan Am jet out of the sky over the small town in Scotland that gave the disaster its name. But outside of that, there wasn't much to distinguish Layton's career with the Bureau. Early on, his superiors had obviously lumped him together with the play-it-safe foot-draggers, even if he was from Harvard and not the usual type of reliable Catholic college boy Hoover always had such belief in for his corps; true, while Layton didn't entirely fit the profile, nobody differentiated him from the common terminally lazy variety of agent, Catholic college or otherwise, just dreaming of retirement and finally paying off a mortgage in some second-tier suburb like Fairfax. Layton admitted the Bureau had wasted his life, or his professional life, anyway; he often thought he would have liked to have gotten a Ph.D., or done just about anything other than put up with as many years as he did of endless Bureau paperwork and office politics. The set retirement age for agents was fifty-seven, but he never made it anywhere close to that. Layton took a cut in pension early when his grown son, whom Layton hardly knew (his ex-wife had remarried), talked him into investing in the son's own business; it was an Internet start-up, a foolish scheme, something to do with selling rock-and-roll trivia to keyboard-clicking, credit-card-wielding fans online. Layton probably went along with it, invested heavily, because he felt guilty that he hadn't been around to raise his son; Layton saw in him a certain vacant lostness that made Layton want to believe that the bragging kid might turn things around, end up making a success of such a far-fetched enterprise, another budding go-getter of a Ted Turner, possibly. Increasingly more money was borrowed against Layton's pension, Layton fell into deep debt, and by the time the Bureau approached him to come out of retirement and do some part-time work — a contractor of sorts, what they referred to as an "asset" — he had no choice but to sign on. The fact of the matter was that after September 11 Layton was suddenly very much in demand, one of the few veteran agents with any substantial time in Arab domestic surveillance; plus, his having handled a Weatherman bombing case and then the Lockerbie bombing case made his dossier more noticeable. He still had his contacts and informants, a list built up through considerable work and despite the legendary FBI stinginess. (While the high-rolling CIA might set up ski lodges and yachts to lure sources, it was different for the FBI; more than once at the Boston FBI office Layton had put in for a voucher to bring an informant to a good restaurant — a Spanish place, specifically, that he liked in a Harvard Square back street — only to have his squad boss balk, suggest he settle for hamburgers at the red Formica tables of Charlie's Kitchen behind the JFK School.) All of which is to say, the game was different now: Layton was *badly* needed, and sending Layton on an errand to yet another country was almost becoming routine. Of course, what was called a "no objection" clearance to allow such foreign work was always applied for and always given, albeit reluctantly, by CIA and State ahead of time. CIA did tolerate activity like FBI bomb squad investigations abroad, but, to repeat, it really didn't like anybody horning in on its own foreign intelligence.

Khaled Khemir had been an informant while a student at MIT.

Layton had already established he was living in Tunis now, but the Bureau seemed nervous about using simple overseas phone contact with him, so this trip was arranged.

On the other hand, Layton didn't like putting pressure on this kid — or a kid back when he knew him, anyway — and he remembered Khaled Khemir in Boston as a rather quiet, brainy sort. He had returned to Tunis and was teaching part-time at the national university in the city.

And in Tunis Khaled Khemir himself was now reluctant, or so Layton detected in the course of two brief local phone calls from the Hôtel Majestic. Then, to complicate the situation, Khaled Khemir announced that he was leaving Tunis for a few days to visit his ill mother somewhere near Sfax, telling Layton they could get together when he returned. So the French girls from Montpellier, having them around, became a way to kill some time for Layton as much as anything else.

III.

Two mornings later, speaking in French, the hotel manager came up to Layton. Layton was walking through the lobby, returning to his room after breakfast with the copy of Flaubert's *Salammbô* in hand. The manager said, "I must say, I admire your taste in women." The manager's name was Youssef, possessor of the nickname of El Bey — translated as more or less "The Ruler" — during his days as a striker with Espérance Sportif.

In his good French suits, Youssef was rather dashing. He exuded sheer confidence, like a former rock star or — better, here in football-crazy Tunis — somebody who actually *had* been a player for Espérance Sportif. He spoke to Layton in a man-to-man way now, almost congratulating him for what Youssef must have seen as Layton's conquest of the duo of sleek blonds. It was all humorous for Layton, who while still lean and athletic at his age, the short military lie-down haircut silver and a perpetual tan from so much travel lately, certainly wasn't the kind of guy for a conquest of the sort the manager was envisioning. Actually, after having seen the girls a couple of times at the cafés on Avenue Borguiba, Layton was just sitting outdoors at the Café des Deux Avenues one afternoon, when the girls took the table next to him. One of them, Véronique, eventually asked for a light, an obvious ploy to start conversation. There was something in their vulnerability. At first they did put on some about how the little jewel of a village on its cliff high above the sparkling Mediterranean, jet-setting Sidi Bou Said, had bored them and so they decided to move to the city, though before long in the talk they unabashedly poured out their predicament — virtually no money, definitely no return tickets, and barely able to stand another night in a hotel beside the patch of soot and dust that passed for a city bus terminal, a place called (Layton appreciated this connection) the Hôtel Salammbô. There followed much talk of the size of the roaches at the Salammbô, the lack of air conditioning at the Salammbô; there was much talk, as well, concerning how their luggage had been confiscated by the expensive hotel in Sidi Bou Said, and how they had, in fact, left there with little more than the jeans and the halter tops they were wearing, plus a couple of dresses and, of course, their cosmetic kits. Without return tickets they had no choice but to try to survive in cheaper Tunis for a while, hope something might happen. Perhaps Layton was the something.

In the course of the conversation, especially beautiful Jeanne-Isabelle, of the bruised-plum lips and mile-high cheekbones, just started sniffling, then her eyes teared up, Jeanne-Isabelle peeling off her big wraparound sunglasses and dabbing those eyes with a paper napkin. Layton, feeling particularly avuncular, told them he would help; he accompanied them to check out of the dim Hôtel Salammbô, and he booked them a room next to his at the Majestic. He knew how to play the expense account game lately, not as tough overseas even with the cheap FBI; it would be easy enough to claim the girls knew Khaled Khemir, say they might be valuable on that front. But when asked about them now, Layton had to be honest with the hotel manager, "They are simply friends, I'm helping them out."

"They seemed tired when they arrived yesterday, *les jeunes filles,*" Youssef said. "They must be sleeping late. Tell them that tomorrow I can arrange for breakfast to be served in the room beyond the regular breakfast time, right up to eleven."

"To be frank, I personally don't have any idea if they're still sleeping," Layton told him. "Though I imagine they might be. Remember, they have their own room. They're in 219, and I'm in 218."

"D'accord," the manager said.

Layton knew the manager must have been picturing what Layton himself was picturing — the single door, cream-enameled and ornate, probably dating back to the "1911" carved in the Majestic's whitewashed façade. It was locked, but a twist of the wrist and an unbolting of the tarnished brass knob would be all that was needed to combine as a single suite the two spacious old rooms; those rooms had long French windows (opening to balconies), grumbling air conditioners, and no shortage of a matching overdone floral patterning (exploding roses, ferns) for the drapes and the spreads and the upholstery on the chairs themselves, the mismatching old furniture all freshly cream-enameled to give some sense of matching, too. The Majestic *was* a find, Layton had decided, no denying its authenticity.

Going through the lobby the next day around noon (he looked at those clocks for the time in different zones above the desk again, maybe he had even dreamed of them the night before), Layton thought he heard voices coming from what should have been the empty dining room, which he knew didn't serve lunch, only breakfast and dinner. He saw the girls with their freshly washed blond hair, loose and stringily wet. They were sitting at a table with Youssef; they were listening, laughing, hanging on his every word surely documenting his legendary soccer exploits, as Youssef made good on that offer of keeping the waiters in their frayed gold jackets around for a very late continental breakfast for the girls.

Though for the moment the man Layton saw sitting there didn't even seem to be Youssef the hotel manager in the least, and with the girls, for the moment, this Youssef was entirely the star player again, "El Bey," the Ruler indeed.

Meanwhile, Layton was beginning to suspect that this errand was maybe not going to be as easy as he had first thought, getting the information on a couple of Khaled Khemir's former grad-student teaching assistant colleagues back at MIT; they had been monitored closely for the last four months, definitely "chatterers," possibly linked to Palestinian resistance organizations. Khaled Khemir was still in Sfax.

To be honest, Layton liked Tunis, liked it a hell of a lot.

He liked this newer part of the city, with wide, tree-lined Avenue Borguiba and its cafés, the French district all around it offering plenty more of the frilly white colonial architecture. He especially liked just letting himself wander in the older part of the city and the Medina proper. Dim tunnels, twisting cobbled lanes so narrow you could spread your arms and touch the ancient walls on either side of you. And once you got away from the few main tourist venues and well behind the Grand Mosque, into the real Medina, it was a contained world in itself, with shops and little banks for the locals, always kids playing soccer against the houses, everything suddenly more Arabic — the workers in smocks and skullcaps, the women wearing headscarves — everything suddenly more dreamlike, too, Layton told himself. In a bit of reading of Flaubert's letters beforehand, Layton learned how on a trip to Tunis and the ruins of Carthage in preparation for writing *Salammbô* in 1858, Flaubert, when not out at the archaeological sites, spent his own share of time in the Medina, completely walled then, carousing with the French trade consuls and sampling the prostitutes, because Flaubert when young never failed to sample a foreign city's prostitutes, apparently. The Medina probably hadn't changed much at all since then, Layton thought: the same smells — sometimes leather from the sandal makers or perfume from the nooks and stands selling their many essences, sometimes just the aroma of bread, the stacked fat loaves pushed in wobbly wooden wheelbarrows through the Medina, often creating a traffic jam — and surely the same sounds — the din of tambour and reed-flute music, from boom boxes if not from actual musicians now, or just the quiet taptapping of a silversmith's hammer in a particularly out-of-the-way alley, even the rhythmic hissing of a weaver at work on another fine exercise in the geometric artistry of the world-renowned carpets produced here. That afternoon, following the encounter with Youssef and the girls, Layton lingered at a café in the Medina. He drank a strong tea and reread some of the lush sentences in *Salammbô* (billed as Flaubert's worst novel, though for sheer richness of prose it could have been the best, having served as almost the literary bible for French Parnassiens and Symbolistes, the Décadents later). When he returned to the Majestic, he detected the coconutty fragrance of shampoo even from the hallway, well before he got to his room. The girls had figured out themselves how to unbolt the door connecting the two rooms, or possibly Youssef helped them, and in Layton's room now, Jeanne-Isabelle was sitting, legs crossed at the knee, on the edge of the made bed while letting the window air conditioner blow-dry her hair, the cooling turned off and the fan on high. Naked except for emerald panties, she was thumbing through a French fashion magazine. She explained nonchalantly, without looking up, that she hoped Layton didn't mind, and she said that each of them, the two girls, needed a shower and a bathroom of her own to get ready for that evening. Youssef was taking the two of them to a disco.

She kept turning the pages, and, after all, toplessness was for French girls just beach etiquette, so she definitely saw it as no big deal. Her breasts were lovely, pert, her shoulder blades sculpted artistry in themselves, the line of her backbone a delicately knotted chain; she lifted up a hand for one of those raking shoves through the damp mane of hair, chin held high, that gesture she and Véronique had near patented, and she continued on with the magazine. Finding her casualness more ridiculous than anything yet, Layton lightly slapped her smack on the derrière, smiling, telling her to scoot and close the door — he said that a phone message had been left for him at the desk and he had a call to make.

Jeanne-Isabelle stood up, pecked a kiss on each of his cheeks as if he were a favorite uncle, then did exactly that, scooted, the two dimples on her backside just above the low line of the emerald panties taking turns winking at Layton, emphasizing the pure absurdity of it all. At the door itself she slowed down, smilingly tiptoed like a kid making a show out of trying to be very, very quiet, the old walking-on-eggshells routine, and returned to the adjoining room, latching the door.

IV.

The next day Layton met Cunningham a second time at the couscous place on Rue du Caire. Once they disposed of the small talk concerning whether Layton minded eating at the same restaurant again ("Best fucking couscous of one's life," Layton told Cunningham, "why toy with a premise like that?"), the conversation did seem to be veering toward one tack. On Cunningham's part, anyway.

"What you want to do is see him," Cunningham said.

They were talking about Khaled Khemir, of course.

"Yeah, it's what I want to do, all right," Layton said. "I don't think he's dodging me — that thing about his mother in Sfax sounded honest enough."

"But you have to see him. Talk to him."

"Of course I have to."

Cunningham's horn-rimmed glasses reflected so that you couldn't quite see his eyes; he was wearing the same seersucker sport coat as last time.

"And not just talk on the phone," Cunningham emphasized.

"He's touchy on the phone."

The waiter brought more bread, Cunningham nodded. Layton got the feeling that Cunningham was a regular here, no doubt knew it was a safe spot to talk.

"I wonder if it would have been easier," Layton said, "if I had come to Tunis more officially, if you know what I mean. There's a contact from the National Police Academy in the central *préfecture* here, I think, he maybe should have handled my visit, no?"

It was something left over from the Hoover regime at the FBI. Hoover's National Police Academy trained a lot of cops from abroad, most of them hanging up on their office walls in police stations back in their own home country framed photographs of themselves with pals from that training course in the States, proud of it, Arab World or not. It gave the FBI, usually wielding only Stateside jurisdiction, international ties, and it was something CIA types didn't like. Cunningham didn't get into that now, but flatly assured Layton the "no objection" approval Layton had obtained from the CIA was a much better way to proceed in this particular case.

"You will see him?" Cunningham asked.

"Yeah, what the hell am I doing here otherwise. Soon, I hope."

Cunningham seemed satisfied with that.

"Harvard," Cunningham then said, as if plucking the word out of the heat of the restaurant.

"What's that?" Layton said.

"You're a Harvard man?"

Layton hadn't heard that term in years, and it appeared Cunningham had done a little background checking on Layton since they had last met, knew where Layton had studied. Cunningham talked of his own time at Brown, also emphatically used the term

Ivy League, as if it was supposed to install the two of them in some club with a complicated secret handshake, perhaps, a shared understanding of life. For somebody like Cunningham in today's CIA, no longer the depository for fellow graduates of the Ivy League that it had once been, Layton's stock had apparently risen considerably — Layton not the usual FBI rube but a, well, "Harvard man."

Cunningham talked about how much he had enjoyed Brown, how the classes were small and you could design your own major, and how the education was decidedly top-notch. It was a standard, to-be-expected spiel from somebody from that so-called Ivy League who hadn't gone to Harvard or Yale and had to trudge through life with a pressing need (Layton had no idea why) to constantly explain why he hadn't gone to (which meant hadn't been admitted to) Harvard or Yale, or at least Princeton.

There was something Layton really didn't like about this guy.

Layton took the trip around Tunisia for several days because Khaled Khemir himself still hadn't returned from Sfax, also because of what was degenerating to the afternoon circus next door. The manager Youssef — El Bey, all right — was spending most of his own afternoons in that room next door with Véronique and Jeanne-Isabelle, keeping room service busy in the ongoing party. Layton saw no harm in that, but the romping made it tough to get some sleep with a nap in the two or three P.M. heat, the kind of napping that Layton had been savoring lately, if truth be known — deep hammer-on-anvil slumber free of the phantasmagoric cinema of constantly dreaming, playing out the reruns of Layton's admitted mess-ups in life.

Layton traveled to Kairouan and then Sousse, making a loop from Tunis.

He relied on the long-distance *louages,* dented white Peugeot station wagons with seven others in the three rows of seats, not counting the driver. The passengers were usually all men, some in work clothes and some in robes and dressy *chechia* caps, "*Bonjour*s" politely exchanged. The drivers liked to convert the dashboard into their own personal "space" with maybe a shag carpet on the deck, anything dangling from the rearview mirror from wooden prayer beads to three (he saw this on one *louage*) empty American 7-Up cans, probably collector's items here; a beaded covering for the huge steering wheel was mandatory. The drivers drove fast and recklessly, never hesitating to dangerously swerve to overtake any top-heavy, wobbling lorry on bald tires out there on the otherwise deserted two-lane; Layton figured they got paid by the number of runs they could complete each day.

The geography was handsome, constantly changing as you got farther inland. First vineyards and olive groves laid out neatly on the hills, then fields of undulating golden wheat, then the sand flats of the oncoming desert in earnest, the first date-palm groves standing like islands, and the occasional robed rustic on a mule gazing at the Peugeot speeding by in a blur for him, surely.

An ancient city with a golden-walled Medina, Kairouan was a place of pilgrimage, "The Fourth Holiest City in Islam," rising impressively out of the level plains. Kairouan was entirely different from, almost the direct antithesis of, the next city he stayed in, very modern Sousse, on the return loop; Sousse was a decided tourist trap of gleaming white hotels along the sweeping miles of Mediterranean beach. Different cities, no doubt, but the experience in each for Layton was quite the same. Layton found himself alone in a hotel room in each place. He found himself reading the copy of Flaubert's *Salammbô* in French, that epic of the passionate, star-crossed, half-perverse (the Flaubertian touch) love between the beautiful young Carthaginian princess Salammbô herself and the leader of the revolt of the mercenary troops against Carthage, the confused young Numidian general Mâtho, who should have been a lyric poet and never any combat commander whatsoever. Layton would be reading, yes, he would be caught up in the words, then he wouldn't be reading. He would be just staring at nothing, as it started again.

He found himself crying for no apparent reason, without the escape of drugging sleep that he had slipped into back in Tunis to ease any of it. And it was little use trying to make some sense or logic out of it, attribute it to a specific known failure, as he did admit to a lot of things — how he had never paid off on what should have been his promise in life, how both his career and marriage went nowhere (he *should* have done something like study French literature, he *shouldn't* have married a woman with whom he had so little in common), while his only child, his son, the one person in life he had always tried to believe in, ended up, if Layton was honest, bilking Layton out of his pension money and what should have been an easier life now, without having to hustle like this for what amounted to pocket change. But there was no reasoning, no cause and effect. It was maybe all one of those nail puzzles that looks like it conforms to the rules of geometry, as you want to believe that if you just concentrate, fully analyze it, and slowly work the disentanglement, it will be miraculously solved, even prove miraculously revealing as it loosens in your trembling hands.

But this puzzle didn't untangle, everything remained locked hopelessly together, and there was just the overwhelming blank frustration that nothing but nothing made *any* sense, there away from Tunis.

There was just stupid crying for Layton. There was just crying for no reason at all because he felt so goddamn sad. There was just catching sight of himself in a hotel room mirror again, a ceiling fan chugging through the feeble air conditioning again, and the near disgust with himself. There was just the old message, "Get a fucking hold of yourself, man."

"I used to dream so much when young of going to the States," Khaled Khemir said.

"I suppose a lot of people do," Layton said.

"No, you don't know what it's like. I mean, that's the problem with being an American, you have no idea what it's like."

The contact with the elusive Khaled Khemir had finally been accomplished, the purpose of Layton's trip to Tunisia, and, if nothing else, Layton felt good about that. They sat drinking leafy, sugary-thick brown tea from small glass tumblers at the outside table of a café up by the university, a clutter of new streamlined buildings on a rise behind the Medina. Layton was doing what he had to do, and Khaled Khemir was doing what he had to do, too, Layton knew, even if Khaled Khemir didn't like it one bit. It was the old game, somebody gave you something because they needed something themselves. When Khaled Khemir had been a contact back in Cambridge and a grad student at MIT, his visa had run out and he wanted an extension. He had a German girlfriend he was head over heels in love with; the girl was working on a Ph.D. in philosophy or linguistics at Harvard, and Khaled Khemir couldn't bear leaving her. In truth, Layton had never gotten much important out of him in Cambridge; Khaled Khemir had known some Libyans in the States who had very vague connections with the Lockerbie bombers, and Layton was never sure whether Khaled Khemir offered the information on them he eventually did because he didn't approve of such tactics at the time or, more likely, there was a long-standing, bad-blood general rift between Tunisians and Libyans. Neither of them trusted the other; why, Khadaffi himself had once tried to *annex* the other country in another typically mad Khadaffi pipe dream, in 1980. Now it was Khaled Khemir's brother who needed something, and while the brother wasn't the scholar Khaled Khemir had been (the brother was taking courses not as a grad student at MIT but as an undergrad at a state teachers' college on the Cape to keep his student visa, and presently he had bad check charges to deal with, about to be deported), Khaled Khemir wanted to see the brother finish his education in America. In other words, Khaled Khemir's cooperating now was more a matter of a family thing than anything else. Khaled Khemir looked different, too. He was no longer the skinny grad student with the reedy voice; he had always seemed so outright scared when Layton was full-time with the Bureau and they met several times amid those, indeed, red Formica tables and gum-chomping middle-aged waitresses in uniforms at noisy Charlie's Kitchen, the Harvard Square hamburger dive. Khaled Khemir now had already told Layton about his part-time lecturing in mathematics at the university, which should lead to a regular appointment soon. He also told Layton of his marriage to a Tunisian woman whose family was a friend of his family (the German girl in Cambridge was only "a stage," he laughed); he had two young daughters. His voice more sure, confident, his body having filled out some, yet he still seemed young, with the dark eyes too big in his skull and making him look perpetually startled, the soft smile. He continued with the story about growing up and wanting to go to America very badly, either Miami or Las Vegas specifically.

"Always Las Vegas," Khaled Khemir smiled some more, "and Miami."

"Really?"

"In my village in the Tell, in the north, the old women used to have songs about it. That was the mythically exotic good life for us to which young men supposedly fled, it would even turn up as a romanticized theme at local bazaars, the wonders of Las Vegas and Miami. Not that anybody ever went there. It must have been the movies that gave us the idea."

"I would have thought it would be France," Layton said, "if you were looking for an icon for flight. Don't young Tunisians often go to France?"

Khaled Khemir sipped his tea, laughed.

"No, France was the colonizer, so there was no dream about them, or their country. France was almost a joke, something you'd see as a long trip that you really didn't want to take, but probably would take. When we were kids, if a kid took a long time going to the shop or whatever, you'd say to him, 'Where did you go? France?'"

Layton smiled. He liked this Khaled Khemir. He also realized, when they got to talking about specific people (the Bureau was involved in investigating a Stateside racket in which Arabs in America were apparently using the widespread wholesaling of knockoffs of brand names — designer handbags, car stereo systems, and such — to raise money for Palestinian resistance activities), yes, Layton also assured himself that when he got back to Boston to file his own report, he wouldn't include everything he had been told. Layton had gotten to the point that he wanted to believe in an America that was different from the internationally bullying one he saw today, an America that people still dreamed of, even if those dreams were merely envisioning the glitz of Miami and Las Vegas; Layton really didn't care about anybody *anywhere* selling knockoffs of *anything*. Actually, most of the last hour or so he just listened to Khaled Khemir speak about how lucky he was to have found his wife — she worked in the government Ministry of Women and the Family — how lucky he was to have two such fine young girls, three and five.

"Or five today," he said, "and I must go back now, the birthday, you know."

"I understand," Layton said.

But what was strange, certainly, was Cunningham from the embassy — and CIA — calling Layton for one last meeting at the couscous place, as if he simply wanted confirmation beyond any doubt that it *was* Khaled Khemir Layton had spoken to.

"Don't be crazy, man," Layton told him, "I dealt with the guy for a full couple of years back in Boston. I know him."

Which was about all Layton was going to give him, and Layton, granting he was abroad, had that "no objection" filed formally and properly, so he didn't have to play this self-satisfied — how should he put this? — *"Brown man's"* game any longer.

"Fuck him," Layton later thought, which made him feel good. "Fuck him, and then some."

V.

The trio of them were almost at the summit there at Byrsa Hill, the site of the gone main temple for what was once ancient Carthage. Layton and the two French girls, Jeanne-Isabelle and Véronique.

The narrow suburban road was steep; it snaked up past fine white villas, the velvety black asphalt strewn with fallen orange flower petals. The temperature must have been an even ninety degrees. The girls exaggerated their trudging behind him, and though they had bought big liter bottles of mineral water at the tiny white and blue stucco Hannibal train station on this the commuter line (the girls halted every twenty paces or so now to take long chugs), they kept complaining like a couple of kids, in French, about how *hot* it was, and how *steep* the road was. That came with accompanying, and comically innocent, old emphasizers, including the functional *"sacré"* and the more classic *"zut alors!"* They didn't look at all chic anymore, though they had retrieved their wardrobes; having taken the same train on their own farther up to the Sidi Bou Said hotel that they had originally fled, they had managed to get their suitcases and clothes. Both of them had on simple white T-shirts and camp shorts now, Jeanne-Isabelle wearing sort of a clown's red and yellow sweat socks with her tennis sneakers and Véronique, sweaty and poutier than ever, cursing herself in her whispery French for not having worn socks, red and yellow clown style or otherwise, with her own chafing tennis shoes. They both wore their big sunglasses but no makeup, looked pretty scruffy by this stage in their travels, if truth be known.

The fun with the hotel manager, "El Bey," now simply Youssef once more, had expired while Layton had been traveling. Apparently Youssef's wife, a heavy woman in full traditional white robe and headscarf, had shown up at the Majestic on the tip of a hotel maid, to cause a noisy scene. And while Youssef was now letting the girls stay a few extra days (he had taken over their tab from Layton), he made clear that it would be no longer than that; the girls had already gotten Véronique's soft touch of a grandmother to wire them the money to get back to Montpellier. So they weren't just scruffy, but somewhat defeated, too, their jet-setting escapade over and both of them having to face the drudgery of their jobs at home — Jeanne-Isabelle a hair stylist and Véronique a secretary in an insurance company, *if* she could get the position back — there in Montpellier, where they claimed it rained and rained *all* winter. Layton had a day left in Tunis himself, and he had decided to, in a way, make good on his cover, a cover that he really hadn't needed, and go out to Carthage, which was now a suburb of Tunis. He wanted to walk through some of the scenes of *Salammbô,* possibly follow the route Flaubert did in 1858 when he visited, F. bumping along on a mule, to research the novel. Back at the hotel that morning, when the girls heard his plans for the day, they insisted, again like a couple of kids, that he take them along, pleading that he couldn't leave them at the boring hotel with *"rien à faire"* — nothing whatsoever to do. And now, like kids, all right, they complained, but Layton didn't mind. It was funny. And he liked them, liked their dreaminess in setting out as they originally had and believing they both would meet playboy millionaires in the course of their trip, a jaunt to posh Sidi Bou Said in Tunisia, what they had hoped would solve their own problems back in rainy Montpellier once and for all.

The empty museum there at the top of the hill was located in a former Christian monastery. And during a bit of strolling through its rooms now, the girls did relax, admiring the Carthaginian jewelry — gold, turquoise, and bursting pink coral — in the showcases; they lingered at the little model of Punic Carthage rebuilt to scale like something in a model train layout, and lingered longer, for the sheer yummy horror of it, at the displays of children's burial urns excavated from the Tophet, or the sacrificial burial site — there, those children apparently had been offered to the goddess Tanit in ancient times, given in trade for divine assistance in war. On the other hand, maybe the girls were on good behavior at last because they were themselves grateful to Layton, their rescuer; he had also promised to treat them to a good late lunch at one of the seaside terrace restaurants back down the hill and on the other side of the suburban train tracks, by the beach and more of the handsome white villas there.

Outside the museum again, the three strolled around an empty wide esplanade of broken columns set upright — all of that from the later Roman settlement, rather than the Punic — above the tumbledown brown stone ruins of what apparently had been a residential quarter of the city of Carthage itself during Salammbô's time; not all that impressive, and the fact of the matter was that the original Punic Carthage had left little evidence of its existence — the most powerful civilization of the ancient world at one time had now become the most vanished of civilizations, the heaps of rocks for these unearthed buildings right below the esplanade about the only remaining trace of it, amid the clutter of weeds and giant sunflowers and an inordinate amount of crumpled plastic water bottles tossed about. Layton wandered off on his own, and Layton started feeling much better. No, not simply better, but really good, which is to say, better than he had felt in a long while.

In years, possibly.

He was at the edge of the esplanade. From that vantage point you saw the hill running down to the old Punic harbors, once within the gone, strong city walls, presently just a couple of distant ornamental ponds surrounded by still more villas next to the sea; across the flat Gulf of Tunis that striped alternatingly sapphire and turquoise in the distance, two jutting peninsulas of jagged mountains opened up to the huge Mediterranean. He looked at the sea. Then he looked down to the center of the maze of ruins just a few dozen or so yards below him, where Jeanne-Isabelle and Véronique now sat on a crumbling brown stone wall, in the shade of a scraggly lemon tree. Véronique had her back turned to Jeanne-Isabelle, who was braiding Véronique's long and lustrous blond hair into a thick rope, the two of them humming a song together.

Most everybody had a dream, Layton knew, as corny as that sounded. The girls had their dream of the easy life, Youssef had his dream of remaining a soccer star forever. And Layton had once had his dream of maybe being a scholar, maybe actually going on a research trip like this in the course of a long and productive academic career of university teaching somewhere, giving his students something, and writing something consequential himself about a book as great as what was considered by some but a minor effort by the master Flaubert, that *Salammbô.* Ancient civilizations even had their massive collective dreams, of conquest and glory, and spreading out from this very hill, there had once been an empire equaled by none, what included not only this North Africa but much of Spain and Gaul, and almost the largest prize beyond that, as Hannibal marched his leathery elephants and his thousands of shivering, sandaled soldiers across the snows of the high Alps, with the City of Rome itself, for a moment, anyway, within his grasp. But maybe here was also the overlooked truth about the dreaming, that everything was gone before it started, and now contemplating what had once been triumphant, the scant rubble of Carthage corporeal, Layton realized that it yielded merely the message of nothing to nothing — or possibly nothing all along, the suspected void, because, when you thought of it, everything was inevitably heading toward nothing before it even started, before it even aspired or had the chance to be something.

Yet the trick, Layton sensed, was to appreciate the few instants of clarity that you are afforded in the course of the brief blur of it all, to be looking out at the most legendary sea of all seas, this Mediterranean that sparkled brilliant, to be looking down to the ruins that could inarguably lay claim to a past of the rarest of glory, though that past adding up to nothing really didn't figure into it either, didn't matter whatsoever. It didn't matter because there was the wonder of a reported here and now that *trumped* everything else, because there were two beautiful, living, long-legged girls in shorts and T-shirts, both happily humming some tune like a duet now, one braiding the other's hair in the shade of a crooked little lemon tree. Layton kept looking at the girls, almost a painting.

The day smelled of heat and flowers; a bee buzzed somewhere.

It was perfect, wonderful, and, damn, did Layton ever feel good. Not only this, but knowing that for once he had definitely bucked the FBI and its meaningless treading in circles, the constant lying and the constant hounding of people, which he had grown tired of. He had bucked, too, the smug CIA itself, gotten the better of the likes of that weasel Cunningham. Layton had decided that in his report he would tell *nothing* significant about information gathered from Khaled Khemir. Or he would tell as little as he had to, just to collect his own agreed-on payment, always straight cash, as well as ensure a visa extension for Khaled Khemir's brother. Layton knew that Khaled Khemir himself, happy at last with a lovely wife and two young kids, simply deserved to get on with his life. *(Layton didn't know then, of course, how Khaled Khemir would disappear when he traveled to an international mathematicians' conference in the Czech Republic the very next month. Layton learned that, and a lot else, only later. As it turned out, the real reason for dispatching Layton to Tunis was basically to confirm firsthand Khaled Khemir's identity, which was why Cunningham wanted to make sure that Layton did literally "see" Khaled Khemir. Cunningham, who kept pressing Layton for that identification, in the end was satisfied that this young man was, in fact, the Khaled Khemir the government had designs on, who knows why. And with that established, Khaled Khemir could be "taken out," to use the absurd term thrown about so lightly and casually even on the evening news lately, because that's the way "potentials" and "suspects" and especially anybody who — as Layton figured in this case — maybe had something on Cunningham's shadowy CIA was dealt with lately, simply imprisoned without a trace or, on occasion, outright gotten rid of. Cunningham was in on it from the start, he was using Layton, and the assignment of Layton's gathering information from Khaled Khemir on Palestinian supporters was only the ruse needed to bring Layton to Tunis. Rather than finally asserting himself, bucking anybody, Layton would have to admit that he had been suckered, he was the one who actually fingered Khaled Khemir, dealt him what amounted to the classic kiss of death in a time when Layton's own country was bent on smooching the whole world to death, or so it sometimes seemed — but Layton surely wouldn't learn any of that about Khaled Khemir till later, much later, it coming out when Khaled Khemir's brother Hosni Khemir was quietly deported, Layton futilely protesting. Plus, to know all of that was getting ahead in time, was to realize how Layton would afterward look back on it, and right now Layton was almost outside of time, somehow absolutely free of its inescapable, persistent thumping.)* Yes, in the blinding sunshine on Byrsa Hill, Layton felt more than good.

He felt fucking great.

The girls were both standing now. Véronique twisted her neck to try to glance down over her shoulder, brushing off her skinny bum in khaki camp shorts, and Jeanne-Isabelle put on an exaggerated studio yawn, extending her bare arms — which themselves looked pretty skinny in the loose, oversize white T-shirt — stretching those sticks of arms this way and that to make her point. No doubt they were ready for that lunch he had promised them.

They looked up to see Layton on the esplanade above, each saying in French something along the lines of, "Can we *please* go now?"

And Layton, smiling, called back to them in his own French that they all certainly could.

KYLE MINOR

A Day Meant to Do Less

FROM *The Gettysburg Review*

REVEREND JACK WENDEROTH carried his mother into the bathroom and sat her on the closed toilet lid, and then he began to undress her. She was wearing her threadbare old housedress, the red one she had worn when he was a child and that had now faded to pink. He had bought her gowns, bathrobes, cotton pajamas, other housedresses, but she would not wear them. She said no by making sounds in the back of her throat. The sounds were terrible, the sounds someone made when she was dying. Which she was.

He knelt at her feet. Her body slumped, and her shoulders tilted to the left, toward the sink and the table that held it and the sharp Formica edgework. He raised himself from his knees and reached up and righted her. Her eyes were alert but not bright. He noticed that he was avoiding them. He noticed that he was noticing himself quite a bit and her not so much. It took effort not to notice her, but it was hard on him to notice her. It required him to acquaint himself with the droop of her face's left side, the gurgling sound her throat made involuntarily, and worst of all the foul smell of her body. He had noticed the smell a few minutes earlier, and that's why he was undressing her.

He did not want to undress her. It was the first time he had undressed her. His wife, Julie, usually undressed her. His mother used to say, when they were young and courting, "Jack and Julie, like the song." It was not a song he knew. He knew "Jack and Jill," the nursery rhyme she had sung to him when he was a boy, to the tune of "The Yellow Rose of Texas." His hands were on her shoulders, righting her, and yet he was touching her with as little of himself as he could. His own body was so far from hers that righting her with his hands made his back and shoulders ache.

He thought he should maybe hold her for a minute. She was watching him with those eyes. He thought maybe she did not want him to hold her. He did not know if she wanted him to wash her. She was not making the noises, and she knew why they were in the bathroom. He had told her. To hold her he would have to straddle her with his legs. He was very aware of the proximity, already, of his parts to hers. When he was small he would lay his head in her lap, and she would stroke his hair, but when he turned twelve he tried to lay his head in her lap so she would stroke his hair and she said there would be no more of that. When he asked her why, she said, "Because you're too old now."

So he stood for another moment, righting her but not holding her. He said, "Mother, I'm going to take off your shoes and socks now, all right?"

Her lips moved but not to form a word. He thought what she was giving was permission. He couldn't be sure, but the smell of her was all over him. He took his hands from her shoulders. She did not topple. He knelt again, and though he did not want to, he wanted to: he put his fingers to his nose and smelled them. They smelled like her body. She was not looking down at him. He did not want her to see that he was smelling his fingers. He was ashamed of the act, and he did not know why. No one had seen except him.

"Your shoes, Mother," he said. He had never called her *mother,* not in his whole life. He called her *mama,* or, later, *mom.* When he was very young, he called her *mommy,* but he had not called her that for a long time. His father had called her Francine, and everyone else called her Franny. She was wearing house slippers, fairly new ones he had bought for her. They were rubber-soled and lined with furry cotton. She could not wear them in the winter, because they built up a charge, and she gave and received a shock whenever she was touched.

He took the slippers from her feet. Then he began to pull at the toe of the black sock on her right foot. She made the gurgling sound. No. He let go of the sock.

"Does it hurt, Mother?" he said.

She did not say anything.

"Does it hurt?"

Nothing.

He stood again and looked at her in the eyes. Mother. "Mom," he said, more kindly. "Does it hurt?"

She winked her right eyelid, twice. Slowly. That was something new.

"I saw that, Mom," he said. "Can you do it again? I want to be sure."

She winked the eyelid again, twice, slowly. Then she lost control of it, and it began to twitch.

"Well, that's something," he said, but mostly to himself. "Okay," he said, to himself, but then, louder, for her: "Okay."

She did it a third time, the eyelid, maybe to affirm her yes, maybe to stop the twitching. "I see it," he said. "I don't want to hurt you," he said. "I'm going to wash you now. I'm going to do it, but not if you don't want me to. I'm going to take that sock off by unrolling it from the top, all right?"

A fourth time she blinked twice. A regular conversation.

He knelt again. This time he began at the top of the sock, and unrolled it slowly down her calf. When he touched her there, he could feel the muscle contract a little. Her skin was cold. He unrolled the sock to her heel. Then he put his other hand beneath her foot and lifted it. He was careful around the heel to stretch the fabric, but when he reached the arch of her foot, she made the gurgling sound again, and he stopped. She inhaled sharply. He was hurting his mother.

The sock had to come off. He tried again, this time stretching the fabric as carefully around the arch as he had around the heel. When sock cleared skin, he saw something like a rash, a reddish-purple blemish that covered most of the arch, surrounded by a deep yellowish-purple ring, a deep, deep bruise.

"Mom," he said, "you've got a nasty sore down here. On the arch of your foot. It's bruised. It's a bad one."

He patted her calf to reassure her, but she tensed at his touch, so he stopped. He said, "The other one now, Mom," and began to work on the other shoe and sock.

Her silence bothered him almost as much as the throat noises had. When he was young her voice was a constant, a drone that must have been the same kind of comfort for her that the television had been for him, in college, when he was lonely and could not sleep without the sound of it. When he was young she chattered, and what mattered to her — he could see it now for the first time — what mattered to her was not the content of her talk, but just its continuation. He remembered something his sister Millie had often said about her, uncharitably: "She just talks to hear the sound of her own voice." But that wasn't true, not entirely. Her voice, which had irritated him so often, especially in his adolescence, when he began to think of her as being more and more ignorant the more books he read, was now, in his memory, taking on some kind of a musical quality, a soft companionable drone.

He took off her right shoe, then began to unroll her sock. He thought that if she could talk now, about nothing — no, that was uncharitable — about, say, the shower curtains, how they were starting to yellow, and how that was the problem with translucent shower curtains, the way they yellowed so quickly and needed to be replaced so often, unlike shower curtains patterned in mostly solid colors . . . if she could talk now, and say things like this, she would be bringing comfort not only to herself, but also to him.

So he said, "Mom, have you noticed the shower curtains?" It felt forced, but he pushed on. "They're starting to yellow, and that's the problem, I think, with translucent shower curtains . . ."

The shoes and the socks were off now, and — this was most remarkable — her breathing had become less labored. Maybe he was imagining it. It was barely discernible, this change in her breathing, but it meant something to him. He heard himself saying, "Julie was thinking of buying some shower curtains to match the hand towels. Maybe something forest green, like the towels, with some purple accents," and it was automatic, this talk. It was not the talk he talked, not usually, but it was the talk that was coming from his mouth. It was received talk, like telephone *hello*s and *goodbye*s, or *how are you doing*s and *see you later*s passing between half-courteous strangers on the street. He found that it comforted him the way he imagined the same kind of talk had comforted his mother. It made him uneasy even as it comforted him. He kept it up because it seemed to comfort her.

The shoes and socks were off, but that meant he would soon have to take off the housedress. He had been moving so slowly, and he knew this was why. He was about to confront his mother's nakedness. To be, in a sense, the cause of it. He considered what other tasks he might perform to delay unbuttoning the front of the housedress and sliding it from her body. He was still talking — ". . . the Formica is so out of date, and Julie thinks it might be nice to refinish all the countertops in the house with tile, but that kind of work takes so much time, so I was thinking about maybe vinyl laminate . . ." — but mostly he was thinking of what else he could do, and then — of course! — he remembered the bath water.

Julie had given him instructions before she left to pick up a few things they had forgotten the night before at the house of their friends, the Marinos. She had said maybe two inches of water, like a bath drawn for a baby. Make the water warm, but not lukewarm, but not too hot either. Test it by dipping two fingers in the bath water near the faucet and splashing a little on the tender skin on the inside of the arm, just below the wrist, where the crossing blue veins could be seen beneath the skin.

Or at least beneath his pale skin. He was still talking automatically, at his mother but not necessarily to her, but his mind was on his skin. He straightened and folded the black socks so he could turn his palms toward his face and get a good look at his own arms, how pale they were, how he had always hated their color. It was a color he had inherited from her. He could look beyond his arms and see the pale skin of his mother's legs. They were the same color, his arms and her legs. He wondered if she had ever hated the color of her skin and almost asked her, then thought better of it.

He was always thinking better of it, had always been thinking better of it his whole life. On Sundays he preached sermons that revealed, say, how love hurt at four o'clock in the morning when Julie was still asleep, her hair piled up on the pillow, and him knowing he had to be off to accompany the out-of-town family of an indigent killed beneath a bridge to identify the body at the morgue, and that he might not be home again until after she had awakened and gone about her day and gone back to sleep again. In those sermons he gave away parts of himself more intimate than those he was willing to share with his mother, except in that public space. He looked at his arms and her legs and wanted to tell her a closely held secret, which was that when he drove the interstates on the way to hospital visits and ministers' meetings and church softball games, he often as not would play cassette tapes of black singers like Al Green or Marvin Gaye or, hell, James Brown. He'd drive down the road and let himself imagine he was himself some famous maestro of soul, be transported to what he imagined must be some rundown bar in Detroit or, who knows, Watts, someplace he had never been and would never go and which for all he knew was nothing like whatever it was he was trying to imagine. But he'd be there, in the car, singing for an audience of twelve or twenty, an appreciative audience to be sure, except maybe a few drunks. And here was the centerpiece of the fantasy. The skin, his skin, would have somehow darkened to a deep brown, a skin tone he imagined would give him access to whole worlds he could never know, and one that would not embarrass him under the lights of that dirty club the way it had always embarrassed him at the beach or on the sandlots or anytime he had to wear shorts to play some ball game or to feign comfort at some overly casual social function.

He was looking at his mother's legs and talking about kitchen remodeling, and then without even finishing his sentence, he stopped talking and began humming. At first he was not aware of what he was humming, and then he realized that what he was humming was "Sexual Healing" by Marvin Gaye. It was not a song his mother would have approved of his singing or even knowing. At once he was aware of the, oh, three dozen ironies that wrapped themselves around his choice of song to hum, of all things Freudian and Jungian, all those blowhards, that his seemingly subconscious choice of that tune might imply. The oedipal and the — good great hell, what was he doing?

What he was doing was undressing his mother. What he was doing was *not* undressing his mother; he could see that well enough. So could she probably. He had been in the bathroom for nearly fifteen minutes and had only managed to take off her socks and shoes. He had not even begun to run the bath water.

He finished folding the socks and placed them neatly on top of the shoes and kept humming Marvin Gaye since no other tune came readily to mind and since he knew, really, it didn't mean anything, and because it was a fine tune, and because, strangely enough, his mother was starting to relax a little. He could see it in her posture, and he could see it in her face.

He turned the hot and the cold knobs and tried to find the right temperature. The phone rang. He let it ring but turned off the water and stopped humming and kicked open the bathroom door with his foot so he could hear the answering machine when it picked up. Technically, he was working. But, technically, he was always working. Always on call, at least. He heard Julie's voice on the machine — *we'll get back with you as soon as we can, and God bless* — that last part, *God bless,* always irritating him because it was a cliché so well worn that it didn't mean anything anymore; except it did mean something to Julie, which irritated him, too, but not so much that he would say anything to her about it.

The machine beeped, and he heard Lindsay Marino, a parishioner for whom both he and Julie had some affection. Lindsay and her husband, Tom, too. A fine couple. She was saying, ". . . Art Miller, room 319, Good Samaritan Hospital . . ." Art was Lindsay's husband's uncle, and a real curmudgeon, the kind of guy who would invite you over to pray for his, say, lack of appetite, then get cranky when you said, "Art, buddy, I'm pretty thirsty. Would you mind if I got a glass of water from your tap?"

Art Miller, Lindsay was saying, had collapsed this morning. Right away they had thought heart attack, but it turned out to be a false alarm, some sort of panic attack that anyway felt like a heart attack, and Art wasn't himself so convinced that it wasn't. "He's asking for you," Lindsay was saying. "This is rich, really rich, Jack, but he says my prayers aren't quite enough to get him through the night. He needs the *man of God.* He keeps saying that. 'Bring me the man of God!' I thought you'd get a kick out of that. So, for serious, Jack, can you come over to Good Sam? He's driving me nuts and I need to get out of here by three so I can take Mike Junior to baseball practice."

The machine beeped again, and he looked at his mother sitting on the toilet lid and could not discern any response coming from her. He wanted to say, *Come on, Momma, say something disapproving,* but of course he would not. Instead, he said it himself. "Art Miller," he said. "Now there's one guy who can wait."

Still, she did not respond, but he thought maybe it gave her some satisfaction. It gave *him* some satisfaction. And was his mother any less a member of his congregation than Art Miller? A man who was in the hospital, sure, but who was, in any case, in better health, even on this panic-attack day, than she was on this or any other day. Jack could not be sure how much she was or was not engaged with all that surrounded her. Already her eyes seemed to be less alert than when he brought her into the bathroom, but how can a person tell, anyway, exactly what another person's eyes reveal? Perhaps she was growing tired, or maybe he was growing tired and looking at her eyes differently.

He turned the hot and cold knobs again and tested the water. When he had regulated the temperature to his liking, he put the stopper in the tub. Then he tested the water again with his hands, adjusted the water some more. Checked the stopper. Measured the depth of the water with his index finger. Tested the temperature again. Made a tiny adjustment to the cold knob. Just a little more cold, so it wouldn't be too hot. In defiance of the words of God as reported by the crazy, exiled, and starved apostle John in the Book of Revelation, Jack's least favorite book of the Bible because it so defied anything like rational meaning: "Because thou art lukewarm, and neither hot nor cold, I will spew thee out of my mouth." No. What he was *after* was something like lukewarm, just a little warmer than lukewarm and two inches deep.

The water had risen to one inch. He had run out of things to do with his hands. He noticed that his back was turned to her. He knew how intentional it was, his back being turned to her. It was turned, he realized, because he was still trying to avoid looking at her.

He forced himself to turn and look at her. There she was. She was sitting on the toilet seat, half-slumped, or at least not nearly as upright as he had left her, resting her weight against the back of the toilet. She was looking at him.

He looked down at her feet and saw that they were bare. Of course they were bare; he had taken off her shoes and socks. But were they cold? Should he cover them?

Then he knew that he was looking at her feet because she was not her feet. She was her face and eyes. She was not her body — God no — not this body, not his mother. But if she was not this body, what was she? What had she become? And if the mother he had known — the mom, the momma, the mommy — had vacated this body, who was it then who sat before him?

Then he knew that he was letting himself be drawn deeper and deeper into these abstractions because it was another way of not looking at her. It was a way of looking but not looking. Of seeing but letting sight lead him to a place not present.

The tub was filling with water behind him, and he turned to see how high he had let the water get. It was four inches, probably. He turned off the faucets, then reached down and pulled the stopper. It wasn't the act of pulling the stopper that got him, that made his throat catch in the same way he had seen hundreds of other throats catch in a way so predictable, it had long since ceased to move him. It was the sound of that stopper. The *plop* and the soft sucking that followed.

He turned again and saw her. She had not moved. His own eyes had not filled with tears, and he knew they would not because he had long since trained himself to do a duty when a duty was called for, and now was the time. The time was now. "Now, Mom," he said. "After I stop the tub, okay?"

She winked her eye twice.

He plugged the tub, and it was about two inches, just right. Then he moved toward her and smelled her stink and put his face near hers, his eyes at the level of hers. He couldn't help but think that the only thing like what he was about to do, what he was in fact doing . . . the only thing that he could recall from his whole experience of life was a certain kind of lovemaking he had once known with Julie, a lovemaking of the most intimate kind, a lovemaking that all but precludes knowledge of the body in favor of a different kind of lostness. A lovemaking punctuated only by the involuntary blinking that for brief but too-long moments breaks the illusion, the spell, of complete connection, two sets of eyes locking upon one another in near-inviolate attention while bodies perform their lesser task. The pleasure of that deepest kind of intimacy, sure, but the terror, too. The complete giving and undoing of self.

He said, "I'm going to put you in the bath now, Momma," but what he meant was harder: *I'm going to take off your clothes now.*

He began to unbutton the big white fake pearl buttons that ran the length of her housedress, starting with the top button, near her neck. He looked into her eyes as he did it. She looked back into his, too. She did not make a sound or wink her eye. She did not do anything but breathe shallowly and watch his eyes.

He worked his way down the front of her, button by button. He was sure to keep a tension on the fabric with his fingers. He did not want to touch the skin on the front of her, only button, fabric, button, fabric. He did not know what he was so afraid of. He had been at so many bedsides, seen so many frail bodies uncovered. He did not know what he was so afraid of.

But then he did know. What he was afraid of was his mother's body. He reached the button near her waist, and then his arms could go no farther without his body moving down with them. He crouched down and tried to keep his eyes locked upon hers, but of course his eyes were at the level of her wrecked, sagging breasts. He was struck by something his father had told him, once, when they had gone on a fishing trip and talked once, only once, about things they never otherwise discussed. His mother's family had been poor, themselves the children of day laborers in rural Kentucky, escaped to better lives in Florida, where his father was a well-point foreman. They had taken up with a circle of friends who tried to convince his mother not to nurse because they found the practice disturbing. Instead, they were weaning their children at two months and offering bottles of Karo syrup and cow's milk. "Your mother didn't take to that talk," his father had said. "Two years she got the silent treatment, but she said, 'No baby of mine.'"

Now, eye level with his mother's breasts, he could not ignore his own speculations about what might have passed between them before he was old enough to know. He continued to unbutton, now the waist, now the lap, now the knees.

The housedress came apart then. The flaps of it flanked his mother on either side. She was sitting with her legs uncrossed. He was almost kneeling now, and his eyes continued to seek hers. The next thing he had to do was lift her and put her in the tub. As he stood he lost her eyes and found himself — for a moment, for less than a moment — staring between her legs. She was almost hairless there, but for some stray white wisps and one large alarming black one.

He did not back away. He reached up, toward her, and pulled her arms free of the sleeves. Then he placed his left arm beneath both her legs. With his right arm he encircled her, lifting carefully so he was holding most of her weight under both her armpits. He lifted her and carried her to the bathtub and lowered her into the bath water and took the washcloth and reached down to touch her body with it. She began to tremble as he moved it toward her, and he said, "Shh, shh." What word could he say to help her be okay? He said, "Mommy, Mommy. It's all right, Mommy."

Then her body began to convulse in the water.

Franny Wenderoth had a secret she kept from everyone: the memory of a tobacco field in summer in Kentucky, she running, and a boy, her cousin, giving chase. It started as a game she called house. They played in the kitchen, her mother's kitchen in the house on John Claremont Hollow Road, a hundred feet from the tobacco field where her father sometimes worked as a day laborer. She said, "You be the mommy, I'll be the daddy."

Her cousin blanched at this. His name was Roy. He said, "I'm not being no mommy." So it was agreed. He would be the daddy, she the mommy. He was eleven years old, she nine. It did not occur to her that they were too old to be playing such a child's game, because it did not occur to her that she was anything but a child, or that he was, or that there was anything but a child to be.

They were in the kitchen, and she put wood in the stove and lit it, and he stoked the flames until they were burning. Her mother was somewhere; she couldn't remember where. Her mother was often enough somewhere. Her mother and her father were gone most of the time, but then so was everyone's mother and father. Roy's mother was laid up and was around all the time. His mother made him fetch her things, and more and more Roy did like his seventeen-year-old brother, Donny — a bad seed, that Donny Prather, her father would say — and found someplace else to be.

"Put the eggs on," she said. He did like she said and cracked the imaginary eggs over the griddle. "Now the bacon," she said, and he did likewise.

Her father would beat her with a switch, and probably Roy, too, if he knew they were burning the wood after all it took to keep it cut and stacked and get the pile high enough for all they would need for winter. Roy stoked the fire some more, and she got nervous and said, "Bacon's done, Roy, and eggs are starting to burn."

It was getting hot in the kitchen. She was starting to panic about the wood. Roy noticed and said, "Good Lord, Franny. I'll cut you some more wood."

"You won't cut it right," she said. Her father would know. Better to just leave be. She was indignant. She liked the feeling of indignant. This kind of playing house was more real, anyway, than cooking eggs or bacon on the stove. She couldn't ever remember a time her father and mother worked in the kitchen together. It was her mother, or if her mother was gone, it was her father. But they had argued plenty in the kitchen. Part of her secretly hoped Roy would haul off and knock her upside the head. It was a revolting thought that made her plenty angry, and she took not a little pleasure in the heat in her cheeks and chest. The mommy and the daddy.

"I will," he said. "I know how to cut wood."

"Not like my daddy," she said.

He grabbed her by the wrist. "That dog won't hunt," he said. He said it good and nasty, and soft, but deep-voiced, like a grown man. The sound of it was weird. Unsettling, like the dark could sometimes be.

She laughed and tried to push him away. He held on to her wrist, and she couldn't get loose. "Let me be," she said. She started slapping at him. "Roy Samuel Prather," she said, "let me be."

But he wouldn't let her be. He dug his dirty fingernails into her wrist and pressed down until she screamed. Then, fast as lightning, he reached down with his free hand and grabbed her by the ankle. He picked her up like that, wrist and ankle. When she tried to kick free, he just let her body hit the ground, hard, without letting go of her wrist and ankle, and he dragged her like that out to the front porch and down the four stairs, her shoulder or back or arms knocking against every step.

When he got her out to the yard, he swung her back, then flung her forward as hard as he could. She landed hard, rolling out as best she could, which wasn't much.

He took two steps back, bent down and picked a blade of grass, put it between his teeth, and chewed on it. He said, casual as can be, "I give you fifty steps and then I'm gonna come and get you."

By now she was plenty sure he wasn't the same Roy Samuel Prather she had known the day before. She got up and ran with all that was in her, which was considerable. She had long legs and could run fast, and not just for a girl. She was barefoot, but her feet were hard and soft at the same time, feet that did not mind stepping on stray stones the way other feet might. In later years she could not remember whether she said it aloud or not, but she did have the distinct memory of urging her feet on, of speaking to them: "Go, feet, go."

She did not count her steps, but it could well enough have been fifty before she heard Roy give an Indian war whoop and then the sound of his bare feet moving through the grass.

She thought she might lose him in the tobacco field. She did not know what he meant to do, but she had been admiring his new brown belt with its metal buckle the shape of Kentucky, and she thought if they really were going to play house, he might just whip her like a daddy would a mommy, and if he did it with that brown belt, he might forget to take off that metal buckle, and wouldn't it hurt to get beat about the buttocks and back by Kentucky.

She tried to keep as low to the ground as she could and still run. She was among the rows of tobacco now. The leaves whipped her face and neck, but she did not raise her arms to protect her head because she needed them to pump. Behind her she heard Roy saying, "Run, Mommy, run!" and she did not know, now, if they were still playing the game or if he was mocking her.

But he was not gaining on her. She was running as fast as she could, and she knew she would not tire before he did. It was a good feeling, a safe feeling. She could outrun danger.

She turned a corner at the place where a strip of dirt divided one acre from another, then plunged ahead directly into a row in the new field, five rows removed from where she had emerged. She could hear his feet behind her, hesitating, then choosing a row, choosing the right row, and then the chase was on again, but she had put some more distance between them.

Her plan was to reach the end of the row, then double back toward the house. All that was beyond these fields was mountain, and though she was not afraid of the mountains, she was afraid of getting too far from home, of not making it back in time to cook supper, and getting whipped by her daddy.

She came to the end of the row and made a sharp turn left. She meant to count seven rows, then make her left-hand turn toward home. She was running flat-out, counting — one, two, three, four — and then, BOOM, some large figure, something twice her size maybe, came out from row five and stood still, and she could not slow herself or dodge it in time to avoid collision. Running flat-out, she hit this massive wall, hit the body of a grown man, and just before impact, the man's body jerked its weight forward, into her, and knocked her backward. She landed hard, like a stone thrown straight at the ground, and bounced like the stone would bounce.

It took her a moment to clear her head. She heard the sound of footsteps behind her, Roy's, and when she looked up she was facing him, and when she turned the other way, she saw that she was facing something ten times more scary.

Roy's brother Donny. Donny Lynn Prather. The bad seed.

He was chewing on a blade of grass. He chewed it just like Roy. He said, "Well, now, what have we here?"

She did not make a move to get up. She dared a look at Roy, and he was grinning ear to ear.

Donny said, "It's a fine morning, ain't it, darling?"

Roy whistled a tune: *Shoo, fly, don't bother me, for I belong to somebody.*

Donny took a step toward her. He said, "Now, who do you belong to, honey?"

"Somebody," Roy said, "is me. I'm the daddy."

"Is that right?" Donny said. He bit off the end of the blade of grass and spit it out. She did not like the way he was smiling at her. His smile wasn't the same as Roy's. For the rest of her life, she would remember that smile. It was the smile of a buzzard in the face of the newly coyote-eaten body of a deer, rotting but not quite dead. "What if I said I'm the daddy."

She looked at Roy. All of a sudden he looked very small. He puffed out his chest and said, "I'm the daddy, I give the whooping. Like you said."

She cheered a little at his words. Her own daddy could give a whipping like you couldn't believe, and she knew how to take it. A whipping wasn't nothing to her. One, two. No matter. She would close her eyes and take it. But then Roy was taking off his belt, and she looked again at that metal belt buckle shaped like Kentucky, and she knew it wasn't Roy was going to get to whip her with it, but Donny. And what damage could somebody like Donny do with a weapon like that?

Roy was on one side, and Donny was on the other, behind her. She could outrun Roy, she had already proven that today, but there wasn't one way she could think of to get loose of Donny. So she turned around. She intended to tell Donny that, sure enough, Roy was the daddy, and she would take her whipping from him. That was the rules of the game.

But when she turned around, she saw that Donny had already

taken his belt off. Behind her, Roy was getting steamed. "It's my whipping, goddamn it," he said. "I'm the daddy."

Franny took two steps back, and neither Roy nor Donny did anything to stop her. Donny stepped right past her and yanked the belt from Roy's hand. He had his own belt in the other hand, and then fast as anything, he swung first his then Roy's at Roy's back and legs, first one then the other, again and again. The sound of them hitting was terrible, the whip crack of Roy's belt followed by the dull thud of the belt buckle.

It didn't seem right for him to beat on Roy like that. Franny took a running start. She jumped on Donny's back, and when she did, he threw the belts into a row of tobacco and picked her off his back with one hand and threw her down.

She had lost her wind. Her whole body hurt from being thrown down so hard, especially her left side, where she had hit. She breathed in hard, trying to suck down as much air as she could as fast as she could.

She could see Roy. He was on the ground, behind Donny, on his butt, shuffling backward. Donny didn't pay him any mind. He looked down at Franny. He said, "Ain't you a lovely thing, Franny Mae."

Then he undid the front of his trousers and took out his worm — she knew what one was but had never seen one before — and it was long and flesh colored and purple at the end.

"You ever seen one of these before?" Donny said.

It made her ashamed. Roy was still sprawled out there on the ground, looking at them with a big dumb face. Donny took the worm between his fingers and pointed it at her, and a hot stream of clear piss came shooting out at her. She screamed, and he laughed and shook it up and down so it covered her up and down, and some of it got on her face. She raised her hands to her face and tried to get up, but he came closer, pissing all the way, and when she was almost up, he pushed her down again.

When he had stopped pissing, he said, "Open up that pretty little mouth, Mommy."

She shook her head no and clenched her teeth and held her lips tight together. She wanted to tell Roy to do something, come help her like she had tried to help him, but she did not want to open her mouth.

Donny reached down and gripped both of her cheeks with one hand and squeezed so hard she thought her teeth would be pushed loose from her gums. He pried her jaws open, and then he put that disgusting part of his body right up to her lips and started pissing again. She tried to shut her mouth, but he was still holding it so she could not. It started to get hard and push against her mouth. The piss was hot in her throat, and it gagged her, and she could taste it most in her nose, where the scent of it rose from the back of her throat like the dust from a field newly plowed.

Then he lost his aim somehow, and his grip on her face, and the piss splashed all over her face. It was Roy. Finally — *finally!* — he had jumped on Donny's back from behind. When Donny turned around, Roy reared back and punched him square in the nose.

Blood began to squirt from Donny's face. He put his hands to his nose and when he pulled them away they were covered in red, and she could see that his nose was bent a little, to the side. He reached up and grabbed his own nose and yanked it back into place, and when he did he made a sound so terrible that it threw Franny into a panic, and she got up again and started to run, but Donny saw it, and reached out his foot to trip her.

She fell hard on her face and knocked free one of her front teeth, a new adult one that couldn't be replaced, and right away she could feel the warmth in her own mouth, the taste of iron overtaking the ammonia musk. As she dug in the dirt, looking for the tooth, she could hear Donny and Roy scuffling, Donny cursing and Roy yelling at him to stop.

She found the tooth and put it in her pocket. She put her tongue to the gum from which it had been knocked to try and stop the bleeding. When she looked up, Roy was on his back, and Donny was sitting with his knees on Roy's chest, his thing still hanging out the front of his pants. He had pinned Roy's arms beneath his legs, and Roy's legs were kicking at the air with no chance of getting the rest of him free. Donny was slapping him in the face — "How's that, you little shit? Does that feel fine?" — pulling his right hand back, then bringing it down full force on Roy's right cheek, then again with the left, then the right again.

She did not want to leave Roy like that, at the mercy of his older brother. She had to think quick. What occurred to her in later years was that, like it or not, Roy had set her up, and because of what he had done, she had lost a tooth and wasn't going to be able to get it back, and that she certainly must have feared losing worse than a tooth. That's how she rationalized it when she was older and needed some way to find peace with herself at having left him to fend for himself against an older brother twice his size, an older brother whose self could not be controlled.

But in that moment, all she knew was the great animal fear that made the deer freeze and the bobcat run. She did not look back. She ran into the rows of tobacco, through one acre and then the next, and then on to her own house, and past it, and down the country road, to the house of her mother's cousin, Miss Lucy. The whole time, running, she could not know whether or not Donny was behind her, giving chase, could not have heard the sound of his running if she had tried, not above the din of her own exertions, the labor of her breathing, and the pounding of her heart. She ran as though he was chasing her, did not even look back when, after banging on Miss Lucy's door with her fists, she ran through the open door, right past Miss Lucy, and into the bathroom, and shut the door and locked it and would not come out, not for hours and hours. Not until her mother came by in the early evening and got her out, first coaxing, then threatening, then promising no harm would come to her by way of her father.

By the time she left that bathroom, Franny had washed her face clean. She did not, would not, speak, and it was not until two days later that her mother discovered that her front tooth was gone. By then they had found Roy's body up in the mountains. By then some dogs had got it, and it was mangled so badly they were hard-pressed to know what the dogs had done and what Donny had done. Everybody knew it was Donny, but nobody could prove it, and when the time came, Donny produced a girlfriend, a truly unreliable witness named Thelma Jane, from up in the hills, from a family well known to let their children run wild, and whose men were all locked up in jails most of the time, most of them on repeated small-time stints in Rowan County Jail, and some doing longer, harder time in state and federal penitentiaries.

For her part, Franny didn't say anything. Not one word. Wouldn't even admit to being there, and even though her parents were sure enough she had been with Roy that day, they did not want any part of the proceedings against Donny. He was family, and it was a family matter, and it was meant to be settled among family. In the end, he was let go for want of evidence. Before his own daddy could get at him to settle it in the family way, he was off and gone, some said to California, others to New Mexico, others to Mexico, out of the country and far away, maybe even as far as Guatemala or El Salvador, or past the equator to Venezuela, Argentina, Brazil.

But Franny couldn't see it that way. She thought about it often as she grew older, Donny and Roy and that awful day, and she wondered what would have happened if Roy had just run off like he could have. Would it have been her they found up that mountain, eaten away by dogs?

It troubled her, and then one day, when she was thirteen years old, she thought of something that troubled her even more, which was that Donny was not the brightest wick in the lamp, and how on God's green earth could anyone be made to believe that he, of all people, could possibly teach himself to know Spanish?

He couldn't be in South America, then. Not there, or Guatemala, or Mexico, or anywhere. And how would he pay his way to New Mexico or California? And what would he do for work once he got there? All he knew was hills, and he knew them the way ants knew their dirt tunnels, could probably find his way through every twist and turn in every creek, knew when and where the waters changed their paths after a rainstorm, knew which caves were empty and which bedded brown bears or bobcats or coyotes.

The truth that became apparent to her, then, and which no one else ever seemed to know, was that Donny Lynn Prather, the bad seed, the murderer, was living in the hills that surrounded her. One evening not long before her fourteenth birthday, she was lying in bed in the middle of the night, not sleeping as always, or barely sleeping, sleeping the light sleep that is less like sleep than like worry, when she heard a tapping at her window. Just a slight tapping. Just a little tap. Just a tap-tap-tap. Three taps, a sound like knuckles rapping against a door.

She looked up, and what she saw was nothing. Or nothing she could be sure about. But when she looked down again at her own covers in the dim, half-moon light coming through her window, she thought she saw — it was not even an impression so much as an impression of an impression, a shadow's shadow's shadow — the figure of a man hovering there. When she looked up again, he was gone. When she looked down again, she thought she saw the movement. She looked up again, and there was nothing there, and then she was afraid to not look anymore.

So she stared out the window. She lay rigid, alert. Staring. She stayed that way the rest of the night, in that nervous state. It was exhausting to spend the night that way, and when morning came, she was so relieved at the sight of the sun that she directly fell asleep. Her mother came in and tried to stir her when she did not show in the kitchen to help with breakfast, but there was no rousing her. She had only the faint memory of opening her eyes and seeing her mother hovering over like a ghost, her face white against a bedroom that had taken on a strange shade of blue.

After that she thought she saw him everywhere. Saw him without actually seeing. He was the squirrel peeking out from behind the trees, so she stopped going off into the woods. He was the whistle of the wind through the exposed roots of the old cherry tree by the creek, so she refused to cross it to go to the well and fetch water. He was hiding behind the wood stove where she and Roy had cooked the bacon and eggs with the wood they had stolen from her father's pile, so she refused to go anymore into the kitchen.

Her world grew smaller and smaller and smaller — her room, the parlor, Sunday church — and then she was old enough to flee. John Wenderoth, a boy at the Free Will Independent Baptist Church, asked her to marry him, and she said she would on the condition they move away — "Anywhere, as long as it's away," she said, when he asked — and as soon as he had saved some money working as a well-digger's apprentice, he spirited her off to West Palm Beach, Florida, where he knew able-bodied men were needed for the construction boom, and then they were gone.

The children came quickly, Eleanor first, and then Millie, and then, after enough years had gone by that they thought they wouldn't have any more, along came John Junior, who they called John Junior until he was old enough to declare himself Jack. The world grew larger again. John came home after work smelling like sweat and dirt, smelling sweet to her taste, like a man should, and she fed him, and together they bathed the children, something other families did not do all together. They prayed at the dinner table, too, and broke bread with great reverence. Life was rich and full.

Eleanor went off to the state university, the first in the family. She did not finish, but then neither John nor Franny had finished high school, and they were proud of their eldest all the same for even going. They bought Florida Gators T-shirts and hung an orange and blue flag from the front porch, parallel to their red, white, and blue American flag.

Then Millie went away, too, to Stetson University, a private Baptist school in the north part of the state, on the east coast. When she told them, Franny thought John would burst a vessel in his brain for worry, but then she said she thought she could get a scholarship, and she did, and the people at the church were so proud that they pitched in for board and books.

Millie finished, too, with a degree in accountancy. John said, "Can you believe it, darling? We don't never have to pay anyone to do our taxes ever again."

Franny beamed. Things were so good. She couldn't believe things could ever get so good.

But then they got better. First, Eleanor married a man from a wealthy family, a dentist named Carl. John said, "Can you believe it, sweet girl? We can get our teeth fixed right." And sure enough they did. Carl pulled all John's bad teeth and fitted him with the most beautiful set of porcelain teeth anybody ever saw. They went to church that Sunday, and people were making over him like nothing he'd ever seen. Franny could not believe that porcelain teeth could bring anyone so much happiness.

But then Carl went to work on her mouth. She had been wearing a prosthetic tooth all these years that John had bought for her when they first moved to West Palm Beach, a belated wedding gift so beautiful she demanded he drive her straight home, and when they arrived she led him to the kitchen table. She told him to sit down, situated him just the way she wanted. Then she took off his shoes and his socks and rubbed and kissed his toes and his feet, pulled off his belt and unzipped his trousers and pulled them off, too. Then she rubbed and kissed his legs, just as slow as she liked him to rub and kiss her. Then she did something she had been refusing to do those early months of their union, had been refusing because of Roy and Donny Prather and what Donny had done to her that day in the dirt behind the tobacco field. She put her face right in his lap and took him in her mouth, and the act was to her every bit as cleansing as she imagined the day of her baptism might have been if she had been old enough to know and understand just what sins — past, present, future — were being washed away. When he was finished, she rinsed her mouth in the sink, and then she hiked up her good dress, and — she could hardly believe it — he was ready already, and she climbed up onto the table, onto him, and when they saw that it would not hold their weight for long, they made their way into the bedroom.

That's the way Eleanor was made, and now this dentist husband of hers, this Carl, was offering to make a new tooth for Franny, not a prosthetic, but an actual tooth that he would implant in her gum. By now her prosthetic tooth had taken on a blackish-blue cast, a navy blue almost, that stood in ugly contrast against the yellow-brown color of her other teeth. Carl made this new tooth white, and colored the yellow teeth to match it, and when he was done and her mouth had healed from the procedure, she looked in the mirror, John standing behind her. "You look beautiful," he said. He had been saying it for many years, but this time, this once, she believed him, thought herself beautiful. She was almost forty-five years old now, and for the first time beautiful.

Then the hard times came back with a vengeance. The year John Junior turned thirteen, Millie married another accountant, a man she met at work, and for two years she all but disappeared. This man, this accountant, had been rude to Franny and especially to John at the wedding, and made some mean-spirited comments about John's blue suit, which the man considered out of fashion, and on which John had spent two hundred dollars the week before the ceremony. That was the second sign of trouble. The first had been his forgetting to ask John for Millie's hand in marriage, but Franny said that it must have been an oversight, that times had changed and it wasn't Kentucky, and weren't they glad for that. But then Millie all but disappeared, and when Franny did see her, usually in passing at the grocery store, she looked haggard. She had taken to wearing dark sunglasses, even indoors, and to speaking in whispers.

After the third time Franny saw her this way — produce aisle, iceberg lettuce display — she told John she suspected Millie was what they called a battered wife. John could hardly bear it. He did not go to work the next day. She saw him in the backyard, pacing. She let him pace but thought a vegetable drink might make him feel better. His brother Larry back in Kentucky had got his cancer, melanoma of the skin, and beat it after buying a juicer and making three times daily drinks out of lettuce, cabbage, apples, carrots, and lemon juice. John thought it was a good idea, and whether or not the juicer had the power to ward off cancer, he sure did look and feel better, though his skin had lately taken on an orangish cast that Eleanor's husband Carl said had something to do with the beta carotene in the carrots.

She watched him while she juiced. He looked up and waved a hand to let her know he saw her, and made his way to the door. She met him there, the orange-brown juice in hand. He took a long sip and said, "I'm gonna have to go over there."

She said, "You might make it worse." But she wanted him to go whether it did or not. She wanted to go herself.

He took another, longer sip, and drained the whole thing. She didn't know how he could do it, but it must've given him time to think what he was going to say next. He swallowed, then he met her eyes with a gaze more direct than she was used to seeing from him. It was a little cold, and she remembered what power he was capable of projecting, and what kind of good man he must be to rein it in at home. He said, "If it's gonna get worse, I'm gonna get her out of there myself. And if she's not going to go, I'm gonna get him out. One way or the other."

What happened next it took her some time to piece together. John didn't say much to her, but he did confide in Carl, and Carl confided in Eleanor, and after a while Eleanor let it slip in fragments, a detail here and one there, until finally Franny was satisfied that she knew. Horrified, too. What happened was it was dark by the time John arrived. There was a light on in the house, and the ugly green curtains were drawn, and he could see Millie and her husband — his name was Erik, the Viking name mismatched with his scrawny body — he could see them in silhouette. He saw Erik's arm reach out and make contact with Millie's head, and Millie pushing back. Erik must have been off balance, and he fell, and when his shadow rose again, it reached out for the curtains and ripped them from the wall. When they came down, he could see that Millie was crying. She was standing there, naked from the waist up except for a frilly brassiere, one of her eyes swollen shut. By this time, John was out of the car and racing for the front door. Inside he heard a lot of yelling. The door was unlocked, which was a good thing, because in that state no doubt he would have kicked it down. When he got in the house, he found his daughter backed into a corner by skinny Erik, who was saying vile things. He turned and saw John, and Erik said, rapid-fire, "This is private; this is none of your concern; you don't know what's going on here, what she's done," and by the time he got to who she'd fucked, John was across the room. He grabbed Erik by the wrist and yanked so hard, he jerked the skinny Viking's arm from its socket. Right away, Millie tried to intervene. She put herself between her husband and her father and said, "Stop it, Dad. Stop it right now. He's my husband!" To John, hearing her saying it like that was like taking a whipping. He took two steps back, looked at his daughter, looked at her husband. All the fight went out of him then, and he looked at Erik and said, "You don't have a daughter. You don't know how it is." Erik didn't say anything. He went into the bedroom and pulled a suit from the closet, walked out the front door, his arm dangling from his shoulder at a grotesque angle, and drove away. Millie was still standing in the corner. John saw her there, and it must have killed him to see her like that, wearing that lacy brassiere above her bare midriff, her eye swollen shut. He went into the bedroom and took the orange velour blanket from beneath the comforter and brought it out into the living room. She had sat down on the couch, and he sat beside her and wrapped the velour blanket around her shoulders so it covered her and made her warm. His arm came to rest on her shoulder, and he let it rest there, lightly, and she didn't resist any. They sat there in silence for a long time. Finally, he said, "I'm ashamed, but it's not you I'm ashamed of."

After that, Millie moved in with Eleanor and Carl for a while. Erik made some overtures toward patching things up, but it was clear his heart wasn't in it. Franny didn't want Millie to even talk to him again except through lawyers, but she knew well enough to keep quiet, and she told John to do the same.

It ended badly, at least as far as Franny was concerned. The dentist who employed Eleanor's husband Carl was nearing retirement age, and his practice was housed on land he owned, land that sat on one of the last mostly undeveloped major intersections in downtown West Palm Beach. The land was maybe twenty or thirty times more valuable than the dental practice, and the old man decided to sell. He offered Carl his client list in exchange for a continuing (and quite large) participation in the business's future income, and Carl gave it some thought, but it would have been difficult to find land to buy or lease in the same part of the city that was affordable enough to ensure the kind of profitability he hoped he might achieve in return for the hassle and risk of taking over the practice. He would have to move the practice to the suburbs, maybe out west of town to Royal Palm Beach or Wellington, where the young families were moving. But then if he was going to move anyway, and no doubt lose most of the clients, who wouldn't want to make the half-hour commute to the dentist's office twice a year, why give a cut to his old employer?

Carl and Eleanor mapped out their reasons for rejecting the offer over a supper of Franny's famous Hungarian goulash, a recipe she had learned from the Cuban woman next door, and John nodded, and inside, Franny was cheering all over again for this man Carl, this dentist who had made Eleanor's life so good, and who even now was making such well-reasoned decisions for himself and her daughter. But then Eleanor said, "Carl's parents say they'll cosign the bank loan for a new practice in Lake Mary. It's only fifteen minutes from where they live, and it's growing so fast. That's the direction Orlando's growing, to the north . . ."

It was like a blow to the chest. Franny and John both lied and told them it was wonderful news. "Best thing me and Franny ever did was move away from Kentucky," John said — gamely, Franny thought — but after they went home, John said, "Do you think they're gonna take Millie with them?"

The thought had not occurred to Franny. She took to calling Carl and Eleanor's house at odd hours, hoping to catch Millie when they weren't home. But one or the other of them always seemed to be home when she called. When she heard their voices, she hung up the phone, and after the eighth or ninth hang-up, she got a call from Eleanor. "Mom, have you been trying to call here?" she said.

"No," Franny said, too fast.

"Mom, I know you have. We had to get the phone company to put a trace on the call. It cost fifteen dollars. Do you know what a trace is, Mom?"

She could figure it out well enough.

"I don't understand, Mom. You call because you want to talk to me, and then you hang up?"

Franny didn't know what to say, so she hung up.

She leaned on the handset for a while where it rested in the cradle and looked at it. Then she lifted it from the cradle and called back. Before Eleanor could even say hello, Franny was off and running. "You're-ruining-my-life-by-leaving-and-you're-taking-my-Millie-too," and "How-could-you-do-this-to-your-father?" Then she hung up again.

Then she made a list, a catalog of all the things she and John had done for Eleanor and Millie, on a ruled yellow legal pad, starting with eighteen combined months of pregnancy and moving on through all the work of infant mothering (item #12: "nursing, no Karo syrup") and getting toddlers ready for school (item #37: "i learned to read better so i could teach it right to both of you") and roller skates and Barbie dolls and braces and even flashy teenage miniskirts ("and i even hid it from your daddy even though it wasnt right to do it") and on and on, filling seven long yellow pages and writing a paragraph on the eighth to the effect that this effort, this "hasty couple pages," was very much an abridgment.

It was Millie who called first. She had been seeing an expensive psychologist, a friend of Carl's, and her mouth was full of three-dollar words. She told Franny what she thought Franny didn't know about boundaries. She said what was being forced on her and Eleanor was nothing less than an extension of the guilt complex Franny had been building in them their whole lives. She said Franny's main goal in life was her own comfort, and that's what all the walking around the house humming and talking about nothing had been about all those years.

"What humming?" Franny said. "What talking to myself? I was singing songs to bring happy to the house. I was talking to you, to cheer you up. It was a habit, a good good good habit."

"It was an unconscious habit," Millie said. "You did it to meet some unmet need in yourself from your marriage or your childhood you haven't found a way to come to terms with." She told her about something called Johari's window, something her psychologist told her, some way of looking into the soul, where there was all different things about you, and some of them were known to you and everybody else, and some you knew about yourself but kept close so nobody else could know, and some were secrets about you, but open secrets that you didn't yourself know but everybody else knew about you.

Or claimed to know, Franny thought, as she listened to Millie go on and on in this high-minded way. Because how could any one person know what was happening inside the mind of another person? What their thoughts were, their intentions, their motivations? Her intentions were pure, she knew that well enough. And her secrets were her own.

Franny said, "Don't throw big words around to try and show me. I'm no dummy. I know what those big words mean. And let me tell you another one I know: *cultivate.* I cultivated every one of those habits. For you. So don't try and tell me, just because you're getting too big for your britches. I raised you. I knew you from when you were not but a speck in your daddy's eye. I knew you before you knowed yourself."

Still, it was the first she'd heard of this talk, and she knew after hearing Millie say it that it must have been said many times before. She thought about that Johari's window and the things she must not know other people thought they knew about her, had been thinking about her all along. She knew, then, that her children were ripping her up behind her back after she spent her whole life trying to make theirs good. There wasn't a child on earth loved her parents as much as her parents loved her, Franny knew that well enough, but what about respect? What about where the Bible said honor thy father and thy mother? That was in the Ten Commandments. It was given to Moses from God, and those girls knew it, too. She had showed it to them in the blue Bible storybook probably a hundred times or more when they were little.

It wasn't long after that she started to get bogged down in thinking about secrets and the way they were kept. Long after Carl moved away and took Eleanor and Millie with him to Lake Mary and his new dental paradise, nearer his own wealthy parents, she played and replayed that conversation with Millie again and again in her mind. John did not say much about it, but she noticed that he had been taking care of even more things around the house than he usually did, which forced him to be around more. He was taking John Junior — Jack, he wanted to be called Jack now — to the high school every morning so Franny could sleep in, and picking him up after baseball practice in the afternoons, too, juggling his own work schedule and saying no to good overtime so he could do it. He was making most of the meals, and he was bringing into the house flowers fresh cut from the backyard, putting them in vases, and changing the water as long as they stayed nice. It was his way; it was what he had always done when he thought she was sad, and kept on doing until her sadness had passed.

But what she was feeling was not sadness. All Millie's talk about secrets and comfort and what is known and to whom . . . all of that had put her in mind again of the Prather boys, her cousins Donny and Roy, and that day Roy had chased her through the tobacco field, toward Donny, who he had to know was waiting there for her, waiting to do bad things to her, even though Roy probably didn't know how bad. The day playing house had gone wrong, and her childhood had ended, and Roy had died.

It was a secret, *the* secret, in fact, of her whole life. She had never told John the story, although he knew well enough about the dog-eaten boy that was found up in the mountain, knew, too, that Roy was her cousin, and that the boy, the brother, who had most likely done it had run off and was never heard from again. But what seemed so remarkable to her, now, forty years after she stopped being nine years old forever, was that her husband John had never once brought it up. Never once asked. Didn't act one bit curious. Wasn't that strange?

Jack came home early that afternoon, saying baseball practice had been cut short by rain, and he had caught a ride home with a girl named Julie. That took Franny by surprise. She looked him over as he walked down the hall toward his bedroom and shut the door. Only fifteen, but from behind he looked just like his daddy did when Franny had first met him, except for Jack's long hair. Same broad shoulders, same thick legs, walked the same way. Good Lord, he was almost the same age John had been then.

She walked back to his bedroom and knocked on the door, and when he said, "Come in," she did. He was lying on the bed, propped up on his elbows over a pad of graph paper full of algebra equations. Franny said, "Who is this Julie?"

"Just a girl, Mom," he said, but from the way he said it, she could tell it wasn't just a girl.

"How old is she?" Franny said. "She's older? She drives a car?"

"She just turned sixteen, Mom," Jack said. "She's in the same grade as me."

Franny frowned. She had been so caught up in the lives of her girls, she hadn't been paying enough attention to Jack, not for a long time. He was so quiet, moved through the house like he wasn't even there. You could almost forget he was there at all.

"Don't worry, Mom," he said. "It's nothing."

He turned his attention back to the algebra. She said, "Did you call your daddy and tell him you was coming home early?"

He acknowledged as much with a wave, not disrespectful but not mindful, either, of her. He had been growing less and less mindful of her. It had been going on for a long time, but she only now noticed it as a pattern.

She went through the motions of making dinner, peas and carrots and potatoes and cubed steak, but she did not find any joy in it. Turning on the burner on the electric stove, she noticed that she was humming. A hymn. *Oh, precious is the flow that makes me white as snow* . . . For just a moment it had made her feel better, and she remembered what Millie had said, and then it made her feel worse, her humming to keep herself company and not even knowing it, like everyone apparently knew she did.

When John came home, he went directly to tend to the backyard without saying so much as hello. She thought he was mad at her at first — the whole world was, it seemed like — but after a while she looked out at him through the window and saw how he was hacking away at the hedgerows that lined the back of their property with his hedge clippers, but he wasn't doing it right, wasn't doing it slow and careful like was his way. He was going fast, clip-clip-clipping. It looked like he was trying to hurt the bushes. She could see his biceps working where they poked out from his shirtsleeves.

She went outside. He did not hear her approaching. He kept on moving, herky-jerky. She called out his name. She said, "John, honey, John . . ."

He turned and looked at her. He had a strange look on his face like he didn't recognize her.

She said, "John, what's wrong? What did I do wrong?"

He softened at this, let the arm, his right arm, holding the hedge clippers drop to his side. He was standing there at a half-crooked angle, those hedge clippers dangling from his right side and his body all slumped to the right like it was following the hedge clippers. He said, "Oh, shit, Franny."

It was maybe four times she had ever heard him say a curse word. She could count on one hand with the thumb finger left over.

"Them girls is gonna move away," he said. He said it like they were dead.

She thought on it a while. He seemed to be looking at her for an answer.

Then she said, "Just like we did."

At that he just nodded his head, slow. Like he was resigning himself to it. He could say a hundred things and more to her without even saying one single word.

Then she said — she could hardly believe she was saying it — "Do you know why we ran away?"

She said it like that — ran away. Not went away.

He picked up on it right off, and said, "We didn't run nowhere at all. We decided. We *chose*. We made a choice, a real good choice, and packed our things, and left in a orderly fashion. We left because you said we ought to, and that was good enough for me, and I stand by it. I'm not ashamed of it."

He must have been trying to make her feel better, she decided. And that's what he would think was called for. That's what he always thought was called for, making her feel better. Good Lord, that was what he lived for. She knew it and had always known it but only realized that she knew she knew it just now. Millie and her Johari window. It was gonna haunt her, and she did not like it one bit.

She said, "That's not what I'm talking about. I'm talking real things here. I'm talking about why we left. Why I told you I wanted to leave. You never did ask. We just packed our things and went."

"And that was good enough for me," he said. "Your word is good enough for me any day of the week."

"No, no, no," she said. Her voice was rising. "I asked you a fair question, and you must have an answer. You, John Wenderoth, are a smart man who thinks of things. And this once I want to know what it is you think. So you tell me. Why did we leave Kentucky?"

He looked down at the ground for a long moment, one that felt like ten or twenty. Then, lifting his head but not connecting his eyes with hers, he said, "Well," and then another long pause, and then he said, "I suppose we left because of your daddy."

He did look in her eyes, then, probably, she thought, to gauge how it was she would respond before he went on. She did not want to give herself away, afraid he wouldn't if she did.

He said, "Your daddy was a mean man, God love him. I know he was. I seen him being rough with people more than once. And you was so quiet. You didn't hardly come out for anything. I saw you there, sitting in the pew at church, and I knew. I knew how it was. He must've been . . ."

Here his voice trailed away, and she knew what he was saying was that all these years her husband John thought her daddy, her sweet daddy, had been beating on her, or worse, the way daddies sometimes did to their daughters in those hills, in those times, the thing that passed among the women in whispers you had to overhear to be privy to, and that was what he meant to rescue her from. She didn't hardly know what to say to it.

He was still looking at her, like it hurt him to almost say it. He said, "It's okay, Francine. He didn't probably mean anything by it. It wasn't your fault. Maybe not even his. It was a hard life back there. People didn't know how to be."

She stood there and looked at him, her secret between them, and all those years, too. One way of looking at it, what she had to tell him was so much worse than the thing he had been thinking all along. But, the other way, it wasn't worse at all. One way it was her cousin did it to her before he murdered his brother, and the other way it was her own daddy did it to her, and murdered her a different way, a way so bad she would have had to keep on living with it. But then she was living with the other thing well on past when it happened, and it hadn't killed her, but then in a way it had, and she had had to resurrect herself, or at least teach herself how to be again.

Around and around she went with herself. Not much time passed, but in the way the mind does when under great pressure, the time inside her grew very slow to her own reckoning even as it must have been very fast when compared to the ticking of the clock on the kitchen wall.

Then she decided. She hung her head. She didn't say a thing.

John walked over to her and wrapped his arms around her, and he said, "It don't matter one way or the other, Francine. You're the whole world and you always was."

She leaned into him in the way he liked because she liked it and told him so. Roy was dead and buried, and if Donny had found a way to live, he was an old man now, and not Donny anymore. Those girls could move away if they wanted, and soon Jack would be gone, too, but what was past was past. She sealed it off inside herself, and there wasn't anyone could touch her heart in the worst way again. It was a cold feeling.

She didn't have her John for long after that. One afternoon he was working on a construction site in Port St. Lucie, where some developer was building a new baseball park, a spring training facility for the New York Mets where their minor league team would also play during the summer. John was excited about it, working on a baseball park. It meant something to him that office buildings and suburban neighborhoods did not. One afternoon he heard some Mets executives and a few ballplayers would be flying down to survey the progress, and he told Jack to take the day off school and come to work with him, meet the players.

Franny watched them drive away that morning. She watched the way they touched each other when they were walking down the sidewalk to the carport. The good-natured arm punching and the horseplay. They had something between them she thought she had once with Eleanor, and then Millie.

They got into the car and drove away, and that's the last time she saw John alive. On the interstate, on the way to the construction site, John clutched his hand to his chest. Jack later said he thought, for a moment, his father would lose control of the car, but just as Jack was reaching for the wheel, John rallied, inhaled with great effort — "He was white as a sheet," Jack recalled — and straightened his shoulders and gripped the wheel and steered the car onto the shoulder and then the grass strip beyond. Then, the car safely at a stop, he slumped over the steering wheel. Jack jumped out of the car and waved his arms frantically at the approaching traffic. A middle-aged woman in a beige Datsun compact stopped, and together she and Jack wrestled John from the car. By then he had lost consciousness, and by the time they reached the hospital, he had stopped breathing. By 8:22 that morning, he had been declared dead. Jack called and told Franny what had happened and asked her to come to the hospital, and she said, "He's dead?" and Jack said — he was crying — "Yes, Mom, he is," and Franny said, "Then there's nothing I can do," and she got him off the phone as quick as she could. Then she went into the bathroom and vomited until she was too weak to get up. She lay on the bathmat and let herself drift into something not sleep but like dreaming. She rested there until she marshaled the strength to get up. Then she got up and went to the kitchen and made some tea. Her hands were shaking. She drank the tea and ate some peanut butter cheese crackers. Then she went into the bathroom, brushed her teeth, and scrubbed the toilet until there was no sign of her illness.

By the time Jack arrived home, Franny had prepared grilled cheese sandwiches and tomato soup. It was ready for him on the table. He came in through the back door by the kitchen, took one look at the food, then hung his head, went into his bedroom, and did not come out until the next day.

Jack never said anything about it, but she always wondered whether he thought her somehow defective as a mother for not going to the hospital to comfort him. He had been sixteen then, and his pain must have been enormous, but what about hers? Who had she had her entire life except for John? Eleanor? Millie? For the duration of their childhoods, maybe, but they were gone now, moved away, off to follow that dentist Carl — no better than a kidnapper, that Carl — to Lake Mary, which may as well have been the red planet Mars. What could Jack know about what she had lost, losing John? What could any child know about what a whole life spent with someone means? Especially a whole life that didn't rightly begin until that someone came along and gave it a reason to keep being after years and years of having no reason at all.

The distance between Franny and Jack widened after that. They shared the space of the house, but they did not have things to say to each other. They were not enemies; there was nothing bitter between them. They were more like strangers. And something else, too. As he grew toward manhood, he continued to have some of his father's features, but as he grew into his face, characteristics from her own family began to assert themselves in ways she could not have expected. His nose and ears grew longer, more like her father's and less like John's. He had been seeing the older girl, Julie — that's how Franny thought of her, even though she and Jack were still in the same grade — and as they grew more serious, there was some glint in his eye that was not of John, some expression of desire she caught a glimpse of now and then when Jack was walking behind Julie and did not know she was watching him. When her son would look at his girlfriend's legs or backside. A directness. Nothing sidelong. An expression of desire that was different in kind from the way she had seen John look at her in the unguarded moments they had shared.

She tried to put it aside, but she could not. She did not remember ever seeing her father in a moment so unguarded, yet she somehow knew it was of her family. She knew in a very general way but would not say to her own self, not even in the privacy of her own mind, that the quality she saw in her son's gaze was in some way reminiscent of something she remembered about her cousin Donny Lynn Prather.

Just once, and only to put it to rest, she put it into words, but not aloud. Only in her head. Just once, just to put it to rest. Because it was not, she knew, any sign of any deficiency in her son. It was just something in the blood, something, in fact, that came from her, that something inside her shared with Donny only because they shared a grandfather. It was not what caused Donny to be what he had been. It was just a speck in her son Jack's eye.

She suspected Jack and Julie were sleeping together but could not put her finger on why. When they went out at night, he always came home at an acceptable hour. He was busy, and stayed busy, with baseball. He had been going to the church more, the Cherry Road Baptist Church the family had been attending ever since they had moved to West Palm Beach, way back when it wasn't even a proper church but instead what they called a mission. John used to stand in the back as an usher one Sunday a month and greet visitors and tell them that he was "a charter member of our church."

Franny wasn't going much anymore. It was too hard to go without John. Worse, it made her think thoughts that ended up in bad places. Like, if God is good and loves those who accept Jesus Christ as their personal savior, then why does He allow so many terrible things to happen in the world? And she wasn't thinking about it in the abstract. The beef with God she was trying to avoid was quite personal. As in: If God is good and loves those who accept Jesus Christ as their personal savior, then why is John dead? And why did Millie's husband beat her? And why did she and Eleanor move away? And why was Donny Lynn Prather allowed to kill his little brother Roy on a day he meant to do less?

Sunday mornings, Jack would rise early, shower, dress, and leave to pick up Julie, and Franny would lie in her bed and pretend to be sleeping.

She went on sleeping in, and not just on Sundays anymore, but also on Mondays and Tuesdays, Wednesdays and Thursdays and Saturdays. Fridays she did force herself to wake, by the alarm clock neither she nor John had needed their whole lives, being children raised in the natural cycles of the sun's rising and setting. Fridays she was in the car by 8:30, and off to Claudia's Beauty Salon in the Cross-County shopping center on Okeechobee Road, where she got her hair done and listened (without participating) to the neighborhood gossip, this ungrateful child and that one, mostly, and wondered at her own restraint, for she by now had as much to say on the subject as anyone.

Jack graduated from high school and went on to college at Stetson University, same as Millie, and he, too, planned to be an accountant. Julie followed him there, and by sophomore year they were married. At the rehearsal dinner the night before the ceremony, Jack sprung on Franny the news that he had changed his major from accounting to something called Bible and Religion, and it was all she could do to keep from screaming in protest: "And how will you feed your family?" Already he was up to his eyeballs in college loans; six months later he told her he was thinking of attending the Dallas Theological Seminary in Texas upon graduation, which he said would now take five years on account of his changing his major so late in the game.

Three years passed. Jack and Julie moved to Texas. Eleanor sent a card every year for Christmas. Millie remarried, a partner in Carl's dental practice named (and this was funny) Dennis, but didn't send Franny an invitation. The backyard ceremony grew nearer and nearer — Franny heard all about it from Sally Cunningham down the street, whose daughter was Millie's lifelong best friend — and finally, when Franny couldn't take it anymore, she called Millie on the phone and said, "Your old mother can't come to your wedding?"

"I sent you an invitation, Mother," Millie said. She said it cold like that. Mother. What kind of way was that to talk?

"I never saw no invitation," Franny said.

"Well, I sent it," Millie said. "And, anyway, you're invited. I'm inviting you now."

But the invitation never came by mail, and to Franny that was message enough. She did not want to go anyplace she wasn't wanted. If John were around he would've smoothed it over, called Millie, calmed Franny, arranged for an invitation to be sent. But John was not around. John was dead and gone and everything good with him. Franny did not go to the wedding, and after that she and Millie did not speak at all.

Franny went out less and less. She stopped getting her hair done once a week. It was a vanity she did not need to indulge, and anyway she was tired of hearing about everyone else's children, what they had accomplished. Now she got her hair done once every three weeks at Mary's Beauty Salon on Military Trail, but the talk there was almost more unbearable, everyone prattling on about their grandchildren and passing along pictures.

What did it say about her that her children, all married, had not produced any grandchildren? Sure, Eleanor and Carl had the good excuse that they weren't able, a problem of Carl's, not Eleanor's. But was this not the age of science, like they said all the time now, and technology? Surely, with the kind of money a Lake Mary dentist must be pulling in, they could afford some of that in vitro fertilization. Shelby Crockett's son-in-law had been shooting blanks all along, but all he did was get his brother to go in a cup, and then they implanted his seed in her daughter, and it was as though the baby was all theirs, instead of three-quarters.

But Millie, well, Millie said she wanted no part of any child rearing. And Jack and Julie had been married going on four years now, and still no news. That saying, no news is good news? Well, it's not so. No news is not good news. Good news is good news. Franny waited and waited, but the good news never came.

Then one morning Jack called, and he said, "Mom, I have some good news." This was it. She was sure of it. She was so excited she began to squeal and jump up and down. She said, "Oh, oh, I'm so happy, I'm so happy for you. For us."

Jack said, "Well, wait a minute, Mom. I haven't told you yet."

And she said, "I'm sorry, it's just I get so excitable these days." She dabbed at her moist eyes with a handkerchief. She sat down in the chair by the kitchen phone and waited to hear it. She wanted to savor every second. In that brief moment she felt forty-five years old and beautiful. She wished John were here to share it with her. She bounced up and down in her seat like a schoolgirl.

"It's me and Julie," Jack said. "We have a big change that's going to happen in our life. We're moving. Back to West Palm Beach. I've been called to be the pastor at the Cherry Road Baptist Church."

She put her hand over the receiver and began to sob, silently as she could. She was shaking at the shoulders.

"There's a few formalities," Jack was saying. "I have to come down and preach. There has to be a vote. But, I mean, they know me and I know them, and I don't think there will be any sort of problems."

She regained her composure. He was waiting for her to say something. He would want her to tell him how wonderful it was, and how happy and proud she was, and, really, it was true, the part about it being wonderful. It was wonderful that one of her children would be moving home. She could be happy about it. It was something to be happy about.

She said, "Jack, I'm happy and I'm proud. The news you are saying is wonderful."

He said, "I want you to come see me preach, Mom. I want you to be there."

She said, "I'll be there, all right. You just watch. I'll be there on the front row, saying amen. Me and Julie, and, who knows, little John Wenderoth the Third maybe . . ."

She went on at some length about what it would be like to be a grandmother. John, for his part, did not say much about it. When he said he had to get off the phone, had to go attend to something for Julie, she still had more things to say, so she called Eleanor on the phone. Carl answered and tried to exchange some pleasantries, but she said if he didn't mind would he get Eleanor on the phone, because she had some important and exciting news to share.

As soon as she heard Eleanor's voice, Franny told her tale, first the news from Jack that he and Julie would be hearing God's call on their lives to come on down to the Cherry Road Baptist Church — that part she told real fast — and then a whole lot of speculation about what it would be like to sit on that front row, in a seat of honor, right there alongside Julie and little John the Third, and, who knows, maybe some little girl, maybe named Francine Mae, after her.

Eleanor interrupted. "What's this about John the Third and Francine Mae, Mother?" she said. Mother. That again.

Franny began to lecture. "That's what people do when they meet and marry and settle down," she said. "That's the normal, healthful, God-ordained way of things."

"Well, what does that say about me and Carl?" Eleanor said. "We don't have any children."

"Well," Franny said. It was her way of saying that she understood the rebuke and did not accept it. Eleanor had crossed a line she should not have crossed. She was the daughter, after all.

Eleanor's voice softened. "Look, Mom," she said. "I don't think you should be saying things like that to Jack and Julie."

"And why is that your business?" Franny said.

"I don't suppose it is," Eleanor said, keeping an even tone. That was even more infuriating than if she had been yelling. It was a point of pride, Franny supposed. Refinement. Class. All those things people think they acquire so they can be better than other people. "But I'll tell you anyway, because I don't think it's fair for you to assume that Jack and Julie are going to move down there and make their choices just to please you."

"They are not going to have any children?" Franny said. "You know this? They told you it?"

"They're busy with their careers," Eleanor said. "The same as a lot of people. Jack just did his internship at First Baptist of Dallas and he was working eighty, ninety hours a week. And Julie's doing the crisis pregnancy counseling. That takes time. You get these poor black girls who don't have anyplace else to go and the man who got them that way sees he can pay a couple hundred dollars for an abortion or spend the next eighteen years paying child support or more likely running from it. You know how they are. That's a lot of pressure she has to try and combat. And they're all confused about love, like any girl that age knows the first thing about it. It takes a lot of time to avert a crisis like that. It's life and death, Mom. She's out there on the front lines of it, and sometimes it keeps her away all hours."

"You're lecturing me," Franny said.

"I'm not lecturing you, Mom," Eleanor said. "I'm telling it to you straight."

And right away, thoughts began to consume her that she could hardly bear. What kind of mother raises three children who themselves think so little of children that they do not want to have any of their own? What kind of trauma do they think they survived? What do they know the first thing about survival anyway? They had it so easy, these children. John working a good job, and Franny staying home and tending to everything. So easy, and the warmth of family all around them, and now every single one of them acting like family itself was some kind of poison they needed to void from their systems.

Franny went to see Jack preach his tryout, but she sat in the back row, not up front with Julie. It was her way of protesting, but no one seemed to notice. Jack acknowledged her from the pulpit, asked her to stand, said, "That's the woman who raised me, who I owe my very self to. I want to say it publicly. I love you, Mom." Then everyone applauded, but it wasn't for anything she had done. It was because that's what they were supposed to do. It was a dog and pony show.

When it was over they voted him in 204 to 16, with 4 abstentions. That was as close to unanimity as the Cherry Road Baptist Church had ever seen. Franny herself abstained, which would have brought the total abstentions to 5, except her vote was invalidated on account of the last time she set foot in the church was seven and a half years ago for the Easter cantata. She was still a member, a charter member at that, but not in good standing. But the act of attending made her eligible to vote again for at least the next five years, and for the rest of the years she lived in her own house, the one she had shared with John, she never missed another vote. She registered strongly her support for air-conditioning improvements and her opposition to hiring a music minister who did not also want to work with the youth, often enough heading up a stubborn bloc of old-timers against Jack. She did it for the same reason she had abstained the day he was voted in. It wouldn't be right to cast a favorable vote just because the pastor was her son. That would be nepotism, and it just wouldn't be right.

Still, there were advantages to being the pastor's mother. Jack was well liked. Women she had known her whole adult life would come up to her and compliment her on her raising him so well. "He's grown into quite the gentleman," they might say, or, those so inclined: "He's grown into quite the mighty man of God."

She began to attend the Wednesday morning women's prayer meetings, which she found were quite useful for catching up on everyone's business. Everyone talked bad about gossip, even while they were doing it. Marjorie Phillips would say things like, "I want to offer a request for intercessory prayer for Mary Jo Abdo. I was at the beauty shop last week and I heard her spreading all sorts of gossip about the women of the church. I want to pray for Mary Jo, in the spirit of love, that she might turn away from idle chatter and toward more edifying kinds of words."

It was delicious. Franny joined in, too. She resumed her weekly hair appointments so she would have more prayer requests to share. Often she was the first to know about illness, divorce, and all kinds of other miseries, which she offered up for prayer. Mary Jo Abdo began coming to prayer meetings and before long told Franny that she considered her to be an A-1 All-American prayer warrior, and something of a mother to her in the faith.

Tuesday evenings she went over to Jack and Julie's house for dinner, and they made over her. Sometimes Julie grilled steaks on the back porch, really nice tenderloin cuts Franny and John never would have bought, and sometimes Jack made some kind of Mexican food, or Japanese food, always something new he was learning from someone he went to visit. He said it made people feel more comfortable if they had something to do with their hands, and it made him more comfortable, too, so when he went to visit people, if they weren't too ill, he would ask them to teach him how to make their favorite meal in the kitchen. He would even offer to buy the ingredients, though almost everyone refused to let him.

One Tuesday evening Julie was out back grilling. Franny and Jack were sitting in the comfortable chairs in the living room, and she was telling him about how Mary Jo Abdo had met a gentleman in his fifties — "A younger man," she said, eyes bright: "The scandal!" — when Jack interrupted her and said he wanted to check on Julie, that he'd be right back.

He was gone a little too long, and she began to worry. If life had taught her one thing, it was that the good times don't ever last, that the bad times come and take them away right when you least expect it. She waited another minute and then she got up and walked toward the back door. Just then, the door opened, and Jack and Julie walked in pushing a brand-new bicycle, a beautiful old-fashioned kind, with high sloping handlebars and a basket and a red horn. "For you, Mom," Julie said, and that was almost better than the bicycle, her calling Franny *mom.* It was the first time she had ever said it.

She began to ride the bicycle in the early afternoon. It felt good to move around some every day. She was sore at first, but then her body adjusted, and then she began to ride in the mornings. Once a week she undertook a long ride to the airport and back, growing fond of passing landmarks like the old Army barracks, the bomb shelter, even the strip clubs and their pink facades.

July 4, 1996, the church gathered at Okeeheelee State Park for an Independence Day celebration. They started early. The men played softball and later basketball, even though it was hotter than blue blazes by 9:30. There was a potluck lunch followed by a potluck dinner. Bill Miller brought his famous banana pudding. There were lawn darts and horseshoes, tetherball and badminton. The older women served the food and rested between meals in plastic lawn chairs beneath the shade of the palm trees. At nightfall the children traced their names in the air with sparklers. At nine o'clock the fire department brought a skiff out onto the lake where the water skiers practiced and shot off fireworks. Oh, what a sight. Red, white, and blue. And then the grand finale, explosion after explosion. Franny covered her ears and dropped her jaw the way the men who got back from the war said people did in London during the air raids. Then, just when the music had stopped and the last lights burned out in the sky, the music started up again, a massive chord played on maybe ten pianos at once, and dozens of fireworks, one last round, went up into the sky and burst into color simultaneously. The pattern they made was the American flag.

When it was over, everyone sat in stunned silence for a long, long time. Then someone put their hands together and began to cheer. That's all it took was one person, and everyone was cheering, up on their feet applauding and whooping like there was no tomorrow, or, better yet, like tomorrow was going to be even better than today, which was saying a lot, because today was as good as it gets.

That was the night she slept in her own bed for the last time. In the morning she woke up feeling fine. She made a cup of coffee, put sugar on her grapefruit, and dug the flesh from the rind with her spoon. Then she got on her bicycle and set off for the airport.

She saw them up ahead, at the corner of Seminole and Cherry. Two Guatemalans — pickers, no doubt; day laborers, like her father had been; but not like her father at all; dirty and unruly — trading blows. The bigger man had the smaller one in a headlock and was punching away at the top of his head with his free fist. The body of the one in the headlock was flailing all around, kicking his legs in the air, trying to spin out of the hold or get the bigger man on the ground, and he was delivering short blows to the kidneys with both hands.

She slowed down, wanting to see what would happen. Her money was on the one in the headlock, the little guy. He had fight; it was plain to see. It was all she could do to not shout her encouragement.

And just then, the smaller man got his legs hooked around the larger man's legs and swept them out from under him, and they went down together on the sidewalk. The smaller man's head hit the concrete first, and right away split open, ran red on the sidewalk. Then the larger man came down on top of the smaller man.

It was horrible, sure, but it was beautiful, all that blood, and the sickening crack of the smaller man's skull as the larger man came down upon it. She was reminded of something she had all but forgotten from when she was very small, a story her father told. There had been a terrible passenger train accident, a section of track just west of Rowan County that had not been mended. Her father happened to be nearby. He was young, maybe fifteen; she couldn't remember. He was hunting deer with his father. They both saw it happen. The train derailed, and forty people died, "But I could see the faces, all them people looking out at me and my daddy through them windows like they never had seen two men holding hunting guns before. Like we was the most beautiful people that ever lived on the planet earth. I don't reckon I'll ever know that feeling again."

And that's how it was for Franny. That Guatemalan picker hit the sidewalk and busted open his head, and then, just briefly, his eyes met hers, and he must have thought he dreamed it, an old lady on an old-fashioned bicycle.

She thought that the man might die, so she held on to his gaze as long as she could. She held on to it, and the act of holding on to it made her forget to keep her eyes on the road ahead. The bicycle rolled slowly into the intersection at Seminole and Cherry. There was the sound of squealing brakes. She looked up and saw a green pickup truck as it clipped her front tire. She lost control of the bike and fell, and the last thing she remembered was a dull cracking sound not unlike the one the picker's head had just made, but coming from the direction of her right hip. Then a searing pain in that hip as it went stationary while her shoulders and head continued their fall. Then for some reason the smell of bay leaves and cinnamon. Then blackness.

She woke to a strange parade of strangers, vagrants in white coats, faces from her past — neighbors, relatives, schoolteachers, themselves but not. She found herself in great pain, the worst of it in her hip and running up and down her leg. She was haunted by the long dead. They spoke to her, and she was confused because their faces did not match their voices, and they had not aged in the years since she had known them in her youth. Time had ceased its orderly way forward. She could not walk, and men came to kidnap her, and when she tried to scream, they strapped her to a gurney and injected her with something that caused her to lose consciousness, but not entirely.

It happened again and again. She could hear them speaking though she could not move. Once she heard them say that she was suffering from some sort of stroke-related dementia and near paralysis. But she knew that it was the world that was changing and not her. She had *clarity.* Once, opening her eyes, she saw that the youngest of the doctors — how could this be possible? — was Bruce Macholtz from Mt. Sterling, Kentucky, one of the doctors who had tended to her when she had the chicken pox at age six. Dr. Macholtz, but younger now than he was then.

And where was her John? It was time for him to come rescue her. She called out for him, or tried to, but her lips would not properly move. She was saying (but not saying), *Let's do it again, John. Take me away from here. Take me anywhere. We can start over again.*

She remembered a magazine picture of a beachfront town near Georgetown, South Carolina. Debourdieu. Oh, it was so beautiful. Beach houses on wooden pilings two hundred feet from the Atlantic Ocean. John appeared to her once, calling her *momma,* and she knew it must be a dream. Debourdieu; she had seen it in *Better Homes and Gardens.* Why would John call her *momma? Sweet girl,* she wanted to say, to John. *Tell me I am your sweet girl.*

In Debourdieu the alligators occasionally approached from the brackish swamp water just north. Mary Jo had told Franny about Debourdieu, had shown her the pictures in a *Better Homes and Gardens* magazine, but the alligator talk she heard from her friend Arlene, who had vacationed in Georgetown. Alligators, walking the streets and beaches of Debourdieu. They had to get the Negroes and Chinamen who worked the rice paddies to come wrangle them away. Oh, for some Indian alligator wranglers. Old-fashioned cowboys and Comanches, John Wayne in a white hat, Tonto. Shirley Temple, remember her? She was a sexpot, a five-year-old tramp in saddle shoes, and no one was allowed to say it. The old men drove to Lexington to see her shake on the silver screen. It was her eyes, Shirley Temple. They spoke lewd things to the old men, those eyes. Oh, in Debourdieu, there, no Shirley Temple would tap her jig. They would feed her to the alligators, and then the Negroes and the Chinamen would hustle it all away.

She and John, there in Debourdieu, growing old, away from their horrid daughters with their dentist husbands, their rejections. But first she would have to find a way to escape. She woke as from a dream and saw the white flecked with black in the ceiling tile squares. White fluorescent lights ran the length of the ceiling. The terrible new Negro music blared from the television. The talking over the boom-boom-boom. Two of them in the room, talking, so not watching. First about men and their bodies. Delicious men, hard men who could be soft as cotton candy. Men worth their runnings around, but just barely. Then praying together. One said, "Take my hand, Sister Charlene," and then: "Oh sweet Jesus, we come to you now with heavy hearts. We lift up our Sister Charlene in her time of trouble . . ."

The television still running. That dialect she could not bear, and the music, or what passed for it. She tried to cry out, to scream. *Oh, sweet Lord, what if I have been taken from your bosom because of my secret. Because I have lied to John. Where is the fire and the brimstone? The heat and the sulfurous smell that lays waiting for the unrighteous?*

The days and the nights intermingled. The woman came and said, "It's me, Mom. It's me, Julie." Called her *mom.* Took her away, but not to Debourdieu. To a house that seemed familiar, which was a comfort, but which she did not recognize. Often in her life she had recognized places she had never been. There was a word for it, in the French. She couldn't remember.

On New Year's Eves she had often longed for confetti, at Christmas for snow to fall in Florida, every other day of the year for Christ to come back on his white horse, the sky to turn red, to be bodily raptured and be with her Father and all the saints in heaven. In this new place, she slowly realized that she could not any more control her body than a small infant could. She'd once heard a preacher say that from dust to dust there is a fall to match every rise. *I know I am not dead by my pain. I know where the branch creek meets the larger creek that flows into the river at the bottom of the mountain and I am walking with my father. I am a good girl and have not known a whipping for more than a week. He has not said go choose a switch from the tree.*

She knew the tree. She knew it was better to pick a stiff switch, one without any give. But not too stiff, because then it would break against her backside, and, "Franny Mae, you're in for a world of hurt now."

She was wearing her red housedress, and this woman Julie was taking it off and then bathing her. The water was not cold and not too hot. She remembered "Goldilocks and the Three Bears," and isn't it nice to have something that is just right. And isn't it nice to feel the warm washcloth against your skin, and the water, and to be lifted bodily from the water and feel the towel around your shoulders, and the hands of the young woman drying you.

The pain was worst in the middle of the night when she was alone and tried to call out and no sound came, so no one came. Then one night the worst of all, the thing she thought she had laid to rest.

Donny Lynn Prather, looking in her window.

He mocked her by standing still, watching and not watching. She could not lift her head to see the window, but she could feel him there, staring, not moving.

One evening he found a way to speak to her so she knew he was not moving his lips but was just speaking from his mind to hers. A violation he had achieved how? He was not using words but instead a liquid fear. She could feel him seeping it into her through her skin and skull. She worried it would melt her.

He was sending her a message and sending. A message he was sending but she could not know the words and what they stood for.

Sending and sending.

And then, all at once, she knew, and it was worse than the melting of her skin from her face, though that was part of what he was promising. The words she could not know because they were spoken in Spanish, so he had gone to Mexico after all. He was saying, "You thought I was a dummy, little girl, but I got something for you." He was saying it in Spanish, but she was hearing it in English. He had been taken by devils for sure. She remembered the preacher when Eleanor was a baby who came one Sunday night to the Cherry Road Baptist Church and said that these devils were all around us, standing on our shoulders, wanting to poke at us but for the blood of Jesus, and it was not that they had got to Donny Lynn Prather just now or even when he was on the run in Mexico. It was that they had got to his momma before he was even born and taken residence in his soul.

Every night he came to her window but did not show her his face by coming in the room. Just let her know he was there so she could not sleep.

She could feel a growing tightness in her chest. She spent most of her days wrung out and half-alive, slumped sideways in a La-Z-Boy chair until the woman Julie brought some couch pillows to prop her up. Like she was a rag doll with sagging flesh, discarded victim of love like the Velveteen Rabbit. Perhaps a dog would come and take her in his jaws and drag her away.

Then one night Donny Lynn came to the window with a new message. "Do you wonder where your John is?" he said but did not say. "Yes, I do," she said. They were talking this way often. They were bound up together now in such a way that neither had need of voice. "You have him, don't you," she said. "You have taken him."

There was a long silence. Then Donny Lynn Prather went away. He did not say anything. The absence of him was worse than his presence, because he was gone and he had John.

Ten days passed, or ten years. She could not be sure when Donny had found a way to reorder time. A day with the Lord, the preachers would say, is like a thousand years. But what about a day with Donny?

She could see him whipping that little boy, Roy, his little brother, in that field, curse that field, with both belts, knocking that belt buckle the shape of Kentucky into his head, and Franny was standing to one side, no, sitting, in that woman Julie's La-Z-Boy chair, slumped to one side, watching Roy's head cave in slowly, while all around her she could hear string music that sounded like heaven, and Julie saying, "Mom, it's Vivaldi, it's so beautiful, isn't it, have you heard it before?" and Roy crying out to Donny, pleading for his life, singing for it "Shoo, fly, don't bother me, for I belong to somebody" — and then Roy looking at her, saying *I'm not being no mommy.*

Then, a time of amazing quiet. She fell asleep one evening and woke the next morning. That evening she fell asleep again, and did not wake until the morning. Mornings she sometimes woke soiled by her own urine, sometimes even her own excrement. No matter. The woman Julie would come and tend to her. Bathe her, dry her, brush her hair.

She came to think of herself as a child, and Julie her mother. It was not true — she was not a child, and her mother was long gone — but then, in its own way, it was true. In her heart she was growing to love Julie.

One afternoon Julie left her in the care of another woman. She said she had to go to the store to pick up a few things. When she returned, she was holding a metal cage, and inside the cage was a green parakeet. She held it up so Franny could see it. The parakeet jumped from its perch to ring a bell near the top of the cage. "His wings have been clipped," Julie said, "but he's not any less lovely, is he, Mom?"

That evening she went to sleep and woke the next morning reeking of drying urine. She waited for Julie to come and get her, but Julie did not come. She waited for a long time. She could hear the parakeet stirring in his covered cage. The daylight from her bedroom had reached him through the white pillowcase meant to comfort him and keep him quiet through the night.

She began to worry about Julie. The Florida sun burned through the window, the heat rising enough she could notice it every few minutes. She worried the parakeet would overheat and die. Tiny birds are fragile. Little green birds.

The door opened. She heard it open, and the relief settled into her. Julie's being there.

Then a voice. But not Julie's. A man's voice, saying Julie's words. "Let's get you cleaned up, Mom."

She had been conscious, sometimes, of the presence of a man in the house. It was not her business. Julie, kind as she was, could do what she wanted. Any comfort there is in the world . . . how could any of it be bad when all we are doing is waiting to get old and die? She wanted to help that parakeet grow its wings and give it the run of the house. You couldn't set a thing like that free, because some cat would get to it, or some bigger bird.

The man leaned over her, and she did not right away recognize who he was. He was so familiar she should have known, but what in the world is easy to know when it is so hot in the room?

He reached his arms under her and picked her up. He was not gentle enough. His way of lifting her hurt her. Hurt her legs and hurt more under her armpits where he was carrying too much of her weight. Who was he? And why was he, and not Julie, moving her?

He carried her into the bathroom and sat her roughly on the toilet, then knelt at her feet. She could not hold up her weight, and she slumped to the side. She had the terrible pain in her hip. He reached up and grabbed her by the shoulders. As he leaned back she caught her first glimpse of his eyes.

It was the eyes. Something about the directness of his gaze. Even for just a moment, so direct. So familiar. It was then that she knew who it was who had come for her, after all these years.

It was Donny Lynn Prather. He had come and took John, and then he had come all those nights to scare her at her window. If he was here, what had come of John? What was he planning for her?

Donny said, "Mother, I'm going to take off your shoes and socks now, all right?" And it was not his way of talking. It was the way the younger people talked in this part of the country.

It was a matter of pride had led her to this. She had all those years thought Spanish was beyond him, but he had learned it. Now he had learned to talk like the people all around. He was like one of those lizards that could change color.

And he was calling her *mother.* She remembered the words so burned in her memory: *Open up that pretty little mouth, Mommy.* What job had he come to finish?

With the greatest force of her will, she tried to scream in protest, but no words would come. His hands were on her shoulders. His hands were so close to her throat. Then he knelt again and was strangely silent. She could hear only the small sounds of his moving.

"Your shoes, Mother," he said, and she felt him take the slippers from her feet. She wondered why if he was going to kill her did he not kill her, and then she knew he had made up a ritual to make her afraid.

She was afraid.

Then he did something to her foot. He hurt her so bad she lost her air. Her throat closed up like it sometimes did without her wanting it to.

He said, "Does it hurt, Mother?"

She tried to still herself. Her chest was burning.

He said, "Does it hurt?" What did he want from her? How could she keep from him the pleasure of letting him know her pain?

He stood, and again those fearsome eyes locked onto hers. "Mom," he said — in his mouth, the word was a curse — "does it hurt?"

Some signal, any, to make him stop. She tried to blink her eyes. She could only feel the right one, could only see out of it. She blinked twice.

"I saw that, Mom," he said. "Can you do it again? I want to be sure."

In hostage situations, give the captor what he wants. That's what they said on the evening news. She did it again, but her muscles got angry, and her eye fluttered, and she thought it might pop out at him. Any other man would feel horror, but he might find satisfaction. She did not want him to be satisfied.

He began to taunt her again. He was cruel. He said, "Well, that's something." He must have thought it was funny to see her like that, not able to move her body like she wanted. "Okay," then louder, to intimidate her, the monster: "Okay."

So she tried to blink again and was relieved that it at least stopped the fluttering. "I see it," he said. Oh, he was cruel.

Then he began his lies. "I don't want to hurt you," he said. Had he said it to John, too? "I'm going to wash you now. I'm going to do it, but not if you don't want me to. I'm going to take that sock off by unrolling it from the top, all right?"

Rape. She had been avoiding the word all her life, and now it popped up from the place he had planted it. Her body offered nothing for him. What pleasure was left in her old body? This was only violence. Only cruelty. Only the pleasures children find on their way to evil, as when they string a cat from a tree, flay it open, strip its skin, and let it die of exposure. Like they say Donny did when he was a small boy. They say, "Why, we knew then he was a bad seed." They say it, they said it, but here stands Donny, and all them dead, and still he only a little older than he was then, to judge by his talk and his eyes. He found a way in Mexico. Must have. Here he is. Here, standing over her.

He was waiting for something. She blinked one more time, to pacify him. That seemed to be what he wanted. He lowered himself again. She felt him touch her on the calf. His skin on hers. He was taking off her sock, like he said. If this was the end of her, he was going to drag it out. She was like that cat, but not kicking. Her body betrayed her.

"Mom," Donny said, "you've got a nasty sore down here. On the arch of your foot. It's bruised. It's a bad one." Then he struck her three times, just enough to hurt, on the calf. "The other one now," he said, "Mom."

Mom. Mother. He kept using the words. He was taking off her shoes and her socks now. Sometimes in the years after he had run off into the mountains and far away, she had suffered from terrible dreams — she in a canoe with Roy, paddling downstream, and suddenly the water filling with snakes, and both of them trying to beat them away with the paddles, but there were too many, snakes filling the canoe, snakes wrapping themselves around paddles, snakes wrapping themselves around limbs and chests and necks, snakes hissing, snakes opening their mouths, snakes showing their fangs, their forked tongues — and there would come a time when she realized she was asleep and dreaming, but that did nothing to make the snakes any less real. She would try to wake from those dreams. She would fight as though trying to escape from her own skin. She would fight and fight, a feeling not unlike trying to get above water to avoid drowning, and the fighting would exhaust her. She would wake alone and wet, her muscles tense, her blood rushing like whitewater rapids.

Her body, now, was not unlike her young girl's body had been in those long moments of not waking. But now she could not wake. Her body had become divorced from her. It functioned to the extent that it functioned and no more. She could not will it to do much more.

She tried to resist the urge, then, to swim upward through herself and try to escape through whatever surface it was that separated her self from her body. Like a swimmer underwater, she could see through the surface well enough to know it was there, to see the light play upon it.

He kept up his patter. "The other one now, Mom," he said.

She began to pray: *Lord, if it is Your will take me now. I've seen enough of this life. I don't want to suffer anymore. Not at his hands.* She did not believe her prayer would be answered. She had been told that faith the size of a mustard seed was enough to make heaven move. Her experience of life said that was not so.

He said, "Mom, have you noticed the shower curtains?" What did he want with the shower curtains? "They're starting to yellow, and that's the problem, I think, with translucent shower curtains, the way they yellow with time. Julie was thinking of buying some shower curtains to match the hand towels . . ." And at this she thought she might vomit. What was he threatening? *Take me, take me, what life do I have left for living? Julie, she is so kind, so kind . . .*

Now she could not hear the words he was saying, so loud was the sound of the screaming in her own head. The screams got trapped inside when she could not give them voice, and inside they reverberated as in an echo chamber, and multiplied, grew louder and louder until all that was in her seemed to be screaming, crying out as the rocks might but in anguish, not in praise.

She waited to hear the sound of water running, knew he was capable of drowning her, knew how little it would take if he lay her face-down in the water. In Rowan County she had known of at least three children drowned in less than three inches of water in nearby creeks. She had known of cats wrapped in burlap sacks and weighted down, dropped in only a bucket of water and killed that way. Donny himself had at age twelve buried a wounded dog up to his neck in sand and brought over chickens to peck at his eyes and deeper, killed him that way. There was no one way to kill a feeble creature.

Donny began to hum. The song he was humming was carnal. She could feel it in her bones. Could tell from the way he was humming it, the sharpnesses and roundnesses of notes, the way they refused to flatten out, the kind of music that was the opposite of hymns, that carried with it the mark of the silvery tongue.

She heard it, knew she was getting bound up, worried that she was giving him what he wanted. Right then she tried her best to think of things outside herself and long ago. The moment John Junior took his first steps at Connie and Millicent Pomeroy's house. They had brand-new white carpeting, made to look marbled on purpose, and Eleanor was so excited at the baby's steps, she ran into the living room carrying her cup of grape juice and spilled it on that carpet, and John said, "I'll buy you new carpet. I'll install it myself!" And he would have, gladly, but Connie said he had extra, would he just patch it, and John did, with Connie's help. She could see them, those two men, cutting a careful square of that white carpet and matching the extra just right, matching one end of the marbling pattern to the other so you couldn't tell unless you put your nose right up to that patch, and then standing back, taking such satisfaction in what they had done, with their hands, with their heads.

The memory calmed her. She could feel it, and hoped Donny could see it, hoped it sped him on his way to whatever it was he intended to do to her, then sped him ever quicker to hell. Surely someone would find her body and go looking for him. Justice was harder to escape than it used to be. They had more than dogs. They had helicopters and computers and television programs. She had watched them every Sunday night, hoping to catch a killer.

She heard the sound of the faucet turning and the water beginning to run. He was still talking, but she was refusing to listen to the words he was saying. She had survived him once before, and she would not be afraid of him now.

The phone rang. She heard him turn off the water, wondered if he would leave her to get up and answer it. Fleetingly, she heard Julie's voice, which alarmed her, because what if she was in the house? But it was the answering machine, because she heard the beep, and then some sort of wrong number, a woman talking the way one woman talks to another, but saying in the course of her yammering, "Bring me the man of God!"

Then Donny said, "Art Miller. Now there's one guy who can wait."

He had turned on the water again. He was looking at her. And then she knew. He meant to kill not just her, but others, too. She tried to pull herself together, but the fear was beginning to rise in her again. She thought of the little green parakeet, and that affected her somehow more than Art Miller. Like people used to say, "Somebody else's baby dies, you wear black to the funeral. Your dog dies, you wear black for a whole year."

That wasn't right, she'd always thought. Now she knew it didn't matter if it was right or not. Like a lot of things. It was so. It was what it was, and there was no changing the ways of people. The way of a man is righteous in his own eyes, like the preachers say. Oh, to save that little green bird.

He turned off the water. She was aware that he was staring at her with those cold eyes. She could not see those eyes, but she knew. It was just like those long nights when he waited at the windows, or those long-ago afternoons when he stalked her tree to tree. She could not hear his voice anymore and knew he was keeping it from her to prolong the silence and create an empty space in it for her fears.

Finally he spoke. "Now, Mom," he said. "After I stop the tub, okay?" As though he were asking for her consent. The sincerity of the venomous snake, its bright colored markings covered in mud. And he put his body near hers, his face near hers, so close they were almost touching, so close they were breathing in one another's air. Close like lovers, his eyes probing hers, his eyes winding their way inside her.

He said, "I'm going to give you a bath now, Momma," and surely this was her end. There was a strange light in his eyes, something stranger than the familiarity. A sadness, almost. Judas kissing Jesus, compelled by some force stronger than his own love. She could see in that moment something of love in Donny's eyes, and the sight of it, the sight of love, was more frightening than anything she had seen in her life. To know that the very face of evil was love. To know that every boundary separating every one thing from another could be wiped away in the last moments of life, which she knew these would be. The true nature of the world letting itself be known in this last hour.

Then he began to undress her. He worked his way down the front of her, button by button. He was pulling against the housedress as he went. She could feel the pull of the fabric against her back. He crouched down, and the dress went open, and his eyes, now, would be gazing upon the breasts of which she had become first ashamed then indifferent. He continued to unbutton, the waist, the lap, the knees, and then the housedress came undone and fell to her sides. He was seeing for the first time the hidden parts of her. She wondered what it meant to him and knew it must thrill him now even more than it would have when she was very young and he meant to ruin her and did.

Then he picked her up again, and she felt a burning in her chest, a great pain. He lifted her, and as he lowered her to the water, he said, "Shh, shh," and then, "Mommy, Mommy. It's all right, Mommy."

Then she began to shake. Then she felt a great pain in her chest. She had always feared she might die alone, but she was not alone.

ALICE MUNRO

Child's Play

FROM *Harper's Magazine*

I SUPPOSE THERE WAS TALK in our house, afterward.

How sad, how *awful.* (My mother.)

There should have been supervision. Where were the Counselors? (My father.)

Just think, it might have — it might have been — (My mother.)

It wasn't. Just put that idea out of your head. It wasn't. (My father.)

It is even possible that if we ever passed the yellow house my mother said, "Remember? Remember you used to be so scared of her? The poor thing."

My mother had a habit of hanging on to — even treasuring — the foibles of my distant infantile state.

Every year, when you're a child, you become a different person. Generally it's in the fall, when you reenter school, take your place in a higher grade, leave behind the muddle and lethargy of the summer vacation. That's when you register the change most sharply. Afterward you are not sure of the month or year, but the changes go on, just the same. For a long while the past drops away from you easily and, it would seem, automatically, properly. Its scenes don't vanish so much as become irrelevant. And then there's a switchback, what's been all over and done with sprouting up fresh, wanting attention, even wanting you to do something about it, though it's plain there is not on this earth a thing to be done.

Marlene and Charlene. People thought we must be twins. There was a fashion in those days for naming twins in rhyme. Bonnie and

Connie. Ronald and Donald. And then of course we — Charlene and I — had matching hats. Coolie hats, they were called, wide shallow cones of woven straw with some sort of tie or elastic under the chin. They became familiar later on in the century, from television shots of the war in Vietnam. Men on bicycles riding along a street in Saigon would be wearing them, or women walking in the road against the background of a bombed village.

It was possible at that time — I mean the time when Charlene and I were at camp — to say *coolie* without a thought of offense. Or *darkie,* or to talk about *jewing* a price down. I was in my teens, I think, before I ever related that verb to the noun.

So we had those names and those hats, and at the first roll call the Counselor — the jolly one we liked, Mavis, though we didn't like her as well as the pretty one, Pauline — pointed at us and called out, "Hey, Twins," and went on calling out other names before we had time to deny it.

Even before that we must have noticed the hats and approved of each other. Otherwise one or both of us would have pulled off those brand-new articles and been ready to shove them under our cots, declaring that our mothers had made us wear them and we hated them, and so on.

I may have approved of Charlene, but I was not sure how to make friends with her. Girls nine or ten years old — that was the general range of this crop, though there were a few a bit older — do not pick friends or pair off as easily as girls do at six or seven. I simply followed some other girls from my town — none of them my particular friends — to one of the cabins where there were some unclaimed cots, and dumped my things on top of the brown blanket. Then I heard a voice behind me say, "Could I please be next to my twin sister?"

It was Charlene, speaking to somebody I didn't know. The dormitory cabin held perhaps two dozen girls. The girl she had spoken to said, "Sure," and moved along.

Charlene had used a special voice. Ingratiating, teasing, self-mocking, and with a seductive merriment in it, like a trill of bells. It was evident right away that she had more confidence than I did. And not simply confidence that the other girl would move and not say sturdily, "I got here first." Or — if she was a roughly brought up sort of girl (and some of them were that, having their way paid by the Lions Club or the Church and not by their parents) she might have said, "Go poop your pants, I'm not moving." No. Charlene had confidence that anybody would *want* to do as she asked, not just agree to do it. With me too she had taken a chance, for could I not have said, "I don't want to be twins," and turned back to sort my things? But of course I didn't. I felt flattered, as she had expected, and I watched her dump out the contents of her suitcase with such an air of celebration that some things fell on the floor.

All I could think of to say was, "You got a tan already."

"I always tan easy," she said.

The first of our differences. We applied ourselves to learning them. She tanned, I freckled. We both had brown hair but hers was darker. Hers was wavy, mine bushy. I was half an inch taller, she had thicker wrists and ankles. Her eyes had more green in them, mine more blue. We did not grow tired of inspecting and tabulating even the moles or notable freckles on our backs, length of our second toes (mine longer than the first toe, hers shorter). Or of recounting all the illnesses or accidents that had befallen us so far, as well as the repairs or removals performed on our bodies. Both of us had our tonsils out — a usual precaution in those days — and both of us had had measles and whooping cough but not mumps. I had had an eyetooth pulled because it was growing in over my other teeth, and she had a thumbnail with an imperfect half moon because her thumb had been slammed under a window.

And once we had the peculiarities and history of our bodies in place we went on to the stories — the dramas or near-dramas or distinctions — of our families. She was the youngest and only girl in her family and I was an only child. I had an aunt who had died of polio in high school and she — Charlene — had an older brother who was in the Navy. For it was wartime, and at the campfire singsong we would choose "There'll Always Be an England" and "Hearts of Oak," and "Rule Britannia," and sometimes "The Maple Leaf Forever." Bombing raids and battles and sinking ships were the constant, though distant, backdrop of our lives.

And once in a while there was a near strike, frightening but solemn and exhilarating, as when a boy from our town or our street would be killed, and the house where he had lived without having any special wreath or black drapery on it seemed nevertheless to have a special weight inside it, a destiny fulfilled and dragging it down. Though there was nothing special inside it at all, maybe just a car that didn't belong there parked at the curb, showing that some relatives or a minister had come to sit with the bereaved family.

One of the camp Counselors had lost her fiancé in the war and wore his watch — we believed it was his watch — pinned to her blouse. We would like to have felt for her a mournful interest and concern, but she was sharp-voiced and bossy and she even had an unpleasant name. Arva.

The other backdrop of our lives, which was supposed to be emphasized at camp, was religion. But since the United Church of Canada was officially in charge there was not so much harping on that subject as there would have been with the Baptists or the Bible Christians, or so much formal acknowledgment as the Roman Catholics or even the Anglicans would have provided. Most of us had parents who belonged to the United Church (though some of the girls who were having their way paid for them might not have belonged to any church at all), and being used to its hearty secular style, we did not even realize that we were getting off easily with just evening prayers and grace sung at meals and the half-hour special talk — it was called a chat — after breakfast. Even the Chat was relatively free of references to God or Jesus and was more about honesty and loving-kindness and clean thoughts in our daily lives, and promising never to drink or smoke when we grew up. Nobody had any objection to this sort of thing or tried to get out of attending, because it was what we were used to and because it was pleasant to sit on the beach in the warming sun and a little too cold yet for us to long to jump into the water.

Grownup women do the same sort of thing that Charlene and I did. Not the counting the moles on each other's backs and comparing toe lengths, maybe. But when they meet and feel a particular sympathy with each other they also feel a need to set out the important information, the big events whether public or secret, and then go ahead to fill in all the blanks between. If they feel this warmth and eagerness it is quite impossible for them to bore each other. They will laugh at the very triviality and silliness of what they're telling, or at the revelation of some appalling selfishness, deception, meanness, sheer badness. There has to be great trust of course, but that trust can be established at once, in an instant.

I've observed this. It's supposed to have begun in those long periods of sitting around the campfire stirring the manioc porridge or whatever, while the men were out in the bush deprived of conversation because it would warn off the wild animals. (I am an anthropologist by training, though a rather slack one.) I've observed but never taken part in these female exchanges. Not truly. Sometimes I've pretended because it seemed to be required, but the woman I was supposed to be making friends with always got wind of my pretense and became confused and cautious.

As a rule, I've felt less wary with men. They don't expect such transactions and are seldom really interested.

This intimacy I'm talking about — with women — is not erotic, or pre-erotic. I've experienced that as well, before puberty. Then too there would be confidences, probably lies, maybe leading to games. A certain hot temporary excitement, with or without genital teasing. Followed by ill-feeling, denial, disgust.

Charlene did tell me about her brother, but with true repugnance. This was the brother now in the Navy. She went into his room looking for her cat and there he was doing it to his girlfriend. They never knew she saw them.

She said they slapped, as he went up and down.

You mean they slapped on the bed, I said.

No, she said. His thing slapped when it was going in and out. It was sickening.

And his bare white bum had pimples on it. Sickening.

I told her about Verna.

Up until the time I was seven years old my parents had lived in what was called a double house. The word *duplex* was perhaps not in use at that time, and anyway the house was not evenly divided. Verna's grandmother rented the rooms at the back and we rented the rooms at the front. The house was tall and bare and ugly, painted yellow. The town we lived in was too small to have residential divisions that amounted to anything, but I suppose that as far as there were divisions, that house was right on the boundary between decent and fairly dilapidated. I am speaking of the way things were just before the Second World War, at the end of the Depression. (That word, I believe, was unknown to us.)

My father, being a teacher, had a regular job but little money. The street petered out beyond us between the houses of those who had neither. Verna's grandmother must have had a little money because she spoke contemptuously of people who were On Relief. I believe my mother argued with her, unsuccessfully, that it was Not Their Fault. The two women were not particular friends, but they were cordial about clothesline arrangements.

The grandmother's name was Mrs. Home. A man came to see her occasionally. My mother spoke of him as Mrs. Home's friend.

You are not to speak to Mrs. Home's friend.

In fact I was not even allowed to play outside when he came, so there was not much chance of my speaking to him. I don't even remember what he looked like, though I remember his car, which was dark blue, a Ford V-8. I took a special interest in cars, probably because we didn't have one.

Then Verna came.

Mrs. Home spoke of her as her granddaughter and there is no reason to suppose that not to be true, but there was never any sign of a connecting generation. I don't know if Mrs. Home went away and came back with her, or if she was delivered by the friend with the V-8. She appeared in the summer before I was to start school. I can't remember her telling me her name — she was not communicative in the ordinary way and I don't believe I would have asked her. From the very beginning I had an aversion to her unlike anything I had felt up to that time for any other person. I said that I hated her, and my mother said, How can you, what has she ever done to you?

The poor thing.

Children use that word *hate* to mean various things. It may mean that they are frightened. Not that they feel in danger of being attacked — the way I did, for instance, of certain big boys on bicycles who liked to cut in front of you, yelling fearsomely, as you walked on the sidewalk. It is not physical harm that is feared — or that I feared in Verna's case — so much as some spell, or dark intention. It is a feeling you can have when you are very young even about certain house faces, or tree trunks, or very much about moldy cellars or deep closets.

She was a good deal taller than I was and I don't know how much older — two years, three years? She was skinny, indeed so narrowly built and with such a small head that she made me think of a snake. Fine black hair lay flat on this head, and fell over her forehead. The skin of her face seemed as dull to me as the flap of our old canvas tent, and her cheeks puffed out the way the flap of that tent puffed in a wind. Her eyes were always squinting.

But I believe there was nothing remarkably unpleasant about her looks, as other people saw her. Indeed my mother spoke of her as pretty, or almost pretty (as in, *isn't it too bad, she could be pretty*). Nothing to object to either, as far as my mother could see, in her behavior. *She is young for her age.* A roundabout and inadequate way of saying that Verna had not learned to read or write or skip or play ball, and that her voice was hoarse and unmodulated, her words oddly separated, as if they were chunks of language caught in her throat.

Her way of interfering with me, spoiling my solitary games, was that of an older not a younger girl. But of an older girl who had no skill or rights, nothing but a strenuous determination and an inability to understand that she wasn't wanted.

Children of course are monstrously conventional, repelled at once by whatever is off-center, out-of-whack, unmanageable. And being an only child I had been coddled a good deal (also scolded). I was awkward, precocious, timid, full of my private rituals and aversions. I hated even the celluloid barrette that kept slipping out of Verna's hair, and the peppermints with red or green stripes on them that she kept offering to me. In fact she did more than offer — she would try to catch me and push these candies into my mouth, chuckling all the time in her disconnected way. I dislike peppermint flavoring to this day. And the name Verna — I dislike that. It doesn't sound like spring to me, or like green grass or garlands of flowers or girls in flimsy dresses. It sounds more like a trail of obstinate peppermint, green slime.

I didn't believe my mother really liked Verna either. But because of some hypocrisy in her nature, as I saw it, because of a decision she had made, as it seemed, to spite me, she pretended to be sorry for her. She told me to be kind. At first she said that Verna would not be staying long and at the end of the summer holidays would go back to wherever she had been before. Then, when it became clear that there was nowhere for Verna to go back to, the placating message was that we ourselves would be moving soon. I had only to be kind for a little while longer. (As a matter of fact it was a whole year before we moved.) Finally, out of patience, she said that I was a disappointment to her and that she would never have thought I had so mean a nature.

"How can you blame a person for the way she was born? How is it her fault?"

That made no sense to me. If I had been more skilled at arguing I might have said that I didn't blame Verna, I just did not want her to come near me. But I certainly did blame her. I did not question that it was somehow her fault. And in this, whatever my mother might say, I was in tune to some degree with an unspoken verdict of the time and place I lived in. Even grownups smiled in a certain way, there was some irrepressible gratification and taken-for-granted superiority that I could see, in the way they mentioned people who were *simple*, or *a few bricks short of a load*. And I believed my mother must be really like this, underneath.

I started school. Verna started school. She was put into a special class in a special building in a corner of the school grounds. This was actually the original school building in the town, but nobody had any time for local history then, and a few years later it was pulled down. There was a fenced-off corner in which pupils housed in that building spent recess. They went to school a half hour later than we did in the morning and got out a half hour earlier in the afternoon. Nobody was supposed to harass them at recess, but since they usually hung on the fence watching whatever went on in the regular school grounds there would be occasions when there was a rush, a whooping and brandishing of sticks, to scare them. I never went near that corner, hardly ever saw Verna. It was at home I still had to deal with her.

First she would stand at the corner of the yellow house, watching me, and I would pretend that I didn't know she was there. Then she would wander into the front yard, taking up a position on the front steps of the part of the house that was mine. If I wanted to go inside to the bathroom, or because I was cold, I would have to go so close as to touch her and to risk her touching me.

She could stay in one place longer than anybody I ever knew, staring at just one thing. Usually me.

I had a swing hung from a maple tree, so that I either faced the house or the street. That is, I either had to face her or to know that she was staring at my back, and might come up to give me a push.

After a while she would decide to do that. She always pushed me crooked, but that was not the worst thing. The worst was that her fingers had pressed my back. Through my coat, through my other clothing, her fingers like so many cold snouts.

Another activity of mine was to build a leaf house. That is, I raked up and carried armloads of leaves fallen from the maple tree that held the swing, and I dumped and arranged these leaves into a house plan. Here was the living room, here was the kitchen, here was a big soft pile for the bed in the bedroom, and so on. I had not invented this occupation — leaf houses of a more expansive sort were laid out, and even in a way furnished, every recess in the girls' playground at school, until the janitor finally raked up all the leaves and burned them.

At first Verna just watched what I was doing, with her squinty-eyed expression of what seemed to me superior (how could she think herself superior?) puzzlement. Then the time came when she moved closer, lifted an armful of leaves that dripped all over because of her uncertainty or clumsiness. And these came not from the pile of spare leaves but from the very wall of my house. She picked them up and carried them a short distance and let them fall — dumped them, in the middle of one of my tidy rooms.

I yelled at her to stop, but she bent to pick up her scattered load again, and was unable to hang on to them, so she just flung them about and when they were all on the ground began to kick them foolishly here and there. I was still yelling at her to stop, but this had no effect, or else she took it for encouragement. So I lowered my head and ran at her and bunted her in the stomach. I was not wearing a cap, so the hairs of my head came in contact with the woolly coat or jacket she had on, and it seemed to me that I had actually touched bristling hairs on the skin of a gross hard belly. I ran hollering with complaint up the steps of the house, and when my mother heard the story she further maddened me by saying, "She only wants to play. She doesn't know how to *play*."

By the next fall we were in the bungalow and I never had to go past the yellow house that reminded me so much of Verna, as if it had positively taken on her narrow slyness, her threatening squint. The yellow paint seemed to be the very color of insult, and the front door, being off-center, added a touch of deformity. The bungalow was only three blocks away from that house, close to the school. But my idea of the town's size and complexity was still such that it seemed I was escaping Verna altogether. I realized that this was not true, not altogether true, when a schoolmate and I came face-to-face with her one day on the main street. We must have been sent on some errand by one of our mothers. I did not look up but I believed I heard a chuckle of greeting or recognition as we passed.

The other girl said a horrifying thing to me.

She said, "I used to think that was your sister."

"What?"

"Well I knew you lived in the same house, so I thought you must be related. Like cousins, anyway. Aren't you? Cousins?"

"No."

The old building where the Special Classes had been held was condemned, and its pupils were transferred to the Bible Chapel, now rented on weekdays by the town. The Bible Chapel happened to be across the street and around a corner from the bungalow where my mother and father and I now lived. There were a couple of ways that Verna could have walked to school but the way she chose was past our house. And our house was only a few feet from the sidewalk, so this meant that her shadow could practically fall across our steps. If she wished she could kick pebbles onto our grass, and unless we kept the blinds down she could peer into our hall and front room.

The hours of the Special Classes had been changed to coincide with ordinary school hours, at least in the morning — they still went home earlier in the afternoon. Once they were in the Bible Chapel it must have been felt that there was no need to keep them free of the rest of us on the way to school. This meant, now, that I had a chance of running into Verna on the sidewalk. I would always look in the direction from which she might be coming, and if I saw her I would duck back into the house with the excuse that I had forgotten something, or that one of my shoes was rubbing my heel and needed a plaster, or a ribbon was coming loose on my hair. I would never have been so foolish now as to mention Verna and hear my mother say, "What's the problem, what are you afraid of, do you think she's going to eat you?"

What was the problem? Contamination, infection? Verna was decently clean and healthy. And it was hardly likely that she was going to attack and pummel me or pull out my hair. But only adults would be so stupid as to believe she had no power. A power, moreover, that was specifically directed at me. I was the one she had her eye on. Or so I believed. As if we had an understanding between us that could not be described and was not to be disposed of. Something that clings, in the way of love, though on my side it felt like hate.

When I told Charlene about her we had got into the deeper reaches of our conversation — that conversation that seems to have been broken only when we swam or slept. Verna was not so solid an offering, not so vividly repulsive as Charlene's brother's pimpled bum, and I remember saying that she was awful in a way that I could not describe. But then I did describe her, and my feelings about her, and I must have done not too bad a job, because one day toward the end of our two-week stay at camp Charlene came rushing into the dining hall at midday, her face lit up with horror and strange delight.

"She's here. She's here. That girl. That awful girl. Verna. She's *here.*"

Lunch was over. We were in the process of tidying up, putting our plates and mugs on the kitchen shelf to be grabbed away and washed by the girls on kitchen duty that day. Then we would line up to go to the Tuck Shop, which opened every day at one o'clock. Charlene had just run back to the dormitory to get some money. Being rich, with a father who was an undertaker, she was rather careless, keeping money in her pillowcase. Except when swimming I always had mine on my person. All of us who could in any way afford to went to the Tuck Shop after lunch, to get something to take away the taste of the desserts we hated but always tried, just to see if they were as disgusting as we expected. Tapioca pudding, mushy baked apples, slimy custard.

Verna? How could Verna be here?

This must have been a Friday. Two more days at camp, two more days to go. And it turned out that a contingent of Specials — here too they were called Specials — had been brought in to enjoy with us the final weekend. Not many of them — maybe twenty altogether — and not all from my town but from other towns nearby. In fact as Charlene was trying to get the news through to me a whistle was being blown, and Counselor Arva had jumped up on a bench to address us.

She said that she knew we would all do our best to make these visitors — these new campers — welcome, and that they had brought their own tents and their own Counselor with them. But they would eat and swim and play games and attend the Morning Chat with the rest of us. She was sure, she said, with that familiar warning or upbraiding note in her voice, that we would all treat this as an opportunity to make new friends.

It took some time to get the tents up and these newcomers and their possessions settled. Some apparently took no interest and wandered off and had to be yelled at and fetched back. Since it was our free time, or rest time, we got our chocolate bars or licorice whips or sponge toffee from the Tuck Shop and went to lie on our bunks and enjoy them.

Charlene kept saying, "Imagine. Imagine. She's here. I can't believe it. Do you think she followed you?"

"Probably," I said.

"Do you think I can always hide you like that?"

When we were in the Tuck Shop line I had ducked my head and made Charlene get between me and the Specials as they were being herded by. I had taken one peek and recognized Verna from behind. Her drooping snaky head.

"We should think of some way to disguise you."

From what I had said, Charlene seemed to have got the idea that Verna had actively harassed me. And I believed that was true, except that the harassment had been more subtle, more secret, than I had been able to describe. Now I let Charlene think as she liked because it was more exciting that way.

Verna did not spot me immediately, because of the elaborate dodges Charlene and I kept making, and perhaps because she was rather dazed, as most of the Specials appeared to be, trying to figure out what they were doing here. They were soon taken off to their own swimming class, at the far end of the beach.

At the supper table they were marched in while we sang.

The more we get together, together, together,
The more we get together,
The happier we'll be.

They were then deliberately separated, and distributed among the rest of us. They all wore name tags. Across from me there was one named Mary Ellen something, not from my town. But I had hardly time to be glad of that when I saw Verna at the next table, taller than those around her but thank God facing the same way I was so she could not see me during the meal.

She was the tallest of them, and yet not so tall, not so notable a presence, as I remembered her. The reason was probably that I had had a growing spurt during the last year, while she had perhaps stopped her growing altogether.

After the meal, when we stood up and collected our dishes, I kept my head bowed, I never looked in her direction, and yet I knew when her eyes rested on me, when she recognized me, when she smiled her sagging little smile or made that odd chuckle in her throat.

"She's seen you," said Charlene. "Don't look. Don't look. I'll get between you and her. Move. Keep moving."

"Is she coming this way?"

"No. She's just standing there. She's just looking at you."

"Smiling?"

"Sort of."

"I can't look at her. I'd be sick."

How much did she persecute me in the remaining day and a half? Charlene and I used that word constantly, though in fact Verna never got near us. *Persecute.* It had an adult, legal sound. We were always on the lookout, as if we were being stalked, or I was. We tried to keep track of Verna's whereabouts, and Charlene reported on her attitude or expression. I did risk looking at her a couple of times, when Charlene had said, "Okay. She won't notice now."

At those times Verna appeared slightly cast down, or sullen, or bewildered, as if, like most of the Specials, she had been set adrift and did not completely understand where she was or what she was doing there. Some of them had caused a commotion by wandering away into the pine and cedar and poplar woods on the bluff behind the beach, or along the sandy road that led to the highway. After that a meeting was called, and we were all asked to watch out for our new friends, who were not so familiar with the place as we were. Charlene poked me in the ribs at that. She of course was not aware of any change, any falling away of confidence or even a diminishing of physical size in this Verna, and she continually reported on her sly and evil expression, her look of menace. And maybe she was right — maybe Verna saw in Charlene, this new friend or bodyguard of mine, this stranger, some sign of how everything was changed and uncertain here, and that made her scowl, though I didn't see it.

"You never told me about her hands," said Charlene.

"What about them?"

"She's got the longest fingers I have ever seen. She could just twist them round your neck and strangle you. She could. Wouldn't it be awful to be in a tent with her at night?"

I said that it would be. Awful.

There was a change, that last weekend, a whole different feeling in the camp. Nothing drastic. The meals were announced by the dining room gong at the regular times, and the food served did not improve or deteriorate. Rest time arrived, game time and swimming time. The Tuck Shop operated as usual and we were drawn together as always for the Chat. But there was an air of growing restlessness and inattention. You could detect it even in the Counselors, who might not have the same reprimands or words of encouragement on the tip of their tongues and would look at you for a second as if recalling what it was they usually said. And all this seemed to have begun with the arrival of the Specials. Their presence had changed the camp. There had been a real camp before, with all its rules and deprivations and enjoyments set up, as inevitable as school or any part of a child's life, and then it had begun to crumple at the edges, to reveal itself as something provisional. Play-acting.

Was it because we could look at the Specials and think that if they could be campers, then there was no such thing as real campers? Partly it was that. But it was partly that the time was coming very soon when all this would be over, the routines would be broken up and we would be fetched by our parents to resume our old lives, and the Counselors would go back to being ordinary people, not even teachers. We were living in a stage set about to be dismantled, and with it all the friendships, enmities, rivalries that had flourished in the last two weeks. Who could believe it had been only two weeks?

Nobody knew how to speak of this, but a lassitude spread among us, a bored ill-temper, and even the weather reflected this feeling.

It was probably not true that every day during the past two weeks had been hot and sunny, but most of us would certainly go away with that impression. And now, on Sunday morning, there was a change. While we were having the Outdoor Devotions (that was what we had on Sundays instead of the Chat) the clouds darkened. There was no change in temperature — if anything, the heat of the day increased, but there was in the air what some people called the smell of a storm. And yet such stillness. The Counselors, and even the Minister who drove out on Sundays from the nearest town, looked up occasionally and warily at the sky.

A few drops did fall, but no more. The service came to its end and no storm had broken. The clouds grew somewhat lighter, not so much as to promise sunshine but enough so that our last swim would not have to be canceled. After that there would be no lunch — the kitchen had been closed down after breakfast. The shutters on the Tuck Shop would not be opened. Our parents would begin arriving shortly after noon to take us home, and the bus would come for the Specials. Most of our things were already packed, the sheets were stripped and the rough brown blankets, which always felt clammy, were folded across the foot of each cot. Even when it was full of us, chattering and changing into our bathing suits, the inside of the dormitory cabin revealed itself as makeshift and gloomy.

It was the same with the beach. There appeared to be less sand than usual, more stones. And what sand there was seemed gray. The water looked as if it might be cold though in fact it was quite warm. Nevertheless our enthusiasm for swimming had waned and most of us were wading about aimlessly. The Swimming Counselors — Pauline and the middle-aged woman in charge of the Specials — had to clap their hands at us.

"Hurry up, what are you waiting for? Last chance this summer."

There were good swimmers among us who usually struck out at once for the raft. And all who were even passable swimmers — that included Charlene and me — were supposed to swim out to the raft at least once and turn around and swim back, in order to prove that we could swim at least a couple of yards in water over our heads. Pauline would usually swim out there right away, and stay in the deeper water, to watch out for anybody who got into trouble and also to make sure that everybody who was supposed to do the swim had done it. On this day, however, fewer swimmers than usual seemed to be doing as they were supposed to, and Pauline herself after her first cries of encouragement or exasperation was just bobbing around the raft laughing with and teasing the faithful ones who had made their way out there. Most of us were still paddling around in the shallows, swimming a few feet or yards, then standing on the bottom and splashing each other or turning over and doing the dead man's float, as if swimming was something hardly anybody could be bothered with anymore. The woman in charge of the Specials was standing where the water came barely up to her knees — most of the Specials themselves went no farther than where the water came up to *their* knees — and the top part of her flowered skirted bathing suit had not even got wet. She was bending over and making little hand-splashes at her charges, laughing and telling them *isn't this fun.*

The water Charlene and I were in was probably up to our chests and no more. We were in the ranks of the silly swimmers, doing the dead man's float, and flopping about backstroking or breast stroking, with nobody telling us to stop fooling around. We were trying to see how long we could keep our eyes open under water, we were sneaking up and jumping on each other's back. All around us were plenty of others yelling and screeching with laughter as they did the same things.

During this swim some parents or collectors of campers had arrived early, and let it be known they had no time to waste, so the campers who belonged to them were being summoned from the water. This made for some extra calling and confusion.

"Look. Look," said Charlene. Or sputtered, in fact, because I had pushed her underwater and she had just come up soaked and spitting. I looked, and there was Verna making her way toward us, wearing a pale blue rubber bathing cap, slapping at the water with her long hands and smiling, as if her rights over me had suddenly been restored.

I have not kept up with Charlene. I don't even remember how we said goodbye. If we said goodbye. I have a notion that both sets of parents arrived at around the same time and that we scrambled into separate cars and gave ourselves over — what else could we do? — to our old lives. Charlene's parents would certainly have had a car not so shabby and noisy and unreliable as the one my parents now owned, but even if that had not been so we would never have thought of making the two sets of relatives acquainted with each other. Everybody, and we ourselves, would have been in a hurry to get off, to leave behind the pockets of uproar about lost property or who had or had not met their relatives or boarded the bus.

By chance, years later, I saw her wedding picture. This was at a time when wedding pictures were still published in the newspapers, not just in small towns but in the city papers as well. I saw it in a Toronto paper I was looking through while I waited for a friend in a café on Bloor Street.

The wedding had taken place in Guelph. The groom was a native of Toronto and a graduate of Osgoode Hall. He was quite tall — or else Charlene had turned out to be quite short. She barely came up to his shoulder, even with her hair done up in the dense, polished helmet-style of the day. The hair made her face seem squashed and insignificant, but I got the impression her eyes were outlined heavily, Cleopatra fashion, her lips pale. This sounds grotesque, but it was certainly the look admired at the time. All that reminded me of her child self was the little humorous bump of her chin.

She — the bride, it said — had graduated from St. Hilda's College, in Toronto.

So she must have been here in Toronto, going to St. Hilda's, while I was in the same city, going to University College. We had been walking around perhaps at the same time and on some of the same streets or paths on the campus. And never met. I did not think that she would have seen me and avoided speaking to me. I would not have avoided speaking to her. Of course I would have considered myself a more serious student, once I discovered she was going to St. Hilda's. My friends and I regarded St. Hilda's as a Ladies College.

Now I was a graduate student in anthropology. I had decided never to get married, though I did not rule out having lovers. I wore my hair long and straight — my friends and I were anticipating the style of the hippies. My memories of childhood were much more distant and faded and unimportant than they seem today.

I could have written to Charlene, in care of her parents, whose

Guelph address had been published in the paper. But I didn't do so. I would have thought it the height of hypocrisy to congratulate any woman on the occasion of her marriage.

But she wrote to me, perhaps fifteen years later. She wrote in care of my publishers.

"My old pal Marlene," she wrote. "How excited and happy I was to see your name in *Maclean's* magazine. And how dazzled I am to think you have written a book. I have not picked it up yet because we have been away on holidays but I mean to do so — and read it too — as soon as I can. I was just going through the magazines that had accumulated in our absence and there I saw the striking picture of you and the interesting review. And I thought that I must write and congratulate you.

"Perhaps you are married but use your maiden name to write under? Perhaps you have a family? Do write and tell me all about yourself. Sadly, I am childless, but I keep busy with volunteer work, gardening, and sailing with Kit (my husband). There always seems to be plenty to do. I am presently serving on the Library Board and will twist their arms if they have not already ordered your book.

"Congratulations again. I must say I was surprised but not entirely because I always suspected you might do something special."

I did not get in touch with her at that time either. There seemed to be no point to it. At first I took no notice of the word *special* right at the end but it gave me a small jolt when I thought of it later. However, I told myself, and still believe, that she meant nothing by it.

The book that she referred to was one that had grown out of a thesis I had been discouraged from writing. I went ahead and wrote another thesis but went back to the earlier one as a sort of hobby project when I had time. I have collaborated on a couple of books since then, as was duly expected of me, but that book I did on my own is the only one that got me a small flurry of attention in the outside world (and needless to say some disapproval from colleagues). It is out of print now. It was called *Imbeciles and Idols* — a title I would never get away with today and that even then made my publishers nervous, though it was admitted to be catchy.

What I was trying to explore was the attitude of people in various cultures — one does not dare say the word *primitive* to describe such cultures — the attitude toward people who are mentally or physically unique. The words *deficient, handicapped, retarded,* being of course also consigned to the dustbin and probably for good reason — not simply because such words may indicate a superior attitude and habitual unkindness but because they are not truly descriptive. Those words push aside a good deal that is remarkable, even awesome — another word to go by the boards — or at any rate peculiarly powerful, in such people. And what was interesting was to discover a certain amount of veneration as well as persecution, and the ascribing — not entirely inaccurately — of quite a range of abilities, seen as sacred, magical, dangerous, or valuable. I did the best I could with historical as well as contemporary research and took into account poetry and fiction and of course religious custom. Naturally I was criticized in my profession for being too literary and for getting all my information out of books, but I could not run around the world then. I had not been able to get a grant.

Of course I could see a connection, a connection that I thought it just possible Charlene might get to see, too. It's strange how distant and unimportant that seemed, only a starting point. As anything in childhood appeared to me then. Because of the journey I had made since, the achievement of adulthood. Safety.

Maiden name, Charlene had written. That was an expression I had not heard for quite a while. It is next door to *maiden lady,* which sounds so chaste and sad. And remarkably inappropriate in my case. Even when I looked at Charlene's wedding picture I was not a virgin — though I don't suppose she was either. Not that I have had a swarm of lovers — or would even want to call most of them *lovers.* Like most women in my age group who have not lived in a monogamous marriage, I know the number. Sixteen. I'm sure that for many younger women that total would have been reached before they were out of their twenties or possibly out of their teens. (When I got Charlene's letter, of course, the total would have been less. I cannot — this is true — I cannot be bothered getting that straight now.) Three of them were important and all three of those were in the chronological first half dozen of the count. What I mean by "important" is that with those three — no, only two, the third meaning a great deal more to me than I to him — with those two, then, the times would come when you want to split open, surrender far more than your body, dump your whole life into one basket with his. I kept myself from doing so, but just barely.

Not long ago I got another letter. This was forwarded from the college where I taught before I retired. I found it waiting when I returned from a trip to Patagonia. (I have become a hardy traveler.) It was over a month old.

A typed letter — a fact for which the writer immediately apologized.

"My handwriting is lamentable," he wrote, and went on to introduce himself as the husband of "your old childhood buddy, Charlene." He said that he was sorry, very sorry, to send me bad news. Charlene was in Princess Margaret Hospital in Toronto. Her cancer had begun in the lungs and spread to the liver. She had, regrettably, been a lifelong smoker. She had only a short time left to live. She had not spoken of me very often but when she did, over the years, it was always with delight in my remarkable accomplishments. He knew how much she valued me and now at the end of her life she seemed very keen to see me. She had asked him to get hold of me.

Well she is probably dead by now, I thought.

But if she was — this is how I worked things out — if she was, I would run no risk in going to the hospital and inquiring. Then my conscience or whatever you wanted to call it would be clear. I could write him a note saying that unfortunately I had been away, but had come as soon as I could.

No. Better not a note. He might show up in my life, thanking me. The word *buddy* made me uncomfortable. So in a different way did *remarkable accomplishments.*

Princess Margaret Hospital is only a few blocks away from my apartment building. On a sunny spring day I walked over there. I don't know why I didn't just phone. Perhaps I wanted to think I'd made as much effort as I could.

At the main desk I discovered that Charlene was still alive. When asked if I wanted to see her I could hardly say no.

I went up in the elevator still thinking that I might be able to turn away, before I found the nurses' station on her floor. Or that I might make a simple U-turn, taking the next elevator down. The receptionist at the main desk downstairs would never notice my leaving. As a matter of fact she would not have noticed my leaving the moment she had turned her attention to the next person in line, and even if she had noticed, what would it have mattered?

I would have been ashamed, I suppose. Not ashamed at my lack of feeling so much as at my lack of fortitude.

I stopped at the nurses' station and was given the number of the room.

It was a private room, quite a small room, with no impressive apparatus or flowers or balloons. At first I could not see Charlene. A nurse was bending over the bed in which there seemed to be a mound of bedclothes but no visible person. The enlarged liver, I thought, and wished I had run while I could.

The nurse straightened up, turned, and smiled at me. She was a plump brown woman who spoke in a soft beguiling voice that might have meant she came from the West Indies.

"You are the Marlin," she said.

Something in the word seemed to delight her.

"She was so wanting for you to come. You can come closer."

I obeyed, and looked down at a bloated body and a sharp ruined face, a chicken's neck for which the hospital gown was a mile too wide. A frizz of hair — still brown — about a quarter of an inch long on her scalp. No sign of Charlene.

I had seen the faces of dying people before. The faces of my mother and father, even the face of the man I had been afraid to love. I was not surprised.

"She is sleeping now," said the nurse. "She was so hoping you would come."

"She's not unconscious?"

"No. But she sleeps."

Yes there was, I saw it now, there was a sign of Charlene. What was it? Maybe a twitch, that confident playful tucking away of a corner of her mouth.

The nurse was speaking to me in her soft happy voice. "I don't know if she would recognize you," she said. "But she hoped you would come. There is something for you."

"Will she wake up?"

A shrug. "We have to give her injections often for the pain."

She was opening the bedside table.

"Here. This. She told me to give it to you if it was too late for her. She did not want her husband to give it. Now you are here, she would be glad."

A sealed envelope with my name on it, printed in shaky capital letters.

"Not her husband," the nurse said, with a twinkle, then a broadening smile. Did she scent something illicit, a women's secret, an old love?

"Come back tomorrow," she said. "Who knows? I will tell her if it is possible."

I read the note as soon as I got down to the lobby. Charlene had managed to write in an almost normal script, not wildly as in the sprawling letters on the envelope. Of course she might have written the note first and put it in the envelope, then sealed the envelope and put it by, thinking she would get to hand it to me herself. Only later would she see a need to put my name on it.

Marlene. I am writing this in case I get too far gone to speak. Please do what I ask you. Please go to Guelph and go to the church and ask for Father Hofstrader. Church of Our Lady Immaculate. Must be personal they may open his mail. Father Hofstrader. This I cannot ask C and do not want him ever to know. Father H knows and I have asked him and he says it is possible to save me. Only I left so late. Marlene please do this bless you. Nothing about you.

C. That must be her husband. He doesn't know. Of course he doesn't.

Father Hofstrader.

Nothing about me.

I was free to crumple this up and throw it away once I got out into the street. And so I did, I threw the envelope away and let the wind sweep it into the gutter on University Avenue. Then I realized the note was not in the envelope, it was still in my pocket.

I would never go to the hospital again.

Kit was her husband's name. Now I remembered. They went sailing. Christoper. Kit.

When I got back to my apartment building I found myself taking the elevator down to the garage, not up to my apartment. Dressed just as I was, I got into my car and drove out onto the street, and began to head toward the Gardiner Expressway.

The Gardiner Expressway, Highway 427, Highway 401. It was rush hour now, a bad time to get out of the city. I hate this sort of driving, I don't do it often enough to be confident. There was under half a tank of gas, and what was more, I had to go to the bathroom. Around Milton, I thought, I could pull off the highway and fill up on gas and use the toilet and reconsider. At present I could do nothing but what I was doing, heading north, then heading west.

I didn't get off. I passed the Mississauga exit and the Milton exit. I saw a highway sign telling me how many kilometers to Guelph, and I translated that roughly into miles in my head, as I always have to do, and I figured the gas would hold out. The excuse I made to myself for not stopping was that the sun would be getting lower and more troublesome, now that we were leaving the faint haze that lies over the city even on the finest day.

At the first stop after I took the Guelph turnoff I got out and walked to the ladies' washroom with stiff trembling legs. Afterward I filled the tank with gas and asked, when I paid, for directions to the church. The directions were not very clear, but I was told that it was on a big hill and I could find it from anywhere in the heart of town.

Of course that was not true, though I could see it from almost anywhere. A collection of delicate spires rising from four fine towers. A beautiful building where I had expected only a grand one. It was grand, too, of course, a grand dominating church for such a relatively small city.

Could that have been where Charlene was married?

No. Of course not. She had been sent to a United Church camp, and there were no Catholic girls at that camp though there was quite a variety of Protestants. And then there was the business about C not knowing.

She might have converted secretly. Since.

I found my way in time to the church parking lot, and sat there wondering what I should do. I was wearing slacks and a jacket. My idea of what was required in a Catholic church were so antiquated that I was not even sure if my outfit would be all right. I tried to recall visits to great churches in Europe. Something about the arms being covered? Headscarves, skirts?

What a bright high silence there was up on this hill. April, not a leaf out yet on the trees, but the sun after all was still well up in the sky. There was one low bank of snow as gray as the paving in the church lot.

The jacket I had on was too light for evening wear, or maybe it was colder here, the wind stronger, than in Toronto.

The building might well be locked, at this time, locked and empty.

The grand front doors appeared to be so. I did not even bother to climb the steps to try them, because I decided to follow a couple of old women — old like me — who had just come up the long flight from the street and who bypassed those steps entirely, heading around to an easier entrance at the side of the building.

There were more people inside, maybe two or three dozen people, but there wasn't a sense that they were gathered for a service. They were scattered here and there in the pews, some kneeling and some chatting. The women ahead of me dipped their hands in a marble font without looking at what they were doing and said hello — hardly lowering their voices — to a man who was setting out baskets on a table.

"It looks a lot warmer out than it is," said one of them, and the man said the wind would bite your nose off.

I recognized the confessionals. Like separate small cottages or large playhouses in a Gothic style, with a lot of dark wooden carving, dark brown curtains. Elsewhere all was glowing, dazzling. The high curved ceiling most celestially blue, the lower curves of the ceiling — those that joined the upright walls — decorated with holy images on gold-painted medallions. Stained-glass windows hit by the sun at this time of day were turned into columns of jewels. I made my way discreetly down one aisle, trying to get a look at the altar, but the chancel, being in the western wall, was too bright for me to look into. Above the windows, though, I saw that there were painted angels. Flocks of angels, all fresh and gauzy and pure as light.

It was a most insistent place but nobody seemed to be overwhelmed by all the insistence. The chatting ladies kept chatting softly but not in whispers. And other people, after some businesslike nodding and crossing, knelt down and went about their business.

As I ought to be going about mine. I looked around for a priest but there was not one in sight. Priests as well as other people must have a working day. They must drive home and go into their living rooms or offices or dens and turn on the television and loosen their collars. Fetch a drink and wonder if they were going to get anything decent for supper. When they did come into the church they would come officially. In their vestments ready to perform some ceremony. Mass.

Or to hear confessions. But then you would never know when they were there. Didn't they enter and leave their grilled stalls by a private door?

I would have to ask somebody. The man who had distributed the baskets seemed to be here for reasons that were not purely private though he was apparently not an usher. Nobody needed an usher. People chose where they wanted to sit — or kneel — and sometimes decided to get up and choose another spot, perhaps being bothered by the glare of the jewel-inflaming sun. When I spoke to him I whispered, out of old habit in a church — and he had to ask me to speak again. Puzzled or embarrassed, he nodded in a wobbly way toward one of the confessionals. I had to become very specific and convincing.

"No, no. I just want to talk to a priest. I've been sent to talk to a priest. A priest called Father Hofstrader."

The basket man disappeared down the more distant side aisle and came back in a little while with a briskly moving stout young priest in ordinary black costume.

He motioned me into a room I had not noticed — not a room actually, we went through an archway, not a doorway — at the back of the church.

"Give us a chance to talk, in here," he said, and pulled out a chair for me.

"Father Hofstrader —"

"Oh no, I must tell you, I am not Father Hofstrader. Father Hofstrader is not here. He is on vacation."

For a moment I did not know how to proceed.

"I will do my best to help you."

"There is a woman," I said, "a woman who is dying in Princess Margaret Hospital in Toronto —"

"Yes, yes. We know of Princess Margaret Hospital."

"She asks me — I have a note from her here — she wants to see Father Hofstrader."

"Is she a member of this parish?"

"I don't know. I don't know if she is a Catholic or not. She is from here. From Guelph. She is a friend I have not seen for a long time."

"When did you talk with her?"

I had to explain that I hadn't talked with her, she had been asleep, but she had left the note for me.

"But you don't know if she is a Catholic?"

He had a cracked sore at the corner of his mouth. It must have been painful for him to talk.

"I think she is, but her husband isn't and he doesn't know she is. She doesn't want him to know."

I said this in the hope of making things clearer, even though I didn't know for sure if it was true. I had an idea that this priest might shortly lose interest altogether. "Father Hofstrader must have known all this," I said.

"You didn't speak with her?"

I said that she had been under medication but that this was not the case all the time and I was sure she would have periods of lucidity. This too I stressed because I thought it necessary.

"If she wishes to make a confession, you know, there are priests available at Princess Margaret's."

I could not think of what else to say. I got out the note, smoothed the paper, and handed it to him. I saw that the handwriting was not as good as I had thought. It was legible only in comparison to the letters on the envelope.

He made a troubled face.

"Who is this C?"

"Her husband." I was worried that he might ask for the husband's name, to get in touch with him, but instead he asked for Charlene's. This woman's name, he said.

"Charlene Sullivan." It was a wonder that I even remembered the surname. And I was reassured for a moment, because it was a name that sounded Catholic. Of course that meant that it was the husband who could be Catholic. But the priest might conclude that the husband had lapsed, and that would surely make Charlene's secrecy more understandable, her message more urgent.

"Why does she need Father Hofstrader?"

"I think perhaps it's something special."

"All confessions are special."

He made a move to get up but I stayed where I was. He sat down again.

"Father Hofstrader is on vacation but he is not out of town. I could phone and ask him about this. If you insist."

"Yes. Please."

"I do not like to bother him. He has not been well."

I said that if he was not well enough to drive himself to Toronto I could drive him.

"We can take care of his transportation if necessary."

He looked around and did not see what he wanted, unclipped a pen from his pocket, and then decided that the blank side of the note would do to write on.

"If you'll just make sure I've got the name. Charlotte —"

"Charlene."

Was I not tempted, during all this palaver? Not once? Not swayed by longing, by a magic-lantern show, the promise of pardon? No. Not really. It's not for me. What's done is done, what's done remains. Flocks of angels, tears of blood, notwithstanding.

I sat in the car without thinking to turn the motor on, though it was freezing cold by now. I didn't know what to do next. That is, I knew what I could do. Find my way to the highway and join the bright everlasting flow of cars toward Toronto. Or find a place to stay overnight, if I did not think I had the strength to drive. Most places would provide you with a toothbrush, or direct you to a machine where you could get one. I knew what was necessary and possible, but it was beyond my strength, for the moment, to do it.

The motorboats on the lake were supposed to stay a good distance out from the shore. And especially from our camping area, so that the waves they raised would not disturb our swimming. But on that last morning, that Sunday morning, a couple of them started a race and circled close in — not as close as the raft of course, but close enough to raise waves. The raft was tossed around, and Pauline's voice was lifted in a cry of reproach and dismay. The boats made far too much noise for their drivers to hear her, and they had already set a big wave rolling toward the shore, causing most of us in the shallows either to jump with it or be tumbled off our feet.

Charlene and I both lost our footing. We had our backs to the raft, because we were watching Verna come toward us. We were standing in water about up to our armpits, and we seemed to be lifted and tossed at the same moment that we heard Pauline's cry. We may have cried out as many others did, first in fear and then in delight as we regained our footing and that wave washed on ahead of us. The waves that followed proved to be not as strong, so that we could hold ourselves against them.

At the moment we tumbled, Verna had pitched toward us. When we came up, with our faces streaming, arms flailing, she was spread out under the surface of the water. There was a tumult of screaming and shouting all around, and this increased as the lesser waves arrived and people who had somehow missed the first attack pretended to be knocked over by the second. Verna's head did not break the surface, though now she was not inert but turning in a leisurely way, light as a jellyfish in the water. Charlene and I had our hands on her, on her rubber cap.

This could have been an accident. As if we, in trying to get our balance, grabbed on to this nearby large rubbery object, hardly realizing what it was or what we were doing. I have thought it all out. I think we would have been forgiven. Young children. Terrified.

Is this in any way true? It is true in the sense that we did not decide anything, in the beginning. We did not look at each other and decide to do what we subsequently and consciously did. Consciously, because our eyes did meet as the head of Verna tried to rise up to the surface of the water. Her head was determined to rise, like a dumpling in a stew. The rest of her was making misguided feeble movements down in the water, but the head knew what it should do. We might have lost our grip on the rubber head, the rubber cap, were it not for the raised pattern that made it less slippery. I can recall the color perfectly, the pale insipid blue, but I never deciphered the pattern — a fish, a mermaid, a flower — whose ridges pushed into my palms.

Charlene and I kept our eyes on each other then, rather than looking down at what our hands were doing. Her eyes were wide and gleeful, as I suppose mine were too. I don't think we felt wicked, triumphing in our wickedness. More as if we were doing just what was — amazingly — demanded of us, as if this was the absolute high point, the culmination, in our lives, of our being ourselves.

The whole business probably took no more than two minutes. Three? Or a minute and a half?

It seems too much to say that the discouraging clouds cleared up just at that time, but at some point — perhaps at the trespass of the motorboats, or when Pauline screamed, or when the first wave hit, or when the rubber object under our palms ceased to have a will of its own — the sun burst out, and more parents popped up on the beach, and there were calls to all of us to stop horsing around and come out of the water. Swimming was over. Over for the summer, for those who lived out of reach of the lake or municipal swimming pools. Private pools were only in the movie magazines.

As I've said, my memory fails when it comes to parting from Charlene, getting into my parents' car. Because it didn't matter. At that age, things ended. You expected things to end.

I am sure we never said anything as banal, as insulting or unnecessary, as *Don't tell.*

I can imagine the unease starting, but not spreading quite so fast as it might have if there had not been competing dramas. A child has lost a sandal, one of the youngest children is screaming that she got sand in her eye from the waves. Almost certainly a child is throwing up, because of the excitement in the water or the excitement of families arriving or the too-swift consumption of contraband candy. And the anxiety running through this, that someone is missing.

"Who?"

"One of the Specials."

"Oh drat. Wouldn't you know."

The woman in charge of the Specials running around, still in her flowered bathing suit, with the custard flesh wobbling on her thick arms and legs. Her voice wild and weepy.

Somebody go check in the woods, run up the trail, call her name.

"What is her name?"

"Verna."

"Wait."

"What?"

"Is that not something out there in the water?"

THISBE NISSEN

Win's Girl

FROM *The Cincinnati Review*

I'M NOT EVER GOING TO BE Win Cryer's girl — still, I'm here at the Quarry Bar to hear him play every Friday, up front, watching him like I *am* someone Win Cryer loves. I get off work at the slaughterhouse at five, and that's enough time to drive home, have a shower, heat something for dinner, open the mail, watch a little TV, and make it to the Quarry to get my table near the stage. By nine the bar's filling up, most folks not even changed from their work clothes — some guys from the cheese factory shooting pool in their coveralls, a young, pimply drunk zipped into his Jiffy Lube jacket hunched over a tall glass of bourbon. Lonny Bondorf — *Officer* Bondorf — walks toward my table like he's ready to arrest me.

I take out a cigarette, and Lonny's there with a lighter so fast he nearly burns my nose off. "Here for Win's show?" he asks.

"Always," I say.

"You think Win knows you? Think he remembers you every week?"

I shake my head. "I don't know."

"So how're things?" Lonny is a thirty-eight-year-old bachelor who'd like not to be. You could probably say nearly the same about me: over forty, not a lot of prospects.

"My money from the accident just came through," I say. Lonny was first on the scene that night they pulled me from my truck, blood running out my knees like garden spigots. I was on my way home from work, stopped at a light waiting for it to go green, when a drunk from Fairfield jumped the divider, plowed me head on. He didn't die either, which I'm glad about.

"You should get something nice for yourself, Doreen," Lonny says.

"I'm thinking I'm going to have the house rewired," I tell him.

"Well, *that's* fun," Lonny chides.

"Funner than frying in some electrical fire. You know how overdue that house is for an upgrade?"

"So you got someone to do it already?" Lonny asks.

"Rudy Hatch had a look at it a while back. Since he moved I've been nervous about finding someone else, getting bids."

"My sister-in-law had some work done on her fuse box couple months ago," Lonny says. "Some guy drives in from Solon. Said he did a good job."

"You remember the name?"

"Duane." He pauses. "Duane . . . Miller maybe?"

"Duane Miller," I repeat. "I'll look him up."

Onstage, Win turns to his bassist. Then a drumbeat starts in, and I'm recognizing the intro of one of my favorites. And for a second, as Win turns back to the audience, I think maybe he's playing it for me, because even if that smile tucked under the shadow of his hat brim is for everyone out here, I'm out here too.

Monday on my lunch break, I call Duane Miller, who sounds like the nicest guy in the world, but he's over his head in work and doesn't foresee an end anytime soon.

"Shoot," I tell him. "I really want to get this done . . ."

"Hey," he says, "I know someone might be able to fit you in. He's union, so it'd be off the record. Got a side business, totally legit taxwise and all, but the union'd bust the hell out of him if they found him out. But it's totally cool," says Duane. "Only way some of these guys can make a go of it."

I'm thinking that Duane surely knows more than me about this. And that maybe it's not a bad idea to have something on the guy I hire, something that'd make him scared to do me wrong.

"Here, I got the number," says Duane. "His name's Rich. Rich Randall. Real good electrician. He'll do you what needs done."

Rich Randall's answering machine says, "Hey, you've reached Rich at A-1 Electric. Can't catch you right now. Leave a message, and I'll give y'a ring." He sounds young and laid back, and I don't feel stupid leaving my name and number, my little story.

He calls back that very afternoon, and the fact that I'm at a desk at work to answer the phone makes me grateful for my accident, again, in that weird way you can be grateful for something bad. I used to be on the floor, standing all day, sawing carcasses, but my legs can't take it now. Lots of people thought I shouldn't have been doing it in the first place, but I'm no small girl. I had the strength.

"Hey, Doreen," says Rich. "Thanks for your message. Love to have a look at your wiring. When's good for you?" He agrees to come over after I get off work. "Look forward to meeting you," he says.

I hang up relieved. I'm taking care of my parents' house the way a grown person should. It's mine since Dad passed away. He was a house painter by trade, a handyman of all sorts, though since he's been gone I've found out my father didn't know quite all he thought he knew about house repair. Last year I started blowing fuses right and left — that's when I had Rudy Hatch in to see what was going on. Rudy was howling at some of the rig-ups my dad had going. Crazy wiring systems strung like daisy chains, all the parts salvaged from junk, hung together with duct tape. The bid he made to bring me up to code came in just under four thousand dollars, which I didn't have then. Plus, it seemed sad to get rid of all my dad's work just like that.

Rich Randall arrives at my house a few minutes behind me, just enough time to clean out the cat box. He's younger than me, maybe thirty, and the first thing I think is he looks like my ex-boyfriend Walter, but in a good way. The bad parts of Walter usually overtake the good ones in my memory. Walter told me he was a roofer. We went out five months before I found out he was making methamphetamines in his bathtub. I'm not someone to date a drug dealer, and a liar on top of it, but somehow, in the end, it was like I got dumped for not being a cool-enough girlfriend for a big-time Iowa meth dealer. Same with the car accident: Lonny Bondorf made me press charges, found me a lawyer and everything. I'd've never done it otherwise. I'd have found some way to think that sitting at a stoplight and getting head-onned by a drunk guy in a Blazer was 100 percent my fault.

Rich removes his cap, holds out a hand. "Real good to meet you."

He reminds me of things I liked about Walter, like he's a little bit of a brute, but sweet too, balding too early but owning up and shaving his whole head. His sweatshirt says LOCAL #329, UNION YES! We go through the house together, him apologizing for every bureau and plant stand he has to push out of the way, me apologizing for them being in the way in the first place. Rich speaks with authority, explains his terms, talks me through what he's doing and stops when I don't understand — "*Pigtail?*" I repeat — and then he hides under the bill of his cap while he backtracks, embarrassed by his own failure as my guide through the world of electricity. "It's just the word we use," he says. "How you attach the new wire to the old wire?"

"Got it," I say.

"You're great," he says. "Most people don't want to know what the hell's going on inside their walls. They're just like *You do it and tell me when you're done.* And then you get done and show them the bill and suddenly they're all *real* interested in what you're doing."

"My dad was a house painter," I say. "He'd get so mad about the people who'd hire you and then sit watching over your shoulder. Or they'd change their mind five times about what color they wanted for the vestibule, and then it's your fault when the paint looked different on the wall than it did on the TrueValue Hardware card. I guess I also just hate feeling ignorant."

"And that's great." He's looking right at me. "Everyone should know as much as they can about stuff." He pauses at the top of the stairs, leaning on the banister. "Take for instance: I play the guitar . . ."

"You do?"

"Yeah, I've got a band, kind of edgy, lots of technology? Samples? So like I was saying, when I need someone to work on my guitar, I want to know what he's doing. I want to know he's not saying *Oh you need new pickups and the action adjusted which'll be like five hours of labor* and then really all he's done is solder one minuscule fucking wire and I'm paying through the nose . . . It's the same thing. I mean, here's this thing you don't know jack about, and I'm here and this is what I *know,* you know? I mean, I *know* electricity. And I could tell you *any*thing, and you'd have to be like *Okay, sure, whatever you say.*"

"I did have a couple other people look at it," I tell him.

"And that's why you're the best kind of customer," he says, "because you're informed. You're not just letting someone tell you what to do."

"I hope so."

"Here's what should happen," Rich tells me. "You need to think about this. Make sure I'm the right person for this job. I can get you some numbers of references, if you want . . ."

I shake my head, embarrassed. He's already been recommended by Duane Miller.

"Well, I can give 'em to you. I'm a good electrician. I'm an excellent electrician, really. You don't have to have any doubt about that."

Downstairs, Rich sits at my kitchen table doing some calculations while I make him a cup of coffee. Then I sit down and we go over them. He points to some numbers: "Here's materials," he says, "and projected labor." He points again: "And here's your total. Might be a little higher than the bids you got before, and I know that I do charge a little more for labor than some, but I stand behind the fact that my work's worth it. I lose some business probably, people who aren't willing to pay for a job to be done right. People who are willing to cut corners. And I'm just not. Not with electricity. We're talking about *safety* here." His bid is not too far over Rudy's, given that he's talking about dealing with the grounding in the basement and the outdoor sockets Rudy never even thought about. "Not to dis your old electrician," Rich says, "but some people don't think of everything, you know?"

I wait a day before I call Rich back to tell him yes, let's start, whenever he's ready. "Actually just had a cancellation on another job," he says. "Haven't wanted to take too much on, with the move and all . . ."

"Oh! You're moving?"

"Yeah, we've been out in Texas part-time a while, back and forth, seeing how hard it's going to be to find work and stuff. My wife's there now, in fact, trying to find us a place, so I'm on kid duty till she gets back. But I can start Monday, if that's good with you, Doreen?"

"You have kids?"

"Seven and three," he says, and for a second I think he's telling me he's got ten children.

"That's great," I say.

"Yeah, we'll see how great it is by the end of the week. They miss Mommy. Tell you the truth, I miss Mommy too."

I laugh a little.

"So I'll see you Monday, Doreen?"

"Great," I say, and it all seems way too easy. "Um, I work, but the door's unlocked. You can just come in . . ."

"That's okay with you?" he asks. "You're okay having me there while you're not home? Some people are funny about that — s'why I ask."

"Oh, it's fine," I say as the doubt washes over me, sudden as a sickness.

Rich hedges. "I hate to bring money into this, but I guess that's what makes work go 'round. The way I usually do it is you give me half up front, for supplies and materials, and half upon completion."

"That sounds fair," I agree. I try to think what I'm supposed to ask. "Should . . . could I leave a check for you on Monday?"

"A check's fine . . . Oh, also," he says, "I just wanted to make sure — Duane told you about the union stuff, right? We all do it — only way to hack it with how everything works nowadays — I just wanted to make sure Duane let you know about that. That you were okay with that and all."

"Yeah," I stammer, "yeah, he said about you doing stuff on the side."

"That man is a fucking prince," Rich says. "When you said it was Duane sent you, I knew I'd take your job. He always puts me on to real nice people."

After the accident the doctor at the hospital assigned me to a lady at the Community Mental Health Center to talk to if I wanted, about the wreck or anything that was bothering me. Honestly, I think it was about my job. When that doctor found out I worked on the slaughterhouse line, he went a little white. Men worry like that, can't believe what I do — what I *did* — for my job. He meant well, so I took the number, and then when I got sort of blue afterward, working in the office, feeling washed-up and old, Sherry, who works next to me, Sherry said, "Why don't you go see that counselor, Doreen?"

The therapist's name was Brianna, pronounced like royalty: Bree-*ahh*-nah. When I first went to see her, she pried a while into the accident, but more into my job, sure I had a whole world of rage under my skin that she was dying to tap. She scheduled another appointment; I was too embarrassed to argue. I see her every other week now. Mostly she tells me the sagas of her love life, which are always turbulent and interesting in a soap-opera kind of way.

The day after I meet Rich, I'm scheduled with Brianna, and when she politely asks how I am before she launches into her latest drama, I find I'm talking about the electric job and about Rich Randall.

"Is this a man you're attracted to, Doreen?" Brianna asks.

"No," I say, too quick. "No, I mean, no, I mean: he's married."

Brianna switches tactics: "Is it . . . ? Are you . . . nervous having this man in your house while you're out? That can feel very invasive, Doreen. Your home is a private place. It's your nest, you know, where you're most yourself . . . Maybe think about taking Monday off work, Doreen? The slaughterhouse can get along without you one day. You let yourself get worked too hard." This is Brianna's perennial suggestion, and I've run out of ways to tell her I'm fine. Unless you're lower than low or happier than God, no one believes a thing you tell them when they ask how you are.

But when my alarm goes off Monday morning, I don't want to go to work. By seven thirty, I've convinced myself I'd be irresponsible leaving my parents' home in the hands of some stranger. For the first time in ten years — not counting after the accident, when I couldn't even walk — I call in sick.

It's almost noon before Rich arrives. "Doreen! Didn't expect you here!"

"I got the day off." I get a rush of panic that he thinks I'm going to scold him for showing up so late, and then I suddenly, desperately, miss my father. Dad took care of things, and even if he didn't know exactly what he was doing, he *felt* like he did, and I felt sure in his sureness. His absence thwacks me in the chest, and I'm breathless.

"Great," Rich says. "Great to see you. Guess I'll get to work then, if that's good with you." Rich hoists his tool belt on his hips and aims for the nearest socket with something that looks like a screwdriver with a crank to wind it like a music box. He unscrews the outlet cover, me feeling dumb just standing there watching.

"How are your kids?" I think to ask.

Rich laughs. "Surviving!" He pauses, leans against the wall as though he needs a rest. He's shaking his head in near disbelief. "They're such a trip, you know?"

"I don't have any." I gesture around the house: no children hidden anywhere.

"Ha! It's a crazy thing . . ."

"Crazy?"

"God, you ever just listen to the things kids'll say? I mean, just the shit that comes out of their mouths? It's such a trip! Kaylee, my daughter, she's three . . . ? She's got these really bad allergies and we have to pump her full of Benadryl at bedtime. And before she goes to sleep, she's wandering around the house all doped up, saying the craziest, trippiest things. Last night some guys from the band were over, and I followed Kaylee around with a mic, just picking up the crazy shit she said. It's going to be awesome when I get it looped onto a track."

I'm laughing, almost not believing what he's saying, but laughing anyhow because he is.

"God, you should totally have kids, Doreen. They're so damn awesome." Rich turns back to the socket then and pulls a wire from the wall, inspects it. "Okay," he says, "I see what we need here. Hey, so, if you've got that check on you now, I can go ahead and get the supplies I need . . ."

"Oh, sure!" I'm way too chirpy. I get my purse and make out a check to Rich Randall for twenty-five hundred dollars. "Don't spend it all in one place," I say, and Rich laughs like I'm actually funny, and I'm grateful for it. For the second time in ten minutes I feel the loss of my dad again so hard it could've been yesterday.

Rich is gone a couple hours, comes back carrying an old, worn cardboard box full of tools and screws and nails and stuff, which he plunks down in the dining room and starts digging through. "Menards was all out of the wire I needed, but I hunted some down through my distributor." He holds up a spool. "So we're good to go." It's nearing three o'clock.

Rich works steadily until four thirty, when he comes and finds me in the living room reading a magazine and tells me he's got to go pick up his kids from his wife's mother's place. "Looking good," he says. "We'll have you all safe and up to code in no time."

"It'll really be a relief," I say. "I never had the money to do it. Until now. I was in a car accident, and the settlement just came through. I mean, I don't *usually* have money. It was this crazy thing . . ."

"It's weird, isn't it?" Rich says. "How you get a bunch of money all of a sudden and you think it'll make everything easier, but it just gets super-confusing. I mean, for instance: me and my wife, we came into a bunch of money kind of recently — like a good chunk of money, you know? And we thought, oh it'll all be so much easier now. But then there's all that shit about what do we spend it on, and her being like *You are not using our money to buy that vintage guitar,* and me being like *I sure as fuck am!*" Rich smiles. "And here you are doing the responsible thing, like my wife'd do, not like me. I'm bad. I've been sober five months now, but before that I used to get into some shit. In my youth, you know? Maybe it's not the most responsible thing, but you gotta live, you know? I mean, you ever do coke?"

I shake my head.

Rich's eyes are almost closed like he's reliving a great pleasure. He breathes in deep. "Oh, boy." He lets his breath huff out in resignation. "Man, we used to do some incredible shit down in Mexico. You know how they make coke?"

Again, I shake my head.

"They do this whole process thing," he explains, "but the guys we knew down there, the guys who were making it, they'd have the purest kind, like the first, most pure stuff, and it'd be cut with peaches, or coconuts. I mean: peach cocaine! You never had anything so incredible! But I got kids now. Family to think about. No more of that shit for me. No more heaven," he says, his head beginning to wag back and forth like he's watching it all slip away.

The next day I go to work, but I drive home on my lunch hour just to see how things are going. Rich isn't there, and it doesn't look like he has been. I make myself a sandwich. When the front door opens suddenly and it's him, I start, like I have something to hide.

"Doreen!"

"I'm sorry! I didn't mean to scare you. I just came home for some lunch." I hold up my dirty plate as evidence.

"I just didn't expect you is all. I'm a little late getting started. It's been a hell of a morning. Jesus," he swears, running a hand over his head. "Jesus, it's been such a fucking morning. And I've got work to do. I've got a job to do here!" He looks around my house like this old place is the most important thing in the world. "I've been on the phone with lawyers all morning!" he blurts out. "They're holding my wife in jail! In Texas! Can you believe that bullshit? They want two thousand bucks bail to get her out. So I'm down at the bank trying to get money fucking wired to Texas or some shit, and trying to get a lawyer out there for her. It's going to be a fucking fortune!"

"Wait," I say, "wait — what? Your wife's in *jail?*"

"It's total bullshit," Rich says. "Something about the place she's working out there. Or the place she worked last year. The company's being investigated for tax fraud or something, and everyone who worked there during that time in question, they came and arrested them all. They're saying my wife knows something, which is bullshit — she doesn't know anything. And now I have to come up with two thousand bucks to get her out of jail. Such bullshit!"

"Wait," I say, trying to slow him down, trying to back this up to where I can understand it. "Wait, here, sit down." I pull him out a chair at the table. He looks like he's about to bury his face in his hands and cry. I take a seat across from him. "Okay," I say, "go slow. Tell me what happened." It's how Brianna would sound, if Brianna ever did her job right.

"Do they even understand the fact that she's got fucking *kids?* That there's two little kids at home saying *Where's Mommy?* Jesus!" He drops his head, and I'm afraid he really is going to cry.

"Okay," I say, "wait: your wife worked for some company that's in trouble with the IRS, and they arrested all the employees? That can't be legal . . . They can't just . . ."

"Yeah, well, they did," he says. "Now I've got to figure out how I'm going to get to Texas and get her out of jail. And I've got this job to do for you, and . . ."

"Rich, you can finish here when you get back. It's okay."

He looks at me, then away, like he can't bear the kindness. "God, I'm glad it's you I'm working for right now. A union job and they'd say *That's shit for luck, man. Your wife's gonna have to find some other way out of prison, 'cause you ain't going nowhere!*" Then there's resolve in his voice: "No," he says. "You know, my wife's mom's got the kids, and there's nothing I can do till the damn lawyer calls me back." He pats his cell. "So I'll stay here and get as much done as I can so I can finish tomorrow maybe and have it off my mind. I tell you what, Doreen: I'll get to work, get a jump on this. Hey, and I'd really appreciate it if you didn't say anything about this, just for the kids' sake, really. I just don't want everybody going around knowing Hailey Randall's in jail, you know? There's people who'll judge you without knowing anything about it, you know?"

"No problem," I tell him. By my watch it's ten past one, and I'm about to be late to work for the first time in my life.

Rich is not there when I get home at five fifteen. At eight thirty there's a knock on the door.

"I'm really sorry to bother you, Doreen," Rich begins, "I'm just trying to get all my business taken care of before I leave for Texas, and I've got a flight out the day after tomorrow, so my kids are with my old partner, Butch, tonight. He's looking after them so I could buy some time, get things finished up. I got everything inside the house done today. I've just got that stuff we talked about in the basement. If I can get that taken care of tonight, then I'll finish tomorrow."

Now, I admit, I'm feeling a little bit scared — wary, like this is too much, too irregular. But he's in such dire straits that I don't know what to do. "How's your wife?" I ask.

"A mess," he says. "She's a total wreck. She's freaking out. It looks worse than she thought. I guess it's looking like she *did* know about what was going on in the office and all, that she was aware and didn't do anything, or just went along with it or something. I don't know what. She's just totally freaking out now." Shaking his head, he stands there a minute, then says, "Hell, might as well get some work done, keep my mind off it all." He starts fast toward the cellar door.

Late in the night when I know Rich is gone I go down to the basement. There's some sawdust on the floor beneath an outlet, which looks new, but I have no way of knowing what he's done. *If* he's done *anything.* In the morning I wake up panicked and take the day off work again. Rich shows up just past nine, looking like he hasn't slept. I have thought up a long story of why I am not at work today, but Rich doesn't even seem to notice I'm home when I shouldn't be.

"How are you holding up?" I ask.

"Tell you the truth, it sucks," Rich says. "To tell you the God's honest truth, it's so much more messed up than I can even describe." He sinks down at the kitchen table. I pour him a cup of coffee.

"What happened?"

"Well," he says, sipping, "the truth is that my wife *did* know about what was going on with her boss and the money and stuff. The thing is, I knew about it too. It was like a totally low-key thing. Sort of a Robin Hood thing. The only people — and I mean *the only* ones — getting screwed were the fucking asshole feds. It was just this thing that had been going on forever at the company, just like something you went along with when you got hired. So now after all those years, they finally get caught, and now it's *my wife* facing jail time! It's so fucking backwards!"

I have no idea what to say.

"There's not that much I have left to finish here," Rich says then. "I'll be done today with pretty much everything."

"What *is* left?" I ask. I wish I had an inventory, had it all written down in front of me, but it's beyond too late for that.

"Well, let's see, there's that fuse box . . ."

"And the outside switches," I remind him.

"Oh, yeah, right: the outside switches."

"And you did all the pigtailing already?" I ask.

Rich smiles, slow and deep, like he's remembering a joy he'd thought was lost. "All pigtailed," he assures me. "Okay, let's see, I'll go out and get those switches now. Could I ask you, Doreen, if you could lay out the money for that? I left my checkbook at home, and . . . this is so fucking embarrassing, but they froze my fucking credit cards while all this stuff gets sorted out. Can you lay out for this material, and we'll subtract off what you still owe me?"

I'm frozen. Somehow I manage to ask how much he needs.

"Fifty'll do it. Or just make the check to Menards, and I'll fill in the amount. Whatever's good."

I am in a panic. Everything in me says *don't give this man any more money,* but he's standing right there, acting like this is just how these things go. And for all I know, maybe it is. I tell myself about the union, that I can report him if I have to. I can give him cash or a check, and I know one of the two is probably safer, but I can't get my head to figure out which. I head for the stairs. "I think have I some money in the bedroom." I tell myself: *Doreen, you are a moron.*

Rich is gone for two and a half hours. I spend them practicing what to say when he comes back: *Rich, you can't tell the person you're working for that you're part of criminal activity. How can someone trust you with their money when you tell them you've stolen, even if it is from the IRS?* When he breezes in the door like he's been gone ten minutes, he unloads a pile of switches that don't look like they came from a store at all.

"Doreen?" he asks. "Do you think I could use your telephone for just a minute?" He looks like he's going to cry again, and I don't know what I can say but "Sure."

He dials, leans against the wall, and waits. "Pumpkin," he says. "Pumpkin, it's Daddy." At least he wasn't lying about the kids. "Hey, sweetheart, go get Uncle Butch and put him on the phone for Daddy now, okay? Good girl."

"Dude," Rich says after a minute, "if she calls, you tell her to keep her mouth shut. I'll be there tomorrow. I'll figure it out. Tell her just to stay quiet till then, okay?" He pauses, listening. "Thanks, man. You're my hero." He hangs up, turns to me. "Oh, Doreen, what a fucking mess." He sinks down at the table and lays his head on the switches and wires.

"Did something else happen?" I am a little kid, squeaky and dumb.

He lifts his head, wagging it back and forth. "What a fucking disaster, this whole thing," he says. "It was supposed to be so easy. We were just going to do it and be done, and that's it. It was so fucking easy." He looks right at me, then back down, like he's ashamed. "I haven't told you the whole story," he says. "There's a lot more going on than . . . It was such an easy plan, and it worked so damn well. This guy, the one Hailey worked for — *works* for, I dunno — he got this RV, you know? One of those huge honking ones? And he got the whole inside hollowed out, and all Hailey has to do, for *two-thirds* the profit — *two-thirds!* — all she has to do is sit in the goddamn passenger seat and pretend the guy's her lover and she's going over to Mexico with him for the day — just going over with her little boyfriend for the day to have their little affair."

I don't want to know this, and still I don't want him to stop until I know it all.

"So they get pulled over on the way back into the States," he says. "Done it five, six times, no problem. *This* time they get pulled over. And you got to understand: the take was so good. You can't say no to money like that. We thought, we'll do it a few times, be able to get the kids some nice Christmas presents, just live comfortable. You know? We weren't trying to strike it rich or anything, just trying to make things nice for our kids."

I'm nodding, I think. At least I mean to be nodding.

"So they get pulled over. And Hailey, Hailey's fucking intelligent. When the cops find the stash — the whole back of the RV's filled with pot — marijuana, you know? — so when they find it, Hailey starts doing a whole act like *What the fuck is going on, you bastard? You invite me to come over the border with you for a little fun and really you're running drugs? You fucking bastard!* She's making like she's got no idea except that she's having a little fling with a married man, no idea about anything in the back of the RV. She's fucking brilliant. Only they bring her in with him anyway, seize the whole fucking RV — we're talking five hundred grand in the back of that bus, sitting in some federal pen — five hundred grand of really fine marijuana, drying out in some government warehouse . . . It fucking kills me!"

"But she *did* know? She knew the pot was there, right?"

"Yeah. Yeah, yeah, yeah. I mean, we all knew. There was just Hailey and me and the guy driving the RV, really. Marshall, Butch's brother." Rich gestures toward the telephone.

I nod. I'm thinking: One-third was Marshall's, and the rest — two-thirds for Rich and Hailey. I'm thinking: I don't know how to live in this world.

When Rich leaves that night, there is a pile of old electrical switches on my kitchen table. When I get home from work the next day, the pile is still there. When I call Rich's number, the machine picks up, same voice as before: "Hey, you've reached Rich at A-1 Electric . . ." Of course, he's in Texas by now. If I believe that much. In the days that follow, I leave so many messages on Rich Randall's answering machine that I'd be scared if he ever *did* call back. I try being nice at first, but then I lose nice. I threaten to report him to the union. I threaten to sue him for the money he's taken, the work he hasn't done. I threaten to report him to child welfare. It's easy to threaten an answering machine. The threat I do not make regards what I know of his drug-smuggling operation. The words *drug-smuggling operation* make me feel like I'm playing Nancy Drew. And for all I know the drug story's as much of a lie as everything else. Maybe Rich Randall hasn't gotten to the end of his tale?

I'm at the Quarry one Friday night, about a month after Rich disappears, sitting at my table just before Win's second set, about to light myself a cigarette, when the bar door opens and there shaking the snow from his wool cap and stamping his feet on the indoor-outdoor rug is Rich Randall.

My stomach hollows. My lighter's shaking so hard in my hands I can't even raise it to my mouth. I just sit there, dumb and shaking and staring. I've had two beers and part of a third, and maybe that's what kicks in once the nausea passes, because what I'm left with is a kind of fury I have never known in my life. I stand.

He recognizes me from a few feet away, a friendly recognition, eyes lit up the way they do when you come back to a place you've been gone from and start spotting the people you used to know. First you don't realize who they are, just that you know them. A split second later they come into focus: a name, or a context, a placement, history. All this happens in Rich Randall's face as I walk toward him across the Quarry Bar. His expression shifts from recognition to realization to fear. And then from fear — a tiny little millisecond of fear that I see, and that I know he knows I see — he crosses seamlessly into disdain: a clear, smirking, righteous grin. He tries to pretend he's never seen me before in his life.

"Did you just plan on never coming back, on never finishing what you started?"

Rich Randall just looks at me, his eyes gone deliberately blank. He blinks. "'Scuse me?" He looks around, like maybe I'm talking to someone else.

"You fucking bastard," I say. "You fucking . . ."

"Whoa, lady." He backs up a step. "Take it somewhere else, sister."

I'm so angry I feel like I'm spitting. Then I realize I'm actually crying: I'm standing in the middle of the Quarry while Win Cryer takes the stage, tears running down my face, and my voice is a threat of death. "Get out of here," I'm telling this stupid, cowardly, criminal man. "Get out of here right now. You don't deserve to hear a note that man plays. You're a thief. Get out. Get out now."

Onstage Win starts strumming, and I can see Rich's body respond to the music, soften and find the beat, relaxed as anything. He looks right at me, then tosses his head and laughs, turning back to the stage, grooving along to the music.

I spin and run for the ladies' room, where I splash my face, pull myself together. Without looking at Rich, I walk back to my table where Lonny Bondorf is sitting now, MGD in hand, staring up at Win like he's in love with him too. I fish a cigarette out of my purse and hold it up for Lonny to light. My hand is shaking, and Lonny sees something's wrong.

"Doreen, are you okay?"

I make a quick glance back at Rich, standing smug in his spot by the door, hands shoved in his pockets, head nodding in time to the music. I say to Lonny: "I don't know." I say: "See that guy over there?" Lonny nods. I say: "I was waiting for the ladies' room, and he started sort of hitting on me, and then he just started saying weird stuff . . ."

Lonny looks like he can't decide what kind of suspicious to be: suspicious like an older brother, or a boyfriend, or like a policeman. "What kind of weird stuff?"

"Sort of crazy stuff, like do I want to see the gun in his pocket, and do I know it's loaded. And that he's got all sorts of other stuff out in his car. And do I want some drugs — he's got pot if I want, or coke. He was trying to get me to come out to his car to smell some peach-flavored cocaine. I said, 'No thank you.' Then he just said, 'Bitch.'"

Lonny stands without a word, sets down his beer, pushes in his chair, and starts walking toward Rich with the kind of purpose in his step that makes people afraid of policemen. Onstage, Win and the band play the final chord of a song, and it's like the whole place is holding its breath. Win's mouth is moving, which makes me realize I'm staring right at him, but I can't hear what he's saying, like it's just his mouth moving but the volume's gone mute, or I've gone deaf, and I'm frozen, staring, waiting for the world to start again, only it's like everyone else is staring too, and who they're staring at is me.

The first thing I hear again, breaking through my ears like they're popping, is some man yelling from the back of the bar, "Yo, lady, what friggin' song you want to hear? Let's get a move on; the man ain't got all night!" And I'm confused and disoriented, and suddenly I'm afraid he's talking to me and I don't know what I've missed, and everyone seems to be waiting for something until finally it's Win who's talking again, and now I can hear his voice, and he's looking like he doesn't understand what's going on either, like I'm crazy as they come, and then to the audience it's like he's saying *go figure,* only what he's really saying is, "Well, I guess we'll just go and choose one ourself," and then he shrugs and turns to confer with the band. From the back of the bar I hear someone say, "What the . . . ?" and I turn and see people clearing the way for Lonny, who's coming up on Rich Randall, and down the path that's cleared for Lonny in the crowd, I can hear him saying to Rich, "Would you please step outside with me a minute, sir?" and Rich is just looking at him, like *No way, fuck off, dork,* so that's when Lonny gets to flash his badge and say, "Sir, I'm going to ask you to step outside, and I'm not going to ask you again."

JOYCE CAROL OATES

The Blind Man's Sighted Daughters

FROM *Fiction Magazine*

"HAS HE EVER talked about it with you?"

My sister lowered her voice as if fearful of being overheard for our father's hearing had sharpened in his blindness. My sister who was fifty-two years old and hardly a child inclined her head in the enigmatic way she'd cultivated as a girl to signal *Don't tell me. I need to ask but don't tell me.*

Adding, unnecessarily, "He never has, with me. At least I wasn't aware if he had."

He, him were the ways in which we spoke of our elderly father in our lowered voices. *He, him* seemed more appropriate than such intimate words as *Father, Dad.*

Really there was no danger of him hearing us: we were in the front room of the house and the old man was at the rear of the house lying in a lounge chair facing a window through which winter sunshine streamed. He could not see the window, he could not see how dazzling white snow heaped outside the window as in a scene of Arctic desolation but he could probably see something of the light and he could feel the warmth of the sun on his face.

Sunning himself like a giant lizard. Almost, you could envy him.

He was eighty-one, he'd become almost totally blind over a period of years. A gradual dimming, fading. His condition was called macular degeneration: a hole in the center of his vision. Initially a pinprick, then it enlarges. You manage to see around it, as long as you can. By this time in the sixth year of his affliction the black hole had seemingly swallowed most of our father's vision but he hadn't entirely given up the effort of trying to see.

It was exhausting! For him, and for me.

Knowing yourself reduced to a blurred shape at the edge of a man's vision. The sudden panic of one about to step off the edge of the earth.

I told my sister no. Dryly I told her I'd have been aware of it, if he had.

We knew what we meant by *it.* This was a code between us, to be murmured with a kind of thrilled shame.

Abigail was watching me closely. She'd been shaken by the deterioration of our father and it was possible, she blamed me. Her nostrils were pinched as if against a bad odor. Her forehead was pinched, her mouth. I wondered what she was seeing. Living with a blind man you gradually become invisible.

"What does he talk about with you, then?"

"Stay with us for a while, Abigail. Talk to him yourself. Then you'll know."

I spoke warmly. Hearing me you'd think *A good heart!* But Abigail knew this was a reproach. Something hot swept up into her face, she smiled quickly to acknowledge yes, all right, she deserved it. But she would bear it for my sake.

Don't hate me! I had to save my own life.

I said, "He doesn't talk. He thinks out loud. I guess you'd call it 'thinking' — a stream of words like TV, if you switched from channel to channel. Old quarrels. People who've been dead for fifty years. Men he'd had business dealings with, who'd 'cheated' him. Not us. He has no interest in us. Anything he did, caused to happen, in this house or out, no memory of it. Sometimes he speaks of 'your mother.' The worst days, he confuses me with her. He never asks about you. He never asks about me. He calls 'He-len! *He-len!*' so he knows who I am. Though I could be a nurse's aide, I suppose." I paused, so that Abigail could laugh. Politely and nervously Abigail could laugh. I'd missed my calling as a TV comic: the kind who's angry and deadpan and provokes laughter in others that's the equivalent of turning a knife blade in their guts. "He asks me to read the newspapers to him, the worst news first, atrocities, suicide bombers, plane crashes, famines, killings and dismemberings in New Jersey, anything lurid to do with politicians or celebrities, he wants to be consoled that the world is a ridiculous hellhole, people are no damned good and the environment is poisoned to hell, only a fool would want to live much longer. I have to describe for him what's on the TV screen, he can work the remote control for himself. He falls asleep and I switch off the damned set and the sudden silence wakes him and at first he doesn't know where he is, maybe he's dead? had another stroke? then he's furious with me saying he hadn't been asleep. 'Trying to put something over on me,' he says, 'sneaky bitch like your mother —'"

"Oh, Helen. Stop."

We were laughing together. Jamming our knuckles against our mouths like guilty children for if our father heard us immediately he would know we were laughing at him.

"Helen, you turn everything into a joke. I wish you wouldn't."

"Everything isn't a joke, Abigail? Come on."

"You've even begun to talk strangely. Your mouth —"

"My mow-th?"

I felt it twist. Like wringing a rag. Had I been doing this unconsciously? Did I do it bringing our father to the medical clinic, speaking with doctors, staff? Buying groceries, buying gasoline, at the drugstore getting prescriptions filled? Mirrors had become so leprous-looking in this house, I hadn't been able to see my reflection for months.

"*He's* the one who had the stroke, Abigail. Not me. My mow-th is as normal as yours."

Earlier in the day when Abigail had arrived for her visit, she had looked extremely normal: the kind of woman, middle-aged but youthful, I sometimes observed, disliking, envious, in public places. She'd embraced me, the younger sister, with a cry like a stricken bird, hugged me tight against her as if she'd meant it. Oh she'd missed me, Oh I'd lost so much weight, Oh oh oh! she was sorry for having been out of touch for so long. She'd been an attractive well-groomed woman stepping into this house at 2:00 P.M. and now at 6:30 P.M. she looked as if she'd been bargain shopping at Wal-Mart on Discount Saturday. She looked as if she could use a good stiff drink but I never kept hard liquor in the house, not even beer or wine. The old man would find it and drink himself into a coma. Or maybe, I would.

Abigail wiped at her eyes with a tissue. I was touched to see that coming to visit Sparta, driving the width of New York State from Peekskill, New York, she'd taken time to apply eye makeup.

"I wish you'd warned me, Helen. You might have."

Warned her about what? The old man wasn't so bad — was he?

"And I'm worried about you, too."

"Me! I can worry about myself, thank you."

"No. Obviously not. You don't look well, you must have lost twenty pounds. The way the house looks, and smells . . ."

Abigail's nostrils pinched primly. I was hurt, and I was offended. "Smells! It does not."

Though it was true: I'd tried to give our father a sponge bath that morning in preparation for Abigail's visit but the old man had refused to let me near him. Couldn't have said when exactly he'd been bathed by me, or shaved. Or when I'd showered, myself. Or changed my underwear which I wore to bed in cold weather, with wool socks, beneath an old flannel nightgown.

But I'd wetted my hair and combed it. Smeared plum-colored lipstick on my mouth. In a shadowy mirror there was no face behind the mouth but the mouth was smiling.

". . . should be moved to an assisted-care facility, Helen. That's why I've come, have you forgotten? Oh, please listen!"

I was listening. I saw my sister's mouth move and I was listening but somehow I seemed to have lost the knack of comprehending words in a coherent sequence as you lose the knack of comprehending a foreign language you have not heard or spoken in some time.

When Abigail called me and static interfered, I hadn't any choice but to quietly hang up. But when someone is speaking to you from a few feet away, you have not that option.

The power I'd been exerting over my sister just a few minutes ago to make her laugh against her will had faded rapidly. I didn't know how I'd lost it, I resented this too.

". . . six-month leave, you said? Unpaid? Aren't the six months up by now, Helen? Have you made new arrangements?"

I thought that I had, yes. I told my sister this.

I'd taken the leave because caring for our father had begun to require more and more time. There was the vague idea too, at least initially, that I would be preparing for the next phase of the old man's life which would be an assisted-care facility. I had put off speaking to him about the prospect. Until Abigail mentioned it, I may have forgotten.

Scattered through the house were glossy brochures from such places. Deer Meadow Manor, Rosewood Manor, Cedar Brook Hall. Abigail had pushed some aside, sitting on the sofa.

She was saying in a brisk voice, having recovered some of her poise, that she would take time off, too. (My sister was a well-paid administrator at a science research institute in Peekskill.) She would help in the "move" of course. And after our father was "settled" in the new residence we would have the entire house cleaned, and painted, repairs made to the roof, then we'd put the house "on the market" . . . "Helen? Are you listening?"

Half-consciously I'd been listening for his uplifted voice at the rear of the house. It did seem time about now for him to call *Helen?* Sometimes the voice was raw and aggrieved, sometimes the voice was uncertain, wavering. Sometimes the voice was angry. And sometimes pleading like the voice of a lost child. *He-len!*

I lowered my own voice that had gone slightly hoarse from not being used much. I said, "Each day I think of it. Already when I wake in the morning the thought is with me."

"What thought?"

"'This day might be it. His last.'"

Abigail stared at me. For a long moment she seemed unable to speak.

"And how — how — how do you feel, Helen? Thinking such a thought?"

"Anxious. Excited. Hopeful."

"'Hopeful.'"

Abigail didn't seem to be challenging me nor even questioning me only just trying out the word.

At the rear of the house the voice lifted querulously: "He-len?"

November 1967. In the night the temperature dropped below zero, the bodies had frozen together. Not in each other's arms but crushed together bloodied and broken in shattered glass in the front seat of the wrecked vehicle that seemed to have skidded off the road to plunge down an embankment above the Chautauqua River north of Sparta. The vehicle was a new-model Dodge sedan that had capsized and stopped short in underbrush on the river-bank, thirty feet below the roadway. If the car hadn't capsized it would have rolled forward and broken through the ice to be submerged in fifteen feet of water, by morning a crust of ice might have formed above it. If snow had continued to fall heavily through the night the car's tracks might have been hidden from view, covered in snow.

The Dodge sedan was registered to the dead man behind the wheel whose name was Henry Claver. The dead woman was not Henry Claver's wife but another man's wife, a woman known to our father Lyle Sebera. She'd been his receptionist at Sebera Construction for several years and it would be said that she and our father had been "involved" for most of this time. Since her separation from her husband, the woman and her five-year-old son had been living in a brick row house in downtown Sparta that was one of several properties owned by Lyle Sebera and it would be said that on those occasions when her estranged husband came to take the boy away for the weekend, to Buffalo where he was now living, Lyle Sebera was a "frequent" visitor in that house.

The woman's name was Lenora McDermid. This was not a name that would be uttered in our house, ever.

That night he'd come home late. By eight o'clock our mother had several times called his office for it was her belief that he was working late. Though possibly he'd been traveling that day, and had neglected to tell her. Our mother was not a woman to ask very many questions of her husband who was not a man of whom a wife might comfortably ask questions.

By eight o'clock my sister and I had eaten dinner and cleaned away our places at the table. Our mother did not eat with us and afterward remained in the kitchen alone. She would call our father's number at Sebera Construction for this was the only number she had for our father. This was an era before voice mail when you called a number and when it rang unanswered you had no choice but to hang up and call again and later you might call again listening helplessly to a phone ringing unanswered.

Where is Daddy? was not a question my sister and I were in the habit of asking.

That night he was working late, very likely. He'd gone to check a building site. There were often business trips: Yewville, Port Oriskany, Buffalo. Lyle Sebera thought nothing of driving ninety miles roundtrip in a single day. Possibly there were financial problems at this time in our father's business but we were not meant to know of such problems as we were not meant to know of any aspect of our father's life guarded by him as zealously as the large cluttered lot behind Sebera Construction was guarded by a fierce German shepherd inside a ten-foot chain-link fence. Some of the problems of which we weren't to know had to do with bank loans, mortgages on investment properties owned by Lyle Sebera in partnership with another Sparta resident whose name was not Claver but the man named Claver was a former business associate of Lyle Sebera's partner whose name was Litz.

McDermid, Claver, Litz. Names not to be uttered in our house.

Yet we knew of these names, that were not spoken in our house or in our earshot. Though no newspapers containing these names were allowed in the house and we were not allowed to watch TV news.

Abigail was thirteen and I was ten. We were in eighth grade and in fifth grade. Quiet girls, obedient, believed to be well-mannered because we were shy. We'd been trained not to test our mother's patience and we had hardly needed to be trained not to displease our father. Yet we scavenged neighbors' trash cans in the alley that ran behind our houses searching for forbidden knowledge. Eager, in fear of being seen, we pawed at newspaper pages smelling of garbage, damp pulp paper that left newsprint on our fingers. "Oh! Look." Abigail whispered pointing at a photograph on the front page of the *Sparta Journal,* of a dark-haired, squinting man with a familiar face.

LOCAL CONTRACTOR SEBERA, 44
QUESTIONED IN DOUBLE HOMICIDE

We were squatting beside trash cans in the alley. Dogs had defiled the snow here. There was a rancid smell of garbage, we swallowed hard to keep from gagging. "Double homicide." Our lips moved numbly. In the cold still air our breaths steamed. "Bludgeoned."

Bludgeoned! I seemed to know what this word meant. This was a word that carried its meaning in its sound.

On the same page were photographs of the dead woman Lenora McDermid and the dead man Henry Claver. The woman was smiling which seemed wrong because she was dead. She was younger than our mother and much prettier than our mother but her lipstick was so dark her mouth looked like a black wound. The man was our father's age and frowning the way our father frowned if he'd heard something he had not liked. *McDermid, Claver* had not died in the car wreck but had been "bludgeoned to death" with a weapon like a tire iron and Claver's car had been pushed over the edge of the embankment to make it seem like an accident.

I was staring at the blurry photograph Abigail had pointed out.

"Is that Daddy? No."

"Silly! Of course it's Daddy."

In those years we called our father "Daddy." We called our mother "Mommy." We must have been instructed in this, we could not have thought of such names by ourselves.

The picture was of a man like Daddy but I did not think it was Daddy. He had heavy eyebrows and a heavy jaw and he was squinting at the camera. His hair was thick and dark lifting from his forehead like a rooster's comb but Daddy's hair was not like that now.

"It isn't. Not Daddy."

"Stupid, it says 'Sebera' right there. *It is.*"

Abigail slapped the wet newspaper in my hands and ripped it. She nudged me with her fist to topple me over into the yellow-stained snow. Still I cried, "It is not *it is not him.*"

Other men were questioned in the double homicide. Other men had been involved with both the dead man and the dead woman and one of these was the dead woman's estranged husband Gerald McDermid whose photograph would also appear in the newspapers we were forbidden to see. Later, Gerald McDermid would be arrested by Sparta police and charged with the double homicide but by spring of 1968 these charges were dropped for insufficient evidence. McDermid's relatives insisted that he'd been with them in Buffalo, he'd brought the child with him for the weekend. No one else was ever arrested. Gradually the names *McDermid, Claver* disappeared from the newspapers and the name *Sebera* would never appear again, ever.

This was a fact: Lyle Sebera had been questioned by police and released. He had never been arrested like Gerald McDermid. Our mother's relatives meant to comfort her as they meant to comfort themselves pointing out this fact in murmured conversations just beyond earshot of my sister Abigail and me. *Yes but. Lyle was never. The other one, the husband. He was the one!*

Our mother had been questioned by police also, more than

once. We had no idea what she told them. My sister Abigail and I were not questioned, we were too young.

When had we heard Daddy come home that night? — maybe we had not heard him at all. Maybe it was windy, snowy. Maybe we'd fallen asleep. Maybe it was some other night we remembered. Or maybe that was a night he'd come home for supper by six thirty which was when my mother had expected him. Memories are confusing, when one memory is stronger than other memories it is the strong memory that prevails.

Daddy! Dad-dy. For there was this to remember, that Daddy could be impatient and angry but Daddy could make your heart lift, also. Daddy brought us presents, Daddy called me Funny Face. Daddy was gone, and Daddy came back, and Daddy whistled for us saying, Hey you two you're my girls, you know that, eh? in his two arms lifting us both so we squealed. Who's Daddy's special girl, Daddy would ask, who loves Daddy best, and Abigail would say, Me! and Helen would say, Me! Me, Daddy! until at last Abigail was too old and held back stiff and embarrassed but Helen was still a little girl eager to hug and kiss Daddy for there was no one like Daddy, ever. The stubble-jaws he called the Grizzly, here's the Grizzly come for a kiss, and Daddy's sweet-strong breath, you shut your eyes feeling dizzy. So maybe it had been one of those nights and Daddy had come home in time for supper and was home all that night as Mommy said. For there were many nights. You could not possibly keep them straight. Our mother spoke sharply to us for it was a school night, we were not to watch TV but do our homework and at 9:30 P.M. go upstairs to bed. And she would check us there, to see. In our beds in the darkened room beneath the eaves except there came headlights against the blind drawn over the window and faint ghost-shapes moving across the ceiling in a way to be confused with crawling things in dreams and these dreams to be confused with wakefulness. *Are you asleep?* one of us would ask and the other would giggle *Yes!* Except not that night for we were frightened. Lying very still on our backs beneath the covers, arms against our sides and elbows pressed against our ribs to give the comfort of being held. Drifting into sleep that night and waking suddenly to see the ghost-lights and later to hear a car turning into the driveway and there was the sound of a door at the rear of the house being opened and then shut and if our mother had been waiting up for him there may have been an exchange of voices, muffled words we could not hear. And so *When had we heard Daddy come home that night* was not a question that could be answered even if it had been asked.

Has he ever talked about it with you my sister has asked. As if she has the right.

Back in December I had to take him for more urinary tract and prostate tests, that had frightened him. By this time he had his way of turning his head to the side, the way you'd imagine a sharp-beaked predator bird turning its head, to fix prey in its sight. He sighted me in what remained of his peripheral vision so that I began to feel panicky, my breath began to quicken as if I were standing at the edge of a steep cliff. It was a dark time of year, winters are long and depressing in this part of the country and I'd taken six months off from work at the local community college where now I had to worry they'd give my job to someone else and wouldn't hire me back, and suddenly our father was asking if I remembered something that had happened when I was a little girl, a car found wrecked out in the country, a man and a woman were found dead in the car, and his voice was hoarse and faltering and I stood very still thinking *Maybe he can't see me, he won't know that I am here.*

I went away. I left him there. He was groping to find the edge of his bed. I was very upset, I had work to do. Vacuuming, housework. I hadn't time for this.

Next day he asked if I would take him to church. To church!

Long ago our parents had been married in St. John's Roman Catholic Church in Sparta. So we'd been told. From time to time our mother had gone to Mass there but our father, never. Neither Abigail nor I was baptized in any church. Our mother had never taken us with her to Mass. She'd wanted to be alone, maybe. She'd become a nervous woman who wanted to be alone much of the time. Or maybe she hadn't believed that our souls were very important because we were children and we didn't require the solace of religion as we didn't, like our mother, require the solace of solitary drinking and painkiller pills. *But Mommy is there God?* once I asked my mother and she turned away as if she hadn't heard.

Now this elderly blind broke-back man who'd been Daddy long ago and was not recognizable as Lyle Sebera was saying, "I want — I want to go to confession."

I was stunned by this. Couldn't believe I'd heard right.

Fumbling I said I didn't think the Church had confession any longer.

"No confession? Eh? Since when?"

He couldn't see me — could he? Not when I stood right in front of him. He was quivering with strain, half-standing, the tendons in his elderly neck were taut as ropes. I feared those eyes that were glassy-hard and discolored like stained piano keys and the pupils the size of caraway seeds.

I tried to smile. I tried to speak reasonably. Observing this scene from the doorway you'd think *What a good heart, that woman!* "There have been 'reforms' in the Church. You know, there's a new Church now. The Latin Mass has been gone for, what? — forty years. If you want to confess sins you say them to yourself, you don't involve others in your messes."

Was this so? I had no idea. Maybe it was so. Maybe I'd read it somewhere. I'd never been religious, it was like being colorblind. *Messes* was to suggest childish behavior, not serious transgressions. *Messes* was to keep distance between him and me.

He was whining, "You can take me to church can't you? That church where your mother used to go? I want to talk to a priest. There must be a priest." He was breathing audibly, sweating. His face was drawn and anxious yet I knew that he was capable of suddenly slapping at me, clawing and kicking at me, even spitting at me if I dared to defy him. "I can't — can't — you know I can't — die without talking to a — priest."

"'Die.' You aren't going to die."

"I am! I'm going to — die! I want to die! Goddamn I want to talk to a — priest — a priest — I want to talk to a — and then I want to die."

I began to tremble. I was frightened but I was angry, too. How like Lyle Sebera to imagine that somewhere close by there was "a priest" to serve him. As, always close by, there was a daughter to serve him. And somewhere at hand there was God to forgive him.

"There aren't many priests today, either. Didn't I just read you that article in the paper, there's a shortage of priests. Remember you laughed, you said, 'Serves them right, assholes think they have all the answers.'"

My father seemed not to hear this mimicry of his voice. I'd thought it was damned funny, myself.

"I want to talk to —"

"— to God? You want to talk to God? That's what you're saying, isn't it, you want to talk to God, ask God to 'forgive' you. But there isn't any 'God,' either. It's too late." I was laughing, a sensation like flames without heat, flames of pure dazzling light passed through me. I was on my way out of the invalid's room leaving the old man gaping after me.

Invalids say things they don't mean. Invalids say things to test their caretakers who are likely to be the only individuals who love them and can endure them.

But often then he began to speak of dying. What I needed to do for him was get the right pills the kind that put you to sleep forever: "'Barbitch-ates.'" Or his own pills, damn-fucking pills, so many he had to take every day, at mealtimes, it was my task to sort out these pills and make sure that he took them, my task (as I'd promised his doctor) to cut the largest tablets (four hundred milligrams!) into pieces so he wouldn't choke swallowing them. So why didn't I dump all the prescribed damn-fucking pills into a pile and pulverize them and dissolve them in a tall glass of gin, he'd lap down thirsty "like a dog." I listened to this, the pleading, whining, cajoling, the threat beneath, always the threat beneath, for this scrawny bent-back old man had once stood six feet tall and weighed somewhere beyond two hundred pounds and he'd been a man who had not needed to plead, beg, cajole you can bet your ass, he'd been a man who controlled his family with a frown, a glance, a sudden fist brought down flat on a table. So as I listened to my father's voice I understood that this was a test being put to me. I was expected to express surprise, alarm. I was expected to plead with him *No Daddy! Not when we love you.* Instead I mumbled something vague and conciliatory as you do when an elderly invalid is whining in self-pity and self-disgust spilling over you like a sloshing bedpan. But at the same time my heartbeat quickened. *He wants to die, I can help him die.*

He said, sneering, "You'd like that, eh! Get rid of the old man. You and —" His hoarse voice trailed off in befuddlement, he'd forgotten Abigail's name.

Not that this was flattering to me, for lately he'd been forgetting my name, too.

But now he'd trapped me: for I couldn't say "Yes" and I couldn't say "No." He laughed cruelly, baring his stained teeth. Stiffly I said, "You're not very funny."

"*You're* funny. 'Hel-len'-got-a-poker-up-her-ass."

Pronouncing my name as if it was a joke. Some TV comic inflection. When I didn't react, he snorted and threw the TV remote control at me, such a lightweight plastic thing it struck me harmlessly on my right breast and fell to the floor. (We'd been watching Fox TV, his favorite program was *The O'Reilly Factor.*) I went away, left the remote control on the floor where he'd have to grope for it partway beneath his bed if he wanted it.

He-len. I suppose the name was a joke.

So the subject of dying, wanting to die, how I might help him die began to surface in our life together in that house. It surfaced and sank from view and resurfaced like flotsam in a turbulent river. I thought that yes, my father was probably serious, I believed that he understood that his condition was terminal, he would never even partway recover his health before the stroke, yet of course I didn't trust him. He was feeling guilt for something he'd done years ago but he'd never once spoken of what he'd done to our mother. How he'd wrung the life from her. How he'd laughed at her, as he laughed at me, speaking her name in mockery. It was the way of the bully daring you to react with anger or indignation and knowing that you could not. Ovarian cancer had swept through my mother like wildfire and when after her first surgery she'd wanted to stay with an older sister to recuperate my father had said yes, that was a good idea, she'd taken his word on faith but after that he refused to see her, even to speak with her, he never allowed her to return to live with him, liked to say he'd washed his hands of her, she'd left *him.* Now he was elderly and blind and whining about wanting to die and yet he continued to eat most of the meals I prepared for him, except when he was actively sick his appetite was usually good enough, especially for ice cream. Elderly invalids frequently want to die and are aided in their deaths by sympathetic relatives and doctors, I knew this of course yet I would not have dared speak to his doctor about this wish of my father's, I would not even speak with my father about it thinking *I am not a daughter who wishes her father dead.* More truthful was the admonition *I must not be a daughter legally liable for her father's death.*

Would I have helped him to die, if I knew I wouldn't be caught?

Would I have held a pillow over his face until he stopped breathing, if I knew I wouldn't be caught?

"'He-len. Good daughter.'"

I laughed. Living with a blind sick old man who dislikes you, you become accustomed to talking and laughing to yourself.

Between us there was an undeclared war. In a distant part of the house I could hear, or believed that I could hear, the old man muttering to himself, laughing also, but meanly, as one might laugh stubbing his toe, and cursing *Damn! Goddamn! Fuck!* loud enough to hear if I wished. For years he had not been able to sleep for more than a few hours at a time, needing to use the toilet frequently, but now his nights were ever more restless, disruptive. I would be wakened in a jolt from my exhausted sleep hearing him prowling and stumbling through the downstairs. I dreaded him falling and injuring himself for already he'd sprained a wrist, sprained ribs, bruised himself badly. After a severe stroke at seventy-eight he'd had smaller strokes, all without warning. Years of heavy smoking, heavy drinking, heavy eating had weakened his heart that had now to be monitored by a "gizmo" in his chest — a pacemaker. And there was the macular degeneration that had begun years ago, to madden and terrify. Old age is one symptom after another, a doctor told me meaning to be sympathetic.

After the initial stroke I'd moved back into the house in which I had spent the first eighteen years of my life for I'd been shaken by my father's rapid decline and I'd been touched by his obvious need for me. For never had Lyle Sebera expressed any need for anyone, and certainly not for me. We'd relocated his bedroom downstairs and close to the bathroom in the hallway and I'd been cheerful and upbeat and he'd been grateful then, at the start. Before more symptoms emerged, that were not going to go away.

Later I would come to realize that my father's gratitude had been a trick to ensnare me. He'd been a man to seduce women, then to speak of them in contempt as "easy."

When Abigail called, I told her none of this. That our father was exactly the man he'd always been except now he was miserable and wished to die and that I wished him to die. That I was furious with her for her shrewdness in leaving Sparta to live hundreds of miles away. Instead I told her coolly, daring her to doubt my words: "Oh, you know Lyle. Hardy as hell, he'll outlive us all." Or: "He's doing as well as we can expect. Good days, not-so-good. Want me to put him on?"

Quickly Abigail would say no! For he seemed always to be agitated or annoyed by her, asking if she was "checking up on him" — "wanting money from him" — and seeming not to remember her name.

"But he asks after you, Abigail. All the time."

"Oh, Helen. He does?"

Abigail was doubtful yet wanting to believe. I had all I could do to keep from bursting into laughter.

Except one day when Abigail was questioning me too closely about our father's property investments, his medical insurance, and his latest physical ailments, I did begin to laugh. I laughed, and I sobbed angrily. For it was the riddle of my life now, how I'd become our father's caretaker. I'd become the "good" daughter as our mother, before her cancer, had been the "good" wife. I told Abigail that it was some kind of grotesque mistake, these past several years. I wasn't a good person, I hadn't a good heart. She, Abigail, was so much the better person. Everyone knew that. I was selfish, cruel, and indifferent to the pain of others, just like our father. My heart was shriveled and hard as a lump of coal yet somehow I was the sister who'd remained in Sparta, New York, while she, Abigail, had gone away to college and married and had children and never lived closer than three hundred miles away. While I'd never married, never been in love. I'd barely graduated from high school and remained in Sparta taking courses at the community college where now I worked in "food services" and had to be grateful for that. Now I was living in this house we'd both been desperate to escape. I wasn't a girl of ten, or nineteen, or even a woman of twenty-nine. I was forty-nine years old and how had that happened?

Abigail said, "Oh, Helen. Of course I'm coming there. We'll make new arrangements. I love you."

I love you would burn in my shriveled heart. Though I had not been able to mumble *I love you, too.*

"Helen, you must let *me.*"

Yes I would let her. I smiled to think *Yes! Try.*

Through this second day of her visit my sister Abigail was suffused with energy, determination, good intentions. Reminded me of when she'd been, for a few ecstatic months in high school, a born-again Christian. She "aired out" rooms long pervaded with the stink of rancid food, soiled clothing and bedding, dried urine. With paper towels and Windex she washed windowpanes long layered in grime. She drove our father, sulky and anxious, to his morning medical appointment. In a voice pitched as if for a deaf or retarded child she spoke to the old man earnestly and cheerfully and tried not to be discouraged when he acknowledged her efforts only in grunts. I thought *He doesn't want your good cheer, he wants anger and hurt. He wants to be punished.*

Never would the old blind man speak intimately to Abigail as he spoke to me. I knew this.

"Why is he angry with me? Is he angry with me? Does he hate me, Helen?"

My sister's voice began to sound wistful, even resentful. She'd sent me away to take the afternoon off — "Spend some time on yourself for a change, Helen" — and when I returned in the early evening she was looking tired, baffled. The old blind man hadn't been grateful for her company but preferred to sulk in his room with the TV turned up loud. He hadn't even seemed to know, or care, who she was! The damned vacuum cleaner had gotten clotted with something gluey and smelly sucked up into the hose. The damned washing machine in the basement had broken down in mid-cycle. The first of several "assisted-living facilities" she'd called had no openings, only waiting lists. Cleaning the kitchen cupboards that hadn't been cleaned for years she'd discovered roaches. Nests of spiders in all the corners of the house. I wanted to ask if she'd noticed how the rear of the old house had begun to sink into muck, to disappear. How the lead backing in the mirrors had begun to eat its way through the glass like cancer.

"How can you live in this house, Helen! How can you bear it!"

Because I am stronger than you. Like a roach.

The rest of the day went badly. I'd warned Abigail that the old man had sharp ears and so he'd overheard her on the phone calling "nursing homes" and he was furious saying he would never leave this house, he would die in this house, nobody could force him to leave this house which was his property, he knew his rights as a United States citizen and he'd go on TV to expose us, if we tried to cheat him. Abigail tried to explain which was a mistake, tried to apologize which was a worse mistake. He shouted, he spat, he threatened, he pummeled the air with his fists, there was nothing to do but assure him *Yes we promise no we will not ever, you have our word.* Abigail's next blunder was to try to feed the old man a "special supper" she'd prepared in place of the sugar-laced frozen Birds Eye suppers the old man was accustomed to eating and I was accustomed to preparing, the first mouthful of poached salmon he spat out onto the table: "Trying to choke me with fish bones, eh? That's why you're here, eh?"

Abigail protested, "Daddy, no. How can you think —"

Daddy caused the old man to snort in derision. He hadn't been *Daddy* in thirty years.

My afternoon away from the elderly blind man's house had been strange as a dream dreamt by someone not myself whom in some way I seemed to know, even to be bound with intimately, like a cousin not glimpsed in many years. Mostly I drove around Sparta. I drove out along the Chautauqua River. I stopped at a liquor store to bring back a bottle of Scotch whiskey and this bottle like a shining talisman I brought upstairs with two freshly rinsed water glasses to share with my exhausted sister Abigail after — finally! — the house was darkened downstairs and the old man sunk into his comatose sleep in the hospital bed installed in his room. As we'd huddled together in our bedroom down the hall as girls so now we huddled together as adults in my bedroom which was our parents' former bedroom that still felt unnatural to me, that I'd dared even to enter this room let alone appropriate it. Sprawled on my back on the rumpled double bed whose sheets hadn't been changed in weeks, a soiled foam-rubber pillow scrunched beneath my head, I balanced my whiskey glass between my flat-sloping breasts and listened to Abigail speak in wayward feverish lunges like a marathon runner who has overexerted herself yet can't stop running, must continue panting and gasping for air until the collapse is complete. We had not undressed for bed. Our clothes were rumpled and smelled of a sickroom. This day that was meant to be my sister's triumph we'd been defeated by the old blind man yet — so stubbornly! — Abigail reverted to her subject of the assisted-care facility we must find for him, as if finding the place was the task, the challenge, and not persuading our father to move into it. Abigail said adamantly that it wasn't possible for me to continue to care for him in this hopeless pigsty, he had to be moved immediately, for his own well-being as for mine, by which she meant, Abigail said pointedly, my physical and mental health. We would have to get power of attorney over his assets, there was no turning back. I told her yes but we'd just promised him, hadn't we: *No we will not ever, you have our word.* But Abigail seemed not to hear.

"If not in Sparta then somewhere else. Peekskill! — there are plenty of 'assisted-living facilities' there."

Abigail was sitting on the edge of my bed sipping whiskey in small mouthfuls. Her weight felt heavy, leaden. Her hair that had been sleek-cut and glossy was nearly as matted now as mine and her skin exuded a sick clammy odor. I said, "He's serious, Abigail. He wants to die here. He wants to *die.*" Abigail laughed angrily, "Well, he just can't *die.* Probably not for a long time."

I gripped the foam-rubber pillow with both hands, behind my head. I said, "We could hold a pillow over his face. He'd struggle like hell and he's strong but there are two of us and his heart will give out." I paused. I giggled. Inanely I added, "It's been done."

Abigail frowned. "Oh, Helen."

Abigail giggled. Abigail drained much of her glass and wiped her mouth with the edge of her hand. "Oh *Helen.* The things you say." Maybe in rebuke, or to comfort or console me, Abigail groped for my free hand, and squeezed. Middle-aged sisters gripping hands. That evening after our disastrous supper I'd overheard Abigail on her cell phone in the room she was staying in, our bedroom when we'd been girls, I stood outside the door listening hearing my sister's lowered voice, she was speaking with her husband back in Peekskill saying things were much worse than she'd expected, so much worse, *can't leave Helen, my poor sister I can't leave until* as quickly I turned away blinded by tears. My sister whose life was so rich and full and superior to my own cared for me! Another person cared enough for me to be anxious on my behalf, my name had been uttered in a tone of dismay. I was very moved though I could feel nothing much, I'd become anesthetized to sensation as a paralyzed limb.

I said, "Where I drove this afternoon? Out along the river? I was looking for where it happened — the wrecked car, the 'double homicide,' remember?" Abigail shuddered and seemed to stiffen but made no reply. She'd become drowsy, lying on her side on the bed, clumsily perpendicular to me, her nearly empty glass against her thigh. I said, "I don't think I found it. The exact site. I'm not sure," and Abigail said irritably, "Well, you'd never seen it, had you? *I* never saw it," and I said, "Supposedly they'd gone off the road, down an embankment. I mean, they were pushed off the road. It's very steep there, down to the river. There was a bridge there, I'd thought. Eventually I found an old iron-girder bridge so maybe that's where it happened. Not where I'd thought but farther out. It's desolate out there, a kind of swampy jungle along the river where the car must have capsized. I remember that word — *capsized.* Like *bludgeoned* — a word that, if you hear it, you can guess its meaning. On my odometer I clocked it, where the wrecked car was found is seven point three miles from this house." Abigail made no reply. I heard her breathing in husky surges. Like depleted swimmers sinking slowly through the water, unresisting we settled in the warm black muck below.

We were wakened suddenly hours later by a noise downstairs of lurching footsteps. Helplessly we lay listening to the blind man make his uncertain way to the bathroom in the hall. I knew to wait for the toilet to be flushed (though sometimes he failed to flush it out of forgetfulness, or spite) and following this it was crucial that he return to his bed for if he did not return to bed, this meant he'd become confused and lost and I would need to go downstairs to guide him back to bed; but more upsetting was the possibility that he'd decided he did not want to sleep but preferred to prowl the house like a trapped animal searching for a way out. I was remembering how a few nights ago I had stopped him at the top of the basement steps, he'd opened the door and was about to pitch forward to break his brittle bones on the concrete floor twelve feet below. And there was the time I'd discovered him in the kitchen where he'd turned on four gas burners emitting a deathly hissing sound for of course (no need to tell me, I knew) the old man's wish to die might not be a wish to die alone. Abigail said, "How can you live like this, Helen!" but in the next moment she was up, slapping her cheeks to wake herself fully, saying, "We have to help him, he might hurt himself." Already I was at the door. I was practiced in such nighttime maneuvers and had no doubt that the old man downstairs was waiting for me and would be surprised that tonight there would be two of me, not just one.

We switched on lights. The downstairs was ablaze with light. A festive occasion here! We were not blind and so we required lights to see and in such dazzling light bracketing the vast and terrible night outside we did see: the old man barefoot and cowering in a corner of the living room, turning his head at an angle to sight us in his vision. Abigail spoke to him and he cursed her. I spoke to him and he cursed me. Though Abigail had cajoled him into changing out of his filth-stiffened flannel shirt and pajama bottoms to put on freshly laundered pajamas, yet he seemed to be wearing the same filth-stiffened things. "Oh, Daddy. Oh!" Abigail advanced upon him recklessly not knowing how quick his blows could come, surprisingly hard stinging blows and his nails were broken and sharp as a cat's, drawing a zigzag of blood in her cheek. We circled him, tried to head him off so he couldn't stumble into the kitchen. He was glowering, panting. He lunged at Abigail sensing she was the weaker of the two of us, he managed to thrust a floor lamp at her, striking her and hurting her, and he grabbed her, "Damn bitch! Want to suck my blood!" and they struggled together, I tried to pull him off her, loosen his talon-grip on her shoulders. He was fierce and writhing as a wounded snake. He fell and pulled Abigail with him, she straddled his bony thrashing body and grabbed a cushion from the sofa and pressed it against his face. Her eyes were bloodshot and triumphant. Her lips were drawn back from her glistening teeth. "Hate hate hate you why don't you die!" I grabbed my sister's wrists and managed to pull her from him. Her thighs were muscular, her bare feet curled with strain. The cushion lay on the old man's face, his body appeared headless. He was breathing feebly but he was breathing. When I tried to help him up he spat at me, he called me the vilest names. He could not have known who I was, he called me the vilest names. On his belly then crawling, and I tried again to help him and was rebuffed and Abigail crouched above us dazed and affrighted as a sleepwalker wakened too abruptly, she seemed not to know what she'd done, what was happening except that it wasn't her responsibility but mine, and I would take charge. After some minutes of resistance the old man gave in, surly and still cursing, but I was able to get him back to bed, he was exhausted now and would sink back into his comatose sleep for a few more hours. "None of this has happened, Abigail," I told my sister, squeezing her icy hands. "He won't remember anything in the morning."

We made no effort to sleep that night. Already it was 4:20 A.M. I helped Abigail undress and ran a bath for her and shampooed her hair in the bath and treated the shallow scratch in her cheek and put a flesh-colored Band-Aid over it. By dawn she was prepared to drive back to Peekskill. She'd repacked her small suitcase, her eyes were socketed in fatigue yet she'd put on fresh lipstick and a bright smile flashed in her face. We thought it best for her to leave without saying goodbye to him. For very likely he wouldn't remember that she had even been here, let alone what had happened in the confusion of the night. Or if he remembered, he would blame Helen. At the door Abigail hugged me tight and kissed me at the edge of the mouth. I held her for a long moment. "Call me, don't forget me," I said, meaning to be playful, and Abigail said, "Oh, Helen. I'm going to help you. I promise." Abigail could not hear what I was hearing, only just audible at the rear of the house: an elderly voice sounding weaker than usual, fretful and anxious. "Helen? *He-len?*" I shut the door after my sister and hurried back there.

NATHAN OATES

The Empty House

FROM *The Antioch Review*

AFTER THE PLATE OF UNDERCOOKED beans and crumbly tortillas, Ryan had half an hour before his bus for Huehuetenango, so he ordered coffee. The waiter, an old man with gray hairs hanging from his nose, said he had something special and hurried into the back. By that evening Ryan would see his old friend Jim. It'd been eight years since they'd spoken and in that time Jim had become a Maryknoll priest, a missionary, posted here in Guatemala. There really was no accounting for life, Ryan thought. The old man came out of the back with a cup, taking small steps.

"Nescafé," he said, setting the cup down and putting his hand on Ryan's shoulder. "Bueno. Muy bueno."

"Gracias," Ryan said, touching the handle of the cup, but the old man stood squeezing his shoulder until he lifted the cup, sloshing a bit over the rim, and took a sip. It was bitter and grainy. He smiled up into the tangle of nose hairs and said, "Deliciosa."

"Nescafé," the man said, delighted. As he went back to the kitchen he glanced over his shoulder, miming sips.

Here Ryan was, in a country covered with coffee plantations, and he was served instant coffee, which probably cost twice as much as local grounds. And this wasn't a Western tourist hotel where the need to impress Americans might drive the owners to such stupidity; he was in a shitty little café near the Guatemala City bus station. There were only two other patrons, both young, scraggly-looking men, asleep over their yellow plastic tables. But this was one of the pleasures of traveling: You were always allowed to marvel at the incongruities that, when they faced you in your everyday life, say, in the suburbs, you simply rolled right past, thinking, big deal, let's get moving. That would be him in a few weeks, back in America, at his sister's house in Florida. Florida! As though they were all retired and worn down and exhausted by life, which, he felt sure, his sister, younger than he by two years, would be soon enough, since she was getting married in a week and would probably have a kid, buy a Volvo, start saving for college. And then if she were in a coffee shop and they served her Nescafé, well, she'd probably just be annoyed. What is this shit, she'd think.

Nescafé, he thought again, sloshing the last bit of coffee around in the slick of grounds, with a sinking feeling that he'd overplayed the moment. The irony wasn't as dense as he'd hoped. Anyway, what good was irony without anyone to share it?

Hooking his blue duffel bag over his shoulder — though travelers were now all using new, internal-frame backpacks, he stuck with his old Diadora bag with a sense of Luddite pride — he went up to the bead curtain that hung between the dining room and the kitchen and called for the check.

In the blue haze of the station men clambered atop buses, shouting at the crowd that tossed up luggage. The drivers, some in gray uniforms, others in white shirts and jeans, chatted together off to the side, smoking, together summoning the strength to plunge these buses out onto the crumbling roads that clung to and wound around the sides of mountains through remote areas purportedly — though who could know how much of the "official news" to believe — full of revolutionaries and bandits.

The highways all over the country, Ryan knew, though he'd not actually traveled much in Guatemala, were spotted, particularly at the sharper turns in the passes, with clusters of white crosses where buses had overshot the road, breaking a window through the jungle canopy, crumpling on the mountainside. He'd seen many such crosses in Chile and Peru, up in the Andes, riding on buses just like these. He wasn't about to be fazed, or worried. Or maybe he was a little bit worried, a tiny, niggling fear that crept through his stomach. But he was used to this fear, and in a way, he thought, it was a comfort: proof, amid the chaos and violence, of his individual, coherent self. The fear was the same each time he boarded a bus or was stopped by the police, and so it was a reminder that, despite all he'd seen and all he'd learned about the terror of the world, at the core he was still Ryan. Himself.

Stuffing his duffel beneath the seat, he flipped through the *Time* magazine he'd bought in Antigua. He scanned the table of contents for familiar names, but didn't recognize any. Most of his friends had gone into television, thinking, rightly, that's where the money was. He was one of the few to stick with newspaper work, and one of the very few to have left the country. For six years now he'd been covering the political troubles in Chile and Argentina. The culture of fear. Though, looking through *Time,* you wouldn't have any idea this was happening. He'd always half-expected his work to make him famous, to win him Pulitzer Prizes, get him on staff at the *New York Times.* This hadn't happened. Four of his articles had been picked up for the *Herald Tribune,* over six years. This wasn't bad. Better than most. But it was never enough. The world just didn't care.

The bus left the middle-class neighborhood around the station, rattled past two large shopping centers, then turned onto a narrow side street. They went through what seemed to be a shipping district: streets were full of trucks, idling up on the curbs, or pulled halfway into warehouses. Men with machine guns herded a crowd of peasants onto the backs of cargo trucks while a fat man in a tight suit brandished a clipboard. After the warehouses the bus passed along the edge of a market where people were screaming at one another across tables loaded with fruit and flies. From there the neighborhoods deteriorated until they were passing the slums along the mountain, shacks with plastic walls, heaps of trash sending up translucent waves in the sun. Then the bus was free of the city.

Earlier that morning he'd taken a different bus over the mountains from Antigua, where he'd been "on vacation" for a week after a long flight from Santiago. He'd managed to make himself into a real tourist, he'd thought: taking a tour of the heavily guarded jade factory, visiting the crumbling cathedral, and breakfasting each morning in the flower-flooded patio of his pension, listening to the elderly British couple at the next table whisper over cups of tea about whose fault it was that they'd missed their charter flight to Tikal or some other failure in their trip. Nights he'd gone to bars, surprised at first by the hordes of gringos there to study Spanish at the language institutes despite the civil war. But then the gringos had their own take on reality. A few had told him earnestly that the civil war was overrated. It wasn't really a *war,* you know. He'd been disgusted by their obliviousness. He was glad to be back on the trail of a news story, a potentially radical and important one.

Jim was a Maryknoll, which meant he was dispensing medicine, teaching literacy skills to the poor, instructing them in the proper way of Catholic worship, and, although of course he'd never admit this, encouraging dangerously leftist ideas. The political naiveté of the Catholic project in Guatemala was the seed of Ryan's projected article. Though he sympathized with the ideals, it was suicidal. There were rumors of recent massacres in the mountains just outside Huehuetenango. Whole villages dumped in the woods. The military blamed the EGP; the Catholic clergy blamed the military; the military blamed the clergy for supporting the EGP; the clergy said they were doing humanitarian work. According to a reporter Ryan had spoken with in Guatemala City, there was a rumor a young woman had escaped, taken for dead amid the pile of bodies by drunk, blood-lusting soldiers. Eyewitnesses were rare. If Jim could hook him up with this woman not even American newspapers would be able to ignore the article. Ryan could, with some luck, make the world care. At least for a moment.

Along the highway the jungle was flattened back a hundred feet. There were gleaming puddles of water in the deep tracks of heavy equipment. Yellow backhoes leaned on piles of earth. Men squatted in the shadows of the wheels, smoking. He knew the trees had been pushed back to reduce the risk of guerrilla ambushes, and that the forests were also ravaged by a beetle that burrowed into pines and cut off the sap flow. The remaining trees were whittled at in the night by local farmers for fuel. He thought this would be a good way to open an article on Guatemala: a new, unused highway and a disappearing forest.

It's possible that not all the buses are quite so broken-down as the one I rode to Huehuetenango when tracing the path Ryan, my older brother, must have taken back in 1982. For one thing it was years later, 1997. The civil war had ended the year before.

I got on the bus early and had a seat, but soon people filled the aisle, bumping each other with bags of vegetables and fabrics. The driver climbed along the side, thrusting his hand in the windows, demanding fares. I gave my seat to an old woman with a chicken in a wooden box. Not far out of Antigua the young woman beside me in the aisle threw up, splattering my shoes, strings of saliva hanging from her lips, her face pale. She grabbed my shirtsleeve for balance. She dry heaved a few more times, then straightened up, wiping her mouth. She was younger than I'd first thought, maybe around my age, mid-twenties, wearing a loose, large T-shirt that said Nike in flaking black script. Her long black hair was pulled into a thick braid that went all the way down her back.

"Gracias," she said. I kept my hand on her arm. She smiled weakly and tucked her head down, shoulders shaking before she got sick again. For an hour we went on like that, I holding her up, she throwing up and dry heaving. It was the closest I'd felt to any Guatemalan while I was down there. When we reached her stop, a small town whose name I didn't know and couldn't find on any maps later, she said something to me, more than just thanks, and I nodded, though I hadn't understood. I wanted to hug her. I didn't want her to go. Maybe, I thought, I should get off the bus, talk with her, make sure she gets home all right. But this was just an excuse, I knew, to avoid going to Huehuetenango.

I'd put off going there until the very end of my trip. I don't want to give the impression that I had any real, tangible hopes of finding my brother still alive in Guatemala. He'd appeared on a list from the State Department, marking him as missing. Disappeared. They'd called my parents two months after the wedding to tell them Ryan had been in the country, but had not been heard from since the day his plane had landed. They knew he'd gone to Huehuetenango, apparently to visit an old friend working as a priest there. That was the last they'd heard.

I went down to Guatemala to see the place where, in some ways, my family had broken apart. But traveling alone down there was harder than I'd anticipated. The country was rough, my Spanish was bad, and after getting violently ill for a week in Panajachel I spent most of my time in Antigua, which was crowded with tourists: Swedes and Americans and Danes shopping in boutiques and drinking all night in the gringo bars and clubs, admiring the city's beauty, the pastel painted walls of the Spanish colonial mansions, the ornate lampposts over cobblestone streets. Antigua felt, beyond the architecture, European and safe.

This is not to say that one doesn't still encounter fear, even there. Once, walking with my camera, taking pictures of flower-dressed ruins destroyed in an eighteenth-century earthquake, I strayed too far down through the city. I lowered the camera and noticed an old man, face-down in the street, as though he'd stopped for a sip of sewer water and died. His hands, flopped out above his head, were cracked and looked as though they were made of chalk. I turned to find my way back uptown when a group of young men spotted me and began following, shouting faggot, pussy: *pinche huecho, concha.* Each time I glanced back the four flung out their arms, like birds defending a nest.

Thinking back I'm not sure how afraid I should've been; maybe the boys just wanted to scare me a little, or maybe they wanted to take my wallet, stuffed with quetzals, my watch, my camera. I hurried past gringo bars and the central park with the ornate fountain, three angels, heads thrown back, hurling white arcs of water. It was near the fountain that the boys fell off my trail. That should have been the end of my fear, but a moment later, on the far side of the park, I passed the police station — two cops were outside smoking cigarettes — and then the fear only got worse, became terror. The boys might've mugged me, at worst kicked me a few times, but these men, with their big stomachs and machine guns, could arrest me on a pretense, murder me, and no one would stop them.

Even in my short time down there I knew this sort of thing happened. I'd met a young Danish man in a bar who'd been thrown in prison for insulting a drunken policeman. In his cell the guards had kicked him until his liver ruptured. His skin was tainted yellow. Patches of green flesh sagged beneath his eyes. He flew back to Denmark for surgery the next day, or that's what everyone at the bar said.

I left all this out of the e-mails and post cards I sent home. I mentioned the flowers, the way people from each of the five towns in the mountains around Lake Atitlan wore different brightly colored woven shirts, like jerseys. I wanted my parents to know I was all right. I was a gringo, and so I could be scared and worried about myself but I'd always be safer than most. But how could I say this to my parents, my mother in particular?

There was, throughout my childhood, a shrine to Ryan in his old bedroom. The room hadn't been left untouched — he'd hadn't really lived there since he left for college — but on one dresser were several photographs of him: his graduation from college, a picture of him in New York before he went to South America, then one he'd sent from Santiago of him at a rooftop restaurant in the early morning, the sheer, snow-capped mountain peaks not yet cloaked in smog. There were the post cards he'd sent along with his news articles in a binder, arranged chronologically. This little shrine wasn't hidden away, or something to be ashamed of. Nor was it something every guest was shown. It was just there.

Ryan went to college when I was five and I remember only glimpses of him: a bag of candy corn he gave me as a present one Thanksgiving — probably just left over from Halloween — while he was in college. I left the candies in their bag on the windowsill, liking the way the streetlight glinted silver off the plastic, until the following spring when they melted in the sun and my mother threw them out; his long hair toward the end of college that our mom hated. "Where are my scissors?" she kept saying at his graduation, lifting up long frizzy locks and snipping them with her fingers. Then he moved to New York and was busy with reporting, then he was off to South America and didn't return home for years.

Though Ryan wasn't physically present, he permeated my life. My mother cried often when I was young, and though I can't be sure it started with Ryan's disappearance, I assume they were related. I remember once going upstairs to tell her I was going to play soccer and finding her sitting on the edge of the bed, sobbing. Her whole body was involved, shoulders shaking, head bobbing, hands clutching at her pants, then coming to her face, then grabbing her hair.

"Mom?" I said, and she looked up, still sobbing.

"Honey, yes, what is it?" she said. It was terrifying to hear her voice, trying to be so normal in the midst of all that awful shaking grief. I couldn't remember why I'd come up there. She came across the room, wiping her tears. She put her hand on my head and asked again what I wanted. I hated Ryan then.

One of his articles, a short thing published in the *Herald Tribune* about the American expatriate community in Santiago, says it's tempting to imagine ourselves the victims, to imagine the violence is because of us, about us, but it isn't, and one needs to always remember the thousands in the mountains, in the cities, who have no voice, whose fear will never be recorded. But what good was this to my mother?

Ultimately, I went to Guatemala with two hopes: perhaps I could find out who *I* was — I'd always felt my self was in some ways missing and was connected to the mystery of what had happened to Ryan — and maybe my trip could bring a kind of solace to my mother. Perhaps through action, through really engaging the world, I could forge clarity out of the mess of life.

Ryan's bus slowed as it reached the small town of Chimaltenango. An old man climbed aboard; his gums were stained black, as though a bottle of ink had spilled in his mouth. He held a sack of avocadoes on his lap like a favorite grandchild.

As the bus pulled clear of the town a clutch of children gave chase, dragging strings tied to plastic bags, trying to fly them. Ryan waved to the kids and one let out a triumphant shout, leaping in the air, his bag jerking along the ground.

He hadn't seen Jim for eight years and wondered if he'd recognize him. But of course they'd be the two gringos at the bus stop. He imagined Jim with the long hair he'd had in college, curling into a loose cloud, though this was hard to match with a pinching white priest collar and those sticky black polyester pants and shirt.

It was difficult to connect Jim, whom he'd always thought of as the smartest of his college friends, with the fact that he was now a Maryknoll. Ryan had a rich, full contempt for religion. One just had to consider the situation here in Guatemala, with General Rios Montt who believed he was some kind of prophet and the massacres were the will of Jesus. But if Jim hadn't turned to religion they might never have connected again. His sister had forwarded Jim's letter. The letter had jokingly said it was Ryan's adventurousness that had helped him decide to leave the States and work in Latin America.

Ryan had written back, saying perhaps he'd come for a visit. Jim had written an encouraging letter: maybe Ryan could even write an article about the work they were doing there in Guatemala? Sure, Ryan wrote back. Maybe.

Reading Jim's letter, he had felt as if a cord, trailing back into his past he'd thought long severed, was suddenly pulling on him. And, over the past five years in Chile, he'd met many expatriates, had so much work, felt caught in something so important, that it was easy to lose track of those back in America living the life you'd not been able to stand the thought of; but here was another friend, someone he'd lost track of, who'd chosen a similar path. They were different from most Americans.

When he called from his pension in Antigua he'd been full of nervous energy. The letter with Jim's number was tattered from a week in Ryan's wallet and from his having read it so many times. A woman who answered, perhaps a nun, said yes, Padre was in.

"Diga?" Jim's voice shouted, so familiar, so wonderful to hear.

"Is this the infamous Father Jim?" Ryan said, feeling his old self, his self from college — naive, ironic, ridiculous — rising up in a rush.

"It just might be," Jim said, with a laugh. "Ryan. I'm surprised you called."

"Of course I called. I was so moved by your letter, I just had to."

"Right," Jim said, then cleared his throat, sounding suddenly older. "So, you're in Guatemala? You said in your letter you might be stopping through."

Ryan said he'd tried hard to be a tourist for a week and Jim responded politely, but there was a distance in the conversation. When Ryan asked if he should come visit, as Jim suggested, the man said, "Of course. Did I say that in my letter? Of course you should."

"Jim, if this isn't a good time, that's fine. I haven't even been up to Tikal yet."

"No, everything is fine. It's fine. You should come." Jim then tried to steer the conversation onto more even ground, asking about old friends, but after a few minutes of this Ryan asked if Jim was frightened.

"Who isn't?" The line was staticky. Maybe they were being taped, Ryan thought.

"Well, me," he said. Was this a lie? He wasn't sure.

"You've always been the brave one."

"That's very true," Ryan said, smiling ironically at his reflection in his room's mirror. "I am incredibly brave."

"Maybe you can inspire me, when you visit." There it was again: the old Jim.

"You haven't given up drinking, have you? Because I'm not sure I can look at you in a priest getup without at least a few drinks."

"Ryan, I'm a priest. All we do is drink. And love Jesus. And mankind and so on." He would meet Ryan at the station, but right then he really needed to go.

The weekend before my own bus ride to Huehuetenango I went to the embassy in Guatemala City. They had no information, not even the records of Ryan's disappearance. Or at least they didn't show them to me. They showed me nothing, though they were polite. They asked how my hotel was. They gave me their business cards. They told me to travel safe. Back in Antigua that night I met a guy from Chicago, whom I'll call Chris. We watched the Red Sox games — this was the only bar in all of Guatemala with satellite TV — and talked about places we'd been, places we thought we were going. He asked if I'd been to Tikal. I said I'd missed it, too hard to get to. We discussed the new highway that was scheduled to open soon from Guatemala City to the ruins, cutting the trip from sixteen hours to four.

The next night, when Chris didn't show up, the bartender from Virginia told me Chris's story. He was traveling with his fiancée. They'd been up in the Tikal region a few months before and had gone camping in the mountains. A group of men had found their campsite and had tied him to a tree and forced him to watch while they raped and beat his fiancée. She was in Antigua, but never left their hotel.

Why would they stay in Guatemala? I asked. The bartender said he didn't know. "But that's crazy," I said. "Why don't they just get out of here?"

"What? Dude, how should I know?" He turned away to watch the Red Sox.

I didn't tell my parents I was going until after I'd bought my plane ticket. My father listened, didn't say anything, and handed the phone to my mother, who said, "What? What's this?" I tried to explain. I told her the countries weren't nearly so dangerous anymore. "Being on an Interstate is more dangerous," I told her. I wasn't sure if this was true, but it sounded right. "You are not going, do you hear me?" my mother said. But what could they do? They couldn't stop me. I needed to get out into the world.

My mother had always encouraged me to live through the imagination, particularly after Ryan disappeared. She made me take typing instead of shop and was always happy when I went upstairs to work on one of my fantasy novels instead of going out to play. I remember once my father came upstairs, home from teaching at the university, and sat me down and said it just wasn't healthy for a kid to spend so much time alone. Out my bedroom window I could see two of my neighborhood friends chasing a couple of girls, shouting and jumping. My mother came up during this talk and told my father to leave me alone. "What's the problem?" she said. "He has an imagination. There's nothing wrong with that. I'm proud of him."

She did this to keep me safe. She'd already lost one son to the world.

But, after graduating from college and working for three years in customer service jobs, I decided I needed to go to Guatemala. I'd been thinking of doing it for years, but had put it off because of my mother, and I'd hoped how I should live my life and who I was would be clearer in the working world. It wasn't, and eventually going to Central America was all I thought about, all I wanted.

What I found during those six weeks in Central America wasn't what I'd been looking for. Nothing had been resolved. I still had no better sense of who I was, or who Ryan had been. After the trip I stayed with my parents for a couple of months, figuring out what to do next. During those months with my parents — they didn't look at my pictures, didn't want to hear anecdotes — I wondered if I'd gone down there *only* for myself? Is that what all this was? Was it all just for me?

With the wedding as an excuse, Ryan felt like less of a coward for leaving Chile. He'd spent too many years there, had angered enough people that if he was murdered the embassy wouldn't be able to guess who'd done it. The article he'd written about a rumor of children stolen from their dissident mothers and given to military families had caused the biggest stir. Death threats had come in, both on the phone and in the mail. He'd come home late from dinner downtown one night to find his front door open. His first impulse was to turn, run. But he pushed the door open, flicked on the light. Nothing, as far as he could tell, had been stolen, but everything was ruined: curtains torn from the walls, the pillows and mattress gutted, books pulled from the shelves, ripped up. Someone had pissed on a pile of pages in the middle of the room. The next day Jim's letter arrived and since he hadn't bought a ticket home yet, Ryan planned his trip through Guatemala.

He leaned his head against the bus window. Dirt blew into his eyes as the stubby landscape scrolled past, dark silhouettes of mountains in the distance, streaked with webs of rain, strands cut, hanging loose.

When he woke, his neck stiff, the old man with his sack of avocadoes had moved a row closer. "Buenos tardes," the man said, his Spanish clipped with an Indian accent.

Avoiding the old man's stares, he tried to read the few reports about the civil war he'd got after two days of asking — the embassy had given him almost no information, and what he did have was mostly blacked out. The heat bore down and he gave in to it, sitting stunned for the next several hours as they pulled in and out of ruined towns.

His flight was in three days. He'd land in Miami. His sister worked in the administration of a small private university along the western coast. Her husband-to-be worked in a chemistry lab.

He'd seen his family only twice in the past six years. And now his sister's world was filling out with the things one's life was supposed to be filled with, while he had only his career; but it was a better career by far than if he'd stayed in America and become a lawyer, a banker, a teacher. It wasn't wrong, he thought, to take a kind of pride in his life.

In Huehuetenango the bus stopped in the street, the station no more than an office with glass doors. Jim wasn't there. Ryan waited on a bench, watching the driver toss cargo from the bus's roof. Maybe Jim had forgotten. Or was just busy.

After an hour it was clear Jim wasn't coming. According to the map the church where Jim worked was just a few blocks away. The sun lit up the tops of the buildings, reflecting off high windows. Though it was still early evening the streets were nearly empty.

The yellow and white church was at the far end of the square, bell towers visible above thick green trees. Flagstone paths wound around flower beds, past empty iron benches. Birds lined the buildings and chased each other off unlit lampposts, disappearing into the dark trees.

Ryan saw the body as the path opened up before the church. At first he thought it was a drunk. He'd seen that before, men passed out in the gutters, along the sidewalks. You just stepped over them and kept going. But as he got closer he knew this wasn't the case. The black clothes were tattered, one pant leg pushed up over a white sock, the dark hairs flattened against the pale skin. The kneecaps had been shot out, jagged, crusted wounds with bright, hard slices of bone. The face was turned to one side, but Ryan knew it was Jim. Pieces of flesh had been torn from his face. Crusted holes where the eyes should have been.

Behind him a car rattled past, small and brown, the windows clouded with dirt. He stepped around the body and went toward the church. The sun had fallen and light struck only the point of the steeple. The strap of his duffel cut into his shoulder. He drew close to the end of the square and then he thought, *Not the church* and turned quickly down a side street. He stopped against the wall. The square was still empty, save the birds and the body he could no longer see. Ryan pulled the map out of his pocket. Four hotels were noted. One a few blocks off, near the local market. He patted his wallet, buttoned the front of his coat, and then unbuttoned it. Through the closed windows overhead he could hear the low murmur of voices.

The concierge was chatting and smoking with the bag boys in the lobby when he pushed through the glass doors. They all followed him to the check-in desk, as though they were old friends, finally together. He ground his teeth until they squeaked in order to control the shakes as he signed in. One of the boys went up with him to his room, though Ryan had no bags other than the duffel, which he carried. The boy leaned against the doorway and nodded, smiling, as though he were waiting for a punch line. Ryan closed the door in his face.

He turned the lock and took off his coat and sat on the bed. His face felt filthy and looked, in the mirror across the room, as though he'd been beaten. He went to the bathroom, splashed water on his eyes and wiped them with a thin, stiff towel.

Had I found the same hotel? I found the one closest to the church, but it was fifteen years later. A lot changes in that much time. Though the war had been over for a year, threat leaked from the city's rundown buildings. I spent one night in the town, then took the bus back to Antigua. I hated myself. Was I trying to pretend it was the same now for me as it'd been for Ryan? Did I want to *be* Ryan? Of course I did, to some degree, and this meant I wanted to face violence. But also to live. To be always on the edge, the way

Ryan had put himself. Glance right and see death, spreading like a stain over life. But then why wasn't I in Haiti? I was a coward. That's why I took notes, always scribbling throughout my time in Guatemala in my small notebook, little fragments of phrasing and descriptions I've put together into this story.

There was a phone on the nightstand beside the bed. He picked it up. The dial tone sounded like a horn intended to drown out screaming. He put the receiver down. There were no buses until morning. He had the numbers for the embassy. They'd tell him to just take the next bus. The phones were probably monitored. He thought of calling his sister. No one knew where he was.

For an hour he watched television and then called for room service. The concierge told him there was no service. Where could Ryan eat? There was, the concierge said, a restaurante, cerca, comida fresca.

Behind the swollen blue lips of Jim's corpse Ryan had seen a line of jagged broken teeth.

The bedspread was a bright paisley pattern and Ryan sat on it with his eyes closed, running his hands back and forth, as though his fingers were inches deep in crumbling petals that loosed up a bright smell into his nose.

The last time he'd visited his sister she was living in Wisconsin, working at a small two-year college. She'd driven him around the depressing town, pointing out the new McDonald's, the small hotel whose restaurant had been the first to obtain a liquor license, and then she'd taken him to her small brick house on the outskirts. Beside the fold-out couch she'd set out a pile of new, green towels. Maybe, he thought, smacking the hotel sheet cover, she'd bought those towels just for him.

After a few minutes he put on his jacket. He'd eat, come back, watch television, sleep, wake up, and get on the bus to Guatemala City. In two days he'd be in Florida. He'd sit with his sister and drink a beer. He'd be able to hear the water, pulling at the pilings of her dock. They could walk down, after the sun had set, having put on warmer clothes against the cool night air, and watch ghost crabs scuttle up the sand.

The bag boys were outside smoking and their whispering seemed to chase him down the street. Curtains were drawn over all the windows, so only slices of yellow light fell onto the dark paving stones. A car rolled past and Ryan felt his legs tighten. He wasn't hungry. Had he ever felt hungry? How was that possible? What the hell was he doing out here? He should've just stayed in his room till morning. But then the restaurant was there spilling yellow light over the cracked street. Behind him in the square church bells tolled nine times.

The restaurant had three round tables, a pair of metal folding chairs at each. On the wall was a dirty soccer pennant. At one of the tables an old man scooped watery beans into his mouth. Ryan sat down as a short overweight woman brought him a pitcher of water and a plastic plate with four thick tortillas on it. He asked for a beer. She nodded and smiled. Her two front teeth were missing. A television crackled — hysterical laughter — out of the back room into which the woman disappeared, the thick rug falling back into place. Flies drifted up off the empty tables and a large beetle hummed furiously about the light.

The old woman delivered his beer. It was warm and bitter, but he finished it before she left the room and asked for another.

It was awful to leave Jim's body in the square. But what could he do? Drag the body out of town? Bury it? Put it in his duffel and take it back to the embassy? The military wouldn't stand for that. But then, maybe the men who'd done this had moved on, had frightened themselves with killing a gringo, a priest no less. Maybe they'd already been reprimanded by their superior, or executed.

With his second beer the woman brought his beans and chicken. The chicken was covered with wilted, almost-brown tomatoes. The beans were warm and crisp on top and he ate them, sipping his beer. When I went out for dinner in Huehuetenango the food was almost inedible, pocked with puddles of water, trembling with parasites. The chicken was sticky and pink. There is no way of knowing if it was the same restaurant, if he'd even gone out to eat at all. Perhaps he'd been too afraid. Perhaps the men had come to his hotel room.

Beetles hummed into the light when the men opened the door. They were all young, sixteen to eighteen. The bulges of guns could be seen on the hips of two, while the third, who remained out in the street, carried a machine gun. They wore cobbled-together suits. The one who stood in front, a short kid, maybe eighteen, wore a baggy pinstripe jacket and tight tuxedo pants that rode up above his military boots.

"Señor," he said and smiled. Dark metal braces pushed out his lips.

Ryan could barely get his beer back to the table.

"Perdóname, señor," the boy said, stepping forward, his hands out. The old man at the next table stared at his plate. The kid in front of Ryan had terrible acne, clusters swollen red. He asked Ryan to please come with them.

Where?

Please, sir, the kid said, smiling. He reached out and put a hand on Ryan's arm and squeezed gently. Ryan stood up and the kid nodded and said, "Sí, señor. Questions, yes?"

Two of the boys walked alongside him while the third, cradling the machine gun, followed. The windows along the street were silent. He could hear the crunch of his shoes on the loose stones. Ryan asked where they were going.

The kid with the acne looked up at Ryan and smiled and nodded and squeezed his arm again. They walked through town to a poorer section. The shacks became conglomerations of tin scraps. Fires could be seen through gaps in the walls, but there were no voices. "Questions," the kid said, massaging Ryan's arm, the fingers pressing down, then loosening, pressing.

The boys stopped Ryan beside a brown car with dirty windows. The doors slammed and the engine clattered and they bounced over the pitted road. The boy with the scarred face sat in the back with Ryan, smiling at him, the dark braces, slick with saliva, catching bits of light. The two up front talked about something Ryan couldn't make out. They drove out of town.

The conversation up front escalated. The boy in back got involved, leaning forward and shouting curse words at the other men. They were talking about soccer teams.

The boy turned to Ryan, grinning and shaking his head. He pointed at the driver and said, "This pendejo says Guate isn't the best team. Can you believe that? What's wrong with him?"

Ryan shook his head and tried to smile.

"Do you love Guate? Are you a fan?" the boy asked, his smile fading. Before Ryan could answer he said, "Because I hope I'm not riding here with two idiots."

"You dumb fucker!" the driver shouted.

The boy leaned forward and slapped the back of the driver's head lightly. "Just drive, you Guate-hating pinche huecho." The boy smiled at Ryan, shaking his head, as though this wasn't to be believed.

Out of town the car stopped. Sounds of the jungle, birds and howling insects, became louder as the men opened their doors. Ryan stayed in the car.

"Please come out. Questions only," the acned kid says, smiling.

Ryan considered letting them shoot him in the car. But then a last hope filled him. It was possible, after all, that they *did* just want to talk. Why would they kill another American? They could just be taking him to talk with someone who would explain that the priest had been the work of the rebels. They'd assure him they were doing all they could to find the communist murderers.

A hand pulled him out of the car and pushed him toward the jungle. He stepped into high grass. The forest was a black wall.

He stumbled and the boy behind caught his shoulder, held him steady. "Cuidado."

Ryan looked at the kid. He thought of his sister in Florida, his family gathering for the wedding, all those aunts and uncles he never thought of, and his younger brother. What was his brother doing now? For a moment Ryan couldn't remember how old he was. Then it came, a sudden rush of memory: ten! When he thought of his brother, he thought of him riding a bike, wobbling and happy.

The boy with the braces and acne told him to keep walking down the path. Ryan didn't see anything that looked like a path. Down there he'd find a man who wanted to talk. Just to ask some questions. Nothing else. It wasn't a big deal. Then he could go. "Nueva York," the boy said, and laughed.

"Bueno," Ryan said. Maybe, he thought, feeling this didn't make any sense, but feeling it deeply nevertheless, rising up, as though from somewhere behind his stomach, like a truth, that if he explained to these men about his brother things would be different. *I hardly know my brother,* he'd say. *He's going to be in Florida. Florida?* the men would ask, glance at one another. *Cuántos años?* Ten, Ryan would say and smile, because ten, they could all understand this. They knew what it meant to be ten and to have a brother and to not know this brother, because who, the men would all be saying together through their looks, knows a brother? They're like strangers, Ryan would say. Very much like strangers you encounter in a crowded city, or perhaps on a trail, out in the woods, walking past, and you both nod hello because you happen to be there, on the same trail in the middle of the forest — How unlikely to encounter another person! What are the two of us doing here on this trail, passing? — and so you nod and say hello.

Ryan walked ahead of the boys who'd all stopped. There was nothing but the dark forest. Somewhere, in there, was a house. Thickening grass pulled at his legs. He just needed to get to the house and for a moment he thought he could make out, between two trees, a path. Already he could imagine what the house would be like; perhaps it even stood, now, at that moment, empty and dark. They'd light some candles, or switch on the generator, and wait in the empty house for the colonel to show up. It was a mistake. It was the communists. And then he would be on the plane, back to Florida, where his sister was waiting for him, where he would see his parents and his brother and he'd tell them all this story, of his run-in with the military in Guatemala, of Jim's death, of the horror that was life down there and everyone, happy from the wedding, dazed with wine and cake, would lean forward and shake their heads, for wasn't it unbelievable, how terrible those countries could be?

JAS. R. PETRIN

Car Trouble

FROM *Alfred Hitchcock's Mystery Magazine*

"THIS TIME," Skig said, "tell you what. Try not to make it stand up at the back, some kind of antenna sticking outta my head."

"It's just the way your hair goes, dear. Nothing I can do. You should be glad to have hair on the top of your head. Some men your age are ready for a comb-over."

"When I'm ready for it, shoot me."

Every month they exchanged this banter. Leo Skorzeny sitting on a straight-back chair in Eva Kohl's kitchen, a sheet around him, snippets of his stiff, iron-gray hair on the floor. Eva, retired from hairdressing maybe ten, twelve years now, click-clicking away with her scissors.

"Tell me about that new car you're buying," Skig said. He shifted his weight, trying to ease the pain in his gut.

She laughed. Took a playful snip at the empty air.

"Not buying — leasing. The way they explained it to me, Mr. Skorzeny, it's cheaper."

"Smaller payments."

"That's right."

"That don't mean it's cheaper. The long run."

"For me it is. It really is. The salesman told me I'm perfect for a lease. I put on hardly any mileage — mostly just shopping."

"You bargain down the suggested retail?"

"The what?" She stopped snipping, puzzled.

"The price."

"No. I thought I explained. I'm not buying, I'm leasing."

Skig closed his eyes, held them shut a second, opened them.

"You got a good trade?"

The snipping started again. "My old car still runs well. They're giving me two thousand dollars for it."

"Your old car's like new. Why not keep driving it?"

"It isn't all that good. And I feel like a change. Anyway, I've made up my mind. I'm signing the papers this afternoon." She ran the trimmer over his neck, cold steel humming against his skin, then handed him a fan-shaped hand mirror. She held a second mirror behind his head, left, then right. "How's that?"

"Perfect," Leo said, "as always. That's why I come to you."

"Don't kid. You come here because I'm cheap. And I'm only just down the street from you."

Before he left, Skig got the name of her dealership.

He trudged heavily back along the sidewalk, one hand under his billowing sports coat to brace the pain there low in his gut. He would get his car out of the garage, head down to the quack's office, and collect the bad news sure to be waiting for him. All those tests last week. The quacks liked to tell him how lucky he was, that he should be dead by now. Yeah, right. How lucky could you get?

Skig lived in an old made-over filling station, bought years ago as an investment. He'd converted the office area to a few livable rooms after Jeanette died — couldn't stay in the house and didn't know why. Or maybe he did. Sensing her presence there was still too much for him, and at other times it was just too empty.

He crossed the large graveled lot, his front yard, fumbled a key out, and heaved open the repair bay door, all blistering paint: no power assist on this baby, built before the friggin' flood. He backed the Crown Vic into the lot, got out, and hauled the big door down, locked it, then eased back in behind the wheel. He rolled off along Railway Avenue at a sedate five clicks under the limit, windows open to blow the stink off. The Crown Vic still reeked after running off the jetty into the harbor one time, but Skig had no interest in replacing it. Why bother if you were one church service shy of a planting, the way he saw it.

The clock on the dash said 2:15. Time enough for that one small matter before he had to be at his appointment.

He found the lot on Robie, not a first-rate dealership, but not too scuzzy a place. The showroom supported a colossal roof-mounted sign that said HAPPY DAN DUCHEK'S AUTO WORLD, with two sculpted *D*s each the size of a grand piano. Another, smaller, sign said WE'RE NOT HAPPY UNTIL YOU ARE! "Right," Skig muttered as he turned in. He rolled slowly between two rows of gleaming new cars. Bigger than it looked from the street. There was even a detailing shop at the back for well-heeled car enthusiasts, Happy Dan covering all the angles. Skig saw movement in the next row over. An extremely pretty young woman, dressed for the office, talking heatedly with her hands to a young man in sagging-butt pants who stared back at her with lifeless eyes.

"Don't argue with that one, dear," Skig cautioned her under his breath, looking for a place to park. Something familiar about the guy.

He found Happy Dan in the manager's office. Shiny hair. Smile on him like it was wired there. Dan had just unwrapped a tuna sub on his desk and was holding out a coffee mug to the extremely pretty young woman Skig had seen a moment ago. She must have nipped inside while he was parking, now in the process of pouring Dan a fill of seriously black joe from a steaming Pyrex pot. Dan didn't look too happy with her. The guy with the sagging pants was nowhere in sight.

As he stepped into the room, Happy Dan met Skig's gaze, his open face brightening in cheery lines. "Good afternoon, sir. Welcome. Time for a new car?" He showed even white teeth.

"Name's Leo Skorzeny," Skig said flatly. "You heard of me?"

Happy Dan raked his memory. Concentrated. Then something clicked and his smile wilted. He set his mug down. "Yes, I've heard of you."

"We need to talk."

Leo then stared at the extremely pretty young woman until she took the hint and stalked out of the room, carafe in hand, trailing an aroma of burned coffee.

Happy Dan edged around a filing cabinet and took up a defensive position behind his desk.

"We were trading stories about vacation resorts," Happy Dan said, with a nervous stab at affability. Silk tie. Gel in his hair like it was spooned on. "You see, I just got back from Aruba, and —"

"What I really come to see you about was the hose job you're planning to do on a nice old lady, Mrs. Eva Kohl, supposed to come in here later today an' sign some papers."

"Mr. Skorzeny, we don't —"

"Sit down," Skig said.

Happy Dan looked uncertain for a second, then sat. Skig lowered himself into the visitor's chair. Jeez, his gut hurt.

"The lady's a friend of mine. I want her treated right."

"Mr. Skorzeny, I assure you —"

Skig's shoulders moved, his big hands on the heavy desk, trapping Happy Dan against the wall. Dan's jaw sagged. Disbelief on his face.

Skig said, "There's not a car salesman alive wouldn't hose a woman like that, unless he's a saint, and you got no halo floatin' over your head." He watched Happy Dan turn purple. "Here's what you do. You come down fifteen hundred on the MSRP — cash-back covers that — an' you give her three, not two, for the trade, which is more what it's worth. That's forty-five hunnerd, good for ninety bucks off the monthly payment, an' you still do okay. An' don't suck it all up with some BS prepping fees, like you polished the mirrors or something, or I'll be back here for more negotiating. You getting all this?"

Sweat droplets gleamed along the hairline of Dan's spiffy do. He managed a bob of his head. Skig held him there a few more seconds, scrutinizing the Aruban tan for signs of perfidy. Satisfied that there were none, he yanked the desk back and heaved himself to his feet.

"An' make sure she gets the free gap insurance the leasing company likes you to forget about," Skig said, not looking back, moving on out the door.

The clinic's parking lot was jammed as usual, the waiting room packed with distressed humanity. But there had been a cancellation, and Skig's name came up quickly. Shown to a room the size of a large closet, he waited until the quack breezed in. Not his usual quack. A specialist. Like most specialists, this guy had the charm of a forensic pathologist.

"Just tell me," Skig said, "am I still gonna die?"

The quack hunched over a child-sized table, briskly flipping through some arcane-looking charts. "We're all going to die, Mr. Skorzeny."

A pathologist *and* a philosopher. Skig crossed his brawny arms above his thick belly, waiting to hear the bad news.

Finally the quack glanced up. Jeez, he was young. How much could a kid this age know about diseases of the colon? Plenty, judging by the framed degrees, diplomas, and certificates tacked to the wall. But Skig wasn't impressed. Paper was paper.

"The tests were inconclusive," the quack said.

"What!"

"The tests were inconclusive. We'll have to run them again."

"Somebody screwed up, you mean."

"There's no need for acrimony."

"There's a need for something. You think it's happy days goin' through all that?"

"You're overwrought."

"No, I'm *under*wrought. When I get overwrought, you'll know it."

The quack was unintimidated. That impressed Skig. With cool detachment, the young man insisted Skig leave another sample for the lab. The Styrofoam container looked just like the kind the Greek at the corner sold his chili burgers in.

When Skig got home, there was company waiting. An unmarked car with two watchful dicks in it, parked in the front yard where the gas pumps used to be. In his younger years he might have cruised on by, circled the block, gave some thought as to how he would handle things. Now he just rolled in and stopped right beside them. What were they after? Someone to shoot? Pick me, Skig thought.

They got out of their car slowly and purposefully, an air of menace hovering about them. Something they learned at the academy: how to get out of your vehicle with an air of menace. Skig got out too. As he straightened, the pain darted inside him like the tip of a cork puller he'd ingested by accident somehow, and he steadied himself.

The dicks were focused, professionally intense. The older one moved in. He was going to fat, wore an old loose-fitting suit, and showed salt-and-pepper hair around his ears. The one who'd been driving was younger, tall and lanky, and dressed like he was going to a job interview.

"You guys collecting for underprivileged cops?" Leo said. "I gave at the office," thinking of the container he had left with the quack. He brushed past the dicks, jangling his keys, and unlocked the repair bay door. When he heaved it up he thought his stomach would bust open and dump some major organ right there on the ground. He swayed.

"Mr. Skorzeny?" the fat one said.

"You know it."

"Are you all right?"

"Top shelf. Right up there with the chips and cheesies."

The dick studied him, taking his measure.

"We've got a few questions. Think we could go inside?"

"No."

The dick held his gaze. Then he shrugged. "Suit yourself." He took a pen and notebook out of his pocket, flipped pages, glanced up again. "You know a man named Dwight Keevis?"

"No."

"Owns a car dealership. Also goes by the name of Dan Duchek. Happy Dan."

"Oh, that Dwight Keevis."

"Then you do know him."

"No."

The dick pinched the bridge of his nose. "All right. Let's go about this another way. An employee says you dropped by to see Mr. Keevis earlier today, unannounced. You didn't come to buy a car, and you weren't very friendly. We'd like to know what you talked about."

"You asked if I knew the guy. I don't." Skig looked the two dicks over again. A mulish-looking couple of plugs. Stubborn as dirt. Better give them something. The truth was best. "I did stop by about a car. I been told I should trade up."

Behind the fat dick, the lanky one stooped over the window of the Vic. He made a sour face. "That might be a plan. This one stinks."

"Funny," Skig said, "it smelled good till you showed up."

The lanky dick's face tightened, and the older one reined him in with his eyes. Then the older one turned back to Skig.

"The employee claims you threatened Mr. Keevis when you left his office today."

"Is that what this is about? I said an unkind word to somebody?" Skig remembered the extremely pretty young woman, the acid look on her puss as she trip-trapped out of the room.

"Well," the dick said, "whether you did or you didn't, Mr. Keevis now happens to be dead. Died of gunshot wounds at the QE Emergency —" He glanced at his watch. "— going on two hours ago."

"You don't tell me."

"I do tell you. And after what the employee said, and seeing as you're not exactly a stranger to us —"

"Got a sheet on you like the Yellow Pages," the lanky dick put in with venom.

"— we thought," the older dick continued, determined to finish, "that it might be a good idea to come by and hear what you had to say about it."

"An' you did. An' I answered you," Skig said. "So take off."

"You won't get far with that attitude."

"I only need to get through that door to my bottle of Scotch. You want to arrest me because some rip-off artist stopped a long overdue slug, go ahead. But my doctor may have something to say about that. And my lawyer will cut you off at the knees."

Skig got back in the Vic, dropped it in gear, and let the fast idle roll the smelly old car inside.

In the gloom of the kitchen, he rinsed a glass in the sink, rattled some ice into it, and topped it up with Teacher's. He pushed the news about Happy Dan around in his head. Not all that surprising. Probably tried to screw the wrong sap, that's all. The sap got wise, dug his howitzer out of a shoebox, and returned to the lot, bent on revising the terms of their understanding. The fat monthly payment and, oh yeah, a little something else.

Skig glanced at the clock. Solly Sweetmore was late. If he didn't show, Skig would have to go to him, give him a slap or two to get his attention.

He sat down in his ratty recliner — collapsed into it, was more like it. Switched on the TV, jabbed the mute button, took a quick slug from his glass. The liquor did what it was supposed to do, burned for a moment, then mellowed him, but it didn't help his gut. He shook out two of the big fat brown capsules the quack had slipped him — samples, he'd said, take one before eating — and washed them down with a swallow of booze.

Then he closed his eyes.

When he opened them again, there were shadows in the room,

the afternoon sun dying fast behind the fly-specked window over the sink. The light from the silent television winked and gamboled on the walls.

A TV news lady was doing a location shot. The background looked vaguely familiar. Skig frowned as two giant double *D*s reared up on the screen — Dan Duchek's rip-off center. It was an earlier tape, sunlight beating down in the background where a bagged stiff was being rolled out on a gurney. He poked the mute button. The TV lady, brushing a sweep of lustrous hair out of her eyes, said, ". . . all police would reveal was that the owner of this downtown dealership was shot dead in his office by an unidentified assailant." Skig wondered if Dan still wore his grin. "CTV has learned that at least one person has been taken into custody . . ." The canned shot changed. And to Skig the monologue faded as a jerky camera lens zoomed in on a gray-haired woman being bundled into a police patrol car. The woman looked dazed. It was Eva Kohl.

"Ah jeez," Skig said.

He made a call to his lawyer Saul Getz, then rolled down to the cop shop in the Vic. Saul was there waiting for him. A thin man with patient eyes, he was thoughtfully stroking his trim, white goatee.

"You talk to her?" Skig asked.

"Yeah, I talked to her. They didn't arrest her. That woman wouldn't shoot a popgun at a plastic monkey to win a coconut."

"You got that right. You pry her loose?"

"Oh sure. She's an unhappy lady, though. Forensics impounded her car. Seems Happy Dan was about to drive it into the shop when the shooter stepped in and popped him. Two hits, one miss. Quite a mess." He smiled. "She's feisty. She says if the police take people's cars away, then they ought to provide loaners. I sent her home in a cab."

Skig said, "They recover the gun?"

"No. But they think it belonged to the victim. He kept a Smith in the desk, according to an employee, and the cops can't find it anywhere."

That helpful employee again. "Anything else?"

"One slug was recovered in pretty good shape. Went into the headrest. When they find the gun they'll do their ballistics thing, and that'll be it."

"They think."

"They're pretty sure. One of the techs took a quick look. He said it ought to be a slam dunk, far as the gun is concerned."

"Meantime, Eva doesn't get her car back."

"Oh, it gets worse. When I showed up and started speaking for her, the detectives figured out the connection pretty quick. I mean, from me to you, then Eva. They brightened a little. The younger one grinned and said maybe they'd bring her back in for more questioning."

"They're outta their minds."

"They seem a little miffed at you, Leo. Did you yank their chains or something?"

He told them how he had been at the lot for a few minutes and how the fat cop and the thin cop had stopped by and braced him later.

"Buying a new car, Skig? Hey, that's a plan."

"Don't start. I was there at the lot just before the guy got it, an' because I'm me, they made a little too much of it." Skig eyeballed a policeman stepping by them in the hall. "I ran them off."

Saul stroked his goatee, thinking. "No, there's more to it. They got that witness. That employee. We don't know what she saw, or what she says she saw. She could be fingering you *and* your friend." He puffed his cheeks out, gave his head a shake. "Did you rub her the wrong way too?" When Skig didn't answer, he added, "Why would she finger a nice old doll like that?"

"I dunno," Leo said, "but I'm gonna find out."

He had just caught a glimpse of the extremely pretty young woman being ushered out of an interview room down the hall.

The sun had gone down fast. Wisps of pink-bellied clouds lingered way out low over the Arm.

Skig sat in the Crown Vic with the blower on and the windows all the way down. The car smelled especially rank today. The sludge at the bottom of the harbor wasn't violets, that was a fact. But minutes later the night breeze was buffeting through the car again, as he trailed the extremely pretty young woman's taillights down Gottingen Street. She drove fast. She tailgated. She yapped into her cell nonstop.

She drove out to Clayton Park, sped north on Dunbrack, then

turned in at a block of apartments that sprawled above the slope to the basin. Shot down the ramp into the underground parking with the phone still glued to her head. Skig found a slot outside in the visitors' lot, angled so that he could watch for an apartment light to go on. He knew he had about a 50 percent chance, and his number came up. Tenth floor, northwest corner.

"Bang," Skig said.

He kept waiting. Imagined the cell phone burning. Minutes later, headlights lit the Vic from behind, a car coming up fast, flashing by him into the visitors' lot, subwoofer pumping out some irritating hip-hop crap. Nice car. A yellow Audi.

"Boom," Skig said.

Skig knew the vehicle. He'd seen it around. A car like that, you might as well have a neon sign over your head jabbing blinking arrows at you. And seeing it here now, Skig suddenly realized who the kid at the car lot had been, the one with the eyes.

The name he went by was Caesar DeLuca. His real tag? Probably not. He was Filipino. Smart with the ladies. Though what young women saw in guys who looked like extras from *Night of the Living Dead,* Skig had never been able to figure out. And DeLuca was mean. He liked to hurt people. It wasn't just an unavoidable part of doing business with him, he enjoyed it. Beyond that, Skig didn't know much about the guy and didn't want to. He couldn't care less what turned DeLuca's crank, but that would change fast if the guy had his rat's nose buried in this business somehow.

DeLuca swaggered from his car to the building, gold chains, body ink, and attitude. Skig considered the setup so far.

A car dealer shot dead. In his proximity, four people: a gentle unassuming older lady, the extremely pretty young woman, and rat boy here, Caesar DeLuca. And himself. Which of these was most likely to have had something to do with it? Since the cops apparently didn't know about DeLuca, Skig was number one on the list. But he had an alibi with the quack. The cops had probably discovered that. Which left the girl — and the older lady, of course, according to Fatty and Skinny. They had sherlocked it out.

Of course, they hadn't seen DeLuca nosing around the car lot earlier, but on the other hand they didn't seem too interested in finding out about him either. Had they asked Skig if he'd seen anybody else there? No. Had the girl volunteered the information? Skig didn't think so.

Upstairs, the window darkened. Somebody had pulled the drapes. After about half an hour, DeLuca sauntered out of the building and squealed away in his thumping pimp mobile. Skig eased out of the old Vic, locked the door, and followed a tenant and his fuzzy white dog in through the front entrance.

The apartment door on the tenth floor had a spray of dried flowers on it and a ceramic plaque that said RUSSELL. The girl pulled open her door and stared at him.

"Name's Leo Skorzeny, Ms. Russell," Skig said. "Remember me?"

Her face paled in alarm, she started to close the door, and he put his foot in the way.

"Tired of talking about what happened to your boss today?"

That stopped her. She hesitated, found that hissy look somewhere inside herself, then stood back and let him in. She waggled her fingers at a chair and flounced down on the sofa, one leg tucked up, lips clamped together tight. Skig didn't like the idea of fighting his way back out of the overstuffed bucket she had consigned him to, so he dragged a kitchen chair out of the ell and sat down gingerly on it. Jeez.

She shot a meaningful look at a table clock, something modern in plastic and glass. "You've got five minutes." She had a harsh voice. He hadn't been expecting that.

"I'll take it. I can use all the time I can get, according to my proctologist."

"Are you trying to be crude?"

"I'm trying to be accurate. You were pretty accurate yourself when you put those holes in your boss."

She brought one foot down hard on the rug, shoving forward at him. "Don't you *dare* imply I had anything to do with that!"

"I'm not implying it. I'm saying it. You shot him, all right, you or your boyfriend did. An' when you couldn't frame me, you had to settle for the old lady."

She jumped to her feet. "Get out!"

"I could do that. An' I could head back down to Gottingen Street and lay it all out for the dicks."

She stood there breathing, dainty nostrils flaring, considering her options. Then she plumped down on the sofa again and gnawed at her lip. He knew he was on the right track then.

"Fine," she said. "Let's hear your delusional idea."

"I got two, three of 'em," Skig said, ignoring the dramatics. "I been thinking down there in the car. First one is, you were cozy with Happy Dan, shining his cars for him, only somethin' went wrong. He took off to Aruba without you, had a good time in the sun, an' when he got back you tore a strip off of him."

She gave a short, barking laugh.

"That's insane. You don't know anything. What makes you think I wasn't with him?"

"Where's your tan?"

It stopped her. But just for a moment.

"Dwight was married. He flew down there with his wife. He couldn't have taken me along if he'd wanted to."

"Oh, there's ways. But we'll put that on hold. Here's delusion number two, coming at it from the other side. The guy was hitting on you, you finally lost it with him, an' you pegged him."

"Oh puh-lease!" She made her eyes go round. "Why would I do that? I could have walked away if what you're saying is true. Do you think I'm out of my mind?"

Skig looked at her. She was struggling. A pretty bundle of raw nerves curled up there on the couch.

"No," he said, "I don't think that. I think your boyfriend's got a loose connection someplace. What's his part? He came to your rescue?"

"My boyfriend? Now what are you talking about?"

"The little weasel I just saw scuttling out of here."

She rolled her eyes again. "I don't even *have* a boyfriend. Nobody left here."

"He was in this building."

"It's a big place."

"Yeah," Skig said. He wasn't ready to mention he'd seen the two of them arguing earlier under the big double *D*s at Happy's place. "Where can I find him?"

She studied Skig a moment. Worked on that lip again. She really didn't want to get going on DeLuca, that was obvious, and suddenly a miracle occurred. Her face turned all sweetness and light. Just like that.

"Look, we can be friends, you know."

"Sure."

"You don't think I'm cute?"

"Puppies are cute. So are Kewpie dolls. You're in there somewhere, I guess."

She threw her drink at him, the glass tumbling past his ear, splatting against the heavy drapes, then falling to the rug, miraculously unbroken. The drapes hadn't fared so well, a broad stain running down them. A few drops darkened Leo's sleeve.

He got up painfully. "Nice to have met you, Ms. Russell."

Two things he'd gotten out of this. Number one, she was scared of the cops. Number two, she was protecting rat boy.

Skig opened his eyes next morning and wondered where the hell he was. Found he was stretched flat out in his recliner. Last night after taking three of the big fat free samples, he had tumbled into Never-Never Land as if someone had batted him with a jack handle. He yanked the chair lever, sat up, and explored his side with his stubby fingers.

Not too bad this morning. The pain was still there, but it was biding its time. Sometimes it did that. Went away to a seminar on how to really rip a guy's innards apart, then came back and practiced on him. The respite would be short.

He showered, ran his razor over his face, and went out the door without bothering to eat. He stopped at a drive-through for a coffee, double milk, no sugar, which he drank in the Vic at the edge of the lot. There was a contest on. Win a TV. Coffee cups had the good news hidden on them. A kid rooting through the trash can by the doors for a winning cup glanced up as Skig held his out the window. He edged over suspiciously and took it from him. "Jeez, mister. Don't you want to win a plasma TV?" Skig started up the Vic. "I already got a TV. I could prob'ly use the plasma, though."

Skig drove to the recycling depot out past Lakeside. A big Loadmaster trash truck was grunting up to the dock, spewing diesel fumes, and a bunch of cars stood around, engines idling while people hauled out bags filled with beer cans, newspapers — bags filled with bags, for crying out loud — to get their four or five bucks. Save the ozone layer. He found Solly Sweetmore in his upstairs office under the corrugated sheet-metal roof.

Skig was overweight. He needed to drop forty pounds. But Solly had such a colossal gut on him he had to straighten his arms to reach his desk. His face, tracked with broken blood vessels, showed alarm when he saw who his visitor was. He set down the can of Coke he was nursing.

"You were supposed to drop by yesterday," Skig said, wincing. The pain was back. The steep stairs killed him.

"I know, Leo, I know." The trashman leaned away from his desk, moving his hands around. "I just got busy. This place is a nuthouse. You can see —"

"Fine with me, Solly," Skig said, "you want to pay another day's juice. Go for it. Only next time tell me, okay? That's what the phone is for."

"About that, Skig, listen —"

"No, you listen. This is how things get outta hand. You keep taking more time, more time, you run outta time pretty fast. Then I got to lean on you. I don't like that, Solly."

"I know. I should've phoned you, Skig, but listen —"

A gaunt man in a knit cap interrupted, thrusting his small balding head in the door. "That compactor crapped out again, boss, the old green one, so maybe —"

Solly surged up and screamed at him. "Will you get outta my face?" He threw his pop at the man, the half-filled can smashing into the door frame, cola fizzing and splattering over a calendar and running down the cheap paneling in streams. The head withdrew.

"Lots of people throwing drinks these days," Skig said, shaking his head. "People need to relax." He tapped the book in his breast pocket. "Six-five, Solly, plus another half a point for today. Pay me now an' that's an end to it."

"But I got other bills."

"Not like mine you don't."

Solly threw his head back and let out an anguished moan. Then he jerked open a cashbox. Counted the six-five out right there on the desk.

"An' the half a point, don't forget," Skig said. Then he held up his hand. "Or maybe this'll work." He leaned in. "You know a guy named Caesar DeLuca? Drives a car like a birthday cake?" Warily, Solly nodded. Skig said, "Tell me about him."

Solly looked even more stressed out, if that was possible.

"What's to tell? I see him on Argyle there, Hollis Street, sometimes down at the casino. He's trouble."

"What kind of trouble?"

When Skig drove away fifteen minutes later, he had his money, and more information on Caesar DeLuca than he needed. The kid was also in the car business. He and Happy Dan had that in common. He did custom work, prime merchandise only, a certain kind of car, a special customer. He got an order, shopped around till he filled it. Then — this part Solly was shaky on — he delivered the wheels out in Sackville, a guy with a long-haul business there. It got loaded on a semi, other stuff packed around it, and a day later it was in New York or Montreal, on its way to the special client.

Skig had said to Solly, "Rat boy. Where does he live?"

"I dunno. Nobody knows. He keeps that to himself."

"This merchandise. Always a special order?"

"Prob'ly not. He wouldn't walk away from something."

Skig thought a minute. "Get a message to him. There's an old Vette, one a them Sting Rays, been parking on the street all night behind the Armories. You don't know why. But you seen it there, an' you want a spotting fee."

Solly had shaken his fleshy face. "Jeez, I dunno, Leo."

"Just do it." Skig shifted his weight. "Do it an' we'll call it square on the point."

"Fine. But I don't like it," Solly said. "I'm telling you that guy is a crazy man."

Back home, Skig dialed Saul Getz. "They pick her up? Eva Kohl?"

"No, of course not. What case have they got? But they're thinking about it."

"Why?"

"Something about her being a suicide risk."

"They're full of it."

"I'm with you. She doesn't look the type. A little bewildered maybe, but who wouldn't be?"

"Whatever happened to a free country?"

"Things are relative, Leo."

"Things are crap. Listen, do what you can for her. They pull her in, I want you there with her."

"Leo, this is costing you. It's adding up fast."

"Just do it. An' don't bring me into it. She thinks she owes me, that's bad for a friendship. It changes things."

"Yeah, well, she is starting to wonder."

"Just be there for her. Say you're court appointed or something. Make somethin' up, you're a lawyer, for cryin' out loud."

"Fine, but I've got to bill you."

"So cheer up." Skig winced. The pain was back. "One more thing. I need to borrow your Vette."

There was dead silence. Then Saul started breathing again.

"You *what?*"

"I know it's your toy, you only drive it to church on Sunday, but tonight I want you to park it behind the Armories, take a cab home, an' forget about it."

"You're not serious."

"Anything happens to it, I'll pay the shot. You know I'm good for it."

There was a short pause. Then Saul said, "You're up to something."

"Go see Mrs. Kohl."

Skig spent the rest of the day at the clinic. The lousy tests all over again. When he got home that evening he felt as if he was a sample of something himself. He ate beans, cold out of the can, and washed them down with Scotch, both food items totally forbidden to him. To hell with it. Then he set his alarm clock — the blender plugged into the timed outlet on the stove — and fell into his recliner. He dreamed Fatty and Skinny, dressed like surgeons, were stooping over him, making a large incision in his belly and smiling about it.

The alarm was howling in the kitchen, the empty blender dancing around on the metal stovetop like it was going to explode. Midnight.

He limped out the door.

He parked one street over from the Armories where through the gap of a vacant lot he could eyeball Saul's money-pit Vette — a '65 fastback, Nassau Blue. Tilted the Vic's power seat back until only his eyes showed above the dash.

He dozed a few times, and then something woke him. The clock read 1:15. A tow truck was backing toward Saul's ride. It stopped and rat boy got out, gold chains flashing under the sodium streetlamp. He held something down low at his side that looked for a second like a long-barreled handgun. It was a cordless drill with a footlong bit in it. Rat boy put the bit to the fiberglass fender and sank a hole into the Vette's engine compartment. An old trick. Drain the battery. That way the alarm wouldn't sound unless there was a backup.

There wasn't. Something to mention to Saul. The guy hooked up the Vette and dragged it away. Elapsed time, three minutes. Slug readjusted his seat and took off after him.

Rat boy would have places to store his cars, places where he could keep them out of sight for a while. Rented garages here and there, probably. After a ten-minute drive out to Spryfield, the tow truck halted before an old swayback shed. The kid was good with the boom and the winch, and the Vette was tucked out of sight in no time.

The rat dropped off the truck — another darkened house a few blocks south — hopped in the Audi, and beat it out of town along Purcell's Cove Road, stereo thumping all the way, a good night's work behind him. Skig gave him room, not wanting to spook him. Maybe too much room. He came over a hill near Herring Cove, overshot the place, and had to double back. Good thing he'd been watching the drives on either side, and caught a flash of brake lights and yellow paint.

The rat appeared to be doing all right for himself. It was a modern chalet in bleached cedar, overlooking the ocean. In need of some TLC but pretty fine all the same. Skig took the Vic back up the hill to a market gardener's he'd spotted, parked in the darkened lot by the greenhouse, got out, and walked back. A short stroll, no more than two hundred yards or so, but on a steep incline. His gut wasn't happy about it.

Partway up the drive to the house, Skig stopped. There were two cars here. The Audi and, in front of it, the car he had followed from the cop shop the previous night. He grunted. It was the car of the extremely pretty young woman.

"No boyfriend, huh?" Skig said.

He heard voices.

The house stood on a brutally unaccommodating chunk of granite, cantilevered over the cliff face to provide a picture-perfect view of the sea. A wide deck embraced it. In the quiet gaps when the surf wasn't pounding, voices drifted from the seaward side.

Skig climbed three broad steps to the deck. Against the house were some sturdy-looking loungers, a plastic cooler filled with ice and beer. Skig helped himself to a beer and sat down on a bench. He pressed the cold can to his side. From here he could make out the voices better.

". . . I brought the beer like you told me, but I didn't think you'd be here this soon," the girl's voice said.

"I told you two, two thirty."

"Yes, but you're never early."

"What's the late-breaking news, it couldn't wait till tomorrow?"

A wave heaved in. "A man came to see me."

"What man?"

"The man I told the cops about — you know who I mean."

"The guy who threatened your boss?"

"Yes."

"So what did he want?"

"He accused me of killing Dwight."

Another pause in the conversation. The guy deliberating. Down below the house a big wave thundered in. Skig could smell the salt.

"Lemme guess. He thinks he can blackmail you."

"No. That's the funny thing. He just made these crazy accusations, then left. I thought about it all day and finally decided I'd better tell you about it."

"This happened yesterday?"

"Yeah. In the evening. Just after you left." She hesitated. "I think . . ." Her voice trailed off.

"You think what?"

"I think he knows something about you. I mean, he asked me where he could find you, and — Stop that! You're hurting me!"

"You waited all this time to tell me?"

"Let go of me!"

There was a scuffle, a muffled slap.

Skig swished his beer around, took another swallow. Then he got up. He walked around to the front of the house and saw him there, rat boy, staring down at the girl. She was crouched on the deck against the railing, one hand to the side of her face.

The guy must have seen her eyes move. He spun around in surprise.

"Name's Leo Skorzeny," Skig said. "You heard of *me*?"

"Where the hell'd you come from?"

"You heard of me?"

"Yeah, I hearda you. Some kinda shy. You heard of me?"

"Yeah. Some kinda rat." Skig looked at the girl. There was a red welt blossoming along one side of her face. Her nose was bleeding. His eyes moved back to the rat, and he shook his head. "What's the matter with you?"

The dead eyes narrowed, and Skig followed their quick shift to a pile of split wood near the door. A weapon on this guy's mind. A hatchet, maybe.

"Don't even think it," Skig said, "'less you want to wear the thing. Walk around with it stickin' outta you, some kinda new body piercing."

"You talk tough."

"It's the mileage," Skig said. "Want to hear what I got?" He finished the beer and set the can down carefully on the railing. "One part of Happy's business, he had that detailing place out back of the lot. The way I figure it, somebody goes through the records there, they can find out who owns what in town. All the good stuff. The best rides. Cars you don't see on the street too much. Practically a catalog to a guy like you."

"So what."

"You come on to Ms. Russell here so you can get your nose in those records." The girl was getting to her feet. Dawning realization on her face, eyes jumping from Skig to rat boy. "Pretty soon, Happy Dan's customers lose a car or two. Maybe a string of them. Happy Dan is scratching his head. Then one day he finds you goin' through his records, your rat's nose twitching, an' he calls you on it. Or no, more likely the girl's doin' it. He threatens to call the cops. You can't have that."

The dead eyes didn't waver.

"There's some shouting. Some more threats. He has to step out to start processing the old lady's trade, an' the girl calls you up, panicking. You panic too. She tells you where the gun is, or she told you about it before. You're back in a minute, an' you use it to make those big holes in the guy."

The rat edged closer to the woodpile. A car started out back of the house. Skig looked for the girl again, but she was gone. He shrugged.

"What you gonna do? I think the girl figures it out. She remembers me sorting out her boss, an' she's thinking — some nutty idea in her head — that she can put the jacket on me. It's a long shot, but it's all you got. An' it turns out I got an alibi. Then there's the gun. You screwed that up too. Not likely I'd pop somebody with their own gun. Not my style. An' bein' a thief it's really tough for you to give up a perfectly good Smith. I bet you still got it. The gun ties you to it."

By this time DeLuca had sidled halfway across the deck, and now he dived for the open door. Skig moved to block him. He saw what DeLuca was reaching for — not the woodpile but something else, his hand thrusting into the room and coming out with the gun. It must have been on the kitchen counter.

Skig brought the heel of his fist down on the rat's arm so hard he heard something pop and rat boy screamed. The gun clattered over the boards. The rat's bony knee came up, and a huge pain shot through Skig's belly. Skig reeled backward, left hand clenched in the rat's shirt, pulling the rat with him as the knee came up again. A wave of nausea. Skig was going down. He grabbed handfuls of the rat's baggy pants with both fists and heaved, putting his shoulders into it. The jolt hammered all the way up his spine when his butt struck the deck, and he sat there a moment, dazed, chunky legs splayed out, hand pressed to his side. There was one good thing though. Rat boy was gone. A flying header over the railing, sixty feet down to rocks and pounding surf.

Boom.

After a bit, Skig got up and put the gun back on the kitchen counter, careful how he touched it.

"You gonna be all right?" Skig asked Mrs. Kohl.

"I'll be just fine, Mr. Skorzeny. Go ahead to your doctor's appointment."

"He can wait. I'm more worried about you. Somethin' happens, who's gonna cut my hair?"

Skig helped her settle into her glider rocker. She smiled up at him.

"That Mr. Getz is an awfully nice man. He's helped me a lot. I was relieved when he told me the police figured out who killed Mr. Duchek. He was a nice man too." Then she frowned. "Mr. Getz isn't very happy with you, though. Something about a car?"

"Could be."

"Cars are an awful lot of trouble."

"They are for some people."

"I'm going out again tomorrow to see if I can lease one."

Skig was silent a moment, then said, "You want some company this time?"

A bright laugh. "You're afraid I'll get cheated. Men have an easier time of it at car lots than women do, is that it?"

"Lemme think about that one," Skig said.

SCOTT PHILLIPS

The Emerson, 1950

FROM *Murdaland*

I.

IT TAKES ME AND Frank Elting about an hour to get to the dirt road outside the little town of Kingman, where half a dozen emergency vehicles sit, leading the way to a tiny clapboard farmhouse, inside which an old woman lays bludgeoned to death on the kitchen linoleum. The house reminds me of the one my grandfather had in Wichita when I was little, tidy and freshly painted white with green trim. Next to a rusted-out Model A, a sheriff's deputy is bagging a spade, its blade mottled with dirt clods and blood, less lighthearted about it than city policemen would be, and as we get out of the car, Frank feels the need to remind me not to be a smartass in front of the locals.

Outside, the dead woman's husband, eighty-seven years of age, a formerly big man shrunken and stripped of muscle, sits on the tailgate of an ambulance with an oxygen mask over his nose and mouth. Inside, the couple's son, fiftyish with a farmer's sun-wrinkled skin and badly scarred hands, the left one crippled-looking, sits without evident emotion on a swaybacked sofa in the middle of the big main room of the house, next to the kitchen. At a dining room table at the far end of the same room, a pair of sheriff's deputies are grilling the killer, who has already confessed, in an attempt to find out why she brained her eighty-four-year-old mother-in-law with a garden spade. While Frank Elting tries to coax a quote from the son about his dear mother's death-by-entrenching-tool, I get a nice shot of the killer in mid-phrase, one cuffed hand upraised and pointing as she explains her afternoon's work.

"Some of your wives and mothers is on that committee, and any one of them will tell you what she was like. Day in and day out, but especially around rummage sale time." She adopts what I assume is a shrill impression of her late mother-in-law: "'That Doris Upchurch thinks she can get away with donating junk she wouldn't even have in her own home. Maelynn Murray sure made herself scarce when it was time to stick prices on them donations. Last year that Warcroft boy come in and bought all the funnybooks and told me he was going to sell them to the other little boys for a profit and I by God won't let him have a one this year. I'm the only one does any real work around this church and that includes Pastor's wife. Me me me me me.'" She takes a deep breath and resumes speaking in her own voice. "You ask any woman at that church if that's what Mother Carling wasn't like. Well by God if it's bad listening to for a few minutes at church a couple three times a week just you imagine what it's like living with the old biddy. This afternoon she got to talking about that rummage sale and how if it wasn't for her the whole church might as well just shut its doors and I thought all right, let's find out how the church does without you, you old butterball, and I went outside and took the spade Jacob'd left by the side of the house and went back inside and you know what? She hadn't even noticed I'd left the kitchen, she was just talking into the air. So I just hauled off and smacked the blade of it up the side of that old gray head of hers and by God that shut her up good. She dropped down to the floor and I thought I'd better get her again, I didn't want her to suffer, Lord knows, and I swung it that time just like a hockey stick. That's how my shoes and stockings got all bloody."

After I've taken four or five nice loony-looking pictures of the younger Mrs. Carling, I set about photographing her victim in the kitchen. One of the deputies comes in to announce that the ambulance is going to take the freshly minted widower to St. Francis in Wichita and, looking askance at me, questions my shooting photos of the corpse. "You're not going to print them pictures of Mrs. Carling, are you?"

"We've printed worse," I tell him.

He looks down at the dead woman. "My mother used to fix her hair. Said she'd come in once't every two weeks and sit in the chair and jaw everyone's ear off, nobody else could get a word in."

You can't read too much into the facial expression on a corpse — a lot can change in the moments after death, before police and press arrive on the scene — but damned if the old bird doesn't look like she was in the middle of a nasty remark when the blade struck. Her tongue is nestled between her upper bared teeth and the lower incisors. Her eyes are crossed just a little, and the left one is all bloodshot and rheumy.

In the other room the son sits, placid, and mostly ignores the deputies' questions regarding his wife and his mother. He's loosening up now, relief revealing itself in his posture, and though he's not smiling, he does look to have been recently relieved of some unnamed burden. I slip into what I'm assuming is the old folks' bedroom and, after getting a picture of the disorder therein, steal a small framed picture of the old lady off the dresser and slip it into the inside pocket of my overcoat.

II.

It's past dark when I get to my great-aunt Ivy's house to fix a faucet, a couple of stalwart kids still playing cowboys in the yard across the street. Next door, from a side window lit yellow against the pale blue of the early evening, a crabbed woman of indeterminate age watches me with unconcealed hostility. She whips her curtain shut as I let myself in the front door.

Ivy's living room is a malodorous wreck, with blankets draped over the furniture to cover ancient stains of uncertain, doubtless horrifying provenance. I've tried to get her to replace the blankets with plastic, but that's too modern and insufficiently homely for her taste. Two or three of Ivy's cats rub against my ankles and meow as I cross the room toward the kitchen. There are six or more litter boxes scattered through the house, at least one of which badly needs emptying.

I find my Uncle Pell seated as usual at the kitchen table with a water glass full of bourbon and the *Evening Eagle,* and he notes my arrival with alarm.

"Who the fuck are you anyway and what the hell're you doing in my house?" He rises, his lumpy old claw clenched into a pink rope-veined fist. With the sleeve rolled to the elbow, his forearm resembles nothing so much as the neck of a very, very large turkey. I'm unaware of any look of amusement on my face — what I feel is pity and horror — but a smirk is what he sees when he looks in my eyes. "You think this is funny? Think you got nothing to be scared of? Everybody does. You think Jesus Christ didn't piss himself up on that cross, you're crazy." He squints at me and calms down a little. "You're Flavey's boy, aintcha. Here to fix the faucet." He sits back down and picks up the paper.

When I'm done with the faucet I fix the hinge on the medicine chest and scrape the caked-on Pepsodent out of the basin. Back in the kitchen I find Pell deep in conversation with an unseen nemesis.

My intent is to leave without disturbing him, but Ivy spoils it by parking in the driveway and making her slow way up to the door. Smelling of lavender and powder she passes me without a glance, her constricted breath rasping in and out. "You won't get your hands on them candlesticks," she says.

"What candlesticks?" I ask, though I know perfectly goddamn well what candlesticks, since they come up every time I visit.

"Between you and the damn neighbors seems like half the people I know's after Mother's candlesticks."

"Which neighbors?"

"Mrs. Severy, next door, and that no-account cripple she's married to. They come poking through here at night. I can hear 'em. Some night I'll put a lead slug into 'em and the law won't touch me."

"You let me know if they need a talking to, Aunt Ivy."

"You won't get your hands on those candlesticks, boy, you or that skinny wife of yours."

I try to explain that the skinny wife is long since gone, but Ivy's done with me and already shuffling back through the debris to her bedroom, muttering to her sister, my grandmother, dead since before the First World War.

"Faucet all you needed me to come out for?" I ask.

She stops and pivots toward me faster than I would have thought possible, her eyes shining and vivacious. "Oh. That's right, I forgot. I'm leaving on the bus in the morning for Cottonwood. Your great-aunt Edna's poorly again and I think this might be the last one." She's always this way when a relation is ill, with death an unpleasant but very exciting prospect. If she returns from Cottonwood with Edna aboveground she'll consider the trip a failure.

Pell grunts. "Something wrong with Edna's woman parts. Always has been."

"May be gone a couple weeks or a month. Need you to take care of Pell while I'm gone."

III.

It ends up being a pretty good work week, starting with a botched robbery at a diner on Meridian. The stickup man came in at a quarter to four and ordered a bowl of chili, and after eating it, pulled a gun, upon which provocation the counterman extracted a shotgun from under the dish rack and emptied out the badman's midsection. Blood and viscera are sprayed all over the back wall and picture window of the diner, the smells of urine and excrement and blood mingling with those of lemon meringue pie and overheated coffee. I shoot the corpse from various angles while the owner argues with the police about how soon they'll be hauling the body off so he can clean up before dinnertime.

The gunman is — was — about thirty, neatly dressed in a lumber jacket and pressed chinos, and looks like he might have had a haircut that very morning. His lips are ever so slightly parted, the edges of his upper and lower teeth just visible, and his half-open eyes are fixed on the ceiling or beyond it, with no hint of surprise or disappointment in them. He looks far too soft to pull off an armed robbery; did some hint of tentativeness on his part give the counterman the nerve to go for the shotgun?

Outside the waning afternoon sun casts orange highlights on the squad cars and the morgue wagon. The sallow-faced, dyspeptic Sedgwick County coroner, Dr. Groff, half an inch of unfiltered cigarette dangling from his lip, takes one last look at the cadaver before ordering the driver and his assistant to load it up. A morgue attendant told me once that Groff scrounged old butts around the office, saved the tobacco, and rerolled them, and I can never look at him without wanting to laugh. As the dead man gets hoisted into the back gate of the wagon Elting and I shoot the bull with Groff and Captain Meeker of Serious Crimes.

"They must have been expecting a goddamn bear to wander in there someday." Meeker lights up a cigarette and shakes his head.

Elting whips out his notebook. "Can I quote you to that effect?"

"Quote me on this: cocksucker was asking for it. Shit, and now the owner wants to fire the counterman 'cause he made such a mess with the shotgun. Do me a favor and make him out to be a hero so they won't shitcan him, okay?"

"Heroes move papers anyway."

I go back inside to ask the counterman if he'll consent to have his portrait taken for the *Beacon.* His big soft face is a distinctly unhealthy-looking milk white with a sprinkling of black stubble, and I'm thinking about ways to accentuate that pallor.

"How about right there in front of the window so's you can see the blood?"

"That's a good idea but the *Beacon* won't run it. If it was up to me . . ." I shrug. If it were up to me I'd have him pose on one knee with the shotgun next to the corpse like a ten-point trophy buck; in any case, the body's gone and an old woman is already hard at work with a mop and a bucketful of ammonia on the human effluvia staining the floor. I have him stand behind his counter, shotgun leaning across his chest, its barrel pointing above his right shoulder toward the light fixture. He's trying to look like a hard man, but earlier the cops told me he'd been into the bathroom three times to puke since their arrival. The odor in the restaurant isn't getting any nicer, either, a mixture now of the aforementioned smells plus the ammonia in the old woman's bucket plus a soupçon of the counterman's vomit wafting over from the men's room, its door open for aeration. The dinner crowd tonight will be, I predict, thin and of necessity hardy.

"Do me a favor," I say to the counterman. "Quit smiling for a second."

He relaxes his facial muscles and widens his eyes. The corners of his mouth extend downward, the very picture of a psychopath. Perfect.

The late gunman's name was Alvin Holroyd, and he lived in an apartment on South Market. Elting has been topping a married college girl in the afternoons, so as a favor to him I go there on my own to get the widow's picture. If she says anything noteworthy I'll add it to his copy, otherwise just jot down her name and address.

The black-eyed girl who answers the door looks eighteen or nineteen, with scarlet blotches on her cheeks and forehead violent against her pale skin and a scattering of freckles across the bridge of her bright red wet nose. Her hair is dark brown and wavy, pulled into a thick chignon that seems on the verge of bursting, a Gibson-girlish style that I find pleasing. I'm guessing she's six months pregnant.

"Seven. Eight, almost," she tells me. My presence seems to have a calming effect on her, giving her as it does something to do with her hands. Her name is Bea, she tells me as she busies herself making us coffee. Though she seems to have been crying for a couple of hours straight she seems also to have an imperfect understanding of what happened to her husband this afternoon, like a child who, though sad about the death of a puppy, still half-expects it to show up at the door yapping to be let in. "Alvin's all panicky about the baby. I can't believe he went and stuck up a place."

"Panicky? How, exactly?"

"Lately he can't sleep, just lies awake thinking about the baby. He's been working at Feldon's trucking, and he's fallen asleep at the wheel twice already. First time he woke up just in time to get the truck back off the shoulder. Second time was last week, and they fired him."

"Did he hurt anybody?"

"No, but he totaled that truck."

"Wait a minute, was that over on George Washington Boulevard? Hit an aboveground gas pipe?"

"Yeah. One of those big green things, sticks up out of the ground? They had to evacuate all the houses around there."

Jackpot. Alvin's mishap was a reasonably big story last week. "How old are you, Mrs. Holroyd, if you don't mind my asking?"

"I'm seventeen. Alvin's twenty-eight. We practically had to put a gun to my dad's head to make him sign the papers so we could get married." She touches her hand to her belly. "One of those deals, you know, where it was kind of important to do it right away." She moves the hand to the back of her chignon, then slides it down to the base of her neck and squeezes a few times before allowing me a rueful half smile.

"You have a job?"

"Nuh-uh. Alvin doesn't believe in that." She picks a handkerchief off of the table in front of her, wipes her eyes, and blows her nose. Because her nose is so stuffed she holds her jaw slack, and it makes her lips look fuller than they are. "I'm sorry I'm so stupid-looking with the crying and everything."

She poses for me by the window. The poignancy of her situation is the only thing that's going to get the picture in the paper, so I tell her to stand sideways for a good belly view. Now that the picture's taken I'm anxious to get away, but the coffee is just now ready to pour so I take my cup and smile as if I just took her picture for an article on the garden society.

"Guess I ought to call my folks and let them know, hadn't I?" She smiles again, as though out of force of habit, and for the first time I feel a pang of regret for poor dumb Alvin. I don't have the heart to steal his picture, so I ask if I can borrow one.

IV.

When I walk into Pell's kitchen a few minutes after sunrise I find him face-down on the linoleum, and to my expert eye in the light of that fifteen-watt bulb, he looks dead. When I grab him by the shoulders, though, and roll him over he lets out a long, pained sigh. His eyes are half-open, pupils rolled upward, and there's blood caked on and under his nose where he hit the floor. I don't like the way his right arm looks, limp and crooked, and he's slow to rouse. When he first comes around he doesn't seem to know me, and when I tell him I'm taking him to the hospital he blows his stack.

"I ain't going to any fuckin' hospital. Nothing wrong with me, I was sleeping until you woke me up, you dirty son of a bitch." He tries to sit up and falls back onto the floor, howling in pain and clutching at his right arm. "Jesus Christ, boy, what the hell'd you do to me?"

"You passed out, fell down, and busted your arm is what it looks like to me. Come on, let's go to the hospital and get that thing set."

"The hell I will. I'm just winged is all. Nothing wrong with me a little drink won't fix." He tries to sit up again and yelps, a seal-like sound I wouldn't have thought him capable of producing, then falls backward again, his head connecting with a dull thud. "Goddamn."

"Pell, are you going to get in the car with me or am I going to have to call an ambulance?"

"Hold your goddamn horses. Help me up and I'll get a snort and then we'll go."

One more drink can't do him too much more harm on top of the fifteen or twenty he probably had last night, and it might make him easier to handle, so after tucking my hands under his armpits — an unsavory task — I pull him up to a sitting position and help him get his feet planted solidly on the floor. With some degree of difficulty we get to the table, whereupon he pours himself a water glass full and downs it. "Let's get going."

In the car the blood is flowing again slowly from his nose, along with tears at the pain in his arm. I turn on the radio and he sniffles quietly, and it isn't until I pull out of the driveway that he speaks, voice cracking with pain and rage.

"Hospital's the other way, you dumb shit."

"Wesley's closest, Pell."

"Fuck Wesley's, I'm a vet, take me to the goddamn VA. They got to take me for free."

I pull into a driveway and turn it around. "You been there before, or are we going to need some kind of proof you're a vet?"

"I go once a month by taxi and see a croaker about my lungs. Get free prescriptions, too."

"I never knew you were in the service."

"Goddamn right. War with Spain, served down in Porta Rica. Damn near got killed, too. Got my fuckin' horse shot right out from under me."

"You were in the cavalry?"

"Sure. I grew up riding horses. My pa fell off a horse when he was drunk, crushed his head on a rock. Six months later my old lady married a mean old skunk and that's when things started turning to shit for old Pell."

"So did you ride up San Juan Hill with Teddy Roosevelt?"

"Shit, no. And neither did he, that was all bullshit. It was a regiment of niggers took San Juan Hill and that cocksucker Roosevelt took all the credit. He didn't ride up 'til after." A drop of blood that's been quivering on Pell's chin drops onto his shirt at that moment, flattening into a circular red stain.

"I never heard that before."

"The colored don't write the damn history books. But you can ask any man who was there and they'll tell you, if they're honest."

It's the most intelligible conversation I've ever had with Uncle Pell. Maybe the pain is cutting through the boozy miasma in his brain. When we get to the emergency room at the VA we have a long wait, during which he says not one word, and when he finally gets in to see a doctor I tell him that Pell's blood is probably about eighty proof at the moment.

"I could have told you that before I even smelled him," he says. "We get our share of boozers here." Tall and skinny with a long face peppered with zits as red as bee stings, he isn't much older than twenty-five, and when he goes into the room I can hear Pell through the door, angrily challenging his competence and credentials.

Ten minutes later he comes out to inform me that Pell is going to be an inpatient for a while.

"For a broken arm?"

"Broken arm, broken nose, alcoholic dementia, liver and kidney troubles, cardiac arrhythmia, you name it. When's the last time he saw a doctor?"

"He told me he comes here once a month for his lungs."

"According to his chart he hasn't been here since February '48, for some kind of bowel complaint. His lungs sound fine to me."

V.

Elting and I spend a good part of the next afternoon at Adams Billiard Parlor on West Douglas, where a regular patron stabbed a young stranger who'd tried to skip out on a debt. The other regulars are in a state of outrage at the unfairness of their friend's arrest, insisting that it was the stabbing victim who, once out of surgery, ought to be delivered to the county lockup.

"That boy come in here looking for a game, wanted to know who was the best player in the house," says the old man behind the cigar counter up front. He identifies himself as the owner and offers us each a free Roi-Tan, which Frank declines and I accept gratefully.

"And that was Mr. Tremaine?" Frank asks.

"Buddy Tremaine." His belt is cinched well above his navel and he nervously adjusts his trousers. "Well, mister, I've seen a few hustlers in the thirty years I've been in this business, and I knew Buddy could take this little shit on without breaking a sweat. You know, one of those fellows who gets to where he can beat anyone in his shitty little one-horse town and thinks he's the next Moscone. Well, he lets Buddy beat him the first time around, and Buddy knows he let him."

"So Buddy's not playing his best game, either."

The old guy laughs, spraying me through his missing eyeteeth. "No, hell no. He figured on taking the little son of a bitch for his whole bankroll. So when the kid's game sharpens up so does his, but just enough so's it's still tight. Finally the kid's desperate, starts shooting his best, and that's when Buddy cleans his clock. Took thirty-five dollars right off him. Now the kid says he wants to play Buddy one more time, double or nothing, and before that he hightails it to the bathroom. Now Buddy tells me to watch the table while he goes out back to the alley, 'cause this ain't the first time someone's thought of going through the men's room window to get out of paying a debt in here. What Buddy wasn't expecting was the kid coming out of there holding a knife. So Buddy drew his and stabbed the little fucker, and all of us here'll swear to that on a stack of goddamn Bibles."

"So how come the money was still in his pocket when he went to the bathroom?" I ask.

"How's that?"

"Don't people usually hand the stakes over to a third party?"

He puffs his chest out and draws up a little taller. "Not here they don't. Isn't that kind of a place."

Frank takes off at that point and I stay to get a picture of the owner standing next to the table on which the men had played the games in question, and another out back, pointing to the high window from which the young stranger had dropped. There's blood on the pavement and on the grass.

"You shoot billiards?" he asks me as we walk back inside.

"A little pool sometimes."

We sit down on a long wooden bench at the front of the hall intended for players waiting for tables, the length of its seat worn to an evenly blond tone, a tarnished brass spittoon at either end of it. "I was State Three-Cushion Billiards champion two years in a row, '15 and '16, and then again in '20 and regional champ in '23, back when you could play tournaments for good money. Won enough in the regional to buy my own parlor." He looks around at the place, at the players and the loafers and the hustlers, and shakes his head. "I must have been out of my fuckin' mind."

VI.

Several weeks into his VA stay Pell is sitting up in bed, lapping at his slumgullion with brio and addressing me with the full force of his contempt, enraged that Aunt Ivy still refuses to leave her sister's bedside in favor of his own. "That roundheel whoretoilet better get her ass back to Wichita before I head out there myself and drag her back with my good arm."

"Anything I can do for you in the meantime?"

"Bring me my fucking bottle. That'd make this shithole a damn sight more interesting." If these weeks of involuntary sobriety at the VA hadn't lightened his disposition, it has considerably improved his enunciation. He still looks pretty close to croaking — hollow of eye and sallow of cheek, the visible portion of his broken arm lavender and red — but out in the ammonia-scented corridor his pimply young doctor tells me he'll have to go home within the week.

"He has a pretty bad sinus infection, got him on penicillin for that, and an ulceration on his ankle, and his ears are full of fluid. I also don't like the sound of his heart. And anything you could do to keep him from drinking once he gets home would be helpful as well. He had some pretty ugly withdrawal symptoms the first couple of days, but his constitution's strong. Keep him off the sauce and he could live another twenty years."

The thought of Pell passing the century mark is horrifying in its own right, but that of being his custodian for weeks on end conjures an urgent, vaguely electrical sensation in my stomach. "Can't he stay here until his wife comes home?"

"Afraid not."

"What about his heart? And the sinus thing. And his ankle?"

"Beds are scarce, Mr. Farmer. This isn't a hotel and it's not a soldier's home anymore."

I find the chief of staff, Dr. Schnitzler, smoking and pawing a homely nurse six inches taller than he is, and when I knock on the open door she scurries out of his reach looking damned pleased with herself. I explain the situation to him and he nods quietly until she interrupts.

"That's the old man on three who called Marjorie a fishcunt."

"Marjorie?" Schnitzler says. "Is she the big blond with a permanent wave and a limp?"

"That's her," the nurse says. "Your uncle's way too sick to leave, by the way. They just can't take him anymore."

Schnitzler grunts. "I'll talk to the administrator and get it straightened out. What's this doctor's name, the one wants to send him home?"

"Hammond's his name, I think."

He nods. "The one with the acne."

The nurse laughs again. "We call him 'the boy.'"

Schnitzler glowers over the tops of his spectacles at her. "That's going to stop right away, you understand? The man's an M.D., even if he does look like he ought to be throwing the morning paper off of a bicycle in his short pants."

VII.

The highlight of the week is a knife fight over a bottle of cough syrup. A couple of hopheads sitting around the living room of a tiny house on South Meridian cracked open a brand-new bottle of codeine-fortified expectorant and the first of the two, a twenty-seven-year-old pipe fitter named Hazel Kilbane, swigged down two-thirds of it. His best friend and roommate, twenty-nine-year-old Billy Ray Steig, an unemployed linotype operator (who had apprenticed, the *Beacon* will be pleased to note in the evening edition, at the *Eagle*), took offense at Hazel's flouting of narcotic etiquette. Slugging down the remainder of the bottle he stumbled to the kitchen, where he took a butcher knife from the cluttered sink and came out looking to stick his pal. Hazel staggered out of the way and hid behind a tattered easy chair, over whose arm Billy Ray stumbled (a quantity of Old Grand-Dad having been consumed earlier over luncheon), cutting himself badly on the soft underside of his forearm. As he howled in pain Hazel laughed, and Billy Ray lunged for the knife and cracked his head open on the wall, still howling. Enraged at his friend's laughter Billy Ray stuck the butcher knife into Hazel's rib cage, noting with some surprise how difficult it was, even with a nice sharp blade. When he saw the amount of blood pooling around Hazel he panicked and called for an ambulance.

During Frank's brief interview Billy Ray sits on a wooden chair with his hands cuffed before him, his forearm wrapped in bloody gauze. He's reasonably lucid, considering the amounts of codeine and alcohol in his depleted bloodstream. Most crime scenes have one particularly bloody spot, but this one is a gory mess from Billy Ray's arm gushing as he ran about the house trying to find something to help Hazel with before the ambulance came. Before we got there one of the uniformed cops slipped on a puddle of it in the kitchen.

"It was just pure dumb luck it slid in through the ribs like that. If I'd'a hit bone I'd'a quit right then and there."

Elting's face lights up at that, and he writes it down trying to conceal a smile, then asks him how long he and Hazel had been roommates.

"Five years, since't I got back from the Pacific."

"You in the Navy?" Frank asks.

"Hell, no," he said. "I'm a fuckin' Marine."

I get a nice picture of the skinny corpse, the skin of its right cheek stretched eyeward by the floor into an involuntary postmortem sneer, and from the top of a dresser that's missing its upper two drawers I pilfer a photo of Kilbane for my album, since it's unlikely I'll find a studio shot anywhere. The stolen photo shows him on a beach, flexing his childlike biceps, "MUCSLE beacH venis caL. June 47" scrawled along the white border.

There's only one bed in the room, and a giant economy-sized jar of Vaseline stands on an orange crate that serves as a nightstand. Frank comes in and gives a snort. "You figure 'em for a couple of homos?" he says. "Maybe there's our angle."

The *Eagle*'s Bucky Kraft comes in from the living room. "Did you say something about homos?"

"That's what it looks like to me," Frank says.

"Bullshit," Bucky says, spitting a little, patches of red moving up from his neck to his cheeks. "That boy Billy Ray's a goddamn Marine!"

"I don't guess that proves it one way or the other, Bucky."

"My name's Buck, goddamn it. The *Eagle* won't print anything about queers anyway, even if it's just innuendo. Far as we're concerned, that particular vice isn't practiced in the Air Capital City." Bucky's gaze is drawn nonetheless to that jar of Vaseline, and after a moment's contemplation he sniffs and leaves the room.

VIII.

The cats must be fed. In Ivy's kitchen they surround me, making horrible mewling noises as though trying to convey to me some message beyond the habitual "feed us." Sure enough, a worse than usual smell hangs in the thick still atmosphere of the house, and I get the unpleasant notion that a weaker version of it has been present the last couple of times I've visited the house, maybe even before Pell broke his arm.

I follow the smell to the bedroom, where a big old tabby lies dead on the bedspread in a state of advanced putrefaction, body cavity crawling with so many vermin that he or she seems to be wiggling pleasurably, individual clumps of fur swaying this way and that. I run outside the house to take a deep breath of cold clean air and consider my options. The solution that appeals is arson: release the live cats into the neighborhood and watch the whole damned house burn to the rafters. Reason prevails and I go back in carrying the Speed Graphic to take a couple of pictures, then grab the ruined bedclothes by the corners like a sling and lift the cat up in the sling, holding my breath.

Kitty has soaked clean through to the mattress. The right thing to do would be to take the whole damned mess to the dump, but since I don't want that smell in my car, not even in the trunk, I haul it all out into the backyard, making a second trip for the mattress.

After some effort I find a spade in the basement, its handle so gray and rotten I have to grip it very near the blade to keep it from snapping in the hard ground. I dig a big shallow hole to toss the mattress in, followed by sheets, bedspread and maggoty corpse.

Even outdoors in the cold the smell is overpowering. Before I finish digging I hear barking, and on the other side of Ivy's rusty chain-link fence a couple of dogs prance and yap, trying to figure out how to get to this gamey bounty. Clearly, better disposal methods are called for.

In the garage I find a can of turpentine, which, poured on the corpse and the mattress, does a good momentary job of masking their smell before it gives up the ghost and becomes just another ghastly odor in concert with the others. There are now four dogs on the other side of the chain link, and with some small measure of trepidation — just how flammable is turpentine, anyway? — I drop a match into the hole and jump back, away from the resultant ball of flame. The smell that wafts from the burning mess is bad but it's an improvement over a moment ago, and its offensiveness diminishes as the fire consumes. The dogs lose interest and wander away, and I spot Mrs. Severy standing in her yard, following me with tiny wide-set eyes. Her brown housecoat and yellow scarf bring out her jaundiced complexion, offset nicely by the greenish-blue circles under her eyes. She must be freezing her tits off, but she shows no sign of discomfort beyond the pinched expression on her face, which I am guessing is more or less a permanent fixture.

"Dead cat," I tell her. "Been dead a little while." I hold my nose in case she doesn't get the drift.

"No one home over there?"

Mindful of Aunt Ivy's suspicions I tell her that they're just feeling under the weather, and she nods and goes back inside.

The mattress is burned down pretty well by now, and I pour some more turpentine on it where the flames are getting weaker. The smoke is thick and gray, and it strikes me I could have left it on the curb for the trashmen.

IX.

The next morning we all experience an unaccustomed sense of revulsion at what should be an ordinary scene of mayhem. Something in the ether seems to have put us all in a state of moody introspection as we peer one by one into a poorly lit elevator shaft in the Greene Building on Broadway, its bottom strewn with gum wrappers, cigarette butts, and other forms of urban detritus. In the midst of it crouch Captain Meeker and another plainclothesman from the WPD, alongside the venerable Dr. Groff. The object of their scrutiny is the shattered body of one Arnold Stennis, age twenty-four, of 2487 South Mildred in Wichita. There's no immediate indication of how Arnold got down the shaft, but the fact that his hands are tied behind his back suggests foul play. According to Captain Meeker, Mr. Stennis was a known associate of Jack Haughtry, a trafficker in narcotics who at this very moment is being roused from bed and taken in for questioning. Meeker tells us all this with none of his accustomed joviality in the face of death, at least the deaths of those he reckons were in for it; you'd think the event was nothing more than an addition to his week's workload.

The giddy elevator operator is the only one in the building showing any signs of animation at all. He's old and tiny, in the tradition of elevator men, and his nose has gone lavender and gray from drink. An errant strand of very long white hair has come loose and falls over his forehead, giving him the look of an elderly adolescent. "Got here this morning and I seen the cage on number two wuddn't down here where it oughtta been, found the goddamn thing up't the tenth floor. Well it's a goddamn good thing I didn't just ride 'er down, 'cause something seemed off to me, I know my machines, see? Went down to the ninth floor and found the doors jimmied open. Boy I knew something was up then, so I shined me a flashlight down there and by Christ there was that son of a bitch lying there. I said to myself I'd damn well better get the police in before the offices start opening up." Frank takes all this down while I get a couple of shots of the old man and of the cops milling around the lobby.

We move off to the side to watch the office workers arriving, gawking at the police and bitching about everyone having to share a single elevator. Frank cheers up at the sight of a leggy blond with a big crooked nose, crossing the lobby to elevator number one. "Look at that one swaying back and forth. Goddamn. Hey, miss," he shouts. When she looks over at him he points at her legs. "Run in your stocking."

She pulls at her skirt and twirls, arching her back provocatively, looking for the nonexistent run, then shoots Frank a look of pure poison. "Creep," she says, nostrils flared, and struts toward the elevator.

He laughs hard and wipes a little tear from his eye. "That's an old one but it still works. Boy, some pins on her, huh?"

X.

On the way home from the Greyhound Station as Aunt Ivy laments her sister Edna and criticizes the funeral — cheap and low-class, in her opinion — I keep my mouth shut about the dead tabby. As soon as she's in her kitchen, though, she starts counting heads and turns to me, half-panicked, half-accusatory.

"Where's Saucy? What have you done with Saucy?"

"Was Saucy the big tabby?"

"She sleeps on my bed! Where is she?"

"Aunt Ivy, I'm afraid Saucy passed while you were in Cottonwood with Aunt Edna."

"Where is she?"

"In the yard."

"I want to see her. I don't believe it. Show me."

"Aunt Ivy, she's been dead for weeks." Here I feel compelled to add, for no logically supportable reason, something Aunt Ivy doesn't have to know: "I cremated her."

Aunt Ivy slaps me across the face. "No one in our family's ever been cremated," she says.

"Aunt Ivy," I amend myself, in a moment of divine inspiration, "I believe your neighbors might have done her in."

This sets off another bell in her old gray head. "My candlesticks." She tears off into the bedroom and screams. "Where's my bedspread?"

"It had to be burned with the cat. I replaced the mattress, too."

Now she's looking under the bed and in the closet, now under a floorboard.

"That's it, call the police. They've stolen the candlesticks."

"How many places did you hide the candlesticks?"

"I ain't telling you where I hid the candlesticks. It's enough they're gone. What are you going to do about it?"

XI.

Late that same afternoon dispatch sends me out to meet Frank in Kechi, north of town, and I park between his car and one belonging to the Kechi police, a black prewar Plymouth with rust damage on the runners. A Sedgwick County sheriff's prowler is parked on the street in front, with Dr. Groff's meat wagon right behind it. What's odd about the scene at first glance is that the operators of all these vehicles, with the exception of the doctor, are all milling around in front of the house, smoking and kicking at the clods of dirt that litter the cruddy yard. A sheriff's deputy writes up a report on a stainless steel tablet while his colleague from the town of Kechi tries in vain to strike up a collegial dialogue.

On spotting me Elting bounds down from the porch and hustles me joyously inside with a warning to hold my breath. This is unnecessary, as it happens, because by the time I'm even with him the stench emanating from the front door is assaultive and unparalleled in my years of covering violent and unusual deaths.

"Guy's been dead damn near three weeks," he whispers, as if it's a secret. This is intriguing, since normally a few weeks will take the punch out of a death smell.

What I find before me is Ezra Groff, breathing intently into a handkerchief and seated on the lid of the toilet. Next to him is a clawfooted porcelain tub filled with what are only inferentially identifiable as human remains, mostly composed of a thick, soupy liquid, but containing what appears to be a human skull partially exposed near the end of the basin opposite the faucet. I turn and, nearly overpowered, race to the front door with Frank cackling behind me. I stand with my hands braced against the building for a minute, filling my lungs with the relatively clean air of Kechi, Kansas, while Frank fills me in on what he knows.

"Son of a bitch weighed three-fifty, four hundred pounds, is what the neighbors are guessing. Groff says maybe more. Looks like he died trying to claw his way out of the tub. Son of a bitch, can you imagine if this'd happened in July or August?"

I'm trying not to, and I go to the trunk of the DeSoto to get my tripod, since the illumination in the bathroom is just right for a shot in natural light. I take it back into the house and, fortified by pride in my craft, force myself to spend a good five minutes within sniffing distance of the corpse, taking three shots, including one of Groff leaning in to examine the skull's dentition with the hankie over his own cadaverous old face. Lovely shots they'll be, once the memory of that smell fades from my olfactory lobe.

From the bedroom I pilfer a photograph of a fat young man, taken at the Kansas State Fair in 1936, according to the caption running along the border. Accompanied by three other boys and a couple of reasonably attractive girls, he sports a souvenir straw hat and looks quite happy. The man in the picture is fat, really fat, if considerably shy of four hundred pounds, and since there are no other photographs evident on the premises I have to take it on faith that the cheery figure in the fair pictures is a younger version of the liquefied man in the tub.

His name was Vernon Ralston, aged thirty-eight, and until three and a half weeks ago he was employed as a baker at the Renfro Bakery on North Broadway. When Vernon stopped coming in to work, Groff tells me outside, his bosses never bothered to find out why, just hired another baker to replace him. Inside the front door the Kechi patrolman who responded to the neighbor's odor complaint found among the three weeks' worth of accumulated mail a curtly worded notice of termination from the bakery. Vernon's date of death, Groff theorizes, may have been the third week in March when the mercury dropped precipitously for a couple of days, since the thermostat is set to eighty. This extra roaring of the furnace sped the rate of decomposition until the gas was, mercifully, shut off for nonpayment, the dead man having already been several months in arrears at the time of his decease.

XII.

"Kill the cocksuckers," Pell rages that evening from his reclaimed spot at the kitchen table. "I'll de-ball that son of a bitch and bury his wife alive."

"If they stole the sticks they're probably in a pawnshop somewhere," I tell them.

"Go find 'em then," Ivy says.

"There's probably twenty pawnshops in this town, so this may take a while. You'd better get ready to go out."

"I'll not set foot in a pawnshop. That's the province of criminals and Christkillers."

"Aunt Ivy, how am I supposed to identify candlesticks I never saw in my life?"

She waddles into the bedroom and returns with a shoebox full of photos, some of them quite old by the look of them. Finally she finds what she's looking for, hands me a Polaroid of her grimacing behind a set of four matched candlesticks that do indeed look valuable.

"How come I never saw the sticks before?" I ask her.

"Wouldn't take 'em out for the likes of you."

On my way out I pass Pell, looking up at the corner where the east and north walls meet the ceiling, his lower lip jutting out in deep contemplation. I look up there too and don't see anything besides a few decades' worth of discolored cooking grease.

XIII.

On Valentine's Day Frank and I cover a shooting in the parking lot of the Bowler Restaurant way out east on Central. The dead man is a dishwasher, the killer the restaurant's manager. The latter suspected that the former was wooing a waitress away from him, and after an altercation in the restaurant witnessed by more than a dozen diners the dishwasher quit. His corpse strikes me as that of an aging lothario, a few years past his stalking prime but still man enough to draw a woman from the arms of the short, portly manager. I photograph the latter handcuffed in the back seat of a brand-new radio cruiser, the very model of the unhinged impulse killer, but for me the shot of the day is the object of the deadly rivalry, one Phyllis Macklin. Mrs. Macklin, thirty-eight years of age, is plump and full of piss and vinegar, with a wry, depraved, mischievous look that might have ensnared me, too, if I worked with her day in and day out. She's distraught, if not overly so for a woman who's just lost a pair of suitors, and her slightly smeared makeup is a nice if not particularly original touch. While Frank interviews the kitchen staff I get a shot of her seated at a booth, making damned sure to show her legs, long and lovely even with her sensible working shoes on.

Back in the car I ask Frank if he could imagine killing for a gal with an ass like hers.

"Wasn't over her," he says. "That's how it started, but the dishwasher got pissed off and quit right in the middle of lunch. That's when the manager went for the gun."

XIV.

In his exuberant youth Wingy Lazar was riding in the passenger side of a Stutz Bearcat with his arm extended through the window, and when the car passed a little too close to a stop sign he found himself a walking, talking cautionary tale for children, with a new and colorful nickname to boot. As I walk into his father's pawnshop — my grandfather's accounting office was upstairs for years — he's explaining to a willowy blond woman the operation of an ancient box camera. As usual the prosthetic arm hangs by a hook on the wall, and the lady is paying as much attention to his foreshortened arm as she is to the camera. Wingy swears by the stump's mysterious aphrodisiac qualities. "It's just a question of waving the stump around like it's a cock," he said to me once. "Once you do that they're as good as hypnotized."

He nods to me and conveys via a slight arching of his eyebrows that he may have a shot at the lady's virtue. I kill the time examining the old coins stapled into little cardboard squares with round cellophane centers, arranged in rows under the glass counter.

"Is this the kind where you just send Eastman Kodak the whole camera and they send it back with the pictures?"

"It's been quite a while since they've done that, ma'am," he says, and for the first time I take a good look at the willowy blond, who turns out to be quite a bit longer in the tooth than I imagined looking at her from behind, with a long, narrow face shiny with makeup and mascara like Theda Bara's. Damned if Wingy isn't pointing things out with his stump instead of his other hand, though, and damned if her voice isn't taking on a distinctly flirtatious tone as the lesson progresses.

After a few minutes the lady leaves, having promised to give the matter some thought. "Oh, yeah, she's gonna be giving the matter some thought all right," Wingy says.

"You should ask if she's got a granddaughter. We could double date."

"Ah, she's not that old." He looks after her through the plate glass as she disappears down the sidewalk. "How old, you think?"

I slap the Polaroid down on the glass countertop. "Someone come in and pawn these candlesticks in the last couple, three weeks, maybe?"

With a cagey show of nonchalance he holds his fist up to his face and studies his lone set of fingernails. "What if someone did?"

"Stolen from my aunt's house."

"Nah, haven't seen 'em. You sure they got pawned?"

"I've been to two-thirds of the hockshops in town and haven't found anything."

"If the owner thinks they're hot then you won't. If they take in hot merchandise they wouldn't show it to you, coming in with a goddamn Polaroid like that. Better take the picture to the cops."

"Problem is I'm not sure they were really stolen. My aunt's kind of batty."

Wingy cocks his head and looks at me with one eye squinted shut, and I understand that I'm wasting his time and mine.

XV.

Late in the afternoon I accompany Frank down to the Allis Hotel, where a sixth-floor suite is the scene of an apparent suicide. The victim hanged himself in the closet, no mean feat since it involved crouching slightly and suffocating himself. Doctor Groff estimates that the process must have taken ten minutes at the very least.

"I guess this one'll go down as a suicide, Doc?" Frank asks him with a snicker.

"That's what I'll write down, but I'm not convinced."

"You think it's murder?"

"Accident. Take a good look at the body."

The dead man is naked except for his socks, which seems like a funny way to check out — my photographs of him are from the chest up, emphasizing his purple mottled face — and his cock rests flaccid and sticky in his hand.

"You know what the sergeants used to say in the Army, drop your cocks and grab your socks," Frank says.

"Now take a look at that on the floor, next to his left toes." A tiny puddle sits congealing beneath the organ, so small you'd never notice it if it weren't pointed out. "I'm not going to check it, but I'd bet money that's human semen."

"So you think he beat his meat one last time before he punched his own clock?"

"I think he was masturbating with a noose around his neck and when the moment of climax arrived the noose tightened as planned and he passed out. Strangled under his own weight."

Frank bursts out laughing, and two of the cops glare at him. The third laughs it up in his turn, and Groff seems not to notice any of it.

"Don't know how it gets around but these boys get the idea that lack of oxygen intensifies the sensation of euphoria at the moment of physical release. First time I saw one of these was in 1919, a farm boy in Sumner County, just fifteen years old. All around him at his feet were dirty French pictures his brother'd brought back from the war. I knew an old sawbones who'd been a medic with the GAR, he'd seen one way back in the early 1870s in Wisconsin. There was a lady's whalebone corset on the floor the boy was jacking off onto."

I half-expect Frank to try and run the story past the city editor with the offending information highlighted, just to hear the apoplectic reaction.

XVI.

Ivy limp-stomps across the kitchen until she's less than a foot from me. "Where's the candlesticks?"

"Nobody's seen them."

She grabs the lug wrench off the kitchen counter, left over from my last attempt to fix the sink, wields it briefly like a shillelagh, and hands it to me. "Then they must still be next door. I've known them no-accounts thirty years or more, and they've never been any good. Their kids were thieves, too."

"Aunt Ivy, you can't just go over there."

"Are you going to let me go alone?" she asks, and I know there's zero chance of convincing this ninety-pound birdlike old thing not to go, so I follow her.

*

My first rappings on the Severys' door go unanswered, but I can hear their radio playing inside. I keep on knocking and the sound stops, and the living room lights go out. "Come on, open up, we need to talk to you."

Ivy pounds on the living room widow. "They must take us for idiots. Look, trying to pretend they're not home. Knock again."

I pound louder and yell some more. It's cold and quiet, except for a chain reaction of dogs barking, egged on by my knocking and hollering.

Ivy tries the doorknob without success. "Let's go around back and see if it's unlocked," Ivy whispers.

"Why don't we just call the police?" I whisper back.

"Don't be stupid, boy. They'll just lie and we'll look foolish."

There's a light on next to the back door. Ivy points triumphantly at a large wooden crate in its glare, broken down into a stack of boards next to the trash can. "Look at what they just spent a bunch of money on."

It's a packing crate for an Emerson television set. While I'm looking at it I hear Ivy rattle the knob, and then I hear the breaking of a pane of glass. The lug wrench has sailed right through into the kitchen.

"Jesus," I whisper, but I don't manage to keep it very low.

"Stick your hand in there and unlock it," she orders, and I obey, understanding finally why everyone in my family has always been so scared of the old gal.

Stepping inside a kitchen only marginally more hygienic than Ivy's I pick the wrench up from among the shards and we march like soldiers to the living room where I turn on the overhead light. The crippled husband sits next to a walker in front of the extinguished television set, his eyes on the carpet like a bad puppy. His wife rises from the easy chair with her knobby index finger outstretched.

"You get out of my house this instant! I'll have the police over here so quick your head'll spin." Her lower teeth are all jangly and thin, with one incisor broken clean in two.

"Go ahead and call 'em. Ask for Sergeant Burton in Burglary Division." Though this is a name I just made up on the spot, it gives Mrs. Severy a jolt.

"You go on and get out of here."

There's real hate on her face, for me and my aunt and for her husband, too, I think. It's easy to imagine this living room as a crime scene, one of them having slaughtered the other, and not sorry for it, either.

I step over to the TV and turn it back on. It fizzes and crackles, and a tiny blue light appears at the center of the gray-green screen and expands until it consumes it altogether. "Nice picture."

The husband speaks up. "They make one bigger than this."

"You should've stolen more silver," I tell him.

"You watch what you say in this house, mister," Mrs. Severy says.

I haven't loathed her up until this moment, but something in her tone makes me want to coldcock the old bat. I take the wrench from Aunt Ivy's bony, papery old fist. "I'm going to bust this television into little tiny bits if I don't get a goddamn pawn ticket and some cash out of you."

"Go ahead. I'll see you in jail for breaking and entering." But she leaves the room, and I can hear her in the bedroom rooting around in drawers. She turns on the radio to KFH, and I can hear their police beat reporter droning about a stickup at a gas station.

Mr. Severy cries quietly, little spasms rocking his body, his pants belted at his solar plexus. He burbles something about his wife's strong will, never quite admitting that they stole the silver but acknowledging his long-standing desire for a television set like the one their son has. When his wife comes back into the room she has her arms folded over her scrawny chest.

"Where's the pawn ticket?"

"What pawn ticket?" she says, placid and confident. "I just called the police on you."

Again I picture the room as a crime scene, an image that has great appeal to me. I tap the lug wrench on the top of the television cabinet and lift it above my head as if to bring it down on Mrs. Severy's matted scalp. She screams, Ivy laughs, and the old man sniffles as I swivel and smash the business end of it against the television screen. Everyone flinches but nothing happens. I swing again, and really put my back into it this time, and I manage to crack the safety glass in front of the picture tube.

Now I go after it like a lumberjack, and on my third try I smash straight through into the guts of the thing. The picture tube implodes with a genuinely frightening noise, not unlike a gunshot, and I feel a genuine sense of accomplishment as it sparks and smokes.

I'm vaguely aware of a keening from one or both of the Severys as I open the door and unplug the set before dragging it with some difficulty onto the porch, where the entire cabinet sits and burns, pale blue flames illuminating its interior and nasty black smoke pouring from the seams.

After a good spraying down with the Severys' garden hose the smoke dies down, though its smell hangs electric and nasty in the night air. Mrs. Severy pushes through the front door, past me and onto her lawn to greet the arriving cops. As she leans into the window of the cruiser and jabbers at its occupants I gaze at the smoldering set and feel a great calm settling on me as I prepare to make my case to the law. This may look bad at first glance, but these men have seen worse.

STEPHEN RHODES

At the Top of His Game

FROM *Wall Street Noir*

ON THE DAY THEY CONSPIRE to put a bullet in my head, I experience an epiphany.

My epiphany is this: a fourteen-year career on Wall Street wears away at your soul, as assuredly as a stream against limestone. It pushes you to a place where you don't fully recognize who you are, or how you got here. Everyone around you becomes a stranger, including — no, *especially* — your own wife. Working sixteen-hour days in those glistening glass towers in Manhattan, engaging in mortal combat with some of the planet's brightest and most power-obsessed bastards who have trained their full concentration on destroying you and stealing the business you've built up over the years — well, it hardens you. Wall Street eats its young, and today the beast has a particular appetite for a certain thirty-six-year-old maverick with seventy-eight people reporting to him (which would be me).

So today they plan to execute me. How do I know this? Well, last night at 9:30 P.M., an urgent BlackBerry message instructed me to report to Howard Ranieri's office at 7:30 A.M. sharp for a mandatory meeting. That particular e-mail was no surprise; a heads-up had come from a friend in HR that my employment would be terminated during this impromptu meeting.

My response: *Bring it on, jerkweed. Bring it on.*

Ranieri is now more than forty minutes late for his own meeting. Typical move for this passive-aggressive, hair-challenged, beer-gutted, no-talent clown. I should mention that Ranieri is my co-head in the Equity Structured Products group.

Outside Ranieri's office, the phones on the trading floor twitter relentlessly. This morning, Goldman Sachs has issued a dire report on certain Latin American economies. As a result, the overseas financial markets are getting walloped.

The twentysomething stress-addicts that populate the trading floor gaze into their Bloomberg screens seeking divine guidance. I hear the voices of my people reporting losses in the overseas markets like breathless wartime correspondents witnessing heavy casualties from the front lines. *The Footsie is getting whacked, hammered, slammed, smashed, crushed, drilled, smoked, spanked, roasted, sewered, bashed. Beaten like a redheaded stepchild, clubbed like a baby seal.* Boom boom, *out go the lights.*

Ranieri's tardiness is driving me to distraction. It's Friday, for chrissakes. I've got a dinner party at the Honeywells' tonight. And I've got a wife who may have been cheating with a kickboxing instructor for God knows how long. Do I really need to have Ranieri playing with my head in the moments before he gleefully fires me?

Abruptly, Howie breezes through the door of his office. "Sparky, glad to see you're here," he burbles as if he's five minutes late for a tennis game. "I'm really truly sorry about this, but —"

"No, you're not."

"Come again?"

I pronounce each syllable slowly. "I said, 'No, you're not.' Meaning, no, you are *not* sorry. You are the polar opposite of sorry. You kept me waiting on purpose."

"*Touché,* Sparky." Ranieri's laugh is a brutish grunt. "Maybe you're kind of right about that."

"Not a problem. I passed the time by reading all your e-mails."

Ranieri inspects me to see whether I'm serious, but my poker face is inscrutable. *Backatcha, jerkweed.*

"Anyhoo," Ranieri says with narrowed eyes, "let's move on to the reason we're here. You know Brian, I presume."

I turn around and see Brian Horgan, a VP from HR, skulking in the doorway, craving invisibility. Brian is a good guy in my book; he was the one who gave me the heads-up about this meeting. I take note of the thick Redweld tucked under his arm — my personnel file, no doubt.

"Um, good morning, Mark." The poor bastard winces as he says this. It's obvious this is anything but.

"*Of course* I know Brian," I say breezily. "We've worked together for what . . . six years?"

"Yeah, six years," he confirms. "Six long years recruiting the best structured products group on the Street, from the ground up."

Ranieri steers the conversation away from my accomplishments. "Well then, I hope we can make this as pleasant as possible for everyone concerned. Given your contribution to the firm, we've moved heaven and earth to be generous." *Translation: You need to sign this piece of paper promising not to sue us, or you walk away with nothing for fourteen years of service.*

I wheel around to my friend from HR. "Your work is done here, Brian."

"It is?" There is a look of palpable relief on Brian Horgan's face.

"Go back to your office, check your e-mail for further instructions."

Ranieri erupts. "Just what the hell are you trying to pull —"

"It's not my doing. Sanderson has taken an interest in this —"

"Bullshit. He's in Hong Kong."

"Exactly. And Sanderson says stand down. Nothing is to happen until he returns to London on Monday."

Ranieri scrutinizes me. "Does Becker know about this?"

"Why would that matter?"

Ranieri scowls venomously, then wheels his Herman Miller Aeron chair over to his flat-panel computer screen. His lips move as he reads the fresh e-mail from Sanderson. Then he slams his open palm on the surface of his desk. "Son of a bitch!"

I turn to Horgan. "Like I was saying. Until this gets sorted out, you're free to go."

Ranieri grumbles with a dismissive wave. "Whatever."

With a surreptitious wink, Brian Horgan reassembles the file and departs.

My co-head makes a big show of closing the door and sealing us off from the rest of the trading floor. "Swift move, asshole. You knew I was leaving for Barcelona with my family tonight, didn't you?"

"Guess you'll just have to postpone your victory dance."

"Maybe . . ." Ranieri regards me with a feral leer. "But you can postpone the inevitable only so long, Sparky."

I lean back and give him a smile that's . . . well, yes, call it *self-satis-*

fied. "Let's recap, shall we? Four months ago, you pull some strings in London with Ian Becker — your Harvard roommate — to conjure up some do-nothing job that suggests to senior management that you're not utterly useless. Lucky me: since I happen to drive the lion's share of revenue in the U.S., Becker drop-kicks you into *my* sandbox as a co-head. Says you've got a lot to learn and you're 'here to help.' Instead, what happens? You steal my ideas, my team, my business, my *revenues.* You systematically bad-mouth me to Becker and the rest of senior management as 'redundant' and 'not a team player.' You and Becker wait for my mentor to be incommunicado somewhere so you can pull this lame-ass coup d'état." I shake my head in disgust. "You're not even worth keeping around to order lunch for my people."

Ranieri leans back calmly. "On the one hand, screw you for messing up my vacation. At the same time, I commend you for pulling off that last-minute clemency from the powers-that-be. Very creative." A slow smile spreads across his face. "But guess what? Turns out your guy is getting a bullet to the head himself from senior management. So looks like we have a do-over first thing Monday morning."

"We done here?"

"For now."

"Good." I bolt upright and regard my mortal enemy with utter contempt. "You'll excuse me, I'm going to go back to the desk and make some money. I'll leave you to whatever it is you do all day."

Bite me, jerkweed. And I'm out of there.

Moments later, I experience an emotional cocktail of mild embarrassment and genuine euphoria when the entire derivatives trading floor erupts in a standing ovation. On the Street, information is the ultimate commodity, and the news that I survived Ranieri's savage assassination attempt causes spasms of joy among the all-star team I've assembled.

"Okay, okay, all right!" I shout over the sustained applause, whistles, and catcalls. "A for effort, but this show of loyalty won't necessarily have a favorable impact on year- end bonuses."

The cheering tapers off into an admixture of laughter and mock boos. I hear a muffled thud behind me as an apoplectic Ranieri kicks his office door shut. I love these people. *Love them.*

"All right, people, show's over. Let's pump it up and make some money for the Brothers."

As if a switch is turned on, the trading floor becomes electrified, crackling with high-voltage activity. The discordant brays of traders fill my ears:

"I'm choking on micro-gamma decay on my long-vol position, and unless they rally I'm gonna be achin' like there's no tomorrow —"

"Johnny Meyer, pick up the double-donuts!"

"I called Tommy at DB for a chinstrap in the double-Monday nasty; the bid's gone to a bad neighborhood —"

"I took the bid up a noogie from 10.2 to 10.25 and oh-fived a sweet-one pick-off of the crowd. Am I a hammer or what?"

This is in my blood, the thrill and agony of trading derivative securities. There's no Betty Ford clinic for this addiction, nor would I voluntarily twelve-step myself away from this high. Come Monday, if Ranieri succeeds in taking this world away from me, I will wish him a particularly painful strain of testicular cancer.

I slide into the Aeron chair at my trading turret. "Morning, Terri. Any news on your mom?"

"She's getting much better, thanks for asking." My assistant is Terri Aronica, a sweet-natured girl from Staten Island. Her freckled presence on the trading floor is akin to a gazelle among lions, so I'm highly protective of her. In return, her loyalty is beyond question. "She's coming out of the hospital this weekend."

"Good. That's great to hear." I try to sound casual. "Hey, listen, Compliance is all over me to do my semiannual supervisory thing. Can you pull all the personal trading records of Howard Ranieri for the last two years? And tell the back office I need it over the weekend."

"Sure thing." When Terri says it's a sure thing, I know she means it.

To: All Equity Personnel
From: Howard Ranieri

It is with deep regret that we announce Mark Barston's resignation from the firm, effective immediately. As Mark steps down as co-head of Equity to spend more time with his family and pursue other opportunities, please join us in wishing him the best and thanking him for effectively teaching me everything I know, which kindness I repaid by stabbing him in the back . . .

It is six hours later, and I'm mentally composing my resignation announcement. It's customary on Wall Street to extend the courtesy of ghostwriting the memo announcing one's involuntary departure, but I'm finding little joy in my imaginings.

Having escaped the offices of Fischer Brothers, I'm on the 4:36 P.M. Metro-North train out of Grand Central to Greenwich. I'm unaccustomed to the brightness that floods the filthy confines of the bar car; for over a decade, my profession has required me to keep coal miner's hours. I've rarely left the office before nightfall. Still, I'm somewhat surprised that the bar car is so well-populated. Must be advertising types.

With their game faces off, the commuters look positively miserable. They are die-hard junior execs with their eyes still on the prize, feverishly making love to their BlackBerries and Dell Inspirons and Motorola RAZRs. I make my way up to the bar.

"Two Absoluts in a cup, straight, wedge of lime."

Just as I get my cocktail, the train pitches suddenly to the left, and someone collides with me, nearly upending my double shot.

A striking blond girl in a pastel sundress murmurs an apology around a dazzling smile. "So sorry."

I'm taken aback. This is a radiant burst of genuine friendliness, and I have an instant attraction to this girl — and not all of it sexual. It's more that she seems a beacon of positive energy on a suddenly very hostile planet. She makes me think of lemon meringue pie.

"It was my fault, actually," I offer.

"I suppose it doesn't matter much either way, does it?" The girl holds my eyes for a moment while I try to place the accent. Australian, I guess, with the vanishing *r*'s. I'm intrigued.

"My name's Mark," I say, surprised at my own cojones.

"Fiona."

"Ah. Can I get you a drink, Fiona? A Coke?"

"I'd much prefer a Foster's, actually. With a vodka chaser." With that, Fiona flips open her cell phone to smile-and-dial.

When I return with the drinks, I tune in to bits of her conversation. It is peppered with an exotic slang, putting me in mind of *A Clockwork Orange.*

"It's choice . . . That's spot-on . . . Did you dip-out for a moment? What a complete saddo she turned out to be . . . Ah, Viv, Ranieri can be such a *drongo* sometimes."

Ranieri. Could it be?

And now I realize I've seen her somewhere before — on the trading floor, maybe . . . ? Fiona accepts the shot and the beer and slugs down four quick throatfuls — *we have a party girl here.*

"*Kia ora,* baby," she says. She snaps the cell phone shut and turns to me. "That was my mate Vivica. She's my cozziebro. I trust her with my deepest secrets." Fiona hoists her beer in a toast. "Thanks for your kindness. I'm not used to that, especially in New York."

"It's nothing really. Are you from Australia?"

"Australia? How insulting."

"I didn't mean any offense —"

"No worries. I'm from New Zealand originally. But for the last year, I've lived in Greenwich."

"I live in Greenwich also." I struggle to sound casual. "I couldn't help hearing the name Ranieri. Would that happen to be Howard Ranieri?"

"Yes," she says in amazement. "I live with Mr. Ranieri."

"You what?"

She choke-laughs, and a geyser of imported beer spews forth, making her laugh even harder. "That came out completely wrong. His family, I should say, I live with his family. I'm an au pair. The Ranieris are my host family in America."

Ranieri's au pair! This makes perfect sense — the trophy nanny to go with the trophy wife. It was all so Ranieri.

"And you just dropped his children off in the city."

"Right," she says.

"At Fischer Brothers. For the family vacation in Spain."

"Which got canceled, thank you very much, and screws up all our plans. Wait a minute — how did you know that . . . ?" Her voice trails off as she tries to decide whether I'm a clairvoyant or a stalker.

"So happens I work with Howard Ranieri."

"Bloody hell!" With a mock-naughty face, she hides the beer behind her back and giggles. "Don't tell him you bought me a beer. He'll flip out."

"Deal," I say conspiratorially. "That is, if you tell me what you meant when you called Ranieri a *drongo.*"

Fiona draws in a sharp breath. "Ah, yes. A drongo. Well, the American equivalent, I guess, would be dickhead."

I double over in laughter. Things are definitely looking up.

*

So, for the next forty minutes I'm treated to a private performance of Fiona Hensleigh's one-woman off-Broadway show that might well be titled *The Greenwich Nanny.*

She riffs animatedly about her adventures since being plucked from Christchurch, New Zealand, and plunked down in Greenwich, Connecticut, U.S.A., the very vortex of history's most excessive bull market. And she dissects the archetypes of the Connecticut Gold Coast in deliciously bitchy detail: the beauty-shop-addicted, Prada-obsessed prima donnas, whose sense of entitlement is without limitation; the insecure, cigar-smoking Master-of-the-Universe wannabes, whose self-worth is measured by the girth of their Range Rovers; and their worshiped, fretted-over, unlovely offspring, spoiled beyond belief and taught at the youngest age that viral disrespect for authority is a virtue.

As Fiona speaks, I'm picturing the Ranieri household, and it's a fascinating insight into my rival's secret world. Mrs. Ranieri, apparently, is something of a bitch on ice. And Ranieri himself is no candidate for sainthood, prone to moodiness and shouting matches with his better half. I bide my time, awaiting an angle, a vulnerability to use against my blood enemy. Fiona tantalizes me with the possibility that she has some juicy tidbits about Ranieri that she wants to share, but she doesn't trust me enough to give up the goods. Smart girl.

Now, I cannot say this with absolute certainty (for I am admittedly out of practice in such things), but I think this Fiona Hensleigh finds me attractive. There is a certain tilt of her face, a certain way she lets the gleaming wisps of her blond hair tumble over her eye. Then, in an instant of startling clarity, I suddenly realize how the distance between our bodies has shrunk. A chill prickles my skin with each incidental contact between us. Unless this is purely my imagination — and I'm willing to concede it might be — there is an unmistakable electricity between me and Ranieri's nanny.

Fiona is telling me how much she misses some dreadful-sounding Kiwi delicacies — Minties, Jaffas, Moro bars, Wattie's tomato sauce, and Vegemite — when the Old Greenwich train station rolls into view.

"My station," I say, and feel a genuine pang of regret that this encounter is coming to an end.

"Well, it was very nice talking with you, Mark."

"Likewise, Fiona." I offer my hand and the New Zealander's equivalent of *aloha. "Kia ora."*

She glances at my wedding band, then locks up my eyes with hers. "And what about tonight?"

Flustered, I manage: "Tonight? What about it?"

"We were planning to have a piss-up at Chez Ranieri, but now it looks like it's moving to the beach. You ought to pop on by."

"A piss-up?" I stand immobilized as other commuters pour around us to the platform. Pressed up against me, her breath is warm on my cheek, and sweet with the tang of lager. *One Night Only — The Nanny's Ball — Live at Greenwich Point Beach.* The thought of me in the midst of a gaggle of out-of-control drunken au pairs? Tempting, but a tad self-destructive. "That's not in the cards, Fiona. I've got a dinner party I'm obligated to attend."

She rolls her eyes in a deliciously feminine way. "Oh, I'm *so sure* that will be loads more fun than our ten-kegger."

"Ten-kegger, huh?"

"Anyway, you change your mind, come by the beach?"

"Yeah. I'll keep it in mind." I walk off the train backward, nearly stumbling into a heap on the platform. They say crack cocaine is instantly addictive. I totally get the concept.

Okay, I know this is sick, but I'm in tell-all mode, so here goes: my BlackBerry has been programmed to tally up the number of days Susan and I have gone without having sex.

It tells me we're at seventy-eight days and counting.

Wait, there's more: just recently, I have discovered that my wife is also surreptitiously keeping track of this ignoble hitless streak. She pencils tick marks into the kitchen calendar, and by her count, we've been on the sex wagon for seventy-seven days straight.

I own up to it: the demise of our relationship is mostly my fault. My struggle with Ranieri over the last months has turned me into someone other than the person she wed in sickness and health so many years ago. And her infertility problems have weighed heavily on us for even longer. In our calibrated attempts to conceive, we've followed to the letter the clinical manner in which teams of doctors have instructed us to copulate, and have spent the last thirty-six months not so much making love, as conducting laboratory experiments.

It's taken its toll.

To wit, I'm convinced that Susan no longer loves me. I suspect she is in love with at least one, if not two others in the Greenwich vicinity, and I often lay awake nights going over likely candidates. Is it Adam, the wacky New Age martial arts expert at her yoga center on the Post Road, the kid with bad teeth who teaches her Tae Bo and promises to launch her on a spiritual journey to discover her inner self? Is it Dr. Lauren, the collagen-lipped lesbian physician who wears no undergarments when she prescribes migraine treatments at Norwalk Hospital? It could be both, I suppose, or neither. Maybe we've just encountered one of those rough patches that couples therapists are always going on about. One of those things we're supposed to "traverse together," before the "next phase" of our "lifelong partnership."

The appearance of Peter I. Tortola's name in my checkbook register suggests otherwise.

This Friday night, I find my wife in the small childless bedroom designated as the Quiet Room. My wife is strikingly pretty, even as the chiseled angles of her face are softening with time, but just now she's an unsettling sight in the darkened room. Susan has an ice pack swirled over her forehead and eyes. On the bureau next to the trundle bed, a spent EpiPen and bottles of migraine medication are arranged in a neat row. Susan — God help her — is in full-blown aura mode with bursts of colors. With her head tilted back and her arms along the armrests of the recliner, she appears to be clamped in an electric chair.

"Susan, you all right?"

"Migraine," she murmurs tonelessly.

"Need anything?"

"Solitude."

Though she can't see me, I nod in the darkness. I realize how my Friday night will play out, and it ain't a pretty picture. But I can't hold myself back.

"Susan?" My tone is the most delicate I can manage.

"Mm?"

"We need to talk about something — but only when you're up for it."

"What is it?"

"It can wait."

"If it can wait, why bring it up? Just tell me, Mark."

I sigh. "A canceled check came in from Citibank. Made out to Peter Tortola."

Susan has no immediate response to this.

I push. "We need to talk about your intentions, Susan. I need to know what that check means."

All is silence. I'm aware of my own labored breathing. Peter I. Tortola? He's Greenwich's most obnoxious pit bull, a vulture, a shark, the lowest of snakes — a high-powered divorce attorney who specializes in going after Wall Street husbands, with the tenacity and teeth of a moray eel. His quarter-page ad is a weekly fixture in the otherwise-good-news pages of the *Greenwich Time* community newspaper. *IT HAPPENS TO THE BEST OF US: D-I-V-O-R-C-E.*

"Susan, we can talk about this later if —"

"You heartless bastard!" Her voice soars to a blood-chilling volume, and I am transfixed by the fury. "You sadistic son of a bitch. Why would you torture me when I'm in this condition? What's the matter with you? Get the hell away from me!"

I dutifully comply. There is little doubt, after this exchange, that we will be more than a little unfashionably late to the Honeywells' dinner party.

Wealth whispers.

For generations past, this was an unspoken code in Greenwich, the humility of old money. After all, darling, living in this town, how shall we say? *Res ipsa loquitur.* But the relentless tsunami of urban barbarians descending upon the Connecticut Gold Coast with fat Wall Street bonuses has killed off any vestige of subtlety here. Now Greenwich is just another brand name to accumulate.

The McMansions roll past as Susan and I wind our way along tree-lined Round Hill Road. It's nearly eight thirty and we have not said a word to each other since our chat in the Quiet Room. I now believe that our conversations are inexorably headed for the same fate as our sex life.

My Aston Martin approaches the Honeywells' seven-bedroom mansion on Larkspur Lane. Rich Honeywell is yet another Greenwich hedge fund asshole, one of those Wall Street guys with marginal talent and a nine-figure chunk of someone else's family money behind him. A once-in-a-lifetime fluke — a federal deregulation of pension plans — has made him obscenely wealthy in his own right, and kept an endless convoy of Brinks trucks dumping mountains of money on the doorstep of his Steamboat Road office.

Rich's house is an eat-your-heart-out monument to his new

wealth, a dramatic custard-yellow contemporary with Hudson Valley stone veneer set on five acres of what was once a fertile onion farm. And it's equipped with all the usual accoutrements: four-car garage, tennis court, THX-certified home theater, mahogany wine cellar, and an Olympic-sized pool. There are two backhoes in the front yard, suggesting further expansion is imminent.

The Honeywells' Belgian-bricked drive is jammed with probably three million dollars' worth of luxury automobiles, and I wedge my convertible into a space between a Porsche Cayenne and a yellow Hummer with personalized plates: *183 IQ*. I turn off the car, and the ensuing silence is deafening. I crave a talk before we go in, a clearing of the air. Perhaps it's naive, but I still hope that we can turn this around before we pass the point of no return and head down the path of mutually assured destruction. As a prelude, I clear my throat — and get no further.

"I want out, Mark. I'm done with this." Susan delivers this statement in a flat, lifeless tone, as she might say, *Looks like rain.* She opens the vanity mirror to check her makeup. "I want sixty percent of everything, and the house as well. You keep the cars and the retirement accounts. I'd like to file the papers next week."

She snaps the mirror closed and exits the convertible. And just like that, it's official: my marriage has begun its slow-motion spiral to the first circle of hell.

We approach the front door wordlessly, trying to assemble a convincing facsimile of a happy and centered Greenwich couple. Rich Honeywell opens the door with a flourish. He's dressed in a pair of black Ted Baker slacks, a charcoal Armani shirt, and Donald Pliner loafers.

"Hey, it's the Barstons!" Honeywell says theatrically, as he hugs Susan (a bit too warmly for my comfort). "Word up, Barston? You get lost on the way or something?" This offhand dig is a passive-aggressive notice that we are the last to arrive, but it's the unintended irony that makes me blink. *Yeah, I got lost on the way, all right.*

"Jennifer's been asking all night, 'Where're the Barstons, where're the Barstons?' She'll be psyched you're finally here." Rich says this breezily as he shepherds us through the palatial, antiseptic interior of his McMansion-in-progress. Like the homes of most of our friends, the design has a predictable look and feel. The furnishings bear the fingerprints of a particular interior designer who specializes in a bland, WASPy décor that appeals to new-money clients with absolutely no sense of style of their own. She's booked up for six months in advance. "Jen, come say hello to the Barstons."

Jennifer Honeywell curtails her lecture to the waiter on how to serve the platter of jumbo Gulf shrimp, and wheels around with exaggerated delight. "It's the Barstons!" she squeals like a teenager, and I remember something I'd heard about her trying out a new antidepressant.

We apologize for being late, then I give Jennifer a kiss, Jennifer and Susan kiss, and Rich takes advantage of the pleasantries to try to score a kiss on the lips with Susan (which she successfully evades). I take note of Jennifer's new body — it has been honed and shaped by spinning classes and Pilates into a rock-hard leanness that teeters on the verge of masculinity. The excessive athleticism has introduced an asexual coarseness to her face. Too bad; she used to be among the most attractive of my friends' wives.

Rich makes a sweeping gesture toward the French doors. "The bartender's got a bottle of Grey Goose with your name on it, kimosabe."

"Let's have at it," I say.

Honeywell directs us to the open-air patio overlooking an exquisitely manicured backyard of Kentucky bluegrass — an emerald carpet gleaming under a full moon. Predictably, Susan and I peel off in different directions. It will be this way for the entire night, but I'm cool with that. The blast of communal energy from the party lifts my spirits.

At the bar, a pimply-faced Greenwich High School kid gives me a double shot of Grey Goose on the rocks. Duly fortified, I meld into a nearby amoeba of acquaintances. They interrupt their debate about Robert Trent Jones golf courses to slap my back, shake my hand, and high-five me.

"I was just saying," Ford Spilsbury says, "that the Lido course on Long Beach is as close to eighteen-hole nirvana as you're ever going to get. The sixteenth hole is the ultimate par five, and you have an eagle opportunity if you can survive the double-water carry."

The five of them — Spilsbury, Foster, Brightman, O'Clair, and Cantwell — are clubhouse friends, and, like me, they are all Wall Street jerks: bankers and brokers and traders and lawyers. The Ivy

League degrees on this patio cost millions in tuition dollars, but they were worth every penny. The diplomas our parents bought for us are a license to steal. Collectively, we siphon off a disproportionate chunk of the country's GNP, and trundle it north to our trophy wives in Greenwich. We buy expensive cars and homes and boats and pools, and go on obscenely expensive vacations, all of which is meant to inform everyone just how much we're taking out of the American economy for ourselves. Our nine-year-olds are infected with this zombie-like consumerism, and are as tragically conversant with the iconic symbolism of Tiffany and BMW and Prada as their parents. We confuse wealth with class; we think they are synonymous, when they most assuredly are not. Inevitably, we will pass the former on to our children, but not the latter.

In this particular fishbowl, we wrap ourselves in an aura of effortlessness. We are expert at concealing the fears that haunt us at three in the morning: the TMJ-inducing toll our careers take on our stomachs and our mental health; the slow decay of our marriages; the warning signs that our children might not end up at an Ivy League university; the velocity at which our spending is outpacing our income. We hide behind the breezy accomplishment of breaking eighty on the course at the Stanwich Club, pretending everything is right in the world when we've come to know that the pursuit of this life is a cancer to the soul. I gaze up at the moon in the star-studded sky and heave a sigh. Maybe my spirits aren't so lifted after all.

I'm mildly surprised to find my glass is empty. I break away from the group for a refill. As I'm waiting at the bar, a call lights up my cell phone. I flip it open. "This is Barston."

On the other end an uncertain pause, then a soft fumble of the handset. A hand slips over the mouthpiece. Heated whispers, shushing, and the musical laughter of drunken young girls — a live feed directly from Fiona's piss-up at Greenwich Point Beach.

I say nothing, just listen. More giggles and whispers, all unintelligible. Her nanny friends put her up to this, I realize, and it is *so* juvenile, *so* immature — a slumber party prank, for chrissakes — and then, the act of chickening out; the curt click of the line going dead. I'm staring at my phone, waiting for . . . I don't know what.

I'm jolted from my reverie by the underage barkeep holding out my replenished drink. I take a greedy slurp, my temples throbbing with the pulse of curiosity over this au pair Lollapalooza taking place just a few miles away.

The night wears on, booze is consumed in disturbingly large quantities, and the conversation becomes edgy. The subject matter is friendship, fidelity, and minding your own damn business. *Would you tell a friend if you knew his wife was cheating?*

Foster says, "No fucking way, it's not my business."

Cantwell says, "Of *course* it's your business. It's your buddy."

Foster: "I can't be the one to tell him something like that. It's too . . . heavy, man. I'd be ruining his life."

Rob Brightman chimes in: "So you'd keep it to yourself? How would you sleep at night?"

O'Clair says: "I get Foster's point. Why is it his responsibility to break the news that the wife is banging the tennis instructor?"

I jump in. "He's your best friend, Chris, that's why. You couldn't look him in the eye at a party like this if you knew his wife was being unfaithful. You're duty-bound to tell him, and let *him* take the appropriate course of action. Case closed."

The passion with which I deliver this point brings the debate to an abrupt end.

Brightman breaks the uncomfortable silence: "So any of you assholes have something to tell me?" The group explodes in laughter. Everyone, that is, but Ford Spilsbury, who has kept conspicuously out of the conversation.

Forty-five minutes later, when a preoccupied Spilsbury quietly approaches me during the Chicken Kiev dinner and asks to speak to me alone, I feel my stomach knot. I somehow know what's coming.

"I heard what you said on the patio," he says, avoiding my eyes. "About friends."

I nod.

Spilsbury almost whispers it. "I think I'm the kind of guy who *would* tell a friend about that."

"You have something to tell me, Ford?" I reply, my voice warbling. But I already know he does.

Friday evening has segued somehow into Saturday morning. Newly armed with the knowledge that my wife has been having an affair for the last six months with her college friend's husband, I plunge through the darkness of the Backcountry, heading to the other side of the looking glass. I recognize this quest can only end badly — scandal, ruination, utter self-destruction — but it no longer matters. I'm powerless to stop the forces that have overtaken me.

A fantasy torments me: *I arrive at the beach and she spies me . . . She pulls away from her friends and comes so close that I can feel her breath on my cheek. "I knew you'd come." She locks up my eyes in hers as she says this, a note of triumph in her voice. She is such eye candy, I can barely contain myself. We are intoxicated — not just by alcohol, but by the electric danger of being so close. I spirit her away to a secluded beach at the ass-end of Sound Beach Avenue. With the languid hiss of low tide in our ears, the au pair steps forward. She kisses my neck, puts her hot hands up my shirt. I grab her apple-bottom ass and pull her toward me. She responds with a tongue-loaded kiss. I can taste the salt on her skin and smell the soap in her hair.*

This is going to happen, I convince myself. *This is redemption. This is revenge. This is justice.*

I punch the accelerator and push on toward Greenwich Point Beach.

I arrive within minutes, and the scene is surreal. Kid Rock's "Bawitdaba" throbs in the background, and yet the Nanny's Ball has come to an undignified end. Five Greenwich police cars have pinned down at least a hundred stoned kids, all tongue-studded, belly-ringed, lip-pierced, and tattooed. Blinding blue and red strobes light the beach in psychedelic hues, and the squawk of the radio dispatcher says backup is on the way. The acrid smell of pot is heavy in the salt air. Six half-naked, soaking-wet party animals are led by in cuffs. I'm numbed by the commotion, but amid the crowd, I see the object of my desire. *Fiona.* Ranieri's au pair is in the epicenter of this frenetic scene, crying her eyes out. She looks scared and vulnerable and . . . *oh, so incredibly young.*

I swing the Aston Martin into a dark corner of the parking lot and kill the headlights. I don't take my eyes off Fiona's face as I begin to formulate a daring rescue mission. *How far away is she? Thirty yards? Forty?* I could edge up on the far side of the crowd, grab her by the arm . . . then a short sprint back to my car, and we're home free. I can almost hear the sweet relief in her voice. *"I knew you'd come."*

I open my car door and step out. And nearly fall.

Just then I realize how intoxicated I am. My head is swimming in

Grey Goose, my legs are jelly, and I'm now bathed in a panic-induced sweat. I climb back in my seat and grip the wheel. Static blasts from a nearby police radio, and I jump. I can't make out the words, but when I squeeze my eyes shut, they become clearer. The words are my own:

Where you going with this, Barston? You put yourself in the middle of this — to what end? So you can wind up in the police blotter for DUI and God knows what else? And for what — some chick who chatted you up in the bar car for less than an hour? This is your grand plan to get back at Ranieri — fucking his nanny?

Another squawk of static and I realize it's coming from the radio of a Greenwich cop glaring my way. As he strides toward my car, I fumble the door closed. The cop is shouting something, but somehow I get the vehicle in gear and kick up a cloud of sand, which I pray obscures my license plate.

Miles from the beach, I pull over. I'm sweat-soaked and shaking, and I rest my head on the steering wheel and gasp for breath. And suddenly I'm pounding the dash in fury and self-loathing.

What were you thinking, you pathetic, sorry-ass son of a bitch?

It's nearly dawn when I get home and stumble to the front door. On the third attempt, I jam the key into the lock. At first I don't see the white envelope propped up against the door, and I kick it across the foyer. I stagger toward the stairs and almost leave it there on the Kashan rug, but something catches my eye and pierces the alcoholic fog around my brain: the Fischer Brothers logo.

I have to sit to retrieve the envelope, but I manage. Cross-legged on the floor, I thumb-wrestle it open and look inside. And I know instantly.

It's nothing short of a miracle: the last-ditch Hail Mary pass thrown desperately with seconds to go, the game-winning homer in the bottom of the ninth, the sudden-death eagle on the eighteenth hole at the Masters — impossible victory from certain defeat. It is the life preserver that will save me from going under for the last time, that will save me from myself.

"Terri," I whisper reverentially, the papers trembling in my hands. I say my loyal assistant's name over and over.

I enter Ranieri's glassed-in corner office on Monday morning, and I am ready to bite the ass off a bear. For his part, my enemy is bouncing a blue rubber stress ball off the windowed wall. He receives me exuberantly.

"Happy Monday, Sparky. How was the weekend?" He resumes throwing the ball against the glass.

"Must you do that?" I ask pointedly.

"You mean *this?*" He sidearms the ball again and smirks. "Why? Does it bother you?" I decline to engage in this lame banter, and silence prevails.

Moments later, Brian Horgan arrives with my thick personnel file. Sauntering in right behind him is Senior Managing Director Ian Becker. Becker is Ranieri's ultimate boss, and mine too — here to see that I'm officially terminated, and that the empire I've created is handed over seamlessly to his Harvard roommate.

"Guess this is showtime," Ranieri says. We lock eyes for a moment and he quickly looks away, shoving the door closed. He ceremoniously circles back to his chair, slouching into an elaborately casual posture. "Let's pick up where we left off on Friday. Ian, you care to kick things off?"

Becker clears his throat and speaks in an authoritative British baritone. "Let me start by saying we commend you for the contribution you've made to this firm. You've gotten us off to a respectable start, a decent standing in the league tables. But, candidly, you've developed something of a reputation for not being a team player, especially when it comes to matters involving your co-head. So, it's the consensus of senior management that we need to have a single focal point for the future of the business. Regrettably, that means that one of the two co-heads needs to move on. It's nothing personal, Mark, but —"

"Not true, Ian. It absolutely is personal."

"If that's how you feel about it, then fine."

"That's exactly how I feel about it. As for my people, let the record show that they consider Ranieri to be a rodent-faced, backstabbing, Mickey Mouse amateur who will crash this business into the ground within a year. By which time they'll be poached away by our competitors."

Ranieri's eyebrows climb his forehead in offense, but he holds his tongue in check.

Becker's face softens in saccharine compassion. "Be that as it may, Mark, you should know that there will be a formal announcement about a restructuring shortly, possibly as early as Wednesday.

I'm working to find a proper place for someone with your skill set, but we've got headcount pressures from upstairs. If these efforts fail, well, we're committed to ensure proper protocol is followed with regard to your termination. We've all pushed hard to be fair — no, to go way beyond being merely fair — and we're —"

I yawn theatrically.

Becker draws back in outrage. "Am I boring you?"

"Matter of fact, yes, you are. Even worse, you're wasting my time."

Becker sputters, furious at this insubordination, when a sharp rap sounds at the door. The cavalry has arrived, and just in time. All heads turn as David Rosenman, the firm's Associate General Counsel, opens the door and leans in.

"Ian, I need to see you," he says.

Ian Becker is annoyed by the disruption. "We should be done here in about fifteen minutes, David. Can we circle up at eight fifteen A.M.?"

"It wasn't a request, Ian," Rosenman says sternly. "Step out of this meeting *now.*"

Becker is puzzled, but there's no mistaking the seriousness in Rosenman's voice. He mumbles something under his breath, rises from his chair, and disappears around a corner with Rosenman.

"What the hell was *that* about?" Ranieri says to no one in particular.

"Oh, that?" I say. I produce a cigar from my jacket pocket and light it. "That would be about the Eagles Mere III CDO. The 'kitchen sink' collateralized unit."

Ranieri freezes, color draining from his face. The transformation is astounding: he ages ten years in an instant — exhausted, pallid, scared. *He knows exactly what I'm talking about.*

I push on. "According to a routine compliance check on personal trading that was run over the weekend, both you and Becker have sizable positions of these Eagles Mere III units in your personal trading accounts. *Sizable* positions."

"You fucking son of a bitch," Ranieri whispers hoarsely.

"So I imagine right now Rosenman is asking Becker how it is that a security that cost him $50,000 a unit is throwing off $11,568 in interest — a *month.* That would be about $140,000 a year, risk free —"

"You're *so* going to regret this, asswipe."

"What kind of security pays nearly three hundred percent interest a year with zero risk? I don't know, I've never heard of such a thing." I exhale a luxurious cloud of smoke. "But maybe — and this is just a theory, mind you — maybe it's a dummy security concocted by you. And maybe — just maybe — it's a little something you cooked up to divert hundreds of thousands of dollars a year from the firm's institutional clients to you and your greedy-ass butt-buddy. Now, why would you do such a heinous thing? I don't know — perhaps as a quid pro quo for Becker naming you to a certain co-head position in equity derivatives? It's just a theory, of course."

"This conversation is *over.*"

"You're goddamned right it's over!" I yell. "Sun Tzu is required reading at *Hah-vahd* b-school, isn't it? You must know *The Art of War* by heart. *A mortal enemy must be crushed completely. More is lost stopping halfway through than through total annihilation: the enemy will recover and will seek revenge. Crush him, both in body and spirit.*"

Ranieri regards me with a superhuman loathing. He remains mute.

"Hey, Brian?" I say, getting up to leave. "I'll be at my desk if you need me."

Brian Horgan is open-mouthed with awe as I shut the door.

Checkmate, motherfucker.

My head is spinning. Events have been set into motion that will be impossible to stop. There will be lawyers and compliance officers and regulators piling onto this situation in the hours, days, and weeks to come. Both Ranieri and Becker will pay an enormous personal price for fucking with my livelihood. There's even a good shot that they will be thrown out of the industry. So be it. *Kill or be killed* — that's Wall Street in its purest form, isn't it?

As I cross the trading floor, I receive another standing ovation. Apparently, Terri Aronica has spread word of the Eagles Mere scandal among the trading floor personnel, and I am acknowledged as the undisputed heavyweight champion of the world. This time, though, I don't bask in the adulation. There is little sense of accomplishment in my Machiavellian maneuver, because with this second bullet dodged comes a second epiphany: *This is no victory.*

I have crushed Ranieri, but his voice is playing in my head: *You can postpone the inevitable only so long, Sparky.* And I know he's right. How many more Ranieris are even now lining up to take what I've built? How many of them are in this room, smiling and clapping for me? And if not one of them, then it will be Susan and her cadre of lawyers. How many more bullets can I dodge?

There are handshakes, back pats, light punches on the shoulder, as I make my way to my seat. The applause subsides and the normal trading room chatter rises. Random static from a speakerphone fills my ears and I think of the other night with Fiona. Even if I'd whisked her off that beach, she too would have turned on me eventually, gotten lawyers of her own, tried to pick my bones clean. Maybe it's destiny or some law of nature: once you're at the top of your game, everyone becomes your enemy — rivals, friends, lawyers, lovers, superiors, subordinates. They plot and scheme and come after everything that matters to you, everything you love and care about.

Terri puts a steaming latte on my desk. Her freckled face beams and her eyes meet mine. It is an intimate moment: together, we triumphed over the forces of evil against great odds. Yet at this moment, absolutely no one is beyond suspicion. *Et tu, Terri?* I force myself to smile back, even as Rich Honeywell's mocking voice unexpectedly fills my head.

You get lost along the way, Barston?

S. J. ROZAN

Hothouse

FROM *Bronx Noir*

A WEEK ON THE LAM.

The beginning, not so bad. In the first day's chilly dusk, a mark handed up his wallet at the flash of cold steel. Blubbering, "Please don't hurt me," he tried to pull off his wedding ring too; for that Kelly punched him, broke his nose. But didn't knife him. Kelly didn't need it, a body. He'd jumped the prisoner transport at the courthouse. A perforated citizen a mile away might announce he hadn't left the Bronx.

Which he'd have done, heading south, heading home, risking the *Wanted* flyers passed to every cop, taped to every cop house in every borough, if he hadn't found the woods.

Blubber's overcoat hid his upstate greens until Blubber's cash bought him coveralls and a puffy jacket at a shabby Goodwill. Coffee and a Big Mac were on Blubber too, as Kelly kept moving, just another zombie shuffling through the winter twilight. *Don't look at me, I won't look at you.* His random shamble brought him up short at a wrought-iron fence. Behind him, on Webster, a wall of brick buildings massed, keeping an eye on the trees jailed inside, in case one tried to bolt. *You and me, guys.* Winter's early dark screened Kelly's vault over. Traffic's roar veiled the scrunch of his steps through leaves, the crack of broken branches.

Five nights he slept bivouacked into the roots of a monster oak, blanketed with leaves, mummied in a sleeping bag and tarp from that sorry Goodwill. Five mornings he buried the bag and tarp, left each day through a different gate after the park opened. One guard gave him a squint, peered after with narrowed eyes; he kept away from that gate after that. None of the others even looked up at him, just some fellow who liked a winter morning stroll through the Botanical Garden.

The grubby Bronx streets and the dirty January days hid him in plain sight, his plan until the heat was off. He thought of it that way on purpose, trying to use the cliché to keep warm. Because it was cold here. Damn cold, bone-cold, eye-watering cold. Colder than in years, the papers said. Front-page cold. Popeye's, KFC, a *cuchifritos* place, they sold him chicken and *café con leche,* kept his blood barely moving. Under the pitiless fluorescents and the stares of people with nothing else to do, he didn't stay. The tips of his ears felt scalded; he got used to his toes being numb.

The first day, late afternoon, he came to a library, was desperate enough to enter. A scruffy old branch, but he wasn't the only human tumbleweed in it; the librarians, warm-hearted dreamers, didn't read *Wanted* posters and were accustomed to men like him. They let him thaw turning the pages of a Florida guidebook. The pictures made him ache. Last thing he needed, a guidebook: pelicans, palmettos, Spanish moss, longleaf pines, oh he could rattle it off. But he couldn't risk the trip until he wasn't news anymore, until they were sure he was already long gone.

Then, last night, a new scent in the air, a crisp cold, a rising wind. Bundled in his bag, his tarp, and leaves, Kelly heard a hush, everything waiting, a little afraid. He slept uneasily, knowing. When he woke, he felt new weight, heard a roar like far-off surf. He climbed from his root den to see more shades of white than he'd ever known. Ivory hillocks, eggshell swells, chalky mounds burdening branches. And huge silver flakes still cascading from a low-bottomed sky. The surf-roaring wind whirlpooled it all around. Ice stinging his face, Kelly was in trouble.

Snow as insulation can work, you in the bag in the leaves in the tarp in the snow. But you can't climb back in; you'll bring it with you, and melt it, and lie in a freezing sodden puddle. Once out, in trouble.

A sudden howl of wind, a crash of snow off the crown of a tree. He tugged his hat low, wrapped his arms around his chest. The wind pulled the breath from him. He wasn't dressed for this, coveralls over his greens, puffy jacket, boots — but he wasn't dressed. Who ever was? Why had anyone ever come to live here, where casualties piled up every year? All the green leaves, the red, yellow, purple, solid or striped, small or gigantic, lacy or fat flowers all dead, the birds gone, the ones who stayed, starving. Every year you had to wait and pray, even if you weren't a praying man, every year, that life would come back.

At home the air was soft, the struggle not to make things grow but to clear yourself a corner in the extravagance, then keep it from getting overrun by the tangle that sprang up the minute you turned your back.

Up here everything ended and you shivered, as he did now. From cold, from anger, from fear. Eight years he'd shivered, the last four in lockup. It had been a month like this, cold like this — but heavy and totally still — when he'd killed her. Would he have, back home?

No. Why? In the warmth and openness, her taunts and her cheating would have been jokes. Back home, he'd have laughed and walked out, leaving her steaming that she hadn't gotten to him. She'd have screamed and thrown things. He'd have found another beach, another jungle, lushness of another kind.

Here, there'd been nothing in the cold, nowhere in the gray, only her.

He shut his eyes, buried the memory. His face was stiff, his fingers burning. He had to move.

Astounding stuff, snow this dense, this heavy. Your feet stuck and slipped at the same time. It was day but you wouldn't know it, trapped in this thick, swirling twilight. Fighting through drifts already to his knees, it took him forever to get near the gate. And the gate was locked. Beyond it, no traffic moved, no train on the tracks. A blizzard so bad the Botanical Garden was closed. It wasn't clear to Kelly he could climb the fence in this icy wind, not with gloves and not without, and not clear there was any reason. No one was making Big Macs or *cuchifritos* out there, no sweet-faced spinsters in the reading room.

Two choices, then. Lie down and die here, and honestly, a fair idea. They said it was comfortable, in the end warm, freezing to death. Maybe keep it as an option. Meanwhile, try for shelter at one of the buildings. He'd stayed away from them, not to be seen, not to be recognized, but who'd see him now?

One foot planting, the other pushing off, leaning on the wind as though it were solid, he made for the rounded mounds of the big conservatory. A city block long, two wings, central dome half-lost in the twisting white. Iron and glass, locked for sure, but buildings like that had garages, garbage pens, repair shops, storage sheds. Someplace with a roof, maybe even some heat, there might be that.

The conservatory was uphill from here, and for a while it seemed to not get any closer. He almost gave up, but then he got angry. It had been her idea to come north. That she'd wanted to was why he was here, and that he'd killed her was why he was *here,* struggling up this icy hillside, muscles burning, feet freezing. Maybe he'd kill himself when he got back home. Then he'd never have to be afraid he'd end up here again. But damn her, damn her to hell, not before.

Snow boiled off the arched glass roof. One foot, the other. He fell; he got up. One foot. The other. A glow stabbed through the blinding white, made his watering eyes look up. Lights. A vehicle. He was insane, the cold and wind had driven him mad. A vehicle? It came closer without vanishing. No mirage, then. Some caterpillar-tread ATV whining across the tundra. Didn't see him or didn't care. Lumbered to the conservatory, growled to a stop at the end of the wing. A figure, dark parka, dark boots, blond hair swirling like the snow itself, jumped down, pushed through the storm. To the door? She was going to open the door?

She did. He followed. When he got to the ATV it was there and real, so he eased around it, inching to where the storm-haired woman had disappeared. He stopped, startled, when through its thick quilt of snow the glass suddenly glowed, first close, then along the wing, then the high dome. She was turning the lights on. And moving toward the conservatory's center, away from the door.

He wrapped numb fingers around the handle. He pulled, and the door came toward him. Slipping inside, he closed it after, shutting the violence out.

First was the silence: no howling storm, no ripping-cloth sound of pelting snow. Then the calm: no wind ramming him, the ground motionless. Slowly, with nothing to fight against, his muscles relaxed. He pulled off his soaked gloves, his crusted hat, felt pain as his ears and fingers came back to life. His eyes watered; he scrambled in his pocket for an aged napkin and blew his nose. Looking down, he watched a puddle spread as melting snow dripped from his clothes.

The smell hit him out of nowhere. Oh God, the smell. Sweet and spicy, damp and rich and full of life. Warm, wet earth. Complicated fragrance thrown into the air by sunset-colored blossoms hoping to attract help to make more like them. *I swear, I'd help if I could. There* should *be more,* Kelly thought. They should be everywhere, covering everything, they should race north and smother this dead frigid pallor with color, with scent, with lavishness.

Amazed, gulping moist vanilla air, he stood amid long rows of orchids, gardenias, who knew what else. He was no gardener. Back home you didn't need to be. Back home these plants didn't need you. Here, they had to have pots, drips, lights, towering glass walls to save them from vindictive cold, from early dark, from wind that would turn their liquid hearts to solid, choking crystals. Here, soft generosity had to be guarded.

He started to walk, farther in. He wanted to walk to the tropical core of the place. He wanted to walk home.

Each step was warmer, lovelier, more dreamlike. But when he got to the giant central room, something was wrong.

Plants with man-sized, fan-shaped leaves roosted on swelling hillsides at the feet of colossal palms. They were colored infinite greens, as they should be, and moving gently, as they would be, under the humid breezes of home. But this was not that breeze. A waterfall of icy air rolled into the glasshouse, vagrant snow flying with it but melting, spotting the high fronds the same way rain would have, but not the same. Outraged, Kelly bent his neck, leaned back, trying to find the offense, the breach. Near the top of the dome, he saw greenery bowing under the cold blast. Trying to shrink away.

And some other kind of movement. The woman with the wild hair. High up, near the gaping hole, pacing a catwalk. He watched her stretch, then jump back as jagged glass she'd loosened tumbled past, crashed and shattered on the stone floor not far from him. The echo took time to die.

She hurried along the catwalk, climbed over something. Machinery whined and a mechanical hoist lowered. A square-cornered spaceship, it drifted straight down past curves, bends, wavering leaves. Kelly flattened into the shadows of a palm's rough trunk.

The woman jumped from the basket. She swept her wild hair from her face, whipped off her gloves, pulled out a cell phone. She spoke into it like a two-way radio. "Leo?"

"I'm here," it crackled. "How bad?"

"Two panes gone. Some others cracked, four at least. A branch from the oak."

"All the way there? Jesus, that's some wind."

"This weren't a blizzard, it'd be a hurricane." She had a breathless way of speaking, as though caught in the storm herself.

"If it were a hurricane," the distant voice came, "we wouldn't have a problem."

"Agreed. Leo, the cracked panes could go. Weight of the snow."

"It's not melting?"

"Too cold, falling too fast."

"Shit. You have to get something up there. You called security?"

On icy air, snow tumbled in, unreasonable, antagonistic. The temperature had dropped already, Kelly felt it.

"Only one guy made it in," the woman was saying. "Wilson."

"Oh, mother of God, that Nazi?"

"On his way. But he won't climb. He already said. Union contract, I can't make him."

An unintelligible, crackling curse.

"I called Susan," the woman said. "She's phoning around, in case any of the volunteers live close."

"And you can't do it alone?"

"No." She didn't justify, explain, excuse. She was gazing up as she spoke, so Kelly looked that way too, watched the palms huddle away from the cold. Stuck here, up north where they didn't belong, rooted and unable to flee. They should never have come. If that hole stayed open they'd die.

"I'm going to make more calls, Leo. See if I can find someone. I'll keep you updated."

"Do. Jesus, good luck. If they clear the roads —"

"Right, talk soon," she cut him off, started punching buttons. A massive wind-shift shook the walls, shoveled snow through the hole. She looked up at the palms. Kelly read fear in her eyes. Fear and love.

He stepped forward. "John Kelly."

She whirled around.

"Volunteer," he said. "Got a call."

Suspicion furrowed her face. "How did you get here so fast?"

"I live on Webster."

"How —"

"Door was unlocked." His thumb jerked over his shoulder, toward the wing. Silent, she eyed his inadequate jacket, his bad boots. His five-day growth. "You've got trouble," he said, pointing up. "We'd better seal that." And added, "That's what Susan told me. On the phone."

It was the best he could do. She'd believe him or not. Or decide she didn't care, needing his help.

She looked him up and down, then: "You good with heights?"

From a supply room they gathered tarps, ropes, the one-by-fours they used here for crowd-control barriers. They dumped them into the hoist, climbed in.

"We'll have to improvise." She flicked a switch and the lift rose, quivering. "The crossbars have bolts and hooks. For emergency repairs. A hundred years, never anything like this." Snow whipped and pounded on the roof, cascaded through the approaching void. "We'll string the tarps where we can. Brace them with boards. I turned the heat up. If this doesn't go on too long, we'll be okay." She turned worried eyes to the trees they were rising through, then swung to him, suddenly smiling. "Jan Morse. Horticulturalist." She offered her hand.

"John Kelly," he said, because what the hell, he'd said it already. Should have lied, he supposed, but he'd been disarmed by the heat. The softness. Her eyes. "You must live close too."

"The opposite. Too far to go home, once the storm started. Stayed in my office."

"And you were worried," he said, knowing it.

"And I was worried. And I was right."

"You couldn't have heard it. The break." He had to raise his voice now, close as they were to the hole, the storm.

"No. Temperature alarm. Rings in my office." She turned her face to the intruding snow, blinking flakes off her lashes. Hands on the controls, she edged the hoist higher. It shuddered, crept up, stopped. "Wait," she told him. She climbed from the basket, prowled the catwalk, inspecting the hole, the glass, the steel. The wind, rushing in, lashed her hair. She shouted back to him, "If we start here . . ."

He'd never worked harder. She was strong as he was, his muscles prison-cut, hers maybe from weights, or determination. Snow melted down his neck, ice stung his eyes. Wind gusted, shifting speed and bearing, trembling the dome. The catwalk slicked up with melted snow. With her pocketknife they slashed expedient holes in the tarps, ran rope through them, raised them like sails in a nor'easter. He wrenched, she tied, he tugged, she held. He wrestled boards between tarp and rope. Like seamen in a gale they communicated with shouts, pointed fingers. Straining to hold a board for her, his feet lost purchase. He skidded, slammed the rail, felt her clutch his jacket and refuse to let go. He'd have gone over, but for that. "Thanks," he said. The wind stole his voice away, but she understood. They worked on, lunging for rope ends, taming flapping tarps, tying knots with bruised fingers. She bled from a forehead cut, seemed not to notice.

Sweat-soaked and aching, it dawned on him that the chaos had slowed. A few more tugs, another pull, and suddenly, quiet on their side of the improvised dam. They stood side by side on the glistening catwalk, breathing hard. Overhead, the overlapped, battened tarps quivered, shivered, but didn't give, not where the hole was or where they'd covered and buttressed the panes in danger. They stood and watched for a long time. Kelly felt the temperature rise.

A pretty sound: he looked up. She was pointing at their handiwork and laughing. "That's really ugly." She shook her wild head.

"You mean we were going for art?" He folded his arms. "Damn!"

She smiled, right at him, right into his eyes. "Really," she said, "thank you."

"Hey. It was fun."

"Fun?"

"Okay, it was terrible. But" — he shrugged, looked around — "I'm from the South."

Her gaze followed his. "I've been looking after them for eight years. Some are rare, very valuable."

"But that's not the point, is it?"

Again, a direct look. Her eyes were an impossible blue, a lazy afternoon on a windless sea. "No."

He smiled too, lifted a hand, stopped just before he touched her. "We'd better take care of that."

"What?"

"You're hurt."

"Me?" In true surprise she put fingertips to her brow. She found blood. That made her laugh too. "Okay," she said, taking a last survey, "I guess we can go down."

They climbed into the basket, leaving the catwalk littered with fabric, with rope.

As the hoist inched down, she asked, "What do you do here?"

"I . . ."

She waited, still smiling. A volunteer, he'd said he was a volunteer. He'd gotten a phone call. How could he answer her? What do volunteers do at a place like this?

"Lots of things," he settled on. "Variety, you know." The start of doubt shaded her eyes. He didn't want that, so he said, "I build things. Temporary barriers, that kind of thing." Every place needed those. No matter how carefully you planned, there were always changes in what was allowed, where you could go, how close.

She nodded. Maybe she was going to speak, but a shout blasted up from below. "Doctor Morse! Is that you in that thing?"

They both peered over the basket rail, found a uniformed man craning his neck below, obscured by foliage. "Of course it's me!" she shouted back, her voice full of disgust. "Wilson," she said quietly to Kelly. "An asshole."

Takes care of Wilson. And when they reached the glasshouse floor, it got worse.

"Who's that with you? Doctor Morse, you know you can't take people up without a signed waiver! You —"

"Shut up, Wilson. This is John Kelly." *Don't tell him my name!* "A volunteer. He almost got killed helping me plug the break. Which you weren't about to do, so shut up." She jumped from the hoist's basket, gave the guard a hard stare. He flushed. Once that happened she turned her back, clambered onto a bark-mulched mound to inspect a broken frond, a casualty.

The red-faced guard regrouped. His glare bounced off her back, her riotous hair, so he turned to Kelly. "John Kelly?" He said it slowly and squinted, and shit, it was *that* guard.

Kelly climbed from the basket too, spoke to the horticulturalist worrying over her plants. "Listen, I better go, see if —"

"Kelly! I thought so!" Wilson's bark was full of nasty triumph. "They gave us your photo. They want you back, boy. Big reward. Saw you the other day, didn't I? At the gate." He came closer, still talking. "This guy's dangerous, Doctor." He said *Doctor* like an insult.

"No," Kelly said, backing. "Keep away."

"You're busted."

"No."

"What's going on?" She jumped down, between them.

"He's a killer. Escaped con."

"I don't think so."

"You're wrong," Wilson sneered. "Cops passed out his picture. He sliced his wife up."

She turned to Kelly.

"That was someone else," he said, and he also said, "I'm leaving."

"No!" the guard yelled, and drew a gun.

"Wilson, are you *crazy*?" Her shout was furious.

"Doctor, how about *you* shut up? Kelly! Down on the floor!"

"No." Walk past him, right out the door. He won't shoot.

"On the floor!" Wilson unclipped his radio, spoke into it, gun still trained on Kelly. "Emergency," he said. "Dispatch, I need cops. In the conservatory —"

That couldn't happen. Kelly lunged, not for the gun, for the radio. Pulled it from Wilson's grip, punched his face, ran.

And almost made the door.

Two shots, hot steel slicing through soft, spiced air. The first caught Kelly between the shoulder blades. To the right, so it missed his heart, but all it meant was that he was still alive and awake when the second bullet, flying wild after a ricochet, shattered a pane in the arching dome. Glass glittered as it burst, showered down like snow, with snow, on waves of icy air Kelly could see. The wind, sensing its chance, shifted, pulled, and tugged, poured in, changed positive pressure to negative and ripped through an edge of the tarp patch. Collected snow slid off the tarp onto a broad-leafed palm. Kelly saw all this, heard a repeated wail: "No! No! No!" He tried to rise but couldn't draw breath.

Looking around he saw blood, his blood, pooling. She knelt beside him, wild blond hair sweeping around her face, and he heard her knotted voice, choked with sorrow not for him. "All right, it's all right. An ambulance is coming."

In this storm? And he didn't want an ambulance, he just wanted to go home. *The trees,* he tried to say to her, watching the palms cringe away from the cataract of frigid air. But he couldn't speak, and what could she do for them? *I'm sorry,* he told the trees. *I'm sorry none of us ever got home.* Sprinkled with glass shards and snow, losing blood fast, Kelly started to shiver. As darkness took the edges of his sight, he stared up into the recoiling leaves. At least it wouldn't be as bad for them as for him. Freezing, they say, is a warm death.

HUGH SHEHEY

The Invisibles

FROM *The Kenyon Review*

THE END OF MY FIFTH summer singled it out forever in the stream of my childhood. Many days my mother and I cooked canned soup on a toy stovetop in our basement, pretending bombs had ruined the upstairs world. And one afternoon at the zoo, surrounded by wild animals in cages and tamer ones in trees, my mother confiscated my snow cone and yanked me behind a hedge. She crouched down and directed my attention to a small, gray-haired woman standing in front of the lions. Her face was wrinkling, rendered almost asexual by neglect and the hair of a person who has stopped trying. Families passed without the faintest interest in her.

"Cynthia, see her. She's more or less invisible, except to the lion, who sees lunch. She's not really invisible, but she might as well be. Wipe away that smile, little girl. We're exactly like her."

My fascinated mother drank from the snow cone until her lips were stained purple. She scowled and jerked her head toward the woman — the invisible, a person who is unnoticeable, hence unmemorable. Mother knew all about invisibles, and kept her eyes open in public. She brought home reports: a woman licking stamps at the post office, an anguished old man in line at the bank, a girl crying by a painting in the museum. The library crawling with them.

"Remember, Cynthia, you're an invisible, too," she said. "Just like me. We're in it together. Forever."

That summer I collected her sayings and built a personality with them. I mastered my bicycle and braved the creeks and abandoned barns that lay within an hour's journey of home, never doubting that if a bad guy appeared, he wouldn't see me and, if he happened to be an invisible, that I moved in the aura of my all-knowing mother. Then, one August day when the corn crop was blowing, giving glimpses of sweet ears ripe for the picking, she disappeared from our house.

Over a decade after she vanished, a strange van appeared in the old parking lot at the Great Skate Arena. At once I knew an invisible drove the thing. Around the corner, in the main lot, honking cars inched forward. The grouchy cop waved his ticket book at drivers seeking a place to release excited children. No one had noticed this van, faded maroon van with a custom, heart-shaped, bubble window on the passenger side near the back. Scabs of rust clung to the lower body, over new tires. It wasn't the sort of car you liked to see outside a skating rink, or anyplace where the typical patron was twelve years old.

"First of all it should go without saying that a guy drives that thing. But mainly I wonder how he got it into the lot." Randall was our tall, brainy boy. He lived for logical problems; the old parking lot where we smoked was separated from the new parking lot by a row of massive iron blocks with thick cable handles that only a crane could have lifted. The back of the old parking lot was closed in by a tangle of vines and meager trees. Beyond this dark thicket, from below, came the sounds of the highway.

"He must have come from below." Brianna squinted at the wall of vegetation. I'd put the purplish paint around her eyes. "There must be a bare patch we can't see."

"I would bet that a pervert drives that baby," Randall observed of the van.

"Vans are too obvious for pervs these days." Brianna took a stance in her vintage black and white stockings. She was little, hot, and good at finding killer vintage clothes in thrift stores. "He's probably some poor escapee from the psycho ward."

They turned to me to decide, these two kids who didn't know what invisibles were, even though they were in the club. They bore the symptoms of invisibles in denial, dying their hair black, punching steel through their lips and nostrils, wearing shirts that pictured corpses. They hung out with me. We hung out at a skating rink with junior high schoolers. No one ever caught us smoking.

Rather than try to explain our metaphysical plight — I'd never been comfortable talking about my mother — I shrugged, faked a smile, and ignored the sickening presence I sensed in the van's heart-shaped window. The mind I detected in that window was that of an all-knowing bully waiting for you to contradict him. "I don't know, but he's probably sleeping in there and either way we don't want to wake him up. Can we go inside now and skate?"

I puffed at my cigarette between breaths, trying to hurry things along, confident that under the dome of the skating rink I'd shake my fear that a knife-swinging but otherwise unremarkable oddball lurked behind one of the dormant air-conditioning units lined behind the skating rink.

Randall absent-mindedly played with his recent nose piercing. "Look at that creepy window. If he's in there he's probably watching us right now."

Through the dusty window we could see the surface of an opaque space. In our own ways we acknowledged the disadvantage of the unknowing souls we'd spied on from behind unlighted glass. Our spines all twitched a little.

"You think he's in there?" Brianna pinched a cigarette above the filter, breaking it as she sometimes did when she was nervous. She let it fall on the cracked lot. Her voice grew quiet. "Why would someone want to sleep here?"

Randall walked over to the van and knocked three times on the heart-shaped window. Against the thick, curved glass, his knuckles made a hollow sound that echoed in my chest. Doing a good job of looking unafraid, he stood looking up at it, then smiled at us. Brianna and I watched the window for a terrible face.

Randall threw back his head and laughed like a cartoon villain who has just tied a woman to train tracks. Even at his most raucous he couldn't draw attention from the main parking lot. He cackled until Brianna snapped another cigarette in her shaking hand, and I put my arm around her tiny shoulders. She looked so helpless, her lip shaking, her sticky palm dotted with tobacco.

"You're such an asshole," she blurted. "I'm not going to couples skate with you if you don't come back right now."

"Okay, okay." Randall returned to the little field of safety we seemed to occupy between the brown steel door and the dormant air-conditioning unit. Above our heads, a light snapped on, and I could see how pale my friends looked, how afraid, and knew they could see it in my face, too. Randall squeezed between our bodies, with an arm for each of us. "Shall we?"

As if he could make us forget the unknown behind the dark window in the maroon travel van, he ushered Brianna and me toward the entrance around the corner, where, if she recognized us each Thursday night, the obese woman in the ticket booth would give no sign.

My mother had bad habits which arose as a result of being an invisible. She stared at strangers. She burst into laughter. These were marks of her frustration. She liked to tell cashiers that she'd already paid, and make them admit that they hadn't been totally attentive. Then she'd give the money back.

One day my father and I came home from the farmer's market to a house that bore all the signs of her presence. The garage door was open, revealing the backside of her blue sedan. In the oven, cooked blueberries pushed through the flaky crust of an unwatched pie. Suspecting she was hiding in one of her usual places, I parted the dresses in her closet, and looked under my parents' tightly made bed. Outside, my father walked the rows of the well-tended vegetable garden, and I balanced myself on the patio rail and stood, searching for her face in the field of swaying cornstalks that enclosed our house. Hiding was a game we played together, and with each shift of my eyes I expected to find her grinning among the rows.

When we grew tired of shouting for her, we went into the house, set the pie out to cool, and waited for her to emerge. I was excited to learn what new hiding spot my mother had found, but my father was upset over her absence. He slumped beside me on the couch and pinched the bridge of his nose. A fidgety, bald-headed man who knew numbers and tax laws, he was always forcing himself to keep his mouth shut around his wife.

The detective we spoke to offered no answer.

"Sometimes people disappear out of their lives," he said. He kept a neat, steel desk with a rectangular wire basket on one corner beside his computer monitor. Beneath a glass reading lamp he'd arranged a scene with cast-iron miniatures, an eyeless, large-chinned policeman interrogating a tied criminal who glared up with red eyes. "They just vanish, you know what I mean."

"Not like this," said my father. The very suggestion she'd left infuriated him. "That's on the highway, on long road trips. Hitchhikers disappear." He didn't quite look at the policeman, directed his ire internally. His entire forehead seemed to throb. He held my hand with incredible gentleness.

The detective tried to disguise his pity with a perplexed smile. He looked at me as if he read my thoughts, then reached for a Rolodex. "I can direct you to someone who's good at talking about this sort of thing."

My father flinched away from these words, said no, thank you.

Early that winter my father told me not to expect her to come home. I stopped asking him about it but continued to watch milk cartons and mail flyers for her face. I'd just begun kindergarten and wanted to tell her she had been right all along. I was an invisible. My new teacher couldn't bring herself to remember my name. Other children never looked at me, and seemed to avoid the spaces where I played at recess. I was stuck wearing my name written on a construction paper label strung around my neck with yarn, long after the teacher memorized my classmates'. For weeks I felt like a unit of space in which a sign floated: CYNTHIA INVISIBLE HERE.

My mother would have laughed. But by then it was just my non-invisible father and I and the non-invisible woman who had begun to hang around, in a restored farmhouse out in the cornfields that ran to forgettable stretches outside the city.

After the rink let us out with a drove of children to waiting parents, Brianna and Randall took off in his car, to go screw in their latest secluded spot. With a mild case of virgin's blues I drove off alone, with a scentless, yellow, leaf-shaped air freshener swinging above my head. My drive toured the well-lighted streets of suburbs, and no headlights followed long enough to make me more than a little cold. For a few years now my fear of the dark had been completely relocated to a fear of people, and especially to the signs of them in the dark, like solitary headlights and the sound of footsteps on a sidewalk. The full, rustling fields of corn I drove among on the road to my township had long been reassuring company. Though I'd seen enough horror films to envision the travel van pulling out of the vegetables, I'd ceased to think much about it.

Before leaving the rink, I'd checked the old parking lot and had seen only weeds bent to the gravel by new autumn winds. I'd asked the police officer who oversaw Great Skate's traffic if the van had been towed. A tall, sour-mouthed man with a crab-red face, he considered me as if I'd claimed to see a UFO.

"What van?" he said. "I've been here all night, and there hasn't been any van. Believe me, I would have noticed a van like that."

"Never mind," I told him. "I must have it mixed up with a creepy van in another abandoned parking lot."

My snappy comeback kept me happy while I drank a chocolate malt in a booth beside a tinted diner window and watched drunk older kids come blaring in to devour large sandwiches and plates of chili cheese fries. They spilled food on their faces, shirts, and arms while getting most of it into their mouths. It was disappointing that the boy my imagination blessed with charm and intelligence stood up to belch with greater force than he could muster sitting down. Completely unseen, I made my careful exit through a fray of shouting and reckless gestures. It was after three by then, and I felt snug in my sleepiness and invisibility.

At home the lights were on, the ceiling fans spinning, but the rooms were empty, the doors that should have been closed, open. The air felt charged with a panic that made me run around the ground level, looking for someone.

On the patio I found my stepmother, an impressive work of self-made beauty with big pale hair, smoking in her black robe. She stood beneath the moon and gazed out over a mile of dark, shining corn. She'd been asleep and since getting up had poured herself a glass of wine. When I came up to the rail near her, she gasped and took a step back.

"Just me," I said. "No psycho killer."

She squinted down, and took a step in my direction. "Your father's looking for you."

I laughed, imagining my father, exploring warehouses, deserted docks, shouting my name. He never worried about me, and never made me come home by a certain time. "Where is he looking?"

"He just needs to feel like he's doing something." When she was sleepy, speech did not come easily to her, and I took her strange look for effort. "I've been watching him drive around the block for an hour." By "block" she referred to the square mile of cornfield fringed every few hundred yards with houses like ours. Across the field, where the highway joined back road after back road, the twin twinkles of headlights turned in the direction of our road, and disappeared into the dark mass of the crops. "That's him now."

As I looked for his headlights, she grabbed hold of my wrist with her cold, hard hand. Something like profound relief came over her. Her grip was strong, and she gazed resolutely into the darkness of the field that lay between us and the sight of my father's headlights. When I tried to pull away, she said, "Stay right here with me until he gets here, please." I'd never heard her voice so grim.

I let her hold my hand and stepped closer to her. We weren't very close and being the more girly of us, she looked almost afraid that I would touch her. Then she hugged me against her and sighed.

"What's happening?"

"Your little friends. Your poor little friends." She could never remember their names, but she could still feel sorry for them. She repeated herself twice, and wouldn't say anything more.

The police had discovered Randall's car in a new subdivision where no houses had yet been built, a street making a wide figure eight among undeveloped plots of land. Through the summer the grass had grown tall and seedy, hiding the view of the new street from the country road that led to it, and it was no shocker that Randall and Brianna had been going back there to get it on. They were connoisseurs of discreet sex nooks, the way some couples criticize movies and people they know. Until then I'd believed that doing it in seclusion was an appropriate pastime for a pair of invisible teenagers, but now I felt ashamed of my joke.

The police had been called about teenagers screaming in the subdivision. When they arrived, they found only the car and no sign of Randall or Brianna, who evidently still had her purse. People agreed that this was a good sign, though maybe just to agree there was a good sign. Both windows on the driver's side of Randall's car were shattered. But there was no blood in the car or on the street, no further signs of struggle, and so the police were hopeful.

Because the detective considered time was an important factor, he questioned me that night in my living room. Eager to help, I rehearsed describing the van while watching our front window for headlights. When they arrived, my father and stepmother left me alone with a youngish, good-looking detective and a couple of policemen. This wasn't the same detective who'd looked for my mother, but his personality made up for the dissimilarity.

Detective Volmar had a scar on his lip and spoke courteously. He sat with his legs crossed and listened as I explained the awful prognostications I'd experienced at Great Skate when I'd seen the van.

"But afterwards you let your friends go home," he said at one point. "Why did you do that?"

"I guess I wasn't scared anymore. I should have trusted my instinct. I knew he was an invisible."

The detective had a mean-spirited, doubtful smirk. "An invisible?"

"It's someone who doesn't get noticed, who for one reason or another isn't memorable. I think maybe some of them go bad, become things like kidnappers, or serial killers."

"That's interesting. How do you know this van driver was an invisible?"

I explained how invisibles stand out to one another, how the traffic cop at Great Skate hadn't even seen the strange van, even though it was parked so conspicuously in the seemingly inaccessible old parking lot. Therefore, I reasoned, the van driver was an invisible.

Detective Volmar told one of the cops standing by to find out who this traffic policeman was, and to get him on a cell phone or radio. "How did you notice him, then? If he was an invisible."

"Because I'm an invisible," I said. "And my friends were, too. That's how he saw us."

After asking a few more questions, Detective Volmar thanked me and said he'd appreciate it if he could question me at a later date, should his investigation require it. I told him I only wanted my friends to turn up.

He laughed, I suppose, at my eagerness. "Gosh, you're a nice kid, um." He glanced at his report for my name, then admitted with a wince that he'd forgotten it. "Sorry."

"Don't worry. Happens all the time."

The suburb was in an uproar for days. The police department issued a temporary sunset curfew, and in every class at school I sat within an earshot of some boy or girl who complained about getting taken into the station or sent home by stern police officers.

There were as many stories about sightings of the maroon travel van, near the trailer park, in the oceanic parking lot of the old supermarket, all of them obviously derivative of urban legend. In the halls you saw the usual theater created around a local tragedy. Outwardly my peers showed sympathy for Randall and Brianna. Many joined hands and wept at the assembly where the principal reminded us that we were one community. Girls who never spoke to me invited me to sit with them at lunch.

I declined, sat in the bleachers by the baseball diamond, as usual, though the absence of my best friends made it impossible to eat anything. The weather was getting colder and windier, the sky higher up, and it was even a little frightening to sit nearby the empty dugout, so far from the school building that no one would have heard me shouting if I'd needed help. But mostly I felt sad, hoped my friends would turn up, and doubted they would. This struck me as the kind of situation where hoping is something you do to allay dread. Our farming region was small, its people interconnected in a way that made secrets short-lived, and I feared that the driver of the maroon travel van and my friends were long gone.

Once my mother explained that invisibility could be an advantage. "I don't want to fill your head with too many possibilities, little girl." We were sitting on swings at the metropark, her shoes mired in wood chips while mine dangled above them, and she was talking on and on while I adored her — our usual rapprochement. "I don't want other people's inventions to get in the way of your imagination. Who knows what you could come up with? I talk too much to have a good idea, so I sure as hell don't know. You seem like a good apple to me. Am I right? Are you a good apple?"

"I'm a good apple," I insisted.

"I know it, little girl. You don't have to tell me. I don't have to worry about you going off the map and doing something crazy."

Going off the map, she'd said. The idea intrigued me, though at the same time it was a disappointment. Hadn't I been off the map my whole childhood? Wasn't I still off the map, a seventeen-year-old whose idea of a good time on a Friday night was roller skating in giant circles in a crowd of twelve-year-olds?

No one knew what I thought, and I was little more than a statistic in attendance and grade books. English teachers wrote little congratulatory notes on my essays, but I only wrote back to them what they'd said in class. And anyway they were invisibles, too. My father had to work all the time. His parenting style consisted of giving me money and trusting me.

The first time I dreamed of Brianna and Randall after they disappeared, my bed was in the middle of the floor at Great Skate. The rink must have been closed, because the music was off and only a few lights were on. We appeared to be the only people in the place. I had awoken there, still wearing baggy pajamas, to find them skating circles around me. My friends had changed. They spoke and skated like Randall and Brianna, but looked older, sickly, their eyes sunk in their faces.

"Hi, Cynthia," said Brianna, whizzing past.

"Hey, Cynth," said Randall, over her shoulder.

"Where have you two been? Everyone's been so afraid for you."

"They shouldn't be," said Brianna.

"No reason to worry about us. None at all."

"You shouldn't keep secrets from your friends," said Brianna, circling again.

"You should have told us we were invisibles, Cynthia."

"You knew."

"I didn't think you'd believe me," I said.

"You should have trusted us," said Randall.

"We're your friends."

"We could have gone off the map a long time ago," said Randall. He frowned, shaking his head. "A long time ago. That would have been best for everyone."

"What did you say?"

"Have you ever thought about going off the map?" asked Brianna.

"I definitely prefer life off the map. It's everything I dreamed it would be."

"Or would have, if someone had told us about it."

"Have you seen my mother?"

Brianna's grinning face glided close to mine. There were frown lines around her little mouth. "You want to know where we heard that?"

Randall stopped with his face in mine. His teeth looked gray in the low light. He was pointing off to the side of the rink, to the shadows around the concessions counter. "We heard it from him."

The moment I became aware of the silhouette of a man standing at the edge of the rink I was possessed by such a desire to scream that I woke up in my bed, back in my bedroom. It was early morning, before seven, and in a few minutes my alarm would go off. Outside, rain fell from a dark sky into the acres of dispirited corn plants.

Though the wait tortured me, I let two weeks pass before investigating the site where Randall and Brianna vanished. Each night my friends met me in the dark skating rink and cautioned me to wait for the police to leave the crime scene alone. Their faces were getting older.

For a few days I stayed home from school and flipped through yearbooks, reexamining pored-over panoramic photos for our faces. In all three yearbooks there were only the standard shots of each of us and, the one year I missed picture day, they hadn't even listed me under *Not Pictured.* Afraid of police by day, afraid of the maroon van by night, I drove around, often taking the road that led past the subdivision where they were heard screaming. I couldn't see over the tall grass that blocked the street inside. I attended unsolicited conferences with the pamphlet-bearing guidance counselor at school, and watched television in an empty house.

One morning, just before I woke for school, Brianna and Randall told me the crime scene would be deserted.

"It's safe to go now," said Brianna.

"If you're still interested, that is," said Randall.

The subdivision-to-be was north of the next township, on a farm road with a few old houses perched jauntily along a deep irrigation ditch. The autumn rain had begun to break down the high grasses in the undeveloped lots, but I still had enough cover back there that I didn't mind getting out of my car to walk around. The weather had knocked down the police tape. Clean light poured out of the sky, drying the few leaves that the brisk wind picked up and flew around the new-paved street.

There was evidence of my friends all over the ground, though the police probably couldn't see that. Dried wads of Brianna's green bubble gum lay like moldy little brains all over the pavement.

Cigarettes only she could have broken. There were the wrappers from the tacos that Randall ordered in what he deemed practical boxes of six. Walking along the concave gutter, passing out of the crime scene, I came to a kind of midden of used condoms and wrappers, blown dry and brittle through the warrens of tall grass. I wondered how many were scattered through the undergrowth, and was overcome with the sense that this was all that remained of my friends.

"I seen you come in here."

When I looked up, I didn't see the old man who had come from across the street to talk to me — I saw the maroon van, idling in front of me, with a tall man beside it. Long, muscled arms hung out of his shirt and he wore faded, tight jeans. His blond hair was long and filthy, his skin a burned red, his black eyes bright and dense. Only a few times in my life had my imagination brought something into this world — usually it took me elsewhere. The vision lasted a second, and then I was looking at an old man in bib overalls, standing a few feet away from me. Seeing he'd scared me, he lowered his shoulders and turned slightly. He'd parted his hair on the right, presumably with the comb in his breast pocket.

"Hi," I said.

"You should go home. The police still come around sometimes, and they wouldn't be happy to run into you back here."

"My friends were the ones who . . . were here." I didn't know how to describe what had happened to them to this stranger.

"The ones got taken." The old man nodded. "I called the cops about it."

It was only then that I noticed the blandness in his face, the lights-out quality that rises in a person's eyes after years of being overlooked. "You saw the van, too?"

From the way he puckered his lips as he nodded, it was obvious he felt responsible for my friends' disappearance. "I used to think, 'Let them have their fun back there.' I know things are different now, but I got married when I was about their age. I always thought any kids who had the nerve to go off like that deserved a little time alone." He looked at me hard and said, "Not all of us find somebody who's exactly like us, if you catch my drift."

My mother pitied my father, who never knew what to do with her. "I know," I said.

"Then I seen him follow them back in here, and I knew I made a mistake letting them have the place." He stood with his hands in the deep pockets of his overalls, staring at the taped-off crime scene, which the wind had broken down into an awkward triangle. "I knew I couldn't help them then. Still I came running back here, and that van almost ran me down."

"Do you think the police will find them?" It was stupid to ask this, because asking him to answer hurt him, more than it did me, watching him struggle to lie.

He gave up and said, "I don't know if I can in good conscience tell you to hope too much."

"I keep dreaming about them," I said.

"I do, too," he said.

Detective Volmar telephoned a few days after I'd visited the subdivision where the driver of the maroon van apprehended my friends. He wanted to know if I was opposed to the idea of a free breakfast. He even offered to come out and pick me up.

"I hate to impose on people in their own homes," he explained a second time, as he drove me through the fields of yellowing cornstalks to the nearby diner where, he couldn't have known, I sometimes ate alone at night. "They get nervous to have a policeman in the house. I guess they're afraid I'll notice the infraction of a tiny law while I'm there, one they don't even know they're breaking. People break laws all the time. Sometimes I think we have so many just so I can arrest someone if I know I need to."

In daylight the restaurant was cleaner and full of shadows, staffed with new cooks and waitresses, strangers to me. We sat down at a booth whose window gave out to a view of the township's main street, the storefronts of old lawyers' offices and a realtor. Detective Volmar said he found all this very quaint. Then he ordered the largest breakfast platter on the menu, and requested extra bacon. He drank black coffee in large gulps, and knew where his mug was without looking at it.

I ordered a cup of yogurt with granola, something I could crunch on and finish without really trying to eat. Between the weird dreams and missing my friends, my appetite still hadn't returned. The detective may have thought I was a dainty eater, though maybe I flattered myself to think he noticed. He listened to me with interest, but his eyes were a critical compound of belief and disbelief applied to my every statement. He must have been thinking things he didn't say.

"The first time we talked, you didn't mention that your mother went missing a long time ago."

"Sorry," I said.

"Not at all. I'm surprised your dad didn't say anything. The case is still officially open, but nobody's working on it anymore. Whoever had it figured her for a deserter." With one skeptical shrug he won my gratitude and trust. "There's no evidence for that, though."

"Do you think the disappearances are connected?"

Detective Volmar smiled with what compassion he could muster. "There's no reason to think so. But I've been thinking about what you told me the night I interviewed you in your living room. I'm curious about the connection you made between invisibles and serial killers."

"You really believed me about invisibles?"

He drained half his water glass and shrugged. "We'll see. You obviously believe in them."

"It's because I mentioned the van, and the old man did, too. Isn't it?"

He turned his head away slightly. "I'd appreciate it if you didn't talk to a lot of people about the details of the case. The public already knows too much. As it happens, we don't know much more than the guy who called us, and apparently, you know as much as he does." He paused and let the waitress refill his coffee mug, smiled at her, then continued solemnly, with his fingers playing together on the paper placemat. "But I cannot afford not to be open-minded about this. Two kids have disappeared."

"What do you want to know?"

"Well, you say you're invisible. Plainly, you're not. So what exactly do you mean?"

"It's hard to explain," I said. "I'm not sure I fully understand it either. My mother was never that clear about it. But think of it this way. How did you find out about me?"

Detective Volmar looked from the streaked window to me. "Your father called the station and said you were missing. I guess he'd heard about your friends and thought you were with them. Then you got home, and he called to say you were there."

"So the whole time you were coming to my house, you were expecting to question a seventeen-year-old girl, right?"

"Right."

"So maybe that helped you to see me a little more clearly. Maybe, if you knew nothing about me, I could sit right next to you, and you would never have known it. Not because I'm literally invisible, but because I don't connect to other people. Some people just fall through the cracks. But most of us want to be seen, so we make an effort. I'm somebody's daughter, and until a while ago I was somebody's friend. My mother was somebody's daughter, somebody's friend, somebody's wife, and somebody's mother, in that order."

"What does this have to do with murderers?"

"I think some people get themselves noticed by taking revenge."

"Why not get noticed in a more subtle way?" Detective Volmar's toast arrived, and he proceeded to question me as he scooped grape jelly from a plastic tub. "Why not become somebody's husband or wife?"

I thought of my friends and my mother, how much it enraged me to see the sunset curfew lifted the week before, and to see life return to normal at the high school. "Because it hurts a lot when someone forgets you," I said. "Taking revenge is one way to make sure no one ever does it again."

There I was, in the dream that had become nightly. I sat up in bed in the middle of the skating rink, watching Brianna and Randall skate around me like a pair of professionals. They'd improved quite a bit, skating so much in my dreams, and they could do things like double axels and land rolling on four wheels. That said about their skating, their bodies looked considerably worse, older, more starved. One of Randall's ears seemed to be coming off, and a sore I hadn't immediately noticed on Brianna's cheek was growing. What fingernails remained were black, and the skin where the others had been was dry, red, and wrinkled.

Their moods grew nastier with their appearances. I didn't say much, mostly just listened to them describe what it was like to drive around in the van with the man who stood at the edge of the rink. He never moved. I'd begun to doubt that he knew we were there.

Sometimes Brianna or Randall would make a teasing reference to my mother, and I would beg them to tell me where she was, what had happened to her. However, my pleading could only last for so long, as I knew a game when it was being played at my expense, and then I would just sit there, my feelings hurt, as they laughed at me.

"So why didn't you tell your *boyfriend* where we are?" asked Randall.

"She's afraid he'll like me better. Even like this, I'm prettier."

"What's the use?" I asked. "He can't come into my dream and put you in handcuffs. He wouldn't be interested in that stuff. Besides, he knows where you are."

"And where's that?" said Randall, as Brianna turned about to skate backward, with her arms crossed over her small breasts.

"You're in the maroon van. With that guy. Isn't it obvious?"

Brianna smiled knowingly at Randall. "Do you want to know what we see?"

"Forests, mountains, lakes, eagles, coyotes, a comet," Randall counted off his list on the fingers of one hand, starting over whenever he reached his thumb. "A nautilus shell, sharks feeding in a school of silver fish, the White House, rattlesnakes, tarantula eggs, the Grand Canyon, your mother, cottonmouths, a panther."

"Your mother," said Brianna. "We saw your mother."

"When?"

"When!" Randall shouted.

"Where did you see her?" I asked.

"Where!"

Brianna shook her head at me. "Is that really what you want to know? Or would you rather know if she asked about you?"

Her insight left me speechless. Yes, this was exactly what I wanted to know. Whether she missed me, thought of me, regretted leaving. Did she plan to come back?

"No, no, no, and no," said Randall, laughing in the villainous way he had beneath the heart-shaped window of the van behind Great Skate, the night of his disappearance.

"Stop, Randall," said Brianna, putting her hands on her sides. I couldn't tell if she was serious; as her face deteriorated it conveyed fewer and fewer variations on a lurid scowl. "You don't know when to quit kidding. Honestly, you'll hurt a girl's feelings that way." She looked at me, the gleaming in her dry eyes limitless. "You can see for yourself. If you meet us. Come to Great Skate this weekend," she said. "You'll know where to find us. But don't tell your boyfriend. We'll know about it, and so will he." She nodded at the silhouetted man at the edge of the rink. The lights in the rink came up then, so I could see the line of his mouth, enough to know that he watched us and disapproved.

Sometimes I thought about what I would have been like if I still had a mother, if I'd look, sound, dress, and think like her. If I would love cruelty like she had.

We would play this joke on my father, when he got home from work.

The joke was only good on certain days. I wanted to play it all the time but my mother knew better. She would stop in my bedroom doorway, interrupting whatever fantasy I had going on. Her toothy smile made me feel like she'd caught me doing something wrong. "Cynthia, should we hide from your father?"

Nodding yes, I would gather up my dolls, as they were necessary props.

"Where should we hide, so he can't see us?"

The pantry worked best. We could watch through a crack in the door as my father walked around the house, his loafers clacking on the wooden floors, his shoulders trying to shrug off his suit jacket. When he shouted our names, my mother would hold me against her, covering my mouth with her hand. If I needed to laugh, she'd told me, I was to bite her.

After a while my father would grow so frustrated that his patience failed, and he would make himself a sandwich. This amused us, because he'd never learned to snack properly. After watching him mutter miserably over his approximation of the perfect sandwich my mother had prepared and hidden in the pantry with us, we'd wait until he took a beer out onto the patio. Then, very quietly, we would emerge from hiding, she to prepare him a plate and fill the sink with sudsy dishwater, I to sit on the tiles at her feet with my dolls. Once we were in our respective swings of wash and play, she would open the window and call to him to come in.

"Where were you?" my father would ask, moving to dump his poor sandwich in the garbage, now that my mother's handiwork awaited him. "I was just in here looking for you."

My mother would wrinkle her eyebrows, and send me a wink when my father wasn't looking. "Why, we were right here the whole time. You walked right past. I don't know why you didn't see us. Sometimes I think you just don't appreciate us."

Night was falling earlier now, and though the maroon van was not in the old parking lot when I arrived at the skating rink, I wasn't completely filled with doubt. If my friends were indeed alive, on the run with the driver of the maroon van, they would need to make an inconspicuous entrance. They were simply waiting for the right moment to appear and send me a signal to join them. I wondered what it would be like, to feel the road passing beneath me, what the van smelled like inside, all the things I would see from the heart-shaped window.

Every Friday in October was Halloween at Great Skate, and that night I waited in a line of fifth- and sixth-grade vampires, witches, he-devils, she-devils, and various other monsters. I had dressed up like the invisible man from the black-and-white movie, by wrapping my face in white bandages and wearing sunglasses. I put my hair up in a bun, under a black fedora, and since I was neither a tall nor a large-chested girl I blended with the younger children.

The heavyset woman in the little ticket booth charged me for a child's admission, an unforeseen bonus that under other circumstances would have thrilled me, but now only disoriented me a little. I entered the booming atmosphere of the crowded skating dome, got a locker, and put on my skates, then glided around the polished wooden floor to sounds of campy eighties hits. On the white walls of the rink, echelons of colored light spots slowly rotated against the flow of disguised skaters. The deep voice of the DJ, hidden away in his booth, announced specially themed skates. All around me boys and girls coasted together, five and six years younger than I, already oblivious to me. It was fine, that had been my childhood, and for a while I had fun being nobody, soaring along to the music. I could do and think anything, be anyone, the only catch being that I had no one to share it with. That's when I noticed the man watching me from the rail of the rink floor, back behind the bathrooms, near the fire exit.

He was tall and strong-looking, leaning over the rail on his elbows, staring directly at me once I'd noticed him. He'd brushed his long, blond hair behind his ears, revealing his ruddy face. He lifted one hand and waved at me. His attempt to smile only seemed to worsen his mood. A person like that you could never touch, only brush, and never truly speak with, only at. At this moment I became sure that my friends were dead. I bent my knees and somehow avoided wiping out on the hard, hot floor. I neither waved back nor turned my head abruptly away, but he continued to watch me as I passed him. He would move his face over, as if to push it into my line of vision, and wink at me.

I tried to think of some way I might slip off the rink floor and telephone Detective Volmar without chasing off the man at the rail. I wanted not only to escape him but to see him hauled off by the police. Nothing short of a complete victory would be acceptable. Under my mask I wanted to cry but knew I had to keep moving. As long as I kept skating, I could find a way out, call for help, and do what I could. I skated until the man relaxed and let his hands hang limp over the floor, as if to say he would wait for me. Then I skated through a large group of angels and, with that blockade behind me, coasted off the floor at the far end of the rink. I skated out into the lobby, where I found the crabby traffic cop eating a soft pretzel as he peered into a vending machine that flattened pennies and stamped them with winged roller skates.

Once I'd pulled away the bandages and sunglasses, he remembered me. Because I was so upset, he hardly needed to hear my story to come running with me around to the back of the rink. It was difficult to run on my skates but I didn't want to lose sight of him, lest I be isolated in a space where no one could see me, the only kind of space where I'd be vulnerable to the man I'd seen next to the rink. The traffic cop barked into his radio as he ran ahead of me around the corner into the empty back lot. I nearly lost my balance when I saw there was no maroon van waiting for us.

The officer didn't need to think twice. "We've been looking for that car. He's probably driving something else." He pulled open the emergency exit door and ushered me inside. "Come on. Show me where you saw him."

We hurried into the red light that filled the domed room, and from the rail along the rink scanned a hundred masked faces for the one I'd seen watching me all night. I looked out on the floor, along the tables by the concessions area, among the few arcade games on the far wall. There was no place where the man could have been hiding, not really. The traffic cop dashed into the men's room and then the ladies' room. A group of little girls came running out, then the cop, looking frustrated.

A minute of confusion passed before the rest of the police came running in. The music was stopped, the children herded off the floor so the cops could search the entire rink. The situation quickly became humiliating and inexplicable, with a lot of adults scowling, tweeners complaining. The man who'd been watching me was gone. None of the twelve-year-olds questioned remembered seeing him at the rail. A few said they might have seen somebody, but their voices were too eager. Their descriptions contradicted each other.

In all there were eight police cruisers in the parking lot, their lights flashing in the pungent autumn night. Some of the twelve or so officers complained while looking at me, to let me know I'd wasted their time. Detective Volmar showed up in an unmarked white car and was very kind to me. He told a few other cops that they couldn't understand what I'd been through, though I had the feeling that he, too, was irritated. He put me in the back of his car with the door open, and told me to put my shoes back on. Then he telephoned my father.

About a year later, the man who became known as the Lake Erie killer was arrested in a small town in southern Michigan, a short drive from our suburb in the cornfields. The police discovered the bones of an estimated thirty-one people in the crawlspace beneath his house. Brianna and Randall's clothes were some of the first pieces of evidence found, and a detective said it was only a matter of time before their skulls were identified. Also found in one of three garages built on the killer's sprawling property was the maroon travel van my friends and I had seen outside Great Skate the night they'd disappeared. I saw this after school, in a news flash I watched in my living room, and saw part of an interview with the killer's mother, and a serial killer expert who compared this killer to others. When the station broadcast footage of the police arresting the man who murdered my friends, he wasn't anyone I recognized. He was older, around average height, with neat brown hair and glasses. He had soft cheeks, the sort of face I would never imagine hid plans to kill somebody.

My father and stepmother were there with me, waiting for me to speak, to say that this was the guy I'd seen in the rink that night the police had tried to come to my rescue. They wanted to see my fear vanish forever. I only shook my head. What if my mother was one of the bodies they'd found, one of those so decayed it would never be identified? The more I thought about it the more possible it seemed, the more I understood I might still be sick. My face must have betrayed my fear, because my father and stepmother suddenly grew ashamed of themselves.

"Let's get out of here," I said. Soon, I knew, the telephone would be ringing, and Randall's parents, Brianna's mother, would be calling to speak to me. There was weeping to do, relief to share, and bitterness to acknowledge, and now there was a figure to blame it on. Out the window behind my father and stepmother, the sun rippled in the golden light above the drying, broken stalks of last summer's corn. It was getting cold again, the days shortening. Soon the outdoor businesses would close for the winter.

"How about ice cream?" I said.

By then I'd stopped dreaming about Brianna and Randall in the skating rink. They appeared in my dreams, but in the usual nonsensical places, their faces no longer marbled with decay, but fresh and young, as I had known them. They didn't seem to remember what had happened to them, even when, during a dream set in my front yard, I saw the maroon van drive slowly past us. In the dream it was sunny, there were birds hunting worms in the grass, and I felt no fear after the van had gone. "I've been wanting to ask you two," I said to my friends. "Is the driver of the van the killer or not? Or is he someone else?"

"What driver?" Randall said.

"I don't know any van driver," Brianna said.

On the day the police caught the Lake Erie killer, we came back from the ice cream stand, having licked our fingers clean. The burned flavor of sugar cones lingered in our mouths, and rather than accept the grim circumstances awaiting us, my father suggested we use the remaining daylight to build a scarecrow in the front yard. He dug an old flannel shirt and a pair of brown corduroys from a trunk of old clothes, and I found a pillowcase we could use for a head. In the yard we stuffed them full of leaves. We posted an old shovel's handle in the hard ground and hung the great grotesque doll on it. I'd painted ferocious blue eyes and a stitched red frown on the head, and my father fastened a gray fedora to it with safety pins. My stepmother sat on the porch's swing chair, bundled up in a blanket, watching as she sipped hot peppermint tea.

The day turned dark over the bare trees, faster than we'd expected, and by the time we joined my stepmother on the porch swing, with leaf scraps clinging to our hair and sweatshirts, the sun was setting, and a wild wind had sprung up. The trees swayed, noisily rattling their branches together. We sat in a tight row on the wooden seat and watched the scarecrow flail its arms in the dusk, casting dead leaves up at the shuddering boughs of our maples, like a wizard trying to rebuild the summer. Inside the house, the telephone rang and rang. The answering machine kept switching on, and we laughed to hear my father gloomily repeating that we weren't home. Maybe that was a little cruel, hiding just then, but we would make up for it later. We would call those people back, and shout, laugh, cry, produce the sounds that people make together. We owed them that much, out of the empathy we felt, listening to them speak slowly, faithfully, putting words into the void of our answering machine, against the chill that grows when a name is said and silence answers.

ELIZABETH STROUT

A Different Road

FROM *Tin House*

AN AWFUL THING happened to the Kitteridges on a chilly night in June. At the time, Henry was sixty-eight, Olive sixty-nine, and while they were not an especially youthful couple, there was nothing about them that gave the appearance of being old, or ill. Still, after a year had gone by, people in this small New England coastal town of Crosby agreed: both Kitteridges were changed by the event. Henry, if you met him at the post office now, only lifted his mail as a hello. When you looked into his eyes it was like seeing him through a screened-in porch. Sad, because he had always been an open-faced and cheerful man, even when his only son had — out of the blue — moved to California with his new wife, something people in town understood had been a great disappointment for the Kitteridges. And while Olive Kitteridge had never, in anyone's memory, felt inclined to be affable, or even polite, she seemed less so now as this particular June rolled around. Not a chilly June this year, but one that showed up with the suddenness of summer, days of dappled sunlight falling through the birch trees, turning the people of Crosby uncharacteristically chatty at times.

Why else would Cynthia Bibber have approached Olive in the shopping mall out at Cooks Corner to explain how Cynthia's daughter, Andrea, who, after years of evening classes, had earned a social work degree, thought maybe Henry and Olive hadn't been able to absorb the experience they'd had last year? Panic, when it wasn't expressed, became internalized — and that, Cynthia Bibber was saying, in an earnest half whisper, as she stood next to a plastic ficus tree, could lead to a depressive situation.

"I see," said Olive loudly. "Well, you tell Andrea that's pretty impressive." Olive, years ago, had taught math at Crosby Junior High School, and while her emotions at times had attached themselves fiercely to particular students, Andrea Bibber had never seemed to her to be anything more than a small, dull, asseverating mouse. Like her mother, Olive thought, glancing past her at the silk daffodils that were stuck in rows of fake straw by the benches near the frozen-yogurt place.

"It's a specialty now," Cynthia Bibber was saying.

"What is?" said Olive, considering the possibility of some frozen chocolate yogurt if this woman would move on.

"Crisis counseling," said Cynthia. "Even before 9/11" — she shifted a package under her arm — "but when there's a crash, or school shooting, or anything nowadays, they bring in psychologists right off the bat. People can't process this stuff on their own."

"Huh." Olive glanced down at the woman, who was short and small-boned. Olive, big, solidly built, towered over her.

"People have noticed a change in Henry," Cynthia said. "And you too. And it's just a thought that crisis counseling might have helped. Could still help. Andrea has her own practice, you know — gone in with another woman part-time."

"I see," said Olive again, quite loudly this time. "Aren't they ugly words, Cynthia, that those people think up — process, internalize, depressive whatever. It'd make me depressive to go around saying those words all day." She held up the plastic bag she carried. "D'you see the sale they're having at So-Fro?"

In the parking lot she couldn't find her keys and had to dump the contents of her pocketbook out onto the sunbaked hood of the car. At the stop sign she said, "Oh, hell's bells to you," in the rearview mirror when a red truck honked his horn, then she pulled into traffic, and the bag from the fabric store slid onto the floor, a corner of denim material poking out onto the gravelly mat. "Andrea Bibber wants us to make an appointment for crisis counseling," she'd have said in the old days, and it was easy to picture Henry's big eyebrows drawing together as he stood up from weeding the peas. "Godfrey, Ollie," he'd have answered, the bay spread out behind him and seagulls flapping their wings above a lobster boat. "Imagine." He might even have put his head back to laugh the way he did sometimes, it would have been that funny.

Olive merged onto the highway, which is how she got home from the mall ever since Christopher, their son, had moved to California. She didn't care to drive by the house with its lovely lines, and the big bowed window where the Boston fern had done so well. Out here by Cooks Corner the highway went along the river, and today the water was shimmery and the leaves of poplars fluttered, showing the paler green of their undersides. Maybe, even in the old days, Henry wouldn't have laughed about Andrea Bibber. You could be wrong thinking you knew what people would do. "Bet you anything," Olive said out loud as she looked over at the shining river, the sweet ribbon of it there beyond the guardrails. What she meant was: Bet you anything Andrea Bibber has a different idea of crisis than I do. "Yup, yup," she said. Weeping willows were down there on the bank, their swooping, airy boughs a light, bright green.

She had needed to go to the bathroom, which she had told Henry that night as they were pulling into the town of Maisy Mills. Henry had told her, pleasantly, she'd have to wait.

"Ay-yuh," she said, pronouncing the word with exaggeration in order to make fun of her mother-in-law, Pauline, dead for some years, who used to say that in response to anything she didn't want to hear. "Ay-yuh," Olive repeated. "Tell my insides," she added, shifting slightly in the darkened car. "Good Lord, Henry. I'm about ready to explode."

But the truth is, they had had a pleasant evening. Earlier, farther up the river, they had met their friends Bill and Bunny Newton, and gone to a restaurant recently opened, enjoying themselves a good deal. The mushrooms stuffed with crabmeat were marvelous, and all evening the waiters bowed politely, filling water glasses before the water had gone even halfway down.

More gratifying, however, was the fact that, for Olive and Henry, the story of Bill and Bunny's offspring was worse than their own. Both couples had only the one child, and Karen Newton — the Kitteridges privately agreed — had created a different level of sadness for her parents. Even if Karen did live next door to Bill and Bunny and they got to see her, and her family, all the time. Last year Karen had carried on a brief affair with a man who worked for Midcoast Power, but decided in the end to stay in her marriage. All this, of course, worried the Newtons profoundly, even though they had never cared a great deal for their son-in-law, Eddie.

And while it had been a really ghastly blow for the Kitteridges to have Christopher so suddenly uprooted by his pushy new wife, after they had planned on his living nearby and raising a family (Olive had pictured teaching his future children how to plant bulbs) . . . while it had certainly been a blow to have this dream disintegrate, the fact that Bill and Bunny had their grandchildren right next door and the grandchildren were spiteful was a source of unspoken comfort to the Kitteridges. In fact, the Newtons told a story that night about how their grandson had said to Bunny just last week, "You may be my grandmother, but that doesn't mean I have to love you, you know." It was frightful — who would expect such a thing? Bunny's eyes glistened in the telling of this. Olive and Henry did what they could, shaking their heads, saying what a shame it was that Eddie essentially trained the children to say these things under the guise of "expressing themselves."

"Well, Karen's responsible too," Bill said gravely, and Olive and Henry murmured, well, sure, that was true.

"Oh boy," said Bunny, blowing her nose. "Sometimes it seems like you can't win."

"You can't win," Henry said. "You do your best."

How was the California contingent? Bill wanted to know.

"Grumpy," Olive said. "Grumpy as hell when we called last week. I told Henry we're going to stop calling. When they feel like speaking to us, we'll speak to them."

"You can't win," said Bunny. "Even when you do your best." But they had been able to laugh, as if something about it was ruefully funny.

"Always nice to hear other people's problems," Olive and Bunny agreed later in the parking lot, pulling on their sweaters.

It was chilly in the car. Henry said they could turn the heat on if she wanted, but she said no. They drove through the dark, an occasional car coming toward them with headlights shining, then the road dark again. "Awful what that boy said to Bunny," Olive remarked, and Henry said it was awful.

After a while he said, "That Karen's not much."

"No," Olive said, "she's not." But her stomach, grumbling and shifting in familiar ways, began some acceleration of its own and

Olive became alert, then alarmed. "God," she said, as they stopped for a red light by the bridge that crossed into the town of Maisy Mills. "I really am ready to explode."

"I'm not sure what to do," Henry said, leaning forward to peer through the windshield. "The gas stations are across town, and who knows if they're open at this hour. Can't you sit tight? We'll be home in fifteen minutes."

"No," said Olive. "Believe me, I'm sitting as tight as I can."

"Well —"

"Green, go. Pull into the hospital, Henry. They ought to have a bathroom."

"The hospital? Ollie, I don't know."

"Turn into the hospital, for crying out loud." She added, "I was born there. I guess they'll let me use a bathroom."

There was the hospital at the top of the hill, bigger now with the new wing that had been built. Henry turned the car in, and then drove right past the blue sign that spelled out EMERGENCY.

"What are you doing?" said Olive. "For God's sake."

"I'm taking you around to the front door."

"Stop the goddamn car."

"Oh, Olive." His voice was filled with disappointment, she supposed because of how he hated to have her swear. He backed the car up and stopped in front of the big, well-lighted blue door.

"Thank you," said Olive. "Now, was that so hard to do?"

The nurse looked up from her desk in a lobby cleanly bright, and empty. "I need a bathroom," Olive said, and the nurse raised her white-sweatered arm and pointed. Olive waved her hand over her head and stepped through the door.

"Whew," she said to herself out loud. "Whewie." Pleasure was the absence of pain, according to Aristotle. Or Plato. One of them. Olive had graduated magna cum laude from college. And Henry's mother had not liked that. Imagine. Pauline actually said something about magna cum laude girls being plain and not having much fun . . . Well, Olive was not going to spoil this moment thinking of Pauline. She finished up, washed her hands, and looked around as she stuck them under the dryer, thinking how the bathroom was huge, big enough to do surgery in. It was because of people in wheelchairs. Nowadays you got sued if you didn't build something big enough for a wheelchair, but she'd rather somebody just shoot her if it came to that.

"You all right?" The nurse, her sweater and pants droopy, was standing in the hallway when Olive emerged. "What'd you have? Diarrhea?"

"Explosive," said Olive. "My goodness. I'm fine now, thank you very much."

"Vomiting?"

"Oh no."

"Do you have any allergies?"

"Nope." Olive looked around. "You seem pretty short on business tonight."

"Well. Weekends it picks up."

Olive nodded. "People party, I suppose. Drive into a tree."

"More often than not," the nurse said, "it's families. Last Friday we had a brother push his sister out the window. They were afraid she broke her neck."

"My word," said Olive. "All this in little Maisy Mills."

"She was okay. I think the doctor's ready to see you now."

"Oh, I don't need a doctor. I just needed a bathroom. We had dinner with friends and I ate everything came my way. My husband's waiting for me in the parking lot."

The nurse reached for Olive's hand and looked at it. "Let's just be careful for a minute here. Have your palms been itching? Soles of your feet?" She peered up at Olive. "Are your ears always this red?"

Olive touched her ears. "Why?" she said. "Am I getting ready to die?"

"Lost a woman in here just last night," the nurse said. "About your age. Like you, she'd been out to eat with her husband and came in here later with diarrhea."

"Oh, for God's sake," Olive said, but her heart banged fast, and her face heated up. "What in hell ailed her?"

"She was allergic to crabmeat and went into anaphylactic shock."

"Well, there you are. I'm not allergic to crabmeat."

The nurse nodded calmly. "This woman'd been eating it for years with no problem. Let's just have the doctor give you a look. You did come in here flushed, showing signs of agitation."

Olive felt a great deal more agitated now, but she wasn't going to let the nurse know that, nor was she going to mention to her the mushrooms stuffed with crabmeat. If the doctor was nice, she'd tell him.

Henry was parked straight in front of the emergency room with the engine still running. She gestured for him to put the window down. "They want to check me," she said, bending her head to him.

"Check you in?"

"Check me. Make sure I haven't gone into shock. Turn that damn thing down."

Although he had already reached over to turn off the Red Sox game.

"Ollie, good Lord. Are you all right?"

"Some woman choked on crabmeat last night and now they're afraid they'll be sued. They're going to check my pulse and I'll be right out. But you ought to move the car."

The nurse was holding back a huge green curtain farther down the hall.

"He's listening to the ball game," Olive said, walking toward her. "When he thinks I've died, I expect he'll come in."

"I'll keep an eye out for him."

"He's got on a red jacket." Olive put her pocketbook on a nearby chair and then sat on the examining table while the nurse took her blood pressure.

"Better safe than sorry," the nurse said. "But I expect you're all right."

"I expect I am," said Olive.

The nurse left her with a form on a clipboard, and Olive sat on the examining table, filling it out. She looked closely at her palms and set the clipboard aside. Well, if you came stumbling into an emergency room it was their job to examine you. She'd stick her tongue out, have her temperature taken, go home.

"Mrs. Kitteridge?" The doctor was a plain-faced man who did not appear old enough to have gone through medical school. He held her large wrist gently, taking her pulse, while she told him about going to the new restaurant, insisting she'd come in here only to use the bathroom on the drive home, and yes, she'd had some terrific diarrhea, which did surprise her, but no itchy hands or feet.

"What did you have to eat?" The doctor asked as though he were interested.

"I started off with mushrooms stuffed with crabmeat, and I know some old lady died from that last night."

The doctor touched Olive's earlobe, squinting. "I don't see any signs of a rash," he said. "Tell me what else you had to eat."

She appreciated how this young man did not seem bored. So many doctors made you feel like hell, like you were just a fat lump moving down the conveyor belt.

"Steak. And a potato. Baked. Big as your hat. And creamed spinach. Let's see." Olive closed her eyes. "Puny little salad, but a nice dressing on it."

"Soup? A lot of additives in soup that can cause allergic reactions."

"No soup," Olive said, opening her eyes. "But a lovely slab of cheesecake for dessert. With strawberries."

The doctor said, as he wrote things down, "This is probably just a case of active gastro reflux."

"Oh, I see," said Olive. She considered for a moment before adding quickly, "Statistically speaking, it doesn't seem you'd have two women die of the same thing two nights in a row."

"I think you're okay," the doctor said. "But I'd like to examine you just the same, palpate your abdomen, listen to your heart." He handed her a blue papery-plastic square. "Put this on, open in front. Everything off, please."

"Oh, for heaven's sake," said Olive, but he had already stepped past the curtain. "Oh, for heaven's sake," she said again, rolling her eyes, but she did as she was told because he had been pleasant, and because the crabmeat woman had died. Olive folded her slacks and put them on the chair, careful to tuck her underpants beneath them where they couldn't be seen when the doctor walked back in.

Silly little plastic belt, made for a skinny pinny; it could barely tie around her. She managed, though — a tiny white bow. Waiting, she folded her hands and realized how every single time she went by this hospital the same two thoughts occurred to her, which is that she'd been born here and that her father's body had been brought here after his suicide. She'd been through some things, but never mind. Other people had been through things too.

She gave a small shake of her head as she thought of the nurse saying someone had tossed his sister out the window like that. If Christopher had a sister he never would have thrown her out a window. If Christopher had married his receptionist he'd still be here in town. Although the girl had been stupid — Olive could see why he'd passed on her. His wife was not stupid. She was pushy and determined, and mean as a bat from hell.

Olive straightened her back and looked at the little glass bottles of different things lined up on the counter, and at the box of latex gloves. She bet that in the drawers of the metal cabinet there were all sorts of syringes ready for all sorts of problems. She flexed her ankle one way, then the other. In a minute she was going to poke her nose out to see if Henry was all set; she knew he wouldn't stay out there in the car, even with the ball game on. She'd call Bunny tomorrow, tell her about this little fiasco.

After that, it was like painting with a sponge, like someone had pressed a paint-wet sponge to the inside of her mind, and only what it painted, those splotches there, held what she remembered of the rest of that night. There was a quick, rushing sound — the curtain flung back with the tinny whoosh of its rings against the rod. There was a person in a blue ski mask waving an arm at Olive, shouting, "Get down." There was the weird confusion, for a second the schoolteacher in her saying, "Hey, hey, hey," while he said, "Get down, lady. Jesus." Get down where? she might have asked, because they were both confused — she was sure of that: she, clutching her papery robe, and this slender person in a blue ski mask, waving his arm.

"Look," she did say, her tongue as sticky as flypaper. "My handbag is right on that chair."

But there was a shout from down the hall. A man shouting, coming closer, and it was the quick thrust of a booted foot kicking over the chair that swept her into the black of terror. A tall man holding a rifle, wearing a big khaki vest with pocket flaps. But it was the mask he wore, a Halloween mask of a pink-cheeked, smiling pig, which seemed to pitch her forward into the depths of ice-cold water — that ghoulish, plastic face of a pink smiling pig. Underwater, she saw the seaweed of his camouflage pants and knew he was shouting at her but couldn't hear his words.

They made her walk down the hall in her bare feet and papery blue robe while they walked behind her; her legs ached and felt enormous, like big sacks of water. A shove smacked into her, and she stumbled, clutching her robe as she was pushed through the door of the bathroom she had been in. On the floor, with their backs against the separate walls, sat the nurse and the doctor and Henry. Henry's red jacket was unzipped and askew, one of his pant legs caught halfway up.

"Olive, have they hurt you?"

"Shut the fuck up," said the man with the smiling, pink, pig face, and kicked Henry's foot. "Say another word and I'll blow your motherfucking head off right now."

A paint splotch of memory that quivered every time: the sound of the duct tape that night, the quick stripping of it from its roll, and the grabbing of her hands behind her back, the wrapping of the tape around them, because then she knew she was going to die — that they would, all of them, be shot execution-style; they would have to kneel. She was told to sit, but it was hard to sit down when your hands were taped behind you and your head inside was tilting. She thought: Just hurry. Her legs shook so hard that they actually made a little slapping sound against the floor.

"Move, you get shot in the head," Pig Face said. He held the rifle, and he kept turning quickly, while the flaps of his vest bulged, swinging when he turned. "You even look at each other and this guy shoots you in the head."

But when did the things get said? Different things got said.

Along the exit ramp now were lilac trees and a red berry bush. Olive pulled up at the stop sign, and then almost pulled out in front of a car passing by; even as she looked at the car she almost pulled out in front of it. The driver shook his head at her like she was crazy. "Hell's bells to you," she said, but she waited so she wouldn't end up right behind someone who had just looked at her like she was crazy. And then she decided to go in the other direction, heading the back way to Maisy Mills.

Pig Face had left them in the bathroom. ("It just doesn't make sense," different people had said to the Kitteridges soon after this happened, after they read about it in the paper, saw it on TV. "It doesn't make sense two fellows barging into a hospital, hoping to get drugs." Before people realized the Kitteridges were not going to say three words about the ordeal. What does "making sense" have to do with the price of eggs? Olive could have said.) After Pig Face left them, Blue Mask reached for the doorknob, locking it with the same click it had made for Olive not so long ago. He sat down on the toilet-seat cover, leaning forward, his legs apart, a small, squarish gun in his hand. Made of pewter, it looked like. Olive thought she would vomit and choke on the vomit. It seemed a certainty; being unable to move her bulky, handless self, she would aspirate the vomit that was on its way up, and she would do it sitting right next to a doctor who wouldn't be able to help her because his hands were taped too. Sitting next to a doctor, and across from a nurse, she would die on her vomit the way drunks did. And Henry would watch it and never be the same. *People have noticed the change in Henry.* She didn't vomit. The nurse had been crying when Olive was first pushed into the bathroom and she was still crying. A lot of things were the nurse's fault.

At some point the doctor, whose white lab coat had been partly bunched beneath his leg that was closest to Olive, said, "What's your name?" using the same pleasant voice he had used earlier with Olive.

"Listen," said Blue Mask. "Fuck you. Okay?"

At different times since then Olive had thought, *I remember this clearly,* but then later couldn't remember when she thought that. Paint splotches of memory, though, of this: They were quiet. They were waiting. Her legs had finally stopped shaking. Outside the door a telephone rang. It rang and rang, then stopped. Almost immediately it rang again. Olive's kneecaps bumped up, like big, uneven saucers beyond the edge of the papery blue robe. She didn't think she would have picked them out as her own if someone had passed before her a series of photographs of old ladies' fat knees. Her ankles, and her toes swollen with bunions, seemed more familiar, stuck out in the middle of the room. The doctor's legs were not as long as hers, and his shoes didn't seem very big. Plain as a child's, his shoes. Brown leather and rubber-soled.

Where Henry's pant leg was caught up, the liver spots showed on his white hairless shin. He said, "Oh gosh," quietly. And then: "Do you think you could find a blanket for my wife? Her teeth are chattering."

"You think this is a fucking hotel?" said Blue Mask. "Just shut the fuck up."

"But she's —"

"Henry," Olive said sharply. "Be quiet."

The nurse kept crying silently.

No, Olive could not get the splotches arranged in order, but Blue Mask was very nervous; she understood early on that he was frightened to death. He kept bouncing his knees up and down. Young — she had understood that right away too. When he pushed up the sleeves of his nylon jacket, his wrists were moist with perspiration. And then she saw how he had almost no fingernails. She had never, in all her years of teaching, come across nails that had been bitten so extremely to the quick. He kept bringing his fingertips to his mouth, pressing them into the slots of the mask with ferociousness; even the hand that held the gun would move to his mouth and he would chew the thumb tip quickly — a big bump of bright red.

"Get your fucking head down," he said to Henry. "Stop fucking watching me."

"You don't need to speak so filthy," Henry said, looking at the floor, his wavy hair headed in the wrong direction across his head.

"What'd you say?" The boy's voice rose like it was going to break. "What the fuck did you say, old man?"

"Henry, please," Olive said. "Keep quiet before you get us all killed."

This: Blue Mask leaning forward, interested in Henry. "Old man. What the fucking fuck did you say to me?" Henry turning his face to the side, his big eyebrows frowning. Blue Mask getting up and pushing the gun into Henry's shoulder. "Answer me! What the fuck did you say to me?" (And Olive, turning down past the mill now, approaching the town, remembered the familiarity of that kind of frenzied frustration, saying to Christopher when he was a child, Answer me! Christopher always a quiet child, quiet the way her father had been.)

Henry blurted: "I said you don't need to talk so filthy." Blurted out further: "You should be ashamed of your mouth." And then the guy pushed the gun against Henry's face, right into his cheek, his hand on the trigger.

"Please!" Olive cried out. "Please. He got that from his mother. His mother was impossible. Just ignore him."

Her heart thumped so hard she thought it made the papery blue gown move on her chest. The boy stood there watching Henry, then finally stepped back, tripping over the nurse's white shoes. He kept the gun pointed at Henry but turned to look at Olive. "This guy's your husband?"

Olive nodded.

"Well, he's a fuckin' nut."

"He can't help it," Olive said. "You'd have to know his mother. His mother was full of pious crap."

"That's not true," said Henry. "My mother was a good, decent woman."

"Shut up," the boy said tiredly. "Everyone please just shut the fuck up." He sat back down on the toilet-seat cover, his legs spread, holding the gun over a knee. Her mouth was so dry she thought the word *tongue* and pictured a slab of cow's tongue packaged for sale.

The boy suddenly pulled off his ski mask. And how startling — it was as though she knew him then, as if seeing him made sense. Quietly, he said, "Motherfucker." His skin had become tender beneath the heat of the ski mask, his neck had streaks, patches of red. Inflamed pimples crowded together high on his cheeks. His head was shaved, but she saw he was a redhead; there was the orangey effervescence of his scalp, the tiny flickers of bright stubble, the almost parboiled look of his tender, pale skin. The boy wiped his face in the crook of his nylon-sleeved elbow.

"I bought my son a ski mask like that," Olive told him. "He lives in California and skis in the Sierra Mountains."

The boy looked at her. His eyes were pale blue, his lashes almost colorless. The whites of his eyes had spidery red veins. He kept staring at Olive without changing his hangdog expression. "Just please shut up," he finally said.

Olive sat in her car now in the far back of the hospital's parking lot, where she could see the blue door of the emergency room, but there was no shade and the sun baked through the windshield; even with the windows open she was too warm. The lack of shade had not been a problem all year, of course. In the winter, she would come and sit with the car running. Never did she stay long. Only enough to gaze at the door and to remember the clean, bright lobby, the huge bathroom with its shiny chrome rail that ran along part of one wall: a rail that right now, perhaps, some old doddering lady was holding on to in order to hoist herself off the toilet, the rail Olive had stared at as they all sat, legs splayed out, hands behind their backs. In hospitals, lives were changed all the time. A newspaper said the nurse had not returned to work, but maybe by now she had. About the doctor, Olive didn't know.

The kid kept getting up and sitting back down on the toilet seat. When he sat, he'd be hunched forward, the gun in one hand, the other hand folded in front of his mouth, chewing the hell out of those fingertips. The sirens did not sound for very long. Or maybe they had sounded for a long time — she had thought about that. It was the pharmacist who'd been able to signal a janitor to call the police; a special unit was brought to negotiate with Pig Face, but none of them had known that then. A telephone kept ringing and stopping. They waited, the nurse rolling her head back, closing her eyes.

Olive's little plastic strip of a belt came untied. The memory of this was a splotch of thick, dense paint. The belt, somewhere along the line, had come untied, and the papery gown was open. She tried crossing one leg over the other, but that made the gown open more, and she could see her big stomach with its folds, and her thighs, white as two massive fish bellies.

"Honestly," Henry said. "Can't you find something to cover my wife? She's all exposed."

"Shut up, Henry," Olive said. The nurse opened her eyes and gazed at Olive, and the doctor of course turned his head to look at her. They were all looking at her now. "God, Henry."

The boy leaned forward, and said softly to Henry, "See, you gotta be quiet, or someone's gonna blow your head off. Your motherfucking head," he added, and sat back. His glance, as he looked around, fell on Olive, and he said, "Oh Jesus, lady," a look of real discomfort passing over his face.

"Well, what am I supposed to do?" she said, furious — oh, she was furious. And if her teeth had been chattering before, she now felt sweat roll down her face; she seemed to be one moist, furious sack of horror. She tasted salt and did not know if these were tears or rivulets of sweat.

"Okay, listen." The kid took a deep, quick breath. He got up and came over to her, squatting down, putting the gun on the tile floor. "Any of you move, I'll kill you." He looked around. "Just give me a fucking second here." And then he tugged quickly on both sides of her papery blue robe, tied the white plastic strip in a knot right there on her stomach. His shaved head, with the tiny glints of orange stubble, was close to her, the top of his forehead still red from where the ski mask had excited the skin. "Okay," he said. He took his gun and went back and sat on the toilet.

That moment, right there, when he sat back down and she wanted him to look at her — that was a vivid paint spot on her mind. How much she had wanted him to look at her right then, and he didn't.

In the car, Olive started the engine and pulled out of the parking lot. She drove past a drugstore, the doughnut shop, a dress shop that had been there forever, and then over the bridge. Farther ahead, if she continued that way, was the cemetery where her father was buried. Last week she had taken lilacs to put on his grave, though she wasn't one who went in, especially, for decorating graves. Pauline was down there in Portland, and this was the first year that Olive had not accompanied Henry on Memorial Day to plant geraniums at the head of Pauline's grave.

There had been that pounding on the bathroom door (locked from the inside by the kid, the way Olive herself had locked it) and the hurried, "Come on, come on, open up, it's me!" And then she had seen — Henry couldn't because of where he was sitting — but she had seen, when the kid opened the bathroom door being pounded upon, the horrible pink Pig Face guy with the rifle hit the boy hard, crack him right across the face, shouting, "You took off your mask! You dumb-shit motherfucker!" Screaming, "You dumb shit!" There was an immediate resurgence of the thickening of her limbs, her eye muscles seemed to thicken, the air got thick: the whole thick, slow feeling of things not being real. Because now they would die. They had been thinking they wouldn't, but they saw again that they would. This was clear in Pig Face's panicky voice.

The nurse started saying Hail Marys quickly and loudly, and as far as Olive could remember, it was after the nurse repeated for the umpteenth time, "Blessed is the fruit of thy womb," that Olive said to her, "God, will you shut up with that crap?" And Henry said, "Olive, stop." Siding with the nurse like that.

Olive, stopping at a red light, reaching down to put the bag from the fabric store back up onto the seat next to her, still didn't get it. She didn't get it. No matter how many times she went over it in her mind, she didn't understand why Henry had sided with the nurse like that. Unless it was because the nurse didn't swear (Olive bet that nurse could swear) and Henry, trussed up like a chicken and about to be shot, was mad at Olive for swearing. Or for putting down Pauline earlier, when Olive had been trying to save his life.

Well, she had said some things about his mother then. After Pig Face screamed at the kid, and then disappeared again and they all knew he'd be back to shoot them, in that blurry, thick, awful part when Henry said, "Olive, stop," she, Olive, said some things about his mother then.

She said: "You're the one who can't stand these Hail Mary Catholics! Your mother taught you that! Pauline was the only real Christian in the world, as far as Pauline was concerned. And her good boy, Henry. You two were the only good Christians in the whole goddamn world!"

She said things like that. She said: "Do you know what your mother told people when my father died? That it was a sin! How's that for Christian charity, I ask you?"

The doctor said, "Stop now, let's stop this," but it was like the switch of an engine had been flipped on inside Olive, and the motor was accelerating; how did you stop such a thing?

She had said the word *Jew*. She was crying, everything was all mixed up, and she said, "Did it ever occur to you that's why Christopher left? Because he married a Jew and knew his father would be judgmental — did you ever think of that, Henry?"

In the sudden silence in the room, with the kid sitting on the toilet seat hiding his hit face in his arm, Henry said quietly, "That's a despicable thing to accuse me of, Olive, and you know it isn't true. He left because from the day your father died, you took over that boy's life. You didn't leave him any room. He couldn't stay married and stay in town too."

"Shut up!" Olive said. "Shut up, shut up."

The boy rose, holding that gun, saying, "Jesus fucking Christ, oh fuck, man."

Henry said, "Oh no," and Olive saw that he had wet himself; a dark stain grew in his lap, and down his trouser leg.

The doctor said, "Let's try and be calm, let's try and be quiet."

And they could hear the crackling of walkie-talkies out in the hall, the sound of the strong, unexcited speech of people in charge, and the boy started to cry. He cried without trying to hide it, and he held the small gun, standing up. There was a gesture with his arm, a tentative move, and Olive whispered, "Oh, don't." For the rest of Olive's life she would be certain the boy had thought of turning the gun on himself, but the policemen then were everywhere, covered with dark vests and helmets. When they cut the duct tape from her wrists, her arms and shoulders ached so that she couldn't put her arms down by her sides.

Henry was standing on the front deck, looking over the bay, when Olive arrived home. She had thought he would be working in the garden, but there he was, just standing, looking out over the water.

"Henry." Her heart thumped ferociously.

He turned. "Hello, Olive. You're back. You were gone longer than I thought you'd be."

"I bumped into Cynthia Bibber and she wouldn't shut up."

"What's new with Cynthia?"

"Nothing. Not one thing."

She sat down in the canvas deck chair. "Listen," she said. "I don't remember. But you defended that woman, and I was just trying to help you. I didn't think you'd want to hear that Catholic mumbo jumbo crap."

He shook his head once, as though he had water in his ear he was trying to shake out. After a moment he opened his mouth, then closed it. He turned back to look at the water, and for a long time neither said anything. Earlier in their marriage they'd had fights that made Olive feel sick the way she felt now. But after a certain point in a marriage you stopped having a certain kind of fight, Olive thought, because when the years behind you were more than the years in front of you, things were different. She felt the sun's warmth on her arms, although down here under the hill by the water, the air held the hint of nippiness.

The bay sparkled brilliantly in the afternoon sun. A small outboard cut across toward Diamond Cove, its bow riding high, and farther out was a sailboat with a red sail and a white one. There was the sound of the water touching against the rocks; it was almost high tide. A cardinal called from the Norwegian pine, and there was the fragrance of bayberry leaves from the bushes that were soaking up the sun.

Slowly Henry turned and lowered himself onto the wooden bench there, leaning forward, resting his head in his hands. "Do you know, Ollie," he said, looking up, his eyes tired, the skin around them red, "in all the years we've been married, all the years, I don't believe you've ever once apologized. For anything."

She flushed immediately and deeply. She felt her face burn beneath the sunshine that fell upon it. "Well, sorry, sorry, sorry," she said, taking her sunglasses from where they'd been resting on top of her head, and putting them back on. "What exactly are you saying?" she asked. "What in hell ails you? What in hell is this all about? Apologies? Well, I'm sorry then. I am sorry I'm such a hell of a rotten wife."

He shook his head and leaned forward, placing his hand on her knee. You rode along in life a certain way, Olive thought. Just like she'd ridden home from Cooks Corner for years, past Taylor's field, before Christopher's house had even been there; then his house was there, Christopher was there; and then after a while he wasn't. Different road, and you had to get used to that. But the mind, or the heart, she didn't know which one it was, but it was slower these days, not catching up, and she felt like a big, fat field mouse scrambling to get up on a ball that was right in front of her, turning faster and faster, and she couldn't get her scratchy frantic limbs up onto it.

"Olive, we were scared that night." He gave her knee a faint squeeze. "We were both scared. In a situation most people in a whole lifetime are never in. We said things, and we'll get over them in time." But he stood up, and turned and looked out over the water again, and Olive thought he had to turn away because he knew what he said wasn't true.

They would never get over that night. And it wasn't because they'd been held hostage in a bathroom — which Andrea Bibber would think was the crisis. No, they would never get over that night because they had said things that altered how they saw each other. And because she had, ever since then, been weeping from a private faucet inside her, unable to keep her thoughts from the red-haired boy with his blemished, frightened face, as in love with him as any schoolgirl, picturing him at his sedulous afternoon work in the prison garden; ready to make him a gardening smock as the prison liaison had told her she could do, with the fabric she bought at So-Fro today, unable to help herself, as Karen Newton must have been with her man from Midcoast Power — poor, pining Karen, who had produced a child that said, "Just because you're my grandmother doesn't mean I have to love you, you know."

MELISSA VANBECK

Given Her History

FROM *Porcupine Literary Arts Magazine*

THE NIGHT MY FAMILY BURNT UP I came to in a ditch. I was real little, and don't recollect if it was the yelling or the smell of smoke and gasoline that brought me to. The smoke came from my house, which looked pretty near done in. The smell of gasoline came off me. Billy's dog, Jake, was hunkered up next to me, and had that flat-eared look he got when Billy told him to do something or other. Billy was my oldest brother and it wasn't usual for Jake to be someplace without him, but he made being in the ditch tolerable and I leaned in close to him and shut my eyes. Jake stayed by me although he whined a bit and trembled some.

When I go to sorting things out about that night, what happened and when, it still gets mixed up and I feel like I'm gonna puke, which Mama said little girls don't do. But sorted or not, Mama and Daddy and Johnny were still burnt up. And all that talk about who set the fire and why, makes me want to do that thing Mama said little girls don't do, but what with me not being so little anymore, maybe doesn't matter so much.

It didn't take me long to reason out that Billy wasn't burnt up with Mama and Daddy and Johnny. Who else would have left me in a ditch with Jake? Billy always treated me bad, and at the time it seemed funny he didn't leave me in the house with everybody else. Also, it seemed peculiar he didn't take Jake with him. Unless it was too hard getting Jake to hop a moving train. And I was pretty sure that was how Billy got out of town. When I say Billy got out of town, I don't mean a real town, but I can't think of what else to call where we lived. There was the railroad station, where Daddy worked, the school, the post office and the little store, where you could get bread and canned pork and beans and Vienna sausages. Most folks lived out of town, on farms. And there was a school bus that went out and got their kids and dropped off their mail.

Daddy had sugar diabetes and when he peed he said his pee was honey. I tended to believe him. Because when I went to the outhouse after he'd peed, the boards were all sticky where he missed the hole. The diabetes made him shaky so he missed it a lot. Billy thought it was funny to catch me in the outhouse and stick my head in the hole. Then he'd laugh and tell me if I squealed on him he'd drop me down in there. I never did squeal. Billy was just mean enough to do what he said. That's why I couldn't figure him putting me in the ditch with Jake.

Nobody knew about Billy not being dead. I was pretty sure he'd come back for Jake — and maybe me. I kept an eye out for him, so when he did come we could take off real fast.

People put Jake and me with one of the schoolteachers. There were only three of them and they picked my third-grade teacher because she didn't have kids. Even at that, they had to do some talking to get Mrs. Clarke to agree to both me and Jake. She just kept staring at me, like she didn't know me, which wasn't true, since I had her most of a year already. Mr. Clarke seemed nice. He was pretty old and had only one eye. Mrs. Clarke was a lot younger and you could tell he liked her a lot. He kept telling her he'd make sure to keep Jake and me from bothering. At first she said she wouldn't take Jake, but Mr. Clarke looked at me real kind and said Jake seemed well behaved. He'd take that back later, if he could — but I'd made up my mind Jake and me was a package deal.

If they'd asked my opinion, I'd told them I'd rather live with the man that got Jake to calm down enough to get us out of the ditch. He was big and smelled like dirt and motors, and his hands were giant and all beat-up-looking. But when he picked me up and petted my hair, saying everything was going to be all right, over and over, they were as gentle as Mama's. Jake only growled a little, then followed us out of the ditch.

Folks were standing around, asking the big man all kind of questions. They called him Juris, which I thought was a peculiar name, but who am I to talk. With a name like April-May I've got no room to cast stones. Juris sort of waved them off with his eyebrows, like you'd do with a bunch of pesky flies. You could tell people had him held up in regard the way they quieted down right away. No one ever treated Daddy the way they treated Juris. We were railroad folks. Mama said all she ever wanted in life was to live in a house that wasn't railroad brown and stay in one place long enough to have a garden and make some friends.

Mr. Clarke let Jake sleep with me. Mrs. Clarke glared every time she looked at Jake until she finally said what was on her mind. If that dog, she called Jake, that dog, was gonna live in her house, he'd better have a bath. I'd never heard of giving a dog, especially Jake, a bath. But that's what me and Mr. Clarke did. I had to admit, Jake smelled a lot better. Being with the Clarkes I was getting used to being clean and having clean things around. Not that Mama was dirty. But we didn't have a real inside bathroom and if we needed bathing, Mama had to heat water on the stove and put it in a tub in the kitchen. Daddy got to use the water first, then Billy and Johnny. Mama made a fresh tub for me and her.

Mama was real skinny and wore bright red lipstick all the time. Daddy made fun of her, saying who did she think was gonna look at her anyway. I wondered that too, but not in the mean way Daddy said it. Once I asked Mama if she would put lipstick on me. She sat me down in front of her and I made my mouth the way she showed me, and right then, she started to cry, leaving me with only my top lip done. Mama was like that. She cried at little things. Then something worth crying about, from how I saw it, like when Daddy hit her, on accident he said, and she'd just act like nothing happened. The Clarkes were real different. He never hollered at her, and I'm pretty sure she never got hit on accident.

About a week or so after the fire, the big man, Juris, stopped by to see how I was doing at the Clarkes, and give me a sack of clothes he said his kids were too big for. They were near new as far as I could tell, and a lot nicer than Billy and Johnny's hand-me-downs. I said, "Appreciate the thought," and he pulled a piece of bubble gum out of his pocket and put one of his big hands on my head, which didn't feel bad, more like a warm hat.

On Sundays Mama got on her knees in front of Daddy to pray and he put his thing in her mouth. After a while he put his hands on her head and said he forgave her.

Then Juris asked if Jake and me liked living with the Clarkes. I tried blowing a bubble so he'd stop asking questions. But he kept on, like giving me a crummy sack of clothes, I owed him. Daddy always said people won't give you nothing unless they want something. I could see how he might be right, so I watched real close to see what he wanted for those clothes and the bubble gum I'd already chewed. He was saying something about Mama and Daddy, and them being in heaven with God. And Johnny, being God's innocent child, was in heaven too. I didn't say anything, not knowing very much about heaven and God's ideas, but I noticed right away he didn't say Billy was in heaven.

Then he outright asked what he'd been leading up to.

"Do you know where Billy is?"

I took the bubble gum out of my mouth and put it on Jake's nose, thinking to get Juris off Billy. But he just kept staring at me, not even giving Jake a glance, so I stuck the gum behind my ear for later.

"Do you?" he said again, like he was trying to scare me into saying something.

Some folks just don't have the knack of scaring little kids. I waited a bit, then fell down on my knees and folded my hands under my chin and stared up at the ceiling, like the Jesus picture Mrs. Clarke had hanging in the kitchen.

"I expect he's burnt up with Mama and Daddy and Johnny." I said it real quiet. Then to top it off I said, "Amen," just the way Mrs. Clarke said it after she prayed over me at night.

It was the "Amen" that did the trick, because he stood up real fast and when he left he didn't tell me goodbye, just stomped out. Then I heard him and Mr. Clarke in the yard talking and I snuck up to the living room window to listen.

Juris was leaning up against his pickup, the way of most all the farmers, smoking a cigarette.

Mama let me comb her hair, and it smelled like vinegar and cigarettes.

Mr. Clarke was standing in front of him with his thumbs in his belt, one foot dragging around in the dirt making circles. Juris was saying, "Keep your eyes peeled. That damn loco kid might just come back to finish off what he started." Then Mr. Clarke said something I couldn't make out, but it made Juris snort. And he said, "Don't be fooled. She knows more than she's saying. Wouldn't put it past that crazy Billy to come back for her. And if he does, stay out of his way."

A couple things made me glad. That I wasn't the only one that thought Billy was coming back to get me, and that Juris saw me as somebody that didn't go blabbing everything. And I hoped Billy knew I wasn't the one that told about him not being burnt up.

Juris didn't stop by again, and more and more I could tell Mrs. Clarke was wishing somebody else would take me and Jake. But like I said, it was a pretty small town and everybody else already had kids. It wasn't that she was mean, but if me and Jake walked into the kitchen and she and Mr. Clarke were visiting, she'd quit talking and leave the room saying she had things to do. Mr. Clarke would look all kind and sad at the same time and ask me something that had nothing to do with anything, just to cover up Mrs. Clarke leaving the room. I could have told him it didn't much matter to me if Mrs. Clarke left the room or not. When Billy came back, we'd be out of her hair.

One day when Mrs. Clarke was shopping and Mr. Clarke was taking a nap, Jake and me went out back to sit in the shade and get out of the heat. There was a cement pond back there. Mr. Clarke built it in his spare time, which he had a lot of, him being old and having only one eye. He was real proud of that pond and had it fixed up so water ran into it all the time and then out to the garden. For a pond, it wasn't very deep and I'd waded in it a couple times, although I wasn't supposed to. Mr. Clarke said it would scare the fish to have me sloshing around. I was dubious about fish feeling scared, but I agreed anyhow. Some of the fish were real special and cost a lot. They were big enough to fry, but all different colors of orange and white.

Daddy once got a goldfish someone left on the train and brought it home in a glass jar. We didn't know what to feed it, so it died and Billy cut it open to see its guts.

Mr. Clarke said these weren't goldfish, they were koi, and came from Japan. Daddy said Japs ate dogs. He could have been lying but just in case he wasn't, I hated all Japs. So when Jake jumped in the pond and started biting fish, I didn't think too much about it. The more he did it the more I saw what a good time he was having, sticking his head under the water and grabbing those goldfish and tossing them out on the grass. There was plenty of splashing around, which is probably what woke Mr. Clarke up. I'd planned on throwing them all back after Jake was through playing with them, and if some of them didn't make it, I'd just play dumb. I wasn't expecting Mr. Clarke to wake up and come storming out of the house, hollering like somebody was poking him with a fork or something. Jake froze he was so dumbstruck, like I was, at the noise coming out of Mr. Clarke. I wanted to laugh at how funny Jake looked, standing like a statue, up to his belly in water, with an orange and white goldfish in his mouth. It was a big one, and its head hung out one side of his mouth and its tail out the other.

By the time Mr. Clarke got to us, he was spitting slobber in all directions. Jake dropped the fish and we took off, and Mr. Clarke, yelling all sorts of things, chased after us. Then he sort of coughed and fell down. Jake and me stopped and waited to see what he'd do next, but he was still as a rock. I thought he might be trying to fool us into coming close so he could grab us, but he was too twisted up to be fooling. Jake trotted over and gave him a sniff, then kind of growled. It wasn't a real growl, more like a grumble. Mr. Clarke didn't even twitch. I figured he pretty much kilt himself with all that yelling.

Mama made a cake and strawberry ice cream for Daddy's birthday. And Daddy fell down from eating too much and Mama hit him in the face over and over.

The grass around the pool was wet from so many fish flopping. Some of them were dead from being out of the water too long, and from being bit. Getting them all throwed back before Mrs. Clarke came home didn't take long. Then we ran back to the house, stopping to see if Mr. Clarke had maybe started to breathe again. But he could have been one of those special fish, the way his one eye stared open, not blinking or nothing.

Daddy gave me a doll somebody left on the train. One of its arms was torn off and its eyes were made of glass.

When Mrs. Clarke got home, me and Jake was in the kitchen eating a jam sandwich, so as to look offhand and get rid of the fish smell on Jake's breath. Not that she would get that close to him, but I wasn't thinking all that clear. She asked me where was Mr. Clarke. I said I hadn't seen him. And then I said Jake and me had just got up from a nap, which was why we were eating a sandwich. She studied me a bit, like she was gonna ask me something else. I stuffed the rest of the sandwich in my mouth. Mrs. Clarke was real strict about talking with your mouth full. She quit looking at me and headed to the bedroom, calling to Mr. Clarke. She didn't call him Mr. Clarke. She called him Poppy. Which, again, and it isn't for me to say, seemed a funny thing to call the man you're married to. Mama didn't call Daddy, Daddy, she called him Bill. Billy was named for him. People should be more careful what they name their kids because a lot of meanness came with that name.

Pretty quick Mrs. Clarke started hollering, "Oh, my God! Oh, no! No! No!" and I figured she'd found Mr. Clarke. So Jake and me ran pell-mell outside, me yelling, "Oh, my God! Oh, no! No! No!" just like Mrs. Clarke. If I'd been thinking more clear, I'd been saying, "What's wrong," like I didn't know he was dead.

She was sitting there on the grass, bawling up a storm, holding Mr. Clarke's head in her lap. He looked pretty bad, with his mouth open, staring at me and Jake with his one fish eye. Also, he'd pooped and peed, and smelled even worse than he looked. I decided right then to make sure and use the toilet before I passed on. None of that seemed to make a difference to Mrs. Clarke, and she kept rocking his head until I was worried it might break off, like when you bend a piece of wire back and forth in one spot. When I thought of Mr. Clarke's head bent off his neck, I giggled. Mrs. Clarke must have thought I'd gone hysteric, because she told me to go back to the house and call Juris.

Nobody ever showed me how to use the phone. I guess because anyone I might have called was burnt up. And I didn't think it was a good time to ask Mrs. Clarke for any kind of instruction. So me and Jake lit out down the street, which was more like a road, me still not thinking clear. But moving was better than just sitting in the house looking at the phone, hoping it would ring Juris by its own self.

Once I got going, I got to thinking. I truly believe people's brains work better when their legs are moving. Anyhow, I never did think in a sensible way when I was sitting down or laying in bed at night. Those times I'd spin a tale in my head, and sometimes make myself scared, or even cry, but nothing of any practical use ever came about.

The Little Store, that's what folks called it, though I don't think that was the real name, was the closest place to the Clarkes. I started running right away, so I'd be out a breath when I got there. Then I'd yell, "Oh, my God! Oh, my God! No! No!" and they'd ask me what's wrong and I'd fall down on the floor and start bawling and say, "Mr. Clarke. Mr. Clarke. Oh, my God! Something's wrong with Mr. Clarke." And then someone would go see.

Everything went just like that, except I got to giggling, which was all right. They thought I was hysteric and gave me a bottle of Coca-Cola to settle me down. Then they took off and left me sitting there. At first I thought we were all alone so I went behind the counter where the candy was.

Jake got to tail-wagging and staring at something in the back of the store, which was where a bunch of folks played cribbage most of the time. Sitting there, still as could be, was an old woman. I'd seen her around. She lived by herself, cross from the Clarkes, and rode a bicycle with a basket on the handlebars. She was treated with regard, not like Juris, but you could tell she had a place in folks' eyes. Near as I could tell, she'd been in town forever. Anyone hadn't been born close by, never got to matter. Not that people were mean, they just didn't ask you over for coffee, and if you asked them, they'd be real polite about having something else they had to do. That used to make Mama cry.

The old woman gave me the shivers, the way she sat, all calm, watching me. I was glad Jake saw her before I took any candy. I got the feeling she could see inside my head, so I made like I was picking stickers out of Jake's feet. After a while she still hadn't moved or said anything and Jake was nosing my fingers away, telling me he'd had enough of my digging. When I looked up she was smiling, if you could call it that. Her head cocked to the side and one eyebrow jacked up. And her hair was all flyaway, like a dandelion flower that's gone to seed.

"So, you're April-May," she said. I nodded, thinking the less I talked the better. She wasn't a big talker either and it seemed like an hour before she said, "My name's Vivian."

I nodded again, remembering Daddy saying some old woman named Vivian owned half the town. Herited it, was what he said, and never had to work a spit. Then she stood up and I saw she wasn't much taller than a midget.

"You and your dog better come home with me. No one is coming back for you." I started to butt in, wanting to call her a liar, but she kept on, like she read my mind. "Folks are busy tending to the Clarkes. They won't think of you until later, and given your history, they won't know what to do with you."

"Well, Ma'am," I said, trying to sound snooty, like Daddy when he made fun of the women in first class, which had beds and toilets. "You have me stumped, since I don't know what history you're talking about."

That must have showed her because she sort of sucked her lips into her mouth and squinted her eyes at me for what seemed like a long time.

"You're flotsam," she said. Her voice was real soft. "You're a stray. People will put their leftovers out for you, thinking they're being kind. But they won't want you."

There was hardly anything in Vivian's house, just stacks of books. I'd never seen so many books in one place. Even school didn't have so many. Some of them were opened like she'd just been reading. There was a rocking chair right by the window and a pair of old lady glasses sitting on top of an empty apple crate that'd been turned bottom side up to make a table. Everything was real clean, like she must have scrubbed it every day, which if she read all those books, didn't seem like she'd have the time. Soon as we walked in the door, Jake started lifting his leg on the walls, squirting out yellow pee. Vivian followed him with her eyes, and when he finished all she said was, "So, Dog, are you home now?"

Waiting for Billy got to be more and more on my mind. Not that I especially enjoyed his company. But I did wonder what he had up his sleeve, not leaving me to burn up with the rest of them. When I thought about Mama and Daddy and Johnny, I could sort of understand how Billy got sick of them. The way they were, they really didn't amount to much. I couldn't even recollect what Johnny looked like, except he always had green snot coming out of his nose no matter what time of year it was. That, and he smelled bad, from some brown cream that came in a white jar. Mama said it was Resinal, but Billy called it monkey puke and made like he was gonna throw up whenever Johnny got within smelling range. Johnny wasn't much younger than Billy but when you stood them side by side, Johnny looked like a plate of leftovers that needed throwed away.

When Vivian wanted to tell me something hard she didn't put any polish on it. She'd say it straight out — to Jake, like going through him first would soften up whatever it was she had to say. "Dog," she'd say. She never did call him by his real name, and after a while he'd answer to Dog, same as to Jake.

"Dog," she said one day after we'd been there most of a month, "Mrs. Clarke doesn't want you living with her. I said you may as well stay with me."

I put my hands over my face and made like I was trying not to bawl. "She never wanted me and Jake. We were just a cross to her."

That made Vivian laugh, which she probably hadn't done more than a couple of times in her whole life.

We lived with Vivian near two years before we heard from Billy. That first year I didn't go to school. Truth is, I never did go to school after the fire, but I don't tell folks that, so they won't think I'm some kind of retard. How I happened not to go to school was, one morning Juris came to see Vivian, and after he left she sat me down and started talking to Jake.

"Dog," she said. "Mrs. Clarke says she'll quit teaching if they let you back in school."

"Mrs. Clarke says. Mrs. Clarke wants." I said this real mean, sort of under my breath. "I guess if Mrs. Clarke wanted all of you to jump off a cliff you'd do that too."

Right away I could see Vivian wasn't finished talking to Jake.

"I told you in the beginning, folks wouldn't know what to do with you. The less they see of you the easier they are with themselves."

I knew she was meaning me, not Jake.

"Well," I said, "I don't much care one way or the other."

All year long we ran around in the sage and scab rock that was behind Vivian's house. Sometimes we'd go down to the willows that grew thick beside the river and catch tadpoles. We'd bring them back in a jar and put them in a pail until they turned into frogs. I never got tired of watching how something that looked like a fish could end up being a frog.

There was an old rabbit hutch in her backyard that had been burnt some. "You may as well use it for a playhouse," Vivian said. "The rabbits aren't coming back."

Mama tried to leave once and Daddy put her head in the slop bucket and said she better never pull a stunt like that again.

"What happened to the rabbits?" I said.

She just shook her head and walked, sort of stiff like, back to the house. One thing we learned about Vivian. Once she made her mind up not to answer a question, no amount of asking would get a good result. And it wasn't until later we found out what happened to those rabbits.

It took me and Jake most of two days to clean and fix up the rabbit house. Vivian watched a bit then came out dragging a board she had stuck under her porch for some reason or other. After that she hauled out a saw and a hammer and a can of nails. We sawed and hammered until we had most of the burnt-out places covered up, which made Vivian smile and me and Jake took some enjoyment from that.

We went pretty near all over, which Vivian let us do. She said, "As long as you're back at a decent hour."

We got a kick out of her saying that. Since she never said what hour she was talking about, we were never late. And when we showed up looking like we'd rolled around in some fire pit — which was all that was left of my family's house — she never made a fuss.

Me and Jake went there and poked around. I never did find anything I remembered. Then one day we were partway there and got sidetracked by a bird, looked like a robin or something, flying around and squawking to beat the band. Jake got to nosing around in the weeds and turned up its baby. It was big enough to have some feathers, which was why it wasn't already dead. I figured it must have jumped out of the nest thinking it could fly. I spotted the nest way up in one of the elm trees that were all over town. The mama bird just kept on screeching and flying around. Me and Jake could see no good result — birds having no hands or arms — was gonna come of all her hollering. Seemed like she should have been watching closer in the first place, which not knowing about the way of birds, it's not my place to cast stones. I picked up the little bird, mindful not to squash it, and looked it square in the face. Its mouth was too big for its head, and it was opened real wide, which looked like it was yelling or hungry. The mama was still flying around, just not making so much noise. Jake was sitting in the dirt, waiting for me to make up my mind what to do with it. Being so little, it didn't amount to much. I could have throwed it away. Jake was pushing at my arm to pet him, which I did. Then real gentle we carried the bird back to Vivian. By the time we got there it was still warm but not moving.

Vivian looked real sad and said it was dead. That made Jake and me feel bad, not so much about the stupid bird but about making Vivian sad. She wrapped the bird in a piece of old shirt I'd outgrown, and we buried it, which made us feel some better. Jake did a couple of tricks, like roll over and shake hands, so Vivian would stop being sad. And I quit thinking so much about poking around the old house.

Vivian knew the names of all the stars, and at night we sat on the porch with her big star book, the one with all the pictures, and we'd look at them in the book and then find them in the sky. Some nights they seemed so close I figured if I was on a mountain, I could touch them. Vivian said it didn't matter how tall a mountain you climbed, the only way you could touch a star was in your mind. She talked like that. Mostly, I couldn't make heads or tails out of these conversations, but me and Jake liked the quiet way of her.

At the end of summer that second year we were with Vivian, it was hot as a pistol. Folks said that instead of hello. Jake and me stayed inside, and I was down to my underwear. We laid out on the kitchen linoleum, which was cool, and ate ice cubes Vivian made out of orange Kool-Aid. And that's where we were when somebody knocked at the front door, which wasn't usual. Most folks just stood on the porch and hollered out a couple of times to see if Vivian was home or not. Sometimes, if she didn't want company, she'd just not answer and no one thought much about it. But whoever was out there knocked again. Me and Jake could tell Vivian was thinking. We were used to her ways so it wasn't a surprise to see her get all red in the face when, whoever it was, started to pound with something heavy, like a rock. That seemed to settle it for her and she sort of stomped to the door, which tickled me and Jake, on account of her being no bigger than a dwarf. And then, right before she grabbed the knob she stopped, like she just thought of something. Then cool as a cucumber she opened the door.

There stood Billy. He'd gotten big, like Juris. Just seeing him made me near too scared to breathe. Jake went crazy, barking and growling.

"Where have you been?" was all Vivian said. Like she knew all along he wasn't dead, though I never told her, and she never asked.

I had hold of Jake. He kept growling and the hackles went up all along his back. The last time I saw him do that was when we'd cornered a rattlesnake and I was throwing rocks at it. Vivian motioned at Jake.

"Hush, Dog." She said it quiet and level-like.

Billy kind of leaned against the doorway, looking over top of Vivian. "Well, hello there, April-May. Ain't you glad to see me?"

"What do you want here, Billy?" Vivian was still talking quiet.

"I jus' come back to see April-May."

"Now you've seen her. Get off my porch."

Billy grinned and I could tell he was missing some teeth. "No, I think I'll jus' come in. Get myself out a the sun."

"You think you can waltz in here? After all you've done?"

He was starting to sidle closer, like he was gonna push Vivian out of the way, and her being not even half his size, she sure couldn't do much to stop him.

"Well, now, old woman, I don't know what you're talkin 'bout."

"I know what you did."

Billy made a sound in his throat, I think was supposed to be a laugh, though his eyes didn't look like they should if something was funny.

"Everyone knows you set the fires. You better get out of here."

Vivian was still sounding calm but I could see Billy's mouth go all slack and his eyes stopped blinking like a snake that's getting ready to do something.

"You burned my rabbits."

"Them was your rabbits? You should a been there. Yeh, I knowed them was your rabbits." Billy was starting to push past Vivian. "They sure did scream. Jumpin around. All lit up."

Mama called me funny bunny when she tucked me in at night. She was warm and soft and her hands smelled like Ivory soap.

Jake was getting hard to hold. He was near pulling me cross the floor, trying to get at Billy. Then I heard myself hollering, "You mean-eyed sumbitch! You tried to burn me up!"

And I remembered that night like I was still in it. The smoke, hanging on to Jake's neck, him pulling me outside, running with him to hide in the ditch.

"I should turn him loose on you! He'd rip your sumbitch throat out!" I was yelling so loud I wanted to cover my own ears.

"April-May! Hold Dog!" Vivian was shouting at me.

It brought me up short, and Jake too. Next thing I knew, quick as a cat, she had the shotgun she kept behind the door and was pointing it at Billy. Billy's jaw dropped, like he never expected the trouble he was into, and started backing away fast.

"You're trash, Billy," was all Vivian said, and pulled the trigger. It caught Billy in the neck, and face, and blew him clean off the porch.

I'd peed all over myself and Jake was licking my face. Vivian stuck the shotgun back behind the door.

"Well, there's an end to it then," she said so quiet I could barely hear.

I started to cry a bit, not being sorry about Billy, but thinking about those rabbits set on fire and not being able to run away.

SCOTT WOLVEN

St. Gabriel

FROM *Expletive Deleted*

THERE are violent hurricanes all the time, in my world.

Five men tried to kill my younger brother over some logging rights money, but he lived. By the time I got to the hospital in Spokane, he was sitting up and eating solid food. Recovering. He talked to me about what had happened to him. The five men set him up, to rip him off. They hadn't counted on his dog being so tough. He never went anywhere without his dog and she'd saved his life that night in the woods. She was dead. I got on the phone and the guys I knew in the Pacific Northwest and across Montana, guys who owed me favors, guys who sometimes paid me to move the index finger of my right hand less than an inch, depending on where the barrel was pointing — lots of eyes started to look for this group of five men. I took my brother home to Bozeman, to keep recovering.

The cost of pain and revenge finally dipped into a range I could afford. I got a late-night call, and when it was all said and done, there were Montana state police questions about five men and their sudden death with my name as the answer and the court decided my house should be made of concrete and steel for about eight years or more. That I should wear an orange jumpsuit. Very little proof let me get off light. Three of the men were shot from three football fields away, most likely the result of hunting accidents. Maybe bullets that overreached their animal mark and struck a human. The other two were shot at distances that were deemed impossible by the court forensic expert. No bullet could be accurate, at that range. That's what the forensic expert said. I went to the private prison in Shelby and made my way to Deer Lodge, like everybody in Montana held accountable for their actions. I read the Bible, the most violent story I've ever known — an eye for an eye — and walked the yard when I could. I left when they told me to leave. It had all become one long night to me and that didn't change when I got out. Things didn't seem real to me anymore. My brother met me at my release, eight years and he was doing well, and after a month, we started to talk about money and work and the aspects of the normal world that needed to be attended to.

My brother and I delivered a load of big timber to Lethbridge and a trucker up there put us on to it.

"Biggest storm ever," he said. "Going to wreck the whole Gulf Coast. Hurricanes, the real shit. Lots of work for loggers with their own gear. Big money in the cleanup. You boys headed south?"

My brother nodded. "We are now," he said.

When we got back into Montana, we stopped in a bar in Bozeman and watched the storm develop on the bar TV. Sat drinking and watching those hurricanes sow the seeds of the future for everybody in the Gulf. People abandoning their homes, running to stay alive. For some of those folks, the wind and water would change everything. They'd move, they'd live a life in a part of the country they didn't know existed, or that they hated. They'd be buried in cemeteries that didn't have any stones with their last name already on them, far away from family. The whisper from a voice can make a train jump the rail. And this was a lot more than a whisper. The endless piles of torn trees were sacks of dollars, to me and my brother.

We drove back to our woodlot and rented house and started sharpening saws and collecting equipment into the big pickup truck.

"Do you want to say goodbye to your girl?" my brother asked.

"Not really," I said. I'd been seeing a girl in town for three or four months.

"Okay," he said.

I stood next to the truck. "I don't have anything to say."

"Sure," he nodded.

We packed some guns too, the rifle and ammo, all in the lock box. Just in case trouble knocked and we wanted to knock back. The drive took us through Nevada and Texas. We stopped and drank with a couple of my brother's friends. Driving into east Texas, the disaster started to show and by the time we hit the Louisiana line, it looked like God had been pretty mad that day. Houses torn from foundations, boats in the streets, abandoned cars everywhere, no power, no sewer, no drinking water. We got some papers that allowed us to work, through a connection of my brother's, and we stayed in New Orleans — signed on to cut trees around high voltage at four hundred and fifty a day each, plus food and lodging. Anything we made on the side belonged to us and it was cash paid at the end of each day. It was tragedy for those folks, but it was a license to print money for the contractors. The whole city smelled, when we first got there. I thought of Sodom. And other things.

St. Gabriel only appears four times in the Bible. Some scholars of God say St. Gabriel is an archangel, on the same plane as Michael, and deals in vengeance and death. St. Gabriel is credited with having destroyed Sodom. Others say St. Gabriel is the angel of mercy, one of God's highest, maybe the highest, messenger. I don't claim to know. Somewhere it says that St. Gabriel never really appeared, that all references to St. Gabriel are actually dreams that God had and St. Gabriel is mercy come to life through God's dreams and that mercy isn't what we understand it to be. Dying can be a privilege, I came to understand that in prison, as much as living can be its own gift. Mercy can be flowers, or making sure your aim is true. Dreams die hard. I know mine did. I don't imagine God's died any differently. Maybe St. Gabriel will appear again sometime.

I met her and it was like meeting life for the first time. She opened the eyes of my heart. In any other city she'd have been a model, not a dancer.

After, I asked her if she wanted me to go get some cigarettes. So she could smoke and go to sleep.

"Yeah," she said. "That would be nice." She smiled in the dark, hugging the pillow. She was all curves and so alive. Beyond beautiful. A for-real woman. We had talked for hours before this, about everything. She was without a doubt the most beautiful woman I'd ever seen. Inside and out. Her voice wasn't that sweet sickly Southern crap — she was Cajun, spoke her mind and had a good laugh. She lived like she meant it.

I put on jeans, a shirt, and my light jacket and walked out into the New Orleans night. The fog was there, the storms had just ended. Crushed cars sat on Canal Street, but on Bourbon it was business as usual. I bought the cigarettes and a lighter and headed back.

She was gone when I got back to the room. No note, nothing. The sheets were still warm from her body, the pillow smelled of her. And I tried to take it like a good thing, that maybe she felt like I did and the possibility of getting closer was much more frightening than she could say. Or that she had a man to get home to and leaving was polite — my karma had come back on me from Montana and I put the cigarettes in a drawer with the lighter.

The mess from the destruction went on and on. My brother and I burned through chains and gas and oil. We'd go out and check downed lines or move them with hot-line tools. Then we'd start cutting, so the scoops and chippers could come along and take care of what we left. When the humidity rose, my shirt was wet all day. The sawdust bounced off my safety glasses. We were cutting hundreds of years of growth. It was all the same to us.

She was at the room when I got back that one day. She was a little drunk, high. She had on a red top and jeans over those long legs. That didn't last. We fucked like champs and kept going. Beyond where we'd been before. She made my cock so hard it hurt and my mouth ached from being on her, everywhere. Hours. We smoked and talked in bed. Drank some beer. She was having problems in town, within the city. The cops were harassing her, her ex was harassing her. The guy she lived with turned out to be friends with dealers. The cops were watching her. They wanted to kill her, as revenge on her man. And she wanted to leave. She had children, two young boys, and wanted to give them a better life and she wanted a better life for herself. We came up with a plan that fit the hurricane. We made a hurricane of our own.

There is a town in Louisiana called St. Gabriel. It's a new town, only been around a couple years. After the hurricane, it was the morgue for all of New Orleans. The women's prison is in St. Gabriel too, they hold all the security classifications together under one roof. Women from Sodom, you might say, kicked out of New Orleans for their crimes. I doubt that anyone at the prison even knows who St. Gabriel is or was supposed to be. And the number of dreams that have died within those walls, countless thousands, even dying now. It could make your soul cry, if you were a sentimental person.

My brother didn't show two mornings later and when he hadn't come around in the afternoon, I went looking. He wasn't at the bar we hung out at. I finally walked over to the police station about two in the afternoon and talked to them. They had grabbed him, thinking he was me.

"Who are you again?" the black cop behind the bulletproof glass asked me. He had the NOPD fatigues on and his gun sat smart at his right side.

"I'm his brother," I said. "I'd like to see him."

"We'd all like things," the cop said.

"Can I see him?"

The cop studied the sheet in front of him. "Lots of charges here," he said. People went in and out of the station house with a dazed look.

"What's the bail?"

"No bail," he said. "Just charges."

"What charges?"

He shook his head. "Felonies." Then he went and got the detectives.

They took us in a cop car and another unmarked car out to St. Gabriel prison. Nobody spoke on the way out. We drove around the facility and pulled up in a parking lot, near the edge of some trees. They had my brother cuffed. We walked out through the mud, until we could see something on the ground in front of us at the very edge of the woods, covered with some dirt and leaves. Half in the woods. It was a woman. In a red top and jeans. A large-caliber shell had passed through her rib cage.

"Do you know her?" the cop asked. The detectives stood back, watching us.

"Not really," I said. It looked like her, but not if you knew her. Up close, like I did.

"She's been shot at long range. We think she was trying to escape and during the hurricane, someone had it in for her and shot her." He shrugged. "Or something."

"That's a good theory," I agreed.

"You wouldn't happen to know any boys from Montana, that have a reputation as long-shot artists, would you?" he asked with a New Orleans slow drawl.

"No," I said. "I honestly don't."

"That's funny," the one cop said. "Because after we ran your sheet and came up with some facts, we kind of thought it might have been you that pulled the trigger."

"I've never shot a woman," I said in truth.

"People change," the other cop said.

"Not that much," I said.

"We were looking for this woman, in New Orleans," the one cop said. "We were watching you."

"She was here," I said, pointing at the ground.

"You know," the one cop said, "during the hurricane, some bad folks in New Orleans disappeared."

"Must have got caught up in the storm," I reasoned.

"Certainly," the other cop said. "That stuff happens."

"This woman here," the one cop said. "This woman got caught by someone else."

"I don't know anything about it," I said. "I don't know why you have us out here."

The head detective walked over to the corpse and kicked it in the head as hard as he could. He watched me. "I've got y'all out here," he said, "because we think you were together and you're a killer. We have established that. What we haven't established is who this woman is. She was just printed the other day and that got destroyed in the storm. If she's the woman from the prison. On the other hand, if she's this woman we were looking for from New Orleans, the one hooked up with that dealer, then we can call that off, because we'd have done this to her anyways." He drew his foot back and kicked the head of the corpse again as hard as he could. The whole body moved off the ground a foot. "So which is it?"

"I know who it is," I lied. "I know her."

"Why'd you kill her?" the detective asked. "Did she owe you money? Drugs?"

"I didn't," I said.

He kicked the corpse right in the mouth and watched my face the whole time as he did it. "Does that bother you?" he asked. "I'm kicking your girl here." He stared at me. "Play tough guy like it doesn't bother you, but I'm going to kick her again."

"She's not feeling it," I said.

He brought his foot back and kicked the head of the corpse three or four times, hard. The sound was a loud wet smack. The body moved up and down. Mud and fluid mixed on his shoes and the gray cuff of his pants.

"This isn't the man we want," the detective said to the other cops. He motioned at my brother. "Uncuff him and let's go." He walked back through the mud to the unmarked car. I was walking behind him for a couple steps. He turned to me, his face white and puffy. "If that's her, and I think it is, you did us a favor." He kept on walking, toward the cars, alone.

One of the cops came forward with keys and uncuffed my brother. The cops walked back to their car and drove off, leaving me and my brother standing there outside the facility. After we walked for half an hour, we hitched a ride with a guy, back into New Orleans.

The hurricane raged through the night and day. An older man in southern Louisiana woke up with a straight razor under his bed, with a pink ribbon on it, like someone might use for a little girl's hair. His wife found her gas tank had been filled with pig's blood. A young man in New Orleans who lived with his dad found the locks to the house glued. A guy from Illinois, a DJ, woke up with his shit in the street, and broken ribs. There was mercy all along, no revenge, no vengeance. That's how you know a human did these things and not God. If it was God that had done them, the answer would all be the same. Death, death, death.

The work ended and we drove back to Montana. We hadn't made millions.

I ask myself that now, am I St. Gabriel? Is the mercy that I once had long gone and who will show mercy on me? What a privilege it will be to die. We create ourselves, or so we believe, and we become locked in, we become afraid not to meet the same person each morning in the mirror. I am St. Gabriel and I will stand accountable for what I do and will hold others to account. I am the highest of God's messengers and no Sodom will stand while I live.

Nobody asks a man why he drinks. Mixed in there with the private darkness of reasons, nobody wants to know the answer from the man who is already drunk. I was drinking to get a woman to come back to me, which is the worst reason of all. The cost of pain. When you see someone so bright, such a bright fire, a diamond, it stays with you and their image is on the inside of your eyelids when you close your eyes. I can still see her, she lights up the night of life. Who wouldn't want her back? Her smile alone could cure you of whatever disease had got hold of you. Oceans of booze couldn't put out that fire.

My brother saw her one time, in a bar, on TV, modeling in Milan. I was covered with sawdust and staggered in. "She's coming," he said. "She'll be in the next clip."

I stared at the screen as it changed. It was her. She walked like a princess and a queen all at once, she fucking owned that crowd and that show and I had to look away. I was proud, so proud of her and all she had done and there was a plan that had worked.

My brother knows better than to ever ask. You don't ask about stuff, because then you can't talk about it on the stand. He asked with his eyes, one night, late. We were standing in the cellar, throwing darts and doing laundry.

"Sure," I said. "Part of it was me. And part of it was her."

"It worked," he said.

"It got her a new life," I said. "She deserved that and more."

"Do you think she misses you?" he asked.

"Not in the way you might think," I said. "Like you might miss an old dog."

"You might be wrong," he said. "I miss my dog every day." He took his shirt off to put it in the wash and even his scars were healing from his trauma. His tattoos always looked amazing. He pulled a clean T-shirt over his head from the dryer.

I drank some beer.

"I really think you're wrong," he said. "She's going to come here and be with you."

"Fuck," I said. "I don't want to be with me most days. What would make her want to be with me?"

"Who else would protect her like that?" he asked.

I nodded. "But I would protect her like that and she doesn't have to be around. I'd do it anyway."

"Does she know you feel like this?"

I shook my head. "Look," I said. "I really don't want to get into all this. Somebody who has kids and is living a life, they don't need crap dumped on them. I can handle whatever I feel, regardless of the situation." I drank my beer. "What does it matter what I feel? I'm a grown man."

"What about being happy?" he asked.

"What's that got to do with anything?"

"Are you happy?" he asked. "Without her."

I drank some more beer. "I'm a big boy," I said. "I'm happy for her. That's all that matters." I shook my head again. "She's under enough strain without me being an asshole."

We threw some more darts and I walked upstairs and went to bed. It has been five years and she hasn't shown up. She won't. At first it was hard, but now it's the same. Sometimes, when I'm in a crowd, if we go to Spokane or all the way to Seattle, my eyes hurt and I have a headache. Because I've been looking for her, all day, among the faces. After an eighteen-hour day of cutting and hauling big timber, even the work can't erase her from my mind. Thinking of her keeps me alive some days. Some people would call that sad. They don't know what I'm talking about. I'm lucky.

When I wake up, I am someplace else in my mind. But she is always there. And I'm happy for her. She died the fake death and will get to live the real life. I will wake up in my coffin underground and be comforted. I'll wait for the hurricane to uproot me from my eternal rest and carry me off. To meet St. Gabriel, to whom I will show no mercy. Even if I am in hell, my aim will be true. Gravity pulls the bullet toward earth. There is friction, recoil energy, computed velocity, measured velocity, free-bore travel, resistance, ratio of powder charge. None of it will stop me, it didn't stop me those nights in Montana when I had those five men in my sights and breathed easy and slowly increased the pressure on my finger until that hammer dropped. The cops of heaven can puzzle over the how and why and look for witnesses that don't exist. Maybe she is my St. Gabriel, appearing briefly and now only in my dreams. At least one of us made it out of the night.

If it weren't for her being alive in the world, I'd turn the gun on myself. Show myself the mercy I deserve. The chance to hear her voice keeps me on earth.

Contributors' Notes
Other Distinguished Mystery Stories of 2007

Contributors' Notes

James Lee Burke was born in 1936 in Houston, Texas, and grew up on the Louisiana-Texas coast. He attended Southwestern Louisiana Institute (now called the University of Louisiana at Lafayette) and later the University of Missouri at Columbia, where he received a B.A. and an M.A. in English literature.

Over the years he has published twenty-six novels and two short-story collections. The stories have appeared in the *Atlantic Monthly, The Best American Short Stories, New Stories from the South,* the *Southern Review,* the *Antioch Review,* and the *Kenyon Review.* His novels *Heaven's Prisoners* and *Two for Texas* were adapted as motion pictures.

Burke's work has received two Edgar Awards for best novel of the year. He is also a Breadloaf fellow and a Guggenheim fellow and has been the recipient of an NEA grant. He and his wife of forty-eight years, Pearl Burke, have four children and divide their time between Missoula, Montana, and New Iberia, Louisiana.

▪ I wrote two short stories in the wake of Hurricane Katrina. The first was titled "Jesus Out to Sea." It dealt with events leading up to the storm and the catastrophe that occurred when the levees broke. Later, I began an account of the evacuees who had fled the Lower Ninth Ward and had ended up in places like my family's hometown, New Iberia, two hours west of New Orleans. But as I worked on the second narrative, I believed that it should deal with more than the storm itself.

In one day, six soldiers from a local National Guard outfit were killed in Iraq. I had come to believe that the events in New Orleans and the events in Iraq were related, part of the same piece, involving the same players. The politicians who were not in New Orleans while their countrymen drowned were the same ones who had taken their country to war in the

Middle East. In my opinion, the victims of the breached levees were in many ways similar to the victims of the war. The protagonist in "Mist" is made a victim twice and finds herself carrying a burden that no human being should have to bear. I believe that Golgotha is an ongoing story, and I believe it is daily acted out somewhere in the world, whether in a desert or in neighborhoods that were largely Afro-American before they went under the waves.

In the story, New Orleans became a pewter chalice filled with dark water and the luminosity of broken Communion wafers that represent those who are broken and rejected by the world. I think that what occurred in New Orleans will remain the greatest shame and scandal in our history. And that's what I tried to convey in "Mist."

Michael Connelly is the author of nineteen novels, many featuring Detective Harry Bosch, and one collection of true crime stories. He is a past president of the Mystery Writers of America. He lives in Florida with his family.

▪ Like probably anybody in the game I am a big fan of the film *Double Indemnity.* I have watched it several times and always wanted to write a story that might have a bit of the same twist. Having lived in L.A. for fourteen years, I was also familiar with Mulholland Drive and its almost mythical lore in the city. I lived nearby it most of my years there and on many occasions came around a curve at night and encountered a coyote in my headlights. If L.A. is a place where anything can happen, then Mulholland Drive is certainly a road that it can happen on. I tried to take these interests and elements and put them into this story about an accident investigator.

Robert Ferrigno played poker professionally before an eight-year stint as a feature writer at the *Orange County Register.* Ten novels later, he plays poker only to clear his head, usually at the Indian casino twenty-three minutes away. His writing has gotten better over the years, but his poker skills have atrophied. Most days it seems like a good tradeoff.

▪ "The Hour When the Ship Comes In" was one of those beautiful writing experiences where I just tapped into the character's consciousness and let my fingers do the walking. It's about a bad man who does an inexplicable good deed and pays the price for it, spending the arc of the story trying to understand why he would have done such a foolish thing. The story contains the distillation of all my moral thinking: it's the little kindnesses that kill us, but what else can we do and still stay human?

Chuck Hogan's crime novels include *The Standoff; The Killing Moon; Prince of Thieves,* which was awarded the Hammett Prize; and the forthcoming *Sugar Bandits.* "One Good One" was his first published short story.

▪ Like many writers, I have files crammed with newspaper clippings, magazine articles, and story ideas — stuff from all over. The oldest clipping is dated November 12, 1984, an article from the *Boston Globe* on the new phenomenon of serial killers, entitled: "They're 'Intelligent' and 'Pleasant' . . . and They Kill for the 'Fun' of It." Entire paragraphs are underscored with red pen. I was seventeen years old. My parents were concerned.

These things pile up over the years, and I use them in my novels when I can. After I met Ed Hoch, the prolific short-story author, at an award luncheon in 2005, it occurred to me that the short format would be a great way to explore these scraps and notions which otherwise might not find their way to print. "One Good One" sprang from an index card (dated 10/13/05, 1:00 P.M. — yes, I time-code them) on which I scribbled this idea for a novel:

Drug user/dealer who tells his mother he's a UC (lie). She mentions to wrong people — his cohorts. Also to cops looking for him. Both sides come after him. Cops play along w/ ruse to further pressure him. Real UC cop is revealed (Main's dealer/friend?); i.e., when heat comes, he thinks it's b/c of him? Crazy Get Shorty*–type tale.*

I initially saw it bigger, bringing in the main character's innocent family (*UC* being shorthand for "under cover") and other interesting lowlifes, and putting everybody in great jeopardy — all this chaos springing from one indolent loser's mendacity. It felt like the setup for an Elmore Leonard novel, which was what I liked about it. The short story included here, of course, has none of that promised craziness, none of the patented Leonard zing. It's a different animal entirely. But what I like about it now, reading it one year later, is that each character has a simple and reasonable motivation for his or her action, and it is the overlapping progression of these actions that drives the story. Each section folds neatly into the next, until what you're left with in the end is a little piece of origami in the shape of a coffin.

Ed Hoch passed away the day before I learned of this story's selection for inclusion in this anthology, and I would be remiss in not tipping my cap, however humbly, from the author of one short story to the author of nearly one thousand.

Rupert Holmes has twice won the Edgar Award from the Mystery Writers of America, as well as several Tony and Drama Desk awards as a playwright, lyricist, and composer. In 2008 his Broadway mystery musical comedy *Curtains* celebrated its first anniversary on the Great White Way. He also created and wrote the television series *Remember WENN*. He is the author of the mystery novels *Where the Truth Lies* (made into a motion picture by Atom Egoyan), *Swing*, and the forthcoming *The McMasters Guide to Homicide*.

▪ It's difficult to say much about "The Monks of the Abbey Victoria" without spoiling its outcome for the reader. However, I can certainly disclose how much I enjoy re-creating other times in America, some of which I witnessed wide-eyed as a boy, others of which I try to reconstruct via immensely pleasurable research. With "Monks," I drop in on the television industry circa 1960, in that "gray flannel Brooks Brothers three-martooni *Executive Coloring Book* THINK let's run it up the flagpole" era of uneasy camaraderie and unbridled chauvinism. It's a time whose time has gone, which is probably a very good thing, but you can visit it in total comfort and safety simply by turning a few pages of this volume. This story was also inspired by — if in no way patterned after — the Gamesmen, a group of extremely honorable and memorable fellows who've allowed me into their midst, and whose activities bear no resemblance to those practiced by the Monks of the Abbey Victoria.

Holly Goddard Jones was a 2007 recipient of the Rona Jaffe Writers' Award. Her fiction has appeared in the *Kenyon Review,* the *Southern Review,* the *Gettysburg Review,* the *Hudson Review,* and *Epoch* and has been reprinted in two volumes of *New Stories from the South.* A graduate of the M.F.A. program in creative writing at Ohio State University, she now teaches at Murray State University, in her home state of Kentucky.

▪ "Proof of God" was initially inspired by a crime that took place several years ago on a college campus near my hometown in Kentucky, though of course I've altered events so much that I have to remind myself now where the real horror leaves off and my fictionalized version begins. I recall that I was so haunted and disturbed by what happened to the young woman upon whom Felicia is loosely based that I couldn't get her out of my mind, and I knew that I had to try to write myself toward an understanding, or at least an acceptance, of the crime. So I did write about it, and my first attempt was a story called "Parts" (the *Hudson Review*), told from the perspective of the dead girl's mother. My writing professor at the time, Lee K. Abbott, mentioned in an offhand way to me that the hardest story to tell is the bad guy's, and so I decided, okay: I'd accept the challenge. Getting into Simon's head — making him on some level sympathetic — was one of the hardest things I've done as a writer. I want to thank Lee for encouraging me to try it and for believing, more than I did, that I'd be able to pull it off.

Peter LaSalle is the author of a novel, *Strange Sunlight,* and three short-story collections, most recently *Tell Borges If You See Him: Tales of Contemporary Somnambulism.* His fiction has appeared in many magazines and anthologies, including *The Best American Short Stories* and *Prize Stories: The O. Henry Awards,* and in 2005 he received the Award for Distinguished Prose from the *Antioch Review.* He currently divides his time between Austin, Texas, and Narragansett in his native Rhode Island.

▪ Well, to be honest, I'm always hesitant about offering outright explanatory comment on a story. I guess I'm dead scared of undermining the fragile magic that a writer has to hope for in any narrative. But I am willing — and happy — to note that the setting of "Tunis and Time" stemmed from an ongoing project I've embarked on in recent years — writing essays for literary magazines about going on trips to places where literature I love is set, as I try to see if anything different happens while reading the work "on the premises," so to speak. I've packed a bag and headed off to reread Borges's stories in Argentina; and the twin essential documents of French surrealism — Louis Aragon's *Paris Peasant* and André Breton's *Nadja* — in Paris; and Flaubert's *Salammbô,* a novel about ancient Carthage, in Tunisia. The last of these excursions, of course, is almost exactly what I have my melancholy, Harvard-educated ex–FBI agent, Layton, use as a cover while on assignment there in this story. When I was in Tunis in mid-2003, it wasn't long after the unfortunate U.S. invasion of Iraq, and believe me, in the train stations and in the cafés, wherever people talked, political matters were certainly in the air, as would be expected in an Arab World country at a time like that. I do hope such edginess comes through here, along with the sheer, undeniable beauty of that wonderful city and environs, a place of so much startling history. As for the created character of Layton himself, immersed in both soul-searching and labyrinthine international intrigue, I'll spare explanatory comment entirely and simply let the man lead his own life somewhat in the shadows — the way anybody in his line of risky work, for better or worse, maybe should.

Kyle Minor is the author of *In the Devil's Territory,* the collection of stories and novellas in which "A Day Meant to Do Less" appears, and coeditor (with Okla Elliott) of *The Other Chekhov,* a selection of Anton Chekhov's lesser-known and more lurid stories. His work has appeared in the *Gettysburg Review,* the *Southern Review, Surreal South,* and Random House's *Twentysomething Essays by Twentysomething Writers.* He is at work on a novel, a graphic novel, and a screenplay and corresponds with readers at http://www.myspace.com/kyleminor.

▪ "A Day Meant to Do Less" owes a few things to writers I admire, among them Katherine Anne Porter, Christopher Coake, and Donald Ray Pollock. I wanted to explore a consciousness altered by illness, as Porter does in "Pale Horse, Pale Rider," and I wanted to play with structure and point of view as Coake does in almost all his stories, and I wanted to give breath and dignity to a kind of character I know in life but rarely find in literature, which is what I've learned from Pollock. I'm grateful to those who read sketchy early drafts and encouraged me to continue, among them Debbie Oesch-Minor, Joe Oestreich, Doug Watson, Bart Skarzynski, Maureen Traverse, and most of all Lee Abbott, and to Mark Drew, Peter Sitt, and Kim Dana Kupperman at the *Gettysburg Review*, for giving my story a good home.

Alice Munro grew up in Wingham, Ontario, and attended the University of Western Ontario. She has published eleven new collections of stories — *Dance of the Happy Shades; Something I've Been Meaning to Tell You; The Beggar Maid; The Moons of Jupiter; The Progress of Love; Friend of My Youth; Open Secrets; The Love of a Good Woman; Hateship, Friendship, Courtship, Loveship, Marriage; Runaway; The View from Castle Rock;* and a volume of *Selected Stories* — as well as a novel, *Lives of Girls and Women*. During her distinguished career she has been the recipient of many awards and prizes, including three of Canada's Governor General's Literary Awards and two of its Giller Prizes, the Rea Award for the Short Story, the Lannan Literary Award, England's W. H. Smith Book Award, the United States' National Book Critics Circle Award, and the Edward MacDowell Medal in literature. Her stories have appeared in the *New Yorker*, the *Atlantic Monthly*, the *Paris Review*, and other publications, and her collections have been translated into thirteen languages. Alice Munro divides her time between Clinton, Ontario, near Lake Huron, and Comox, British Columbia.

▪ The story grew out of my memories of summer camp, and the almost casual yet ritualistic brutality of children. An irresistible, terrible act, to be carried through life by two decent, normal women. How *do* they manage it? Two mysteries, really: Why do they do it? And how do they live with it?

Thisbe Nissen is the author of the novels *Osprey Island* and *The Good People of New York* and the story collection *Out of the Girls' Room and into the Night*. She's also the coauthor/illustrator of *The Ex-Boyfriend Cookbook*. A graduate of Oberlin College and of the Iowa Writers' Workshop, she's taught in the M.F.A. programs at Iowa and Columbia, at numerous conferences including Eckerd College's Writers in Paradise, and is currently the Fannie Hurst Writer-in-Residence at Brandeis University. She's at work on a novel, *The Screen Doors of Discretion*, and a story collection, *How Other People Make Love*, in which "Win's Girl" will appear.

▪ I wrote "Win's Girl" out of a desperate yearning for some sort of revenge against the electrician who (ostensibly) rewired my house when I was a brand-new first-time homeowner. He told me practically every one of the stories Rich Randall tells Doreen and then, five thousand dollars later, disappeared. Feeling like a moron, I thought of something my mother always says when my life isn't going the way I'd like it to and I'm heartbroken or otherwise miserable. She says, "Thiz, you'll write this. You'll write this." It doesn't usually make me feel much better, but this time I thought:

I'll write this. I'll show you, you mean nasty electrician. And so it is with no small amount of smirking, gloating self-satisfaction that I express my honor and thrill at seeing "Win's Girl" included in this anthology. I revel in my tiny vindication!

Joyce Carol Oates is a winner and six-time nominee of the National Book Award and has thirty-five books selected as a Notable Book of the Year by the *New York Times.* Among her most recent books are *The Gravedigger's Daughter* and the first volume of her *Journals,* both nominated for the National Book Critics Circle Award.

▪ "The Blind Man's Sighted Daughters" is a nightmare mix of memory, invention, and that air of haunting mystery we feel in hearing of a small-town crime that has never been "solved" — though clearly individuals associated with the crime, survivors and perpetrators and their families, have a very good idea what the solution should have been, if local police had been capable of discovering it. Specifically, the genesis of the story sprang to mind during a trip — by car, our usual mode of travel to upstate New York — when we were staying overnight in a small town near the Mohawk River. Vividly it came to me: what is life like, for the unmarried sister who stays behind in one of these forlorn upstate cities, now a caretaker for her once-murderous father, who has become an ailing blind man? What does she feel for the married sister who moved away, and who lives a very different life? It seemed to me that both sisters, in complicity with their once-murderous father, have been involved in criminal acts that will never be defined or resolved. The caretaker sister has in effect sacrificed her own life and is her father's most unwitting victim.

Nathan Oates's stories have appeared in the *Antioch Review, Juked, Mississippi Review, Fugue,* the *Louisville Review,* and elsewhere. He earned his M.A. from the Writing Seminars at the Johns Hopkins University and his Ph.D. from the University of Missouri. He is an assistant professor at Seton Hall University and lives in New York with his wife, the writer Amy Day Wilkinson, and their daughter, Sylvie.

▪ As is true of much of my work, "The Empty House" developed out of a story my father heard while traveling abroad. I knew immediately I wanted to write this story, but I wasn't sure how to do so. At first I thought maybe it was the start of a novel, then imagined it to be the first in a linked collection, and over the course of a year I wrote subsequent chapters, then stories that connected, but it never felt right. My attempts were either too slight for the subject, or so bloated that the narrative energy was diffused. Through these failures, I figured out it was a short story, but how to make it feel complete remained a problem. I'd traveled twice to Guatemala in my early twenties and one night in a bar in Paris a Swedish woman told me that, for her, Central America was like Disneyland: exotic little people running around in bright clothes. I was appalled, but of course I'd also been just a tourist, sitting in a bar full of Americans, with my camera and cash. Ever since I've been trying to write about my interest in Guatemala, particularly about America's complicated role in the decades of civil war. When I began writing the narrator's contemporary line I saw that "The Empty House" is about what happens to Ryan and the way that mystery, and the emptiness surrounding it, affects those who are left behind. From there it was only a matter of years of revision, of swelling and shrinking the story until it found the right shape. I'd like to thank the following people for their support: my parents, my brothers, Robert Fogarty, and, of course, Amy.

Jas. R. Petrin was born in Saskatchewan in 1947. He began his working life as a busboy, a tailor shop gofer, a truck driver, and once, briefly, "a guy in a bakery who poked the stones out of cherries with a pair of giant tweezers." He went on to become a sheet-metal worker, then spent many years as a musician in various lounge acts and traveling bands before settling in as a telephone network job engineer and planner. Throughout much of this time he flirted with writing. In 1985 he sold a story to *Alfred Hitchcock's Mystery Magazine* and has placed some sixty stories in those pages since then. He has won the Canadian Arthur Ellis Award and his work appears in many anthologies. His story "Mama's Boys" was produced as a TV drama. He now lives in Mavillette, Nova Scotia, with his wife, Colleen, and is hard at work on a novel featuring Leo Skorzeny.

▪ When I thought up the aging moneylender Leo (Skig) Skorzeny, I worked hard, as a writer will, to imbue him with a credible nature. Not a sympathetic nature, especially, just a credible one. I wonder now if I overdid it. I say this because I'm alarmed at the number of people who tell me they have come to like him. *I* like him, but that's permissible. A writer must empathize with his or her characters, or at the very least gull those characters into believing as much, or they may refuse to cooperate, become wooden and unresponsive and lurch around the pages like zombies. But Skig is not a nice guy. He doesn't play well with others. In his first appearance ("Juice," *Alfred Hitchcock's Mystery Magazine*) he commits a grave breach of social etiquette which he carries with him throughout his subsequent escapades. He is capable of warm feelings, but to him regret and remorse are something weaker people are afflicted with. Skig's world, the world he has always known, bristles with treachery, deceit, and violence.

As a reader I find a well-crafted tale akin to visiting the zoo. Here are all these creatures, some of them vicious, going about their day just beyond that sheet of safety glass. As a writer I like to show people my own collection of dangerous creatures. I thank Eleanor Sullivan, Cathleen Jordan, and Linda Landrigan for making it possible for almost twenty-five years. I thank Otto Penzler and George Pelecanos for this fresh and unique (to me) opportunity.

Scott Phillips lives in Missouri, after stays in Paris and Los Angeles and Wichita, where he was born. He is the author of three novels: *The Ice Harvest, The Walkaway,* and *Cottonwood.*

▪ "The Emerson, 1950" started life as a series of unconnected vignettes that were intended to form the backbone of a novel about a newspaper crime photographer/smutmonger in postwar Wichita. The novel never quite came together, but I was sufficiently fond of the characters and incidents that I tore the book apart by the spine and put them into this story. (The business with the candlesticks is very loosely based on something that happened after my great-great-uncle Fred died in Wichita in 1965.)

Stephen Rhodes is the pen name for Keith Styrcula, a novelist and fourteen-year derivatives executive on Wall Street. A 1991 graduate of Fordham Law School, he is the author of two suspense thrillers, including the critically acclaimed financial doomsday thriller *The Velocity of Money* (William Morrow and Avon Books), which was translated into four languages (http://www.thevelocityofmoney.com). "At the Top of His Game" is an excerpt from his forthcoming thriller of the same name. He lives in Westport, Connecticut.

▪ The inspiration for "At the Top of His Game" was a career-long observation that the big gears of the Wall Street machine are engineered to enrich the morally corrupt while destroying the good-hearted — which is not to say that the good-hearted ever escape their dog years on the Street with a soul unscathed. Mark Barston is emblematic of this premise, and the seeming disintegration of his entire world over the course of a single weekend reflects the perils of a life devoted to high finance and its glistening, seductive suburbanite trappings. The core elements of "Game" are based on true events — accordingly, the first draft came quickly: just over ten days. Soon thereafter, though, a positive critique from *Esquire*'s fiction editor, Adrienne Miller, sent me tearing through several drafts over the course of the next year, working to create the pitch-perfect final version. The elusive ambition for me was to create a work of short fiction that was as satisfying as William Hauptman's classic "Good Rockin' Tonight" (published in *The Best American Short Stories 1982*), a story about an insurance-salesman-turned-Elvis-impersonator immediately following the King's untimely death. (Hauptman's story was jam-packed with enough plot, characters, and narrative to be the basis for a full book, yet it instead achieved its brilliant results in *one-twentieth* the length of a novel — a shining example of the magnificence of the short-story form.) Eventually, the breakthrough for "Game" was the privilege of working with *Wall Street Noir* editor Peter Spiegelman (*Black Maps*), who preserved Barston's voice while perfecting the pace of the narrative and the convergence of plot twists that become his final redemption — well, *kind of* a redemption, sort of . . .

S. J. Rozan, a lifelong New Yorker, has won many major crime-writing awards, including the Edgar, Shamus, and Anthony. She's served on the national boards of Mystery Writers of America and Sisters in Crime, and as president of Private Eye Writers of America. In 2003 S. J. was a speaker at the World Economic Forum in Davos, Switzerland, and in 2005 she was guest of honor at Left Coast Crime in El Paso, Texas.

▪ When I wrote "Hothouse" I was aiming for old-school noir, a story in which a character's earlier life reaches out and stops him from becoming the new person he wants to be. To echo that contrast, I wanted to work with the extreme contrasts of the conservatory in winter: the warm jungle damp, the smells and stillness inside, and the frigid, biting, roaring blizzard outside. And I had just gotten back from three weeks at an artists' colony in Florida and I was pining for my cottage in the palms.

Hugh Sheehy's short fiction has appeared in the *Kenyon Review,* the *Antioch Review,* the *Southwest Review,* the *New Orleans Review,* and other magazines. He lives in Atlanta and teaches at Georgia State University.

▪ I hope it will amuse and excite readers from the Toledo area to find a story based on familiar landmarks, particularly a creepy skating rink parents have long trusted to preoccupy their children. And I hope the skating rink (and all the desolate places in Lucas County) will continue to drive the imaginations of myself and others. It's difficult to say where the story comes from, or, you know, what it's *really about.* I do remember conceiving of it, from beginning to end, in an instant. It was one of those epiphanies writers are always on the listen for, rarely getting. A striking order of characters, setting, plot, and phrase is revealed. So you sit and write the thing.

Elizabeth Strout's most recent novel is *Olive Kitteridge.* Her previous novels are *Abide with Me* and *Amy and Isabelle,* which won two national awards and was nominated for others. Her stories have appeared in the *New Yorker* and a number of other magazines. She is on the faculty of the low-residency M.F.A. program at Queens University in Charlotte, North Carolina, and makes her home in New York City.

▪ This story originated in my fascination with the Stockholm Syndrome, a condition deriving its name from a bank robbery that took place years ago in Sweden, where the women who were taken as hostages developed feelings of love for their captor. It is a situation that has long held my imagination and I knew someday I would use it in a story. As I began to write about the character Olive Kitteridge, I saw that she would be the one who could carry this off, and then it became a matter of finding the proper form for the story. Also, I am always interested in what people say and do in moments of great pressure, and so the idea of Olive being held in a hospital's bathroom with her husband and two strangers was invigorating for me, and hopefully for the readers as well.

Melissa VanBeck was raised on a cattle-and-wheat ranch in Klickitat County, the dry side of the Washington Cascade Mountains. The struggle to live on land where rain is an unreliable landlord is never far from her fiction. Melissa and her husband live in Spokane, where she works as a psychotherapist. Her fiction has appeared in the *Chicago Quarterly Review, Phantasmagoria, Whiskey Island,* the *Red Rock Review,* and *Porcupine Literary Arts Magazine.* She is currently working on a novel.

▪ "Given Her History" is a story I waited a long time to tell. In part, I wasn't certain I had the maturity to follow the young April-May from the violent death of her family through her spiral into sociopathy and subsequent redemption through Vivian. Doing that while maintaining her voice seemed daunting. Jake the dog and I were loyal throughout. The town I describe as it was in my childhood. John Day Dam was built across the neck of the Columbia River in 1968, and the town is now submerged. Although I know different, I imagine things continuing as they were — the people, the buildings, growing up, growing old — all under the waters of the Columbia. It took four years and many drafts before I finally got it right.

Scott Wolven is the author of a short-story collection, *Controlled Burn,* and a forthcoming novel, *False Hope.* His stories have been selected seven years in a row for *The Best American Mystery Stories* series. Wolven teaches creative writing in the Professional Writing Program at Champlain College in Burlington, Vermont.

▪ "St. Gabriel" allowed me to place a somewhat mysterious figure from the Bible into a story set against the background of the devastation of the Gulf Coast and more specifically, New Orleans, directly after the two hurricanes, Katrina and Rita. I worked in New Orleans for more than a year after the disaster and when I arrived, it seemed as if God had crushed things. The combination of devastated landscape and displaced people and death influenced my ideas of noir and how to weave that into storytelling. I'm sure I'll write more stories about it in the future — and my heart goes out to the folks who lived there. They deserved much more help than they received. I felt lucky when Jen Jordan asked me to contribute a story to an anthology she was editing. Special thanks to Ben Leroy of Bleak House Books, DMC, M, and WSBW.

Other Distinguished Mystery Stories of 2007

ABELLA, ALEX
Shanghai. *Havana Noir,* ed. Achy Obejas (Akashic)

ALEAS, RICHARD
The Quant. *Wall Street Noir,* ed. Peter Spiegelman (Akashic)

BAKER, KEVIN
The Cheers Like Waves. *Bronx Noir,* ed. S. J. Rozan (Akashic)

BOLAND, JOHN C.
The Return of Jasper Kohl. *Alfred Hitchcock's Mystery Magazine,* April

CHERCOVER, SEAN
The Non Compos Mentis Blues. *Chicago Blues,* ed. Libby Fischer Hellman (Bleak House)

COLEMAN, REED FARREL
Due Diligence. *Wall Street Noir,* ed. Peter Spiegelman (Akashic)

DAVIDSON, HILARY
Anniversary. *Thuglit,* July

DEE, ED
Ernie K.'s Gelding. *Bronx Noir,* ed. S. J. Rozan (Akashic)

DENT, CATHERINE ZOBAL
Half Life. *Crab Orchard Review,* Winter/Spring

GORDON, ALAN
Bottom of the Sixth. *Queens Noir,* ed. Robert Knightly (Akashic)

HARPER, JORDAN
Red Hair and Black Leather. *Thuglit,* October

HARVKEY, MICHAEL
KFC, Three A.M. *Mississippi Review,* Spring

HAYDEN, G. MIKI
A Murder in Marcus Garvey Park. *Alfred Hitchcock's Mystery Magazine,* January/February
HUGHES, ROBERT J.
A Visit to St. Nick's. *Bronx Noir,* ed. S. J. Rozan (Akashic)
HUNSICKER, HARRY
Vivian and Bobby Ray. *Murdaland,* Fall/Winter

LOCK, NORMAN
The Monster in Winter. *New England Review,* vol. 28, no. 3

MCDONALD, CRAIG
These Two Guys . . . *Thuglit,* November
MOSLEY, WALTER
Mr. In-Between. *Dead Man's Hand,* ed. Otto Penzler (Harcourt)
MUSTO, EDWARD
Wedding Album. *Coffee Cramp eZine,* January

NARVAEZ, R.
Roachkiller. *Murdaland,* Fall/Winter
NOONAN, DAVID
Town Car. *Wall Street Noir,* ed. Peter Spiegelman (Akashic)

ORTIZ, OSCAR F.
Settling of Scores. *Havana Noir,* ed. Achy Obejas (Akashic)

PICCIARELLI, PATRICK W.
The Prince of Arthur Avenue. *Bronx Noir,* ed. S. J. Rozan (Akashic)
POISSANT, DAVID JAMES
Lizard Man. *Playboy,* October

QUIGLEY, EDWARD A.
Sundown at Trimble. *New Letters,* vol. 73, no. 3

SOLOMITA, STEPHEN
Crazy Jill Saves the Slinky. *Queens Noir,* ed. Robert Knightly (Akashic)
STEINHAUER, OLEN
Hungarian Lessons. *Expletive Deleted,* ed. Jen Jordan (Bleak House)
STEVENS, ATHENA
What Are You Waiting For? *The Sun,* January

THE BEST AMERICAN SERIES®

THE BEST AMERICAN SHORT STORIES® 2008

Salman Rushdie, editor, Heidi Pitlor, series editor

ISBN: 978-0-618-78876-7 $28.00 CL
ISBN: 978-0-618-78877-4 $14.00 PA

THE BEST AMERICAN NONREQUIRED READING™ 2008

Edited by Dave Eggers, introduction by Judy Blume

ISBN: 978-0-618-90282-8 $28.00 CL
ISBN: 978-0-618-90283-5 $14.00 PA

THE BEST AMERICAN COMICS™ 2008

Lynda Barry, editor, Jessica Abel and Matt Madden, series editors

ISBN: 978-0-618-98976-8 $22.00 POB

THE BEST AMERICAN ESSAYS® 2008

Adam Gopnik, editor, Robert Atwan, series editor

ISBN: 978-0-618-98331-5 $28.00 CL
ISBN: 978-0-618-98322-3 $14.00 PA

THE BEST AMERICAN MYSTERY STORIES™ 2008

George Pelecanos, editor, Otto Penzler, series editor

ISBN: 978-0-618-81266-0 $28.00 CL
ISBN: 978-0-618-81267-7 $14.00 PA

THE BEST AMERICAN SPORTS WRITING™ 2008

William Nack, editor, Glenn Stout, series editor

ISBN: 978-0-618-75117-4 $28.00 CL
ISBN: 978-0-618-75118-1 $14.00 PA

THE BEST AMERICAN TRAVEL WRITING™ 2008

Anthony Bourdain, editor, Jason Wilson, series editor

ISBN: 978-0-618-85863-7 $28.00 CL
ISBN: 978-0-618-85864-4 $14.00 PA

THE BEST AMERICAN SCIENCE AND NATURE WRITING™ 2008

Jerome Groopman, editor, Tim Folger, series editor

ISBN: 978-0-618-83446-4 $28.00 CL
ISBN: 978-0-618-83447-1 $14.00 PA

THE BEST AMERICAN SPIRITUAL WRITING™ 2008

Edited by Philip Zaleski, introduction by Jimmy Carter

ISBN: 978-0-618-83374-0 $28.00 CL
ISBN: 978-0-618-83375-7 $14.00 PA